Advance Praise for
The Great Abraham Lincoln Pocket Watch Conspiracy

"Historical fiction takes a deft hand to do well, and Jacopo della Quercia mixes fact and fiction seamlessly in *The Great Abraham Lincoln Pocket Watch Conspiracy*. It is an adventure tale filled with thrilling incidents, fantastic inventions, international conspiracies, and great characters. How can you not love a book starring a gluttonous and heavyweight-boxing president, the brilliant oldest son of Abraham Lincoln, and an irreverent, cigar-chomping secret service chief? This is a Jules Vernian thrill ride through American history like I've never experienced—and I couldn't put it down."

—Jason Emerson,
author of *Lincoln the Inventor* and
Giant in the Shadows: The Life of Robert T. Lincoln

"With the sweep and scope of a Jules Verne adventure, *The Great Abraham Lincoln Pocket Watch Conspiracy* not only charts its own fantastic course through a dizzying alternate history of the United States presidency—it takes on literary history itself, turning anachronism into action, politics into pop, and a handful of America's commanders-in-chief into the stuff of potent yet poignantly humanized myth. If you think Honest Abe and his brethren have been resurrected to death (so to speak), think again; Jacopo della Quercia has brought the speculative presidential yarn to another level."

—Jason Heller,
Hugo Award–winning author of *Taft 2012*

"High concept and high adventure collide in a dizzying and thoroughly riveting adventure. Insanely entertaining." —Jonathan Maberry,
New York Times bestselling author of *Code Zero*

"Move over, Jules Verne. From the secret passages through the steam tunnel labyrinth beneath the Yale campus to a mid-ocean battle upon which hangs the future of humanity, Jacopo's fantasy novel stretches time and space across a carefully detailed real past. Aboard a floating White House, the pugilistic gourmand President William Howard Taft and a cast of other larger-than-life characters jump out of the past in a rollicking race to save the world from the forces of darkness. What a ride!"

—Marc Wortman, author of *The Millionaires' Unit:
The Aristocratic Flyboys Who Fought the Great War and Invented
American Air Power* and *The Bonfire: The Siege and Burning of Atlanta*

The Great Abraham Lincoln Pocket Watch *Conspiracy*

Jacopo della Quercia

St. Martin's Griffin
New York

THE GREAT ABRAHAM LINCOLN POCKET WATCH CONSPIRACY. Copyright © 2014 by Jacopo della Quercia. All rights reserved. Printed in the United States of America. For information, address St. Martin's Press, 175 Fifth Avenue, New York, N.Y. 10010.

www.stmartins.com

The Library of Congress Cataloging-in-Publication Data is available upon request.

ISBN 978-1-250-02571-5 (trade paperback)
ISBN 978-1-250-02572-2 (e-book)

St. Martin's Griffin books may be purchased for educational, business, or promotional use. For information on bulk purchases, please contact Macmillan Corporate and Premium Sales Department at 1-800-221-7945, extension 5442, or write special markets@macmillan.com.

First Edition: August 2014

10 9 8 7 6 5 4 3 2 1

For students and teachers of history everywhere

Acknowledgments

Any work of history is like a watch with many wheels, and this book would not have been possible without the help of many people.

First and foremost, I must thank my parents and my entire family for their constant love and encouragement. Every act of my life is a product of the time we have always shared. I would also like to thank Jonathan Maberry; my agent, Sara Crowe; my editor, Michael Homler; Lauren Jablonski; and the many people at St. Martin's Press for allowing me to share this book with the world. To all of you, my deepest thanks.

Special thanks go to Ray Errol Fox for his timeless friendship and guidance; Erzsébet Fazekas for her love, support, and feedback; Daniel Eltringham for being my ingénieur; Anthony Losorelli for his bare-knuckle fight choreography; Kate Resler for her expertise on turn-of-the-century costumes and etiquette;

Harry R. Rubenstein of the Smithsonian's National Museum of American History for his exhaustive research on Abraham Lincoln's pocket watches; Marc Wortman for his profound writing, research, and understanding of Yale life; Barbara Narendra at the Yale Peabody Museum of Natural History for her assistance and kindness; Judith Ann Schiff and Bill Landis of the Yale University Library Manuscripts & Archives Department for helping me break into the Skull and Bones Tomb—in 1911, of course; Ray Henderson of the William Howard Taft National Historic Site for his help; Roger and Eric at the Ford's Theater National Historic Site; Eric Frazier at the Rare Book and Special Collections Division of the Library of Congress; the staff and volunteers at Hildene, The Lincoln Family Home in Manchester; the staff and volunteers at the Morgan Library & Museum; the library at the United States Military Academy at West Point; the White House Historical Association; Jane E. Gastineau at the Lincoln Financial Foundation; Brian Richards of the New York Yankees Museum for his undying love of baseball; my professors at Susquehanna University and Syracuse University in Florence for everything they taught me; Pennsylvania Region 6, the "DO IT LIVE!" region; Colin Hicks for being right all the time; Tim Lieb and F. James Walton for their friendship; Eden for her frequent insight; David Mitchell for always listening to me no matter how busy he was; Professor Lawrence Beaston for always telling me that I should be a writer; Nadejda Golovchanova for her assistance in nineteenth-century Russian; the Latin/Greek Institute at the Graduate Center, CUNY for always helping me with my Latin; *The New York Times* for their online article archive; the countless historians, historical societies, and veterans groups who dedicate their lives to their causes; everyone who reviewed this book; everyone at Crisan Bakery who put up with me as I wrote it; and all the good people at Cracked.com, particularly its awesome readers.

And lastly, I would like to give a very special thanks to Dr. Don Housley of Susquehanna University for encouraging a certain sophomore to explore new ways to make history more enjoyable for all audiences. Such as humor.

The Great
Abraham Lincoln
Pocket Watch
Conspiracy

Prologue

April 14, 1865

FLO

[throwing arms around Mary's neck]

What treason is this, Mary? No one to love you, eh,

what's the matter? You've been weeping, and I met

that American Savage coming from here . . .

Abraham shifted anxiously in his wooden rocking chair. It had nothing to do with the play, mind you. On the contrary, Abraham was enjoying the show quite a bit. Miss Laura Keene, the star player and one of the most gifted actresses in the country, was giving everyone at Ford's Theatre an unforgettable farewell performance of *Our American Cousin*. The theater was packed with nearly two thousand patrons, among them the president of the United States; his wife, Mary; Miss Clara Harris of New York; and her fiancé, Major Henry Rathbone of the Union

Army. The four were seated in an ornate, imposing state box overlooking the stage. For this particular evening, the box was draped in American flags.

Abraham stirred again, this time slightly more bothered than before by an unseen, unknown nuisance he could not quite put his finger on. Mary, completely misreading her husband's countenance as absorption in the play, coyly cradled his hand and shot him a playful look. Abraham returned to reality and smiled lovingly at his wife, whose bright face was lightly haloed by the crimson walls around them. As she turned back to the stage, however, her husband's smile faded. His busy mind wandered inward and went straight back to work. He scratched his beard with his left hand while Mary continued playing with his right. Something refused to sit well with the president in that theater, and it seemed determined as the devil to interfere with his evening.

Was it something unresolved from earlier? Abraham doubted this. He had been on his feet since seven o'clock and briskly moved through his day with supreme satisfaction. In Charleston Harbor, Major General Robert Anderson proudly hoisted the same flag over Fort Sumter he had taken down in defeat exactly four years ago to the day. In Washington, Abraham's eldest son, Robert, was home from the war with stories to share and a future to build. His father looked forward to discussing both subjects in greater detail the next morning. The presidential cabinet, now charged with the delicate task of reconstruction, met with the Union hero General Ulysses S. Grant that midday. Abraham could not have been more pleased with Grant's report on Confederate General Robert E. Lee's surrender at Appomattox and expected more good news to come from General William

T. Sherman in North Carolina. Abraham's afternoon carriage ride was calm and pleasant, and so unusually full of cheer that even Mary was surprised by her husband's euphoria. Between Lee's surrender and the triumphant return of the battered Stars and Stripes to Fort Sumter, the nation's great civil war finally appeared to be over.

So, why did it feel like something was gnawing at Abraham like a tick with each passing second?

Did he forget to bring something? Abraham glanced at his hat, shawl, and greatcoat stacked neatly on a chair alongside his ebony walking stick in the far corner of box 8. Although he was too far away to reach them, he was confident everything was accounted for, right down to those ill-fitting white kid gloves Mary always insisted he carry. Those tacky, loathsome burdens were safely stowed in his left coat pocket, completely and deliberately un-used all evening.

Still searching for answers, Abraham's thoughts returned to his cabinet meeting. Something stood out there for some reason, and he had a feeling it involved that strange dream he had shared with his secretaries: the one where he was standing on a vessel floating toward a vast, unknown shore at fantastic speed. The dream preceded every major Union victory of the war, but this was the first time Abraham discussed the subject with his staff. Grant dismissed the idea that the dream foreshadowed any develop-ments for Sherman, but Abraham could not ignore the shared ex-pression on so many faces in that room: his naval secretary Gideon Welles, Assistant Secretary of State Frederick Seward, and . . .

With that last name, Abraham instinctively moved his left hand to his timepiece, only to find an empty pocket where his new pocket watch should have been. Abraham looked down at his waistcoat, aghast. A rather magnificent pocket watch, one unlike any he had ever seen or dreamed possible, was missing. As was its gold chain and gold watch fob.

The watch was gone? *The entire watch?* The whole world around Abraham seemed to slow. He started patting his pockets frantically, but caught himself once he realized Mary was still in possession of his other hand. Fortunately, she was too focused on the play with her binoculars to notice her husband's quandary, sparing him some embarrassment. If Mary learned the president's pocket watch was missing, Abraham suspected she would have the Army lock down the whole building just on principle. The flummoxed chief executive scanned the carpet for anything that glittered, but to no avail. Reddened, Abraham sank deeply into the scarlet damask of his wooden rocker. He had not felt so robbed since Robert nearly lost his first inaugural address four years beforehand.

Abraham knew the only option left was to empty his pockets. If the watch was indeed missing—or worse, stolen—he would have to send his messenger Charles Forbes to notify the Seward household, Allan Pinkerton, and possibly even the War Department. However, the president was mindful that he had to choose his next moves carefully. His position within the state box offered fantastic privacy from the audience, but he did not wish to alarm anyone in the opposing boxes or the orchestra, never mind any of the actors onstage. He looked over his right shoulder at his greatcoat, and then slowly peered at the audience from behind the Treasury Guard flag to his left. Abraham was up to something, and he wanted to keep it safe from the picklocks of history. His demeanor exuded cool indifference, but his mind was all clockwork.

"I'll be right back," he whispered to Mary.

She turned her head in surprise. "Are you all right?"

"I'm fine. I just feel a slight chill coming. I should get my coat." It sounded like a perfectly satisfactory and even halfway honest excuse.

"But you're sweating."

Abraham froze. "Am I?" A cold mixture of sweat and pomade was trickling down his forehead and neck. "I better get my shawl as well." Abraham smiled uneasily, and then darted toward his bundle in box 8. Mary, completely mystified by her husband, shook her head and returned to Laura Keene with her glasses.

Abraham checked his hat—empty—and carefully put on his coat, which, even during times like these, he appreciated as one fine item from Brooks Brothers. He then glanced at Miss Harris and Major Rathbone, who, though preoccupied with the play, were still a little too close for Abraham's comfort. In need of privacy, the president quietly opened the door to his left and stepped into the darkened narrow passage connecting the state box to the theater's dress circle. The sole light in the vestibule was a peephole cut into the box 7 door, but otherwise the corridor seemed to disappear into total darkness.

Abraham stood with his back to the passageway and started searching his coat until he heard what sounded like a board creaking behind him. The president turned and stared into the Cimmerian hallway. For a second, he swore he could hear someone breathing. "Parker?" he whispered, thinking it might be his bodyguard. There was no reply and the breathing stopped, so Abraham dismissed the sound as either nothing or just an actor.

Within the open doorframe to this chamber, Abraham rummaged through his pockets and took inventory:

One pair of spectacles folded in a silver case.

One padded lens polisher.

One pocketknife: six blades, ivory with silver mounting.

One Irish linen handkerchief with "A. Lincoln" embroidered in red. Abraham quickly wiped his brow with it and continued.

A second pair of spectacles: gold-rimmed, mended in one hinge with string, in a second case marked "Franklin & Co Opticians, Washington, D.C."

One sleeve button: dark blue enamel with a gold "L" initial.

One wallet: brown leather lined with purple silk, containing a small pencil, eight newspaper clippings, and a five-dollar Confederate note Abraham found in Jefferson Davis's desk in Richmond the previous week.

And . . .

Eureka! Abraham felt a hard, heavy lump in his left coat pocket, beneath his gloves. He reached in and pulled out a bauble that beckoned him back to the flickering gaslights of Ford's Theatre. It was a watch fob: pyramidal with a gold setting and a single polished fragment of gold-bearing quartz. The alluring stone looked like liquid gold frozen in icy marble that shimmered like a glacier beneath the northern lights. Although its timepiece and chain were nowhere to be found, Abraham could not help but admire the fob's tiny, whispering gold specks in awe.

Unfortunately, Abraham was out of time. The audience was clapping, signaling an end to Scene 1 along with the president's futile search for his pocket watch. Defeated but not empty-handed, the president slipped the fob into his waistcoat and dutifully adjusted the gloves in his coat pocket—the latter something Mary caught with her keen blue eyes. Abraham threw his shawl around his shoulders and returned to his wife as the stagehands readied Act III, Scene 2 of *Our American Cousin*. In his hurry, it never dawned on Abraham to shut the door to the passageway behind them.

The president probably should have dispatched his messenger once it was evident his pocket watch was missing, but something stopped him. As Abraham brooded in his rocking chair for the next few minutes, an image even more captivating than the watch fob seized him: a large outstretched eagle surrounded by Union shields and bearing a banner in its beak reading "One Country, One Destiny." The eagle was stitched into the lining of the president's greatcoat, and he always made a habit of reflecting on it whenever he put the coat on. As the image of this great eagle fanned its wings across Abraham's mind, the president instantly deduced the one place in the world his pocket watch had to be.

A smile spread across Abraham's face and he clasped Mary's hand tightly. Mary, feeling the warmth returning to her husband's fingers, embraced him dearly and directed him back to the play.

MRS. MOUNTCHESSINGTON

I am aware, Mr. Trenchard, you are not used to the
manners of good society, and that, alone, will excuse
the impertinence of which you have been guilty.

Abraham raised his eyebrows in anticipation.

ASA

Don't know the manners of good society, eh? Well,
I guess I know enough to turn you inside out, old gal;
you sockdologizing old mantrap!

Abraham and Mary grinned brightly as Ford's Theatre exploded with the sound of laughter.

"Hey, Bob. You awake?"

Secret Service Chief John E. Wilkie, the mustached, choleric character on Robert's right, gently nudged his aging neighbor back to the world of the living.

"Yes, I am." Robert nodded, slightly jaded. He scratched his beard and straightened himself on his wobbly barstool.

"I've never seen someone sozzled on Darjeeling before." Wilkie grinned. He had a dying cigar in his mouth and a full set of stained yellow teeth.

Robert looked down at his lonely teacup, which by now had completely lost its warmth. "Sorry. My mind was worlds away." The sixty-six-year-old adjusted his spectacles and reacclimated himself while sipping cold black tea. 1865 became 1910, Washington faded like a photograph into London, and the thespian temple that was Ford's Theatre decayed into a crowded, noisy pub: the Lamb & Flag. Colloquially known as the "Bucket of Blood," this Covent Garden locale was a favorite of Samuel Butler, Charles Dickens, and other greats smart enough to avoid it on evenings like this one: an unlicensed British bare-knuckle boxing championship.

"I hear John Dryden was nearly beaten to death outside this place," said Robert. "He was poet laureate at the time."

"No kiddin'. Was he here for the fight as well?" Wilkie lit a fresh cigar that filled his pince-nez with flame.

"I don't think so. It was over two hundred years ago."

"Great," Wilkie puffed. "That means I don't need to know

about him." The Secret Service chief turned around and scanned the scene behind a growing cloud of smoke. The three agents he had planted throughout the pub saw their signal and immediately converged toward the bar. Like their boss, they were wearing bowler hats to blend in with the crowd this evening.

"I admire your ardor for your work," remarked Robert as he finished his tea.

"What is this, a date? Quit twaddling about sweet nothings. I'm here to bring you upstairs, Bob. The big man is ready."

Robert nearly swallowed his teacup. "He's not already up there, is he?"

Every glass and bottle in the pub started shaking. "You tell me." Wilkie winked.

Overhead, Robert and Wilkie could hear the growing rancor of a makeshift coliseum. The wooden boards above them were trembling, raining flakes of centuries-old dust and dirt onto their heads. A heavy barrage of foot stomps shook every inch of the pub like thunder. All the beams in the building were creaking as though moaning with pain. And high above it all: chanting. The feral, heart-stopping chanting of an insatiable, blood-frenzied mob of drunk Londoners.

"You sure those boards can support two hundred people?" Robert asked the Secret Service chief.

"Who are you, the building inspector?" Wilkie sneered as he smacked the dirt off his derby.

"I figured you more than anyone should know."

Wilkie shrugged his shoulders and looked up at the beams. "I guess it depends on the building."

"This one predates the great fire."

"Chicago?"

"No, London. The great fire of 1666."

Wilkie's cigar drooped in his mouth. "In that case, I'm amazed our man hasn't fallen through the floor yet."

As Wilkie conferred with his three agents, Robert pushed his empty teacup forward and unfolded a one-dollar silver certificate from his wallet. He stared blankly at the banknote's large, out-stretched eagle atop an American flag flanked by portraits of two late U.S. presidents. The one on the right was Ulysses S. Grant, and the other was Robert's father.

"Hey, Mr. Lincoln," Wilkie interrupted. "The Treasury's got your tab. Besides, I don't think they take horse blankets here." Wilkie snapped his fingers and his agents forged a path to the staircase. "Up and at 'em, Bob. We're late."

Robert stuffed the banknote in his pocket and followed Wilkie up the steps, his right hand never leaving the magnificent pocket watch in his coat as he walked.

Chapter I

"Taft! Taft! Taft!"

" T aft! Taft! Taft! Taft!"
... The enthusiastic crowd was on their feet, heralding the man's arrival like a howl of banshees. The atmosphere was a thundercloud of smoke, sweat, and shouts. Tickets were clutched tightly in every fist around the ramshackle arena. Secret Service agents cleared a path for their fighter. Women rushed forward to touch him. An unabating London crowd simultaneously cheered, cursed, and chanted his name. In a darkened corner, one surreptitious spectator casually smoked a cigar, while next to him stood a transfixed Robert Todd Lincoln.

It was Friday night, July 15, one minute to midnight, which translated to high noon in the Bucket of Blood. Its four fighters, all champions, stirred anxiously on their sawdust-covered canvas as their enormous opponent thudded toward them. He was six feet, two inches tall, three hundred fifty pounds, and endowed with both the build and the grace of a bear. His torso was a medical atlas of stretch marks and scars. His boxing trunks, though frayed with age, were an unmistakable Stars and Stripes. A vast entourage of staffers and secretaries studied his every move. Spectators screamed, the brazen hearts of four challengers pounded, and every eye in the arena focused like spotlights on the fight's main attraction: William Howard Taft, the twenty-seventh president of the United States of America.

The man-mountain moved slowly, but not lazily. In his fifty-two years of living and thirty-five years of fighting, he had long ago mastered how to steer his huge frame. He entered the ring like a toddler who had outgrown his crib, and his baby blue eyes greeted his adversaries as if they were playmates. His opponents, from left to right, were an Irishman with a checkered past, an Englishman who hated America, a Welshman who hated every-one, and a Scotsman who had once killed a man over haggis. All were tested, seasoned fighters, battle-hardened and spoiling for a fight with the single greatest underground boxing champion the world would never know of. There were no reporters, no po-licemen, no referees, and no rules. For the challengers, this was a fight for personal glory, a last-ditch attempt by the British Isles to put America back in her place. For Will "Big Bill" Taft, this was exercise.

The president twitched his blond mustache.

The audience froze.

The fight started.

The first man to move was the Englishman, who instinctively took a step back to study his foe. The Irishman feinted to Taft's left and the Scot charged in from the right. As effortlessly as a gentleman tipping his hat, Taft seized the screaming Scotsman and tossed him into the Irishman like a bag of potatoes. With Taft's right flank exposed, the wiry Welshman made his move. He rushed in and struck the president hard and fast to the chest, ribs, and head. Despite the echoing smack of the Welshman's fists against Taft's ample flesh, the president was not even tickled. He locked eyes with his aggressor and felled him with a single, openhanded smack upside the head. A quarter of the audience groaned as the Welshman slipped out of consciousness. The fight had barely started and there was already a man on the floor.

With the president's right flank secured, he revisited his remaining foes. As Taft considered his next move, the unsporting Englishman interrupted him by kicking sawdust in his face. The crowd roared with laughter as the president stumbled backward. The Englishman knew this would be his only opening: He leaped onto Taft with all his weight and wrestled him to the ground. Cheers erupted as the Irishman and Scotsman piled onto the president. As the presidential entourage watched intently, a female aide covered her mouth with her hand. For a brief moment in the Bucket of Blood, it appeared to be a good day to have been born an Englishman.

But then he got Tafted.

A deafening, bloodcurdling scream rang through the building as Taft unleashed an old favorite from his Yale days: the dreaded "Skull and Bones." He gripped the Englishman's face like a bowling ball, digging into his eye sockets with one hand while his other hand crushed the man's genitals between his thick fingers. The Irishman and the Scotsman backed away as Taft slowly rose to his feet, lifting the Englishman over his head in a towering clean and jerk. It was a harrowing sight that left much of the audience in tears, some out of pain and others out of disbelief.

The president hurled his maimed opponent into the English section of the crowd, but was careful not to hurt anyone. The defeated Englishman landed face-first on a piano. Taft then brushed the sawdust from his shoulders and turned to face the two remaining fighters.

Now that the Irishman and Scotsman understood the unstoppable beast facing them, they agreed with a nod to take down their foe as a team. The Scot came at Taft from his left and delivered a powerful kick to his knee. The mob cheered wildly as the seemingly invincible warrior nearly collapsed under his own weight. The Irishman, tasting victory, dashed in from the right to deliver a potentially fatal kick to Taft's skull. That is, if only the Irish were so lucky. Taft caught the fighter by the leg and swung him into the air as if he were showing the Scot how to tee off at St Andrews. The president hopped back onto his feet and let the flying, screaming Irishman out of his grip. The Irish section groaned painfully as their prizefighter hit a beam on the ceiling and landed facedown in the sawdust.

Taft turned his back on the dizzied Irishman to confront the last fighter standing. The enraged Scotsman put up his dukes and challenged Taft to fisticuffs, which the president graciously accepted. Taft glided across the floor like a dancer, throwing several punches that the young Scot was quick enough to dodge. However, the skirmish came to a quick end when Taft landed a right cross that would have staggered a Pamplona bull. The Scotsman was stunned and barely able to stand. After consulting the vast library of wrestling moves in his head, Taft threw his arms around his opponent for a finisher that no one of Scottish descent at the Bucket of Blood would forget. The president heaved his hapless foe in the air and suplexed him against the pub's hardwood floor. The Scotsman, much like the Scottish section of the crowd, was no longer moving.

The battle was all but over until one sore gambler raised the stakes. A puukko knife was thrown toward the Irishman as the dazed fighter regained consciousness. Once he saw the weapon, the irate Irishman grabbed the knife and made a final, screaming lunge toward the president. The room gasped. Several Secret Service agents reached for their pistols, including an otherwise indifferent Chief Wilkie, but only Taft knew how little danger he was in. The president turned, met his screaming adversary with a smile, and sent him flying across the sawdust circle with a solid kick to the chest. The response from the crowd was deafening. The fight was over, the president had won fairly, and he claimed the Irishman's puukko knife as a souvenir.

Taft studied the weapon with curiosity before turning to his staff. "Ready the flying machine," he requested.

Chapter II

The Flying Machine

Airship One, President Taft's personal aircraft and floating headquarters, was a marvel of engineering unlike anything the world had seen. Originally envisioned by Theodore Roosevelt as an "airborne hunting lodge," President Taft's wife, Nellie, ballooned the project into its ultimate incarnation. It had promenades, lounges, full course gourmet banquets, a vast selection of champagnes and sparkling wines, a humidor room, hardwood floors, Persian rugs, posh furniture, patriotic artwork, and a near-perfect replica of the recently remodeled West Wing built into it. The elegant vessel was a flying fortress that any president could rule the nation from, capable of traveling more than three times faster than any steamship and virtually unassailable from land or sea. The sky liner stretched more than eight hundred feet from bow to stern, had a top speed of nearly ninety miles per hour, and was reportedly capable of reaching altitudes in excess of twenty thousand feet. The ship was also rumored to contain a few surprises known only to Robert Todd Lincoln, president of the Pullman Company that built the vessel, and Captain Archibald Willingham Butt, President Taft's chief military aide and trusted skipper aboard Airship One.

Technically, the titanic zeppelin was a generation ahead of its peers in every way. Its wireless telegraph room alone boasted more than forty patentable inventions from Nikola Telsa. Its pressurized cabins could accommodate well over one hundred passengers and crew in comfort. Environmental controls permitted smoking anywhere on the airship, from its dining hall to its exercise room to its seldom-used ladies' lounge. Diesel engines propelled the vessel as quietly as a cloud across oceans. And according to Captain Butt, the aircraft handled like the gloves his dear mother used to knit him every Christmas.

Inside and out, Airship One was a soaring triumph of modern technology. A Renaissance masterpiece of ingenuity proudly made in America. A flying sanctuary for President Taft from the endless worries of Washington. A floating palace so steady you could play billiards in its game room—which, incidentally, was where the president blithely abandoned his star-spangled boxing trunks. He left them behind the eight ball.

Taft walked out of his private washroom in a presidential bathrobe, moving with a comfortable gait that clashed noticeably with the swarm of secretaries around him.

"Mr. President," hurried one staffer, "we received an urgent message from Postmaster Hitchcock. Your decoy is stuck in the bathtub again."

"Confound it! I keep telling them its exhaust port is not submersible! Someone get Nikola Tesla on the telegraph. Tell him I'm tired of plugging holes in the backside of Thomas Edison's engines!"

"Yes, Mr. President."

"I really hate Edison," Taft whispered loudly to Butt, who followed closely alongside in a dashing blue uniform. "We need an automaton that works, Archie. Not the goddamn Tik-Tok of Oz."

"I disagree, Mr. President," the airship captain replied. "I've been told that even Tik-Tok worked on occasion."

"What was it doing in the bathtub anyway?" Taft asked his staffers.

"It was melting, sir. Mrs. Taft wanted it readied and shipped to the summer home in Beverly. She's concerned you won't arrive in time for her departure on Monday."

"I guess we'll have to contact Madame Tussauds as well," Taft sighed. "Also, please tell my wife not to worry. I intend to take her on our vacation as fast as we can fly there."

"Yessir . . ." the staffer responded uneasily.

"Bully!" Taft brightened, clapping his hands. "So, what's going on in the rest of the world?"

"Mr. President, the German zeppelin *Erbslöh* exploded over Leichlingen," a different staffer reported. "Five people were killed, including its aeronaut, Oskar Erbslöh."[1]

"Did we do this, Archie?"

"No," Butt assured.

Taft nodded and turned to the staffer. "Very well. Have Ambassador Hill offer our condolences to the German people. And send a basket of cheese and sausages to the embassy."

"Yes, Mr. President."

---

1 "Five Men Killed in a Dirigible," *New York Times,* 14 July 1910.

"And send some flowers," Taft added. "German cornflowers."

"Excellent choice, Mr. President."

"And some chocolates," Taft continued, his eyes glistening like fine pastries. "And an assortment of Bavarian pastries to go with them. The fluffy puff kind with cream on the inside. And I want them all in a basket on my desk within the next fifteen minutes."

"Yes, Mr. President." The staffer bowed his head and rushed to the kitchen.

"I think we handled that well," Taft confided to his captain. "So, what else happened these last few days?"

"Mr. President, the Portuguese clashed with pirates on Colowan Island this week.[2] The fighting lasted from Wednesday until yesterday," said Captain Butt.

"Co-lo-wan?" Taft mouthed.

"Macau. It's in the Orient, sir."

"By jingo, that's close to the Philippines! Archie, I want you to find out who wins and what this piracy means for our friends in the Pacific."

"Mr. President, the Portuguese won," the captain replied. "And I'd say the fewer pirates in the area, the safer it will be for everyone."

"Oh. Well, good work, Archie!" The president slapped Butt on his back, jingling his medals and shoulder cords. "Well, is there anything else you have for me?" Taft asked the assembled.

"Yes, Mr. President." The heavily mustached Attorney General George W. Wickersham stepped forward. "U.S. Marshal William Henkel of the Southern New York District secured

---

2 "Pirates Raise White Flag," *Washington Post*, 16 July 1910, 4.

those four-point-five million ice-cream cones we discussed. The FDA raid was a success."[3]

Taft's eyes lit up like a Christmas tree. "I don't believe it. That's fantastic news, George! As soon as we get home, I'm treating you to ice cream!"

The attorney general moved within whisper range of the president. "Will, are you sure this is the best use of our resources? I have top men—*top men*—out there impounding ice-cream cones by the millions."

Taft put his hand on the attorney general's shoulder, bringing the entourage to a halt in the West Wing's main corridor. "George," Taft said softly, "I received a letter the other day from a little boy in New York. He told me the first thing he did this summer was buy an ice-cream cone with a penny his mother gave him. After he bit into the cone, he spit out a piece of newspaper with my name on it. As he shared the cone with his brothers, one of them coughed up the vice president, and another hacked on William Jennings Bryan's long name. As long as I'm president, I will not let factories produce ice-cream cones out of pencil shavings and shredded newspapers. Inaction would almost certainly come back to bite us worse than these poor children did. But thanks to you, Georgie"—Taft shook the man proudly— "every little boy and girl in New York will be enjoying their ice cream this summer, and I am confident their parents will remember which party made that possible: the Republican Party! The Grand Old Party! The Party of Lincoln! Huzzah!"

"Huzzah!" All but one staffer cheered. She had fair skin, blue-gray eyes, and voluminous auburn hair put up in a pompadour

---

3 "Millions of Cones Seized," *Washington Post*, 12 July 1910, 1.

like a Gibson girl. She stood a little over five feet in a blue women's suit with black high-heeled shoes. She was scribbling away in a black leather notebook in shorthand, but lifted her eyes once she realized everyone on the airship had fallen silent. Waving her pencil like a small pennant, she gave the president a belated "Huzzah."

The president grinned brightly. "Who is she?" Taft whispered to Captain Butt through his teeth.

"Miss Knox, sir," the captain replied. "One of Wilkie's men—uh, women." Truth be told, Miss Knox was the first and only female agent in the United States Secret Service, never mind the only woman on the airship in months. Out of modesty, Taft secured the enormous belt on his bathrobe and straightened its lapels like a jacket. Had he known there would be a lady present, he would at the very least have put on some pants.

"Miss Knox . . ." Taft pondered. "Any relation to Secretary Knox, young lady?" Philander Knox was the president's secretary of state.

"He's my uncle, Mr. President."

"Ah, then you're already part of the family!" Taft chuckled. "That spares me some embarrassment! Welcome aboard Airship One, Miss Knox. You are a most welcome addition." Taft's handlebar whiskers curled into a cheery smile.

"Thank you, Mr. President."

One of the airship's cartel clocks chimed, reminding Taft that it was long past midnight. "Well, if that's everything, I'd like to meet with my cabinet. Excellent work this week, everyone. You may disperse." Taft's secretaries scattered like partridges throughout the airship, leaving only Captain Butt with the president in the hallway.

"Is there anything else I can do for you, Mr. President?" The tall captain looked like he was posing for a statue with his gloved hand on the hilt of his saber.

"Yes, Archie. I was hoping you could join me for a Surprise cabinet meeting." The president had a playful twinkle in his eye.

"Only water when I'm on duty, sir. Same as every night."

"Then take the night off!" Taft insisted.

Captain Butt smiled, but as always his responsibilities came first. "Sorry, Will. There are some clouds on the horizon that could delay us a day. If I don't get you back to Mrs. Taft before Monday, hell hath no fury like the maelstrom we'll be descending into."

Taft nodded, brimming with confidence in the man. "If anyone can steer this ship through Scylla and Charybdis, it's you. Head back to the bridge and fly us home, Captain."

"We'll move like Mercury, Mr. President. Have a good night."

"You too, Archie."

Archie Butt disappeared down the airship's vast corridor as Taft shoved open one of the four white doors to the Oval Office.

Chapter III

The Surprise

Taft's personal workplace aboard Airship One was a facsimile of the new Oval Office he built into the White House's West Wing. Modeled after the mansion's grand Blue Room, the airy abode offered far more space than Theodore Roosevelt's cramped nook. The office's olive green walls with gold accents gave the room the charm of a poker table from the Old West. A matching green rug stretched over the room's hardwood floor: a checkerboard of bleached oak and majagua from the Philippines. The office's rich chairs and sofas were upholstered in red caribou leather with brass studs. Electric candles from a chandelier and brass wall sconces illuminated the room with a soft sepia hue. Across from the marble mantel, matching white bookcases flanked a duplicate of the massive desk that had faithfully served Theodore Roosevelt throughout his presidency. And behind the desk, an enormous chair surrounded by potted palms and green curtains awaited its owner. The chair was far sturdier than the one Taft destroyed his first few weeks in office.

For all its similarities, the Oval Office on Airship One differed from its Washington counterpart in three aspects—four if you count its "surprise." Firstly, the airship's design made any possibility of a working fireplace impossible, hence the mess of maps and papers inside it. All sensitive information had to go into special bags to be burned later. Secondly, the White House's Oval Office had only one hanging portrait: a framed photograph of Theodore Roosevelt looking determined to knock his head through the wall. Aboard Airship One, Taft forged a path to his desk using a golf club to find a photograph of his beloved wife, Nellie, enshrined in gold rococo above the bookcase to his right. As for the room's third departure, its triple bay window offered a spectacular view not of the South Lawn, but of the starry, sweeping landscape gently drifting past the president. Taft was flying six hundred fifty feet over the English Channel at eighty-eight miles per hour, with the Milky Way to his left and the setting moon shimmering over the southwest horizon. After scanning the night sky for one last glimpse of Halley's comet, Taft settled for the next best thing and hopscotched to his Surprise cabinet.

One of the many surprises aboard Airship One was the president's liquor cabinet, which was made out of timbers from the HMS *Surprise*. Taft opened the two doors of the cabinet, disguised as the bookcase beneath his wife's picture, to reveal a cache of his favorite champagnes and spirits behind dummy books and rotating shelves. Taft chose a bottle of 1858 comet vintage already on ice, which he brought to his desk along with its ice bucket. After removing the cork with his new puukko knife, Taft held the bottle under his nose and took a deep breath of its heavenly air. The president reclined in his chair, taking swig after swig from the bottle like a victorious athlete, while holding a handful of ice against the welt on his face where that damned Welshman hit him. As the melting ice dripped down his cheeks like tears of sweet bliss, Taft closed his eyes and let the comet vintage take him away. He was floating . . . barreling down an endless kaleidoscope of comets and nebulae on a journey through time and space, interrupted only by a sudden desire for steak. A thick rib eye and some lobster à la Newberg to go with it. Steak and lobster. He nodded. And a Welsh rabbit.

There was a knock at the door.

"Go away!" Taft shouted. "I'm in a meeting!" Unfortunately, repeated knocking spelled a quick end to the president's delectable fantasy. At the very least, Taft figured he would have to pass his order to the kitchen through someone. The president removed the ice from his face and opened his eyes. "All right, come on in."

One of the office's four white doors opened. Robert Todd Lincoln and John E. Wilkie stepped into the room.

"Mr. Lincoln!" Taft welcomed them with outstretched arms, splashing champagne from his bottle. "Mr. Wilkie. To what do I owe this surprise visit?"

"Good morning, Will," Robert greeted. "We saw your fight."

"Ah! What did you think?"

Robert's silver beard hid the faint hint of his smile. "With no disrespect to Jack Johnson, I think we just witnessed the real fight of the century."

"Oh, that's the ticket!" Taft clapped. "Between you and me, I think Jack Johnson could have mopped the floor with those featherweights!"

"Between you and me, I think you're cockeyed," the Secret Service chief huffed.

"Ha! That's rich coming from a man who smokes cigars on a zeppelin!"

"Wilkie's upset someone threw a knife into the Bucket of Blood," Robert intermediated.

"The hell I am! There's no way anyone could have slipped a shiv past my men. Someone planted it there."

"Wilkie, I have a better theory. It's called Occam's razor!" Taft stabbed his puukko knife into the Roosevelt desk to punctuate this. "Someone brought a Finnish blade to a fight, and I finished him. End of story. Happy ending, too! I needed a new office knife. You wouldn't believe how many letters I've been getting since I tossed that ball at the Nationals game!"[4]

The Secret Service chief sneered at the weapon sticking out of the fine tabletop. "I'm afraid I have to take that, Will. Fingerprints."

"I won't allow it. It's a souvenir!"

"It's evidence."

The president fell back into his chair, rolling his eyes. "John, why is everything an assassination attempt to you? First it's a bomb in the White House, then it's anarchists at Carnegie Hall, and then it's Mexican revolutionaries out to kill me *and* President Diaz. Not even Teddy Roosevelt was in as much danger as you tell me I am! I think all that yellow journalism you used to write has rubbed off on a lot more than your fingers."

Wilkie chewed his cigar and narrowed his eyes. "Colonel

---

4 "Taft Tosses Ball," *Washington Post*, 15 April 1910, 2.

Roosevelt didn't receive as many threats as you do. He wasn't such a big target." A big fat target, in Wilkie's private opinion.

"Wilkie, if you want this hard-earned knife to go with that hard-boiled attitude of yours, it'll cost you a penny. That's how it is! In fact, I'm surprised a Treasury agent like you doesn't know that." Taft took a long guzzle from his champagne bottle while Robert studied Wilkie's reaction.

Incensed, Wilkie pawed through his pocket and flipped a shiny new penny onto the table—so as not to cut whatever remained of his threadbare friendship with the president. But as the Secret Service chief reached for the puukko knife with a saffron handkerchief . . .

"By the way, you may want to put out that cigar," Taft recommended. "Since you're *so* concerned for my safety."

Wilkie took a long, hard look at the man he was sworn to protect but deep down could barely stand. Taft wasn't a president; he was a puzzlewit. A flubdub. A fathead with brains of about three-guinea-pig power. He was an unworthy successor to Theodore Roosevelt philosophically, psychologically, and unquestionably physically. Horses—full-grown horses—had collapsed under his weight. The man was so fat he couldn't even bend over to set a golf ball on a tee. His presidency was an unmitigated disaster that threatened to destroy the Republican Party. And his wife? Dear lord, his wife . . .

"Ticktock," Taft prodded.

Wilkie took one last puff from his cigar and flicked it into the ice bucket on Taft's desk. It extinguished with a long, unhappy hiss.

"Mr. President." Wilkie nodded.

"Yes, Mr. President," Taft reminded.

The Secret Service chief fumed out of the Oval Office with the puukko knife in his pocket. "I think he got the point," Robert observed. The door slammed in response.

"Oh, he'll be back to his old self halfway between here and the men's room. He just needs to cool off." Taft put his champagne on ice, smothering the Secret Service chief's cigar beneath the bottle. "So tell me, Bob, what can I do for you?"

Robert looked around the messy office. "May I sit down?"

"Of course! Make yourself comfortable." Robert took a seat in the only armchair not covered with papers. "Sorry about the mess. Norton's been working overtime to cover our tracks this past week."

"Yes, I saw him in the wireless room on my way over. You know we probably won't arrive home in time for your vacation, I'm afraid."

"That's what Archie told me," Taft lamented. "But I don't think it will cause too much harm if we're late. I'll just have Archie drop me off on the *Mayflower* while it's at sea. Nellie couldn't possibly stay angry at me if I arrived on the yacht with a bottle of her favorite champagne!" On that subject: "Ooh! Care for some bubbly water? Or something stronger, perhaps?"

"Just some coffee, please. Very black."

An amused Taft pushed a brass button under his desk. "NORTON! Bring my friend here some coffee strong enough to float an iron wedge!"

Robert, who knew every inch of the airship, noted, "That's not a radiophone."

"It isn't?" The confused president looked at the button. "What does it do?"

"I don't know." Robert shrugged. "It was on the original Roosevelt desk. We think it fired a pistol concealed beneath the tabletop."

"Oh." Taft drew his hand back. "That's odd. I've been using this thing to page Norton for months."

"If you were shouting for him at that volume, I imagine he heard you through the walls."

Taft raised his eyebrows in shock. "I thought the walls were soundproof in this office!"

"They are, but only on the inside," Robert explained. "It's an electromagnetic device Dr. Tesla invented. After your incident with the chair, we had to ensure that the Secret Service agents outside could hear you in the event that you needed assistance."

Taft twitched his mustache. "Ah, well. I guess that means you'll be getting coffee soon enough. So, what shall we talk about?"

Robert adjusted his chair, preparing to give the most difficult report in his life. But then he remembered: "Oh, by the way, how's Nellie?"

The jovial air around Taft disappeared. "She's better, she's getting better," his voice tumbled out. "It's been over a year since her illness robbed her of so many things. My dear Nellie . . ." Taft looked at her photograph with eyes awash with emotion. "Fortunately, I believe the worst is behind us. Her sisters have been a godsend, and Helen has been so good to play hostess at the mansion while her mother recovers. With their help, Nellie has been walking and talking again for months now. She has such vast reservoirs of strength, Bob. At times, she makes me feel so small." The somber president sipped from his bottle with eyes downcast.

Taft considered mentioning how disastrous his wife's illness had been for his presidency, but Robert already knew this better

than most people. Nellie had spent her whole life with her mind
fixed on the White House, having vowed as a girl not to marry
a man unless she was convinced he would be elected president
someday. William Howard Taft was that man, and through her
husband, Nellie became one of the most powerful political minds
in the country. She engineered Taft's whole career, from Cincinnati to Washington to the distant Philippines. She even vetoed
then-President Roosevelt's offer to make her husband chief justice of the Supreme Court even though it was something Taft
had longed for his whole life. Nevertheless, when William
Howard Taft was inaugurated the twenty-seventh president of
the United States in 1909, it was his brilliant, daring Nellie who
shattered all precedent by riding alongside him to the White
House. Nellie, his dearest love. His closest confidant. His madam
president. And that's when she wasn't drinking beer, smoking
cigarettes, playing poker, driving fast cars, bobsledding, bathing
in the rivers of Philippine jungles, or surfing at Waikiki Beach.
That's right, Nellie surfed.

But then, two months into Taft's presidency, a sudden illness
nearly took Nellie from him. She could not speak, half her body
was lifeless, and her face—her dear face—was frozen in a horrific
contortion. Taft did not know what to do. All the best doctors
in the country were unable to help her. For all his powers, President Taft felt like the most impotent man in America as he stood
at her bedside. And to make matters worse, Taft's presidency
was crippled without his wife's guidance. Every major decision
in his life had always been part of Nellie's design. Everything.
Even the airship and automaton were ultimately Nellie's cre-
ations: trinkets to keep her husband amused and out of the

mansion while she expertly steered the nation into the twentieth century.

It was unfair to have so much hinge on the loss of one person, but Taft did not need to explain this to Robert Todd Lincoln. As the only son of Abraham Lincoln to reach adulthood, Robert knew all too well what life and loss was like in the White House.

The president took a deep breath, and the pained expression on his face faded. Such are the powers of comet vintage. "Where were we, Bob?"

Robert leaned forward in his chair. "Will, I'm relieved to hear that Nellie is recovering, but—"

"Thank you. And I hope Mary and your daughters are well."

Robert ignored this. "Will, we need to discuss something that will not be easy for either of us."

"I understand."

"No, you don't, Will. This situation, it's . . ." Robert shifted anxiously in his chair. "I think it's unlike anything we have ever dealt with."

"You mean you and me personally?"

"No. I mean 'we' as a nation. Maybe even as a people."

As a people? Taft's whiskers perked. "Bob, what do you mean by that?"

Robert shook his head with frustration. "I don't know. The whole world looks upside down to me lately."

Taft could not help smiling coyly. "Bob, what could possibly have you so wound up? World war?"

Robert's eyes widened. "Will, I hope to God not!" He pushed himself up from his chair and walked across the room. Taft watched in bewilderment; his friend was moving like a man with a gun to his back. As Robert approached the bay window, he clasped his hands behind his back and studied the stars.

"I think I will have a drink after all," Robert decided.

"Ah, that's the spirit! Help yourself to whatever you like from the cabinet." Taft went back to suckling his bottle while Robert poured himself a large glass of aged brandy. Robert downed the stuff quickly, but it did not dent his sobriety.

"Will, do you remember that scare we had with Halley's comet?" Robert stared into his empty glass as he spoke.

"What do you mean, do I remember? Of course I do. It was all over the papers."[5]

"Yes, well . . ."

Taft raised an eyebrow, hoping he was not going to hear what he was expecting. As he anticipated, Robert Todd Lincoln remained silent. "Bob, that better not be what this is about." Taft snickered. "Five months ago, in this office, you convinced me the world was going to end. You said, standing there silently just as you are now, that Halley's comet was going to gas everyone on this planet like termites."

"How could I have said that if I was standing here silently?"

Moving along. "There was panic in the streets, Bob, but the world did not end. I thank God it didn't, but frankly, I had more than enough on my plate this Valentine's Day without bringing Armageddon into it. You're a brilliant man, Bob. As far as I'm concerned, you're a second Leonardo da Vinci, but even great men make mistakes. Just ask Thomas Edison. He said something about perspiring and taking credit for other people's inventions. I don't remember."

---

5 "Comet's Poisonous Tail," *New York Times,* 8 February 1910.

An ashamed Robert glanced at one of the room's electric lights. "Will, I know the duress I caused you could not have come at a worse time, but you have to believe me when I say that our caution was not taken in vain. I found something, Will. Something that changes everything."

"Whatever it is, Bob, it's probably nothing. Everything that was keeping you up at night turned out to be a big fat nothing. Halley's comet came and went, and we're still here. Earth won!" The president lifted his bottle with cheer and guzzled the remains of its contents.

"Will," said Robert, looking straight at the president, "my father's assassination was not nothing."

Taft froze, trying with all his ability not to spit his champagne. He unplugged the bottle from his mouth and sat up in disbelief. What could Robert Todd Lincoln possibly be talking about? Was he mad? Was he beginning to go down the same sorry path as his mother? Not knowing what to say or how to say it, Taft's eyes wandered to the copper coin Wilkie flipped onto his desk earlier. It was one of the Treasury's new Lincoln cents resting heads-up as if the ghost of Abraham Lincoln had placed it there to eavesdrop. Taft looked up at Robert, the last living heir of the greatest president in history. He had his father's prominent nose, large ears, and pensive, intelligent eyes. They were eyes this president knew he could trust.

"Please continue," Taft urged.

With his glass still in hand, Robert paced the Oval Office as he spoke. "Two months ago, I put out a wire asking universities, observatories, Army bases all over the country to monitor their skies in case Flammarion was right about Halley's comet producing enough cyanogen to wipe out all life on Earth. Fortunately, the bulk of Flammarion's fears were unfounded. The cyanogen was too dispersed to harm us when we passed through the tail of the comet. However, there was one part of North America that showed unusually high readings of . . . something in its atmosphere. Something strange. Whatever it was, Will, it was definitely *not* cyanogen."

"It was probably Mark Twain riding the comet to heaven." Taft smirked.

"No, Will. This wasn't Connecticut. The phenomenon took place over Alaska. The Wrangell mountain range, to be precise."

"The Wrangell Mountains!" Taft jumped. Robert patiently awaited the president's response. "That's . . . where J. P. Morgan and the Guggenheims are digging."

"I know. The Alaska Syndicate." The Morgan-Guggenheim syndicate was the cause of the single biggest scandal in Taft's administration: the Ballinger affair, the authorized use of Alaskan lands set aside for conservation under President Roosevelt. The controversy took place during the height of Nellie Taft's illness, and with it her husband's helplessness. Attorney General Wickersham swore Secretary of the Interior Richard Ballinger did not break any laws by permitting private use of the land, but legality does not always translate into good policy. Without Nellie's guidance, the crisis had exploded beyond anything Taft could control.

"You don't think the Kennecott mines have anything to do with this, do you?" asked the president. The mines were the heart of the syndicate's activities in Alaska.

"It's too soon to tell, Will. Additional research is needed. It will require soil samples from parts of the world few people can reach by rail."

Taft narrowed his eyes. "You're here about the airship, aren't you?" he asked, grinning. The president hoped to get a smile out of Robert, but instead the last son of Lincoln merely nodded. Fortunately, that was good enough for Taft to celebrate. "Well! I'm sure Archie should be able to help you. Nellie and I will be at sea for ten days, so please consider the zeppelin yours until we return. Just try to keep a low profile, Bob. The Department of the Interior is a circus right now. I want you to avoid them. Speak with John Hays Hammond instead. He was Guggenheim's chief engineer for years and is an old friend of mine from Yale. He's a good man, Bob. I want you to know you can trust him."

"Thanks, Will. And yes, I know John quite well."

"Ah, then you're already ready!" Taft cheered. He considered popping open another bottle of champagne to celebrate, when something hit him like a meteor. "But then, you could have done all this yourself. You knew Nellie and I would be on vacation. The airship was yours for the taking. Why take a boat across the Atlantic to ask me in person? You could have just sent me a wire. Also, what does any of this have to do with . . ." Taft hesitated. "Your father's death?"

Robert set down his glass and slipped his hand into his right coat pocket. "For two years, I have been going through my father's papers for his centennial. Every letter, every correspondence, everything John Hay and I packed before we moved out of the mansion." Robert paused, his brown eyes staring deep into Taft's. "Before the Fourth of July, I found a slip to a safe-deposit box the government opened with the Safe Deposit Company of New York. The account was dated May first: the company's first day of business and two weeks after my father was murdered.[6] I paid the bank a visit before I steamed over here. The account for the box was still open. I found this inside."

Robert pulled a bulky folded handkerchief out of his pocket and rested it gently on the president's desk. He carefully undressed the bundle, revealing a magnificent gold pocket watch along with a gold chain and a dazzling fob made out of gold-bearing quartz.

Its loveliness glistened in the president's eyes. "Was this your father's?" Taft asked.

"I'm not sure," replied Robert. "My father had several pocket watches, but I never saw him wear this one. However, this piece"—Robert tapped the watch fob—"was in his pocket the night he was assassinated. In all my research, I could never determine how that fob got into his pocket. There is no receipt of sale or repair, no photograph of my father wearing it, no mention of it in any letters; nothing. For decades it tortured me. It shouldn't exist."

"You always had the fob?"

"Yes, but not the pocket watch or the chain. I found those in the safe-deposit box."

Taft moved his hand toward the watch. "May I?"

Robert nodded.

The president gently lifted the timepiece into his thick hands. The watch had the weight of pure gold. At first instinct, Taft gently pressed on its winding crown, opening its lid to reveal a white dial with thin Roman numerals. It was a hunter's watch, but neither its hands nor its second dial were moving. Taft tried adjusting its time, but the crown would not budge. The elegant device was silent and still.

---

6 "The Safe Deposit Company of New-York," *New York Times*, 1 May 1865.

"How are you supposed to wind this thing?" Taft asked.

"That's what's so confusing to me. It's not meant to be wound. That watch has no keyhole in its case back, no way to adjust its time, and look here." Robert traced his finger along a cauterized seam on its edge. "I did that. It was the only way I could take a look at its works. The watch was totally sealed when I found it. Waterproof, even. It was as if the watch was not meant to be opened or adjusted. Ever."

Taft looked at Robert and then back to the timepiece. "Did you find anything unusual inside?"

Robert was near speechless. "Will, this watch is the most unusual device ever built! It has no working power source and no sign that it is anything other than ornamental, but I know for certain that it is functional. Its inner workings show wear as if the device had been running without interruption for decades! Maybe even until recently."

Taft ran his fingers over the watch's elegant engravings. For all its technical peculiarities, it was still an enchantingly beautiful work of art. But as Taft admired the timepiece, something marked inside its lid caught his eye:

Сдѣлано

въ

Америкѣ

Taft immediately recognized the Cyrillic script. "Wait a minute. This thing is Russian?"

Robert could not believe he forgot this. "Sorry, Will. I did not see the forest for the trees. You would think that inscription means the watch comes from Russia, but it doesn't. I shared a rubbing of this with Ambassador Rosen's people in Washington, and they assured me that the engraving reads 'Made in America.'"

Taft stared at Robert, surprised.

"There's more. It may not be the answer we're looking for, but it's the best theory I have: Before we purchased Alaska in 1867, the official name for the territory was Russian America."

"Ah yes, Seward's folly," Taft recalled, along with the laughter then-Secretary of State Seward received for the Alaska Purchase. "You know, my father was ambassador to Russia back in the eighties. I wonder if he knew anything about this." Taft gently set the watch back on its handkerchief as he remembered his late father. "Have you considered asking Frederick Seward about this?"

"Yes, I did," Robert said with some sadness. "I was hoping he knew something I didn't about the watch fob, but he's eighty years old, Will. All he remembers from April fourteenth is the part where his father was stabbed a dozen times while he lay helpless in bed. That madman Lewis Powell nearly murdered the whole Seward household that night. Frederick's own mother died two months later from the shock of it all. I can't blame him for only having nightmares to hold on to at this point in his life. Believe me, Will. I know what it's like." Robert stopped, not wanting to go into detail about his recent bouts with insomnia.

Judging from Taft's response, Robert did not need to. "Bob, I would never presume what that terrible night meant for you or for Frederick. But as president, I know full well what it did to this country. If this watch was in any way connected to your father's murder, I will spare no expense to get you the answers you deserve. But I must know, Bob. What could this pocket watch, or for that matter your father's assassination, possibly have to do with the recent passing of Halley's comet?"

Robert stood tall and put his hands behind his back as he spoke. "Mr. President, this pocket watch on your desk is a historic and scientific anomaly. It likely found its way into the White House when Washington, DC, was the most fortified city on Earth. A piece of it somehow found its way onto my father the night he was killed despite there being no evidence it ever came into his possession. There is no mention of it in any of the government's inquiries on the assassination. It does not work, it should not work, and yet it somehow functioned flawlessly without human contact up to the turn of the century. And in addition, this watch was supposedly made in one of the most remote, desolate, unknown parts of the world using technology far more advanced than anything from its era or ours."

"So you're saying this watch has something to do with the activity you monitored in Alaska?"

"No, Will. I'm saying this watch is proof that there is something in Alaska completely alien to this planet, and that it might have been one of the last things my father learned before he was murdered."

Chapter IV

Meanwhile . . .

W ould someone please get the president some damn coffee! I can hear him shouting from here!"

In the bustling, noisy wireless room aboard Airship One,
Charles Dyer Norton was hard at work trying to diffuse the most
persistent presidential problem since George Washington's den-
tures. Not too long ago, Norton had such high hopes as the
nation's new secretary to the president. He was charismatic,
assertive, and so shamelessly full of himself that he used to refer
to his full title as "assistant president." Well, Nellie Taft put a
quick end to that. Two months later, Norton was working more
than one hundred hours a week on a misinformation campaign
to keep the president's new exercise routine a secret. He had a
whole team on the airship producing fraudulent interviews, fake
letters, doctored photographs, and even forged journal entries to

make Taft appear everywhere in the world he was not. For a government employee as self-important as Norton, it was like using a pair of chopsticks to clean up after an elephant. The man was disheveled, exhausted, and surviving on a steady diet of tobacco and coffee. And that was before having to deal with a president as uncontrollable as William Howard Taft's decoy.

"Dr. Tesla, this is not a matter of money!" Norton dictated over the wireless. He had a cigarette in his hand and another in his mouth as he spoke. "It's a matter of national security that we maintain the illusion of our presence at Beverly. We need a fully functional android in the president's likeness by Monday to avoid any suspicion about his"—Secretary Norton had to shut his eyes as he said it—"prizefighting."

Tesla's reply arrived promptly on the airship's modified Burry ticker.

TESLA

NO EXPLANATIONS ARE NECESSARY RE OFFICIAL MATTERS. PUTTING FAITH IN EDISON WAS UNFORTUNATE. A TELAUTOMATON OF THE PRESIDENT'S SIZE WILL TAKE MANY MONTHS TO DEVISE.

"Dr. Tesla, this is dire! We need something now! If it can walk up ramps and wave at crowds without bursting into flames, we'll take it! Can you do this with any of the designs we sent on the phototelegraph?"

TESLA

ONE MOMENT PLEASE. THERE IS A—

A loud popping sound was picked up on the wireless, forcing Norton and his operators to cover their ears.

"What the dickens?" Norton grimaced.

"Interference, sir," said one of the wireless operators. "Probably another one of Dr. Tesla's experiments."

"God damn these wizards!" Norton cursed. "There's a malfunctioning automaton in the White House, we're an Atlantic Ocean away from where we should be, and the only man who can help us is testing an earthquake machine!"

"Sir, I think we have a transmission incoming."

"Good! What does Dr. Tesla have to say?"

The Burry ticker started printing an unusual array of letters:

LAANI LELLS ANIAA AILAS ISIII AILAN ENNAI IISLN
AALLI INALL IINA

"What the devil?" Norton studied the ticker tape as it printed. "Consarn it! Are you lollygaggers playing correspondence chess on the wireless again?"

"No, sir!"

The ticker continued whirling:

LAANI LELLS ANIAA AILAS ISIII AIEAA ISLIE A
LLEIL SLSII

"Gadzooks!" one of the operators ejaculated. "This looks like a ciphertext!"

"Are we expecting any encoded messages?" asked Norton.

"Not like this, sir. This encryption isn't one of ours."

"Fiddlesticks! Keep the ticker rolling, gentlemen. I'll be right back."

"Aye, sir," the operators responded, one of them surreptitiously hiding his chess card from Norton.

Norton opened the white door behind him and rushed into his office. Assistant Secretaries Rudolph Forster and Wendell W. Mischler looked up at their boss from behind tall towers of paper. "Something's afoul in the wireless room, boys," Norton said. "Summon Captain Butt and the attorney general immediately." Norton ducked back into the telegraph office while his assistants fanned through the airship.

"Any word?" Norton asked as he closed the wireless room's three doors.

"Not a dit."

"Damnation. Well, just keep the channels clear! I don't want anyone jamming our lines with—"

The Burry started ticking again.

TESLA

DID YOU JUST SEND ME AN ENCRYPTION?

"Finally!" Norton threw his hands up, losing a cigarette in the process. "Tell Dr. Tesla that we did not send any coded transmissions. And forward him a copy of the ciphertext we received."

"Aye, sir."

Norton lit himself a new cigarette. He always carried a third one behind his ear.

From behind him: "Secretary Norton? The attorney general and Captain Butt have arrived."

"Good, send them in."

Wickersham and the captain stepped into the wireless room, which by now was overflowing with well-tailored men. Somehow, Secret Service Chief Wilkie was already in the room as well.

"Wilkie! When did you get here?"

"I was on my way to the gents' room to let off some steam. I just wasn't expecting there to be an office party."

Norton groaned. "Fine, you can stay." Wilkie sat on the edge of a table and lit a new cigar, which made the already cramped room so hot that its operators were wiping sweat off their brows. Attorney General Wickersham and Captain Butt were deep in discussion, Assistant Secretaries Forster and Mischler were standing outside the door, and everyone from the staff room next door filed into the halls of the West Wing for a look. Norton, dizzied by the commotion brewing around him, dabbed his face with a handkerchief and desperately tried to contain the mob.

"Gentlemen," Norton called to order. Through the crowd, he saw a slender arm waving a pencil. ". . . and Miss Knox. We intercepted an encrypted message from Nikola Tesla in New York. He says he—"

The Burry ticker responded:

TESLA

I RECEIVED THE SAME TRANSMISSION MINUTES AGO. MORE INCOMING. WILL REWIRE MESSAGES AS THEY COME IN.

"Thank God in heaven," praised Norton. "Operator, please send Dr. Tesla our thanks."

"There's more to this?" asked Captain Butt as he examined the ciphertext.

"Relay that question," Norton ordered.

TESLA

YES. NOT THE FIRST TIME THIS HAS HAPPENED. NEIGHBORS AND UNFRIENDLY BUSINESSES USE LAB'S LINES WITHOUT PERMISSION. SAVES THEM MONEY AND JAMS OUR FREQUENCIES. POLICE DO NOTHING.

"Sounds like Commissioner Baker needs to be taken off easy street and put onto early retirement," Wilkie observed while blowing smoke rings onto the back of Norton's head.

"Sergeant," said Captain Butt. "Tell Dr. Tesla this encryption is not used by the Army or Navy. Ask him if there is anything he can tell us about it."

"Aye, Captain." The operator tapped this out on his Triumph telegraph key. Tesla's reply arrived before the operator even finished his message.

TESLA

THE TRANSMISSION IS IN A POLYGRAPHIC SUBSTITUTION CIPHER. VERY BASIC. PROBABLY AMATEUR.

Everyone looked to Captain Butt for some answers, but he had none. "Who would flood Nikola Tesla's private lines with encoded messages?" he asked.

"Sweethearts?" Wilkie suggested with a wink to the captain.

"Unlikely," said Butt. "Dr. Tesla, can you decipher this message for us?"

TESLA

I HAVE ALREADY BEGUN TO. THE MESSAGE IS IN EN-
GLISH. JUST A MOMENT.

All eyes were on the Burry ticker. Its silence seemed to stretch
on forever.

"Is that thing still on?" Captain Butt asked Wilkie.

"What the hell are you asking me for?"

With a jolt of blue lightning, the machine roared to life like a
locomotive.

GENTLEMAN FROM NEW YORK

AHOY HOY.

GENTLEMAN FROM PARIS

HULLO.

GENTLEMAN FROM BRUSSELS

HELLO.

GENTLEMAN FROM BOMA

GENTLEMAN FROM PHILADELPHIA

GREETINGS.

GENTLEMAN FROM PARIS

GOOD DAY TO YOU. IS THIS EVERYONE?

GENTLEMAN FROM NEW YORK

ALL BUT BOMA.

GENTLEMAN FROM PARIS

BOMA? PLEASE RESPOND.

GENTLEMAN FROM BRUSSELS

BOMA IS FINE. PLEASE CONTINUE.

GENTLEMAN FROM PARIS

VERY WELL. GENTLEMEN, IT IS A PLEASURE TO SPEAK WITH YOU ONCE AGAIN. I BELIEVE OUR BUSINESS PARTNER IN NEW YORK HAS SOMETHING HE WOULD LIKE TO SHARE WITH US?

GENTLEMAN FROM NEW YORK

I RESPECTFULLY DEFER TO THE GENTLEMAN FROM PHILADELPHIA.

GENTLEMAN FROM PARIS

VERY WELL. PHILADELPHIA?

GENTLEMAN FROM PHILADELPHIA

THANK YOU, SIR. GENTLEMEN, I AM PLEASED TO ANNOUNCE THAT THE DAY SO MANY OF US INVESTED MILLIONS OF DOLLARS INTO HAS ARRIVED. THE BONANZA HAS BEEN BREACHED. REPEAT, THE BONANZA HAS BEEN BREACHED.

GENTLEMAN FROM BRUSSELS

DOES IT CONTAIN WHAT YOU SAID IT WOULD?

GENTLEMAN FROM PHILADELPHIA

WE BELIEVE SO.

GENTLEMAN FROM BRUSSELS
PARIS? CAN YOU VERIFY THIS REPORT?

GENTLEMAN FROM PARIS
I CAN, SIR. IF THEIR FIGURES ARE CORRECT, THERE IS MORE THAN ENOUGH MATERIAL AT THIS SITE TO SUPPLY OUR WHOLE OPERATION.

GENTLEMAN FROM BRUSSELS
EXCELLENT. HOW MANY SURVIVORS? PHILADELPHIA?

GENTLEMAN FROM PHILADELPHIA
I RESPECTFULLY DEFER TO THE GENTLEMAN FROM PARIS.

GENTLEMAN FROM BRUSSELS
PARIS?

GENTLEMAN FROM PARIS
NONE, SIR.

GENTLEMAN FROM BRUSSELS
AND THE BODIES?

GENTLEMAN FROM PARIS
THEY HAVE ALL BEEN COLLECTED. THEY ARE PER-FECTLY PRESERVED FOR RESEARCH.

GENTLEMAN FROM BRUSSELS
VERY GOOD. I MUST SAY I AM IMPRESSED WITH YOUR RESULTS, GENTLEMEN.

GENTLEMAN FROM PHILADELPHIA
THANK YOU, SIR.

GENTLEMAN FROM NEW YORK
THANK YOU.

GENTLEMAN FROM BRUSSELS
HOW LONG UNTIL WE CAN BEGIN EXTRACTION?

GENTLEMAN FROM PHILADELPHIA
IT HAS ALREADY BEGUN. TRAINS SHOULD START GOING OUT ABOUT ONE YEAR FROM NOW.

GENTLEMAN FROM BRUSSELS
PARIS? WILL THIS INTERFERE WITH YOUR OPERATIONS AT BELFAST?

GENTLEMAN FROM PARIS
NOT AT ALL. WE ARE CURRENTLY AHEAD OF SCHEDULE.

GENTLEMAN FROM BRUSSELS
VERY WELL. I WILL WORK WITH BOMA TO FACILITATE YOUR DELIVERY. WE WILL BE WAITING FOR YOU.

GENTLEMAN FROM NEW YORK
THANK YOU.

GENTLEMAN FROM PARIS
I BELIEVE THAT IS EVERYTHING IN TODAY'S AGENDA. ARE THERE ANY OBJECTIONS IF WE ADJOURN?

GENTLEMAN FROM BRUSSELS

NAY.

GENTLEMAN FROM NEW YORK

NAY.

GENTLEMAN FROM PHILADELPHIA

NAY.

GENTLEMAN FROM BOMA

.

GENTLEMAN FROM PARIS

VERY WELL. THAT WILL BE ALL, GENTLEMEN. YOU
MAY TAKE FULL PRECAUTIONS.

An earsplitting screech rang through the office.

"What the devil was that?" Norton winced as he covered his ears. "Are we under attack?"

"We're not under attack, you fool!" Captain Butt shouted. "Everybody be calm!" The captain rushed to Miss Knox's aid while the rest of the West Wing appeared to descend into chaos.

"Sir!" shouted an operator once the screeching stopped. "The noise was coming from Dr. Tesla!" Right on cue, the Burry ticker started printing, but any attempt to read it aloud was lost amidst the uproar in the hallway.

"Quiet, please!" Norton tried to holler over the crowd, but to no avail. "Everyone hush!" faired even worse due to "hush" being such an inherently quiet word.

With no hope of Secretary Norton quieting the mob, Wilkie drew his pistol and pulled a Morgan silver dollar from his pocket. He flipped the coin in the air and shot it at point-blank range with a .38 Special, causing everyone except Miss Knox and Captain Butt to hit the floor. The coin caught the bullet and imbedded itself in the wireless room's ceiling, narrowly saving everyone on the hydrogen-filled aircraft from a fiery death. With both the screeching and screaming muzzled, the crowd was controlled.

"Miss Knox," Wilkie asked as he tapped the ash from his cigar, "would you please read what the good doctor Tesla just sent us?"

"Yes, Mr. Wilkie." Miss Knox walked out of Butt's embrace and read Nikola Tesla's message aloud from the Burry:

TESLA

I APOLOGIZE FOR MY TEMPORARY LACK OF COMMU-
NICATION. THERE HAS JUST BEEN AN ATTEMPT ON MY
LIFE.

"His life?" Norton gasped while Wilkie reloaded his revolver. Miss Knox continued:

TESLA

YES, MY LIFE. DO NOT WORRY. I AM UNHARMED AND
MY ATTACKER HAS BEEN NEUTRALIZED. I APOLOGIZE
THERE WILL BE NO BODY FOR THE CITY'S CORONERS
TO COLLECT, BUT PLEASE ASSURE UNITED STATES
ATTORNEY GENERAL WICKERSHAM THAT MY ASSAIL-
ANT IS THOROUGHLY DECEASED.

One of the telegraphs sparked eerily as Miss Knox read that last part.

TESLA

PLEASE KNOW THAT I TOOK THE LIBERTY TO WIRE SOME OF THE REPEATER STATIONS USED THROUGHOUT THIS COMMUNICATION. I REGRET TO SAY THAT ALL THEIR LINES ARE DEAD. I AM AFRAID YOU MIGHT HAVE A MASS MURDER ON YOUR HANDS, SPANNED ACROSS SEVERAL COUNTRIES.

AND LASTLY, WHILE I IMAGINE THIS IS OF LITTLE IMPORT, IT MAY INTEREST YOU TO KNOW THAT THE KEYWORD TO THE CIPHER I DECRYPTED WAS "ALIENS."

Miss Knox looked up from the ribbon. "And that's all he wrote," she said.

Without saying a word, Secretary Norton filled his arms with the heap of ticker tape on the floor and leaped out of the office, colliding with two stewards carrying a large wicker basket and some coffee in the hallway. Now covered in equal amounts of Bavarian cream, cigarette ash, Belgian chocolate, coffee, Limburger, and flowers, Norton threw his tape into the steward's basket and rushed to the Oval Office. He kicked open the door to find President Taft at his desk with Robert Todd Lincoln standing in front of him, and with a gold pocket watch on the table. Robert coolly pocketed the timepiece just as Norton delivered the overflowing pile of paperwork to the president.

"Mr. President!" Norton gasped as half the West Wing peered in from the hallway. "Aliens!"

Taft took one look at the mound of paper on his desk and then turned back to Robert.

"I don't like the sound of that, Bob."

"Me neither," said Robert.

However, the assortment of cheese and sausages in the basket looked first-rate to the president.

Chapter V

"Hail to the Chief!"

. . . our invincible commandant.

Hail to the Chief! He hath bested one and all. [In combat!]

Hail to the Chief twice as strong as Andrew Jackson.

Here comes the President William Howard Taft!

Airship One moored over Washington's National Park to the surprise and delight of all in attendance. The Cleveland Naps were playing the Nationals, it was the bottom of the ninth, and Cy Young was just three outs away from making major-league history.[7] It was a great day for baseball, but President Taft stole the show by eclipsing the sun with his spectacular zeppelin. The ivory airship was dressed vibrantly in fluttering banners and flags, and its windows rained a patriotic downpour of ticker tape in red, white, and blue. The president received wave after

---

7 "Young Makes a Record," *New-York Daily Tribune*, 20 July 1910, 5.

wave of applause as he strutted onto the ball field to the ruffle of drums and the flourish of trumpets. Never before had a president demonstrated such open love for the sport, and the response from the grandstand to the bleachers was euphoric. Taft had the vox populi in his back pocket and the best damned recording of "Hail to the Chief" blasting down from the airship's loudspeakers.

> *Like a Greek god, he looms o'er our mighty nation*
> *From Airship One, Earth's most awesome machine! [An aircraft!]*
> *Down on our knees, we acclaim in adulation:*
> *"Hail to the Chief of Chiefs, President Taft!"*

"I love baseball," Taft sighed as he waved to the fans. "Such a good, clean, straight game. Such a healthy amusement."

"That's beautiful," cooed Wilkie. "I'm sure it'll go great with our pictures in tomorrow's newspapers." The president's staff was mortified by the spectacle Taft was forcing them into.

"Who wrote those lyrics?" asked Captain Butt as he looked up at the airship.

"Do you like them?" Taft grinned. "I had Nora Bayes write and record everything with the Marine band. With some creative input from yours truly, of course." Taft ran his thumbs down his jacket's lapels as if they were the enormous suspenders holding up his trousers.

"Will, why is Nora Bayes recording songs for the U.S. government?" asked Attorney General Wickersham.

"It's funny you of all people should ask!" Taft laughed. "I got the idea from a letter a constituent in New York sent me."

"The kid with the ice cream?"

"No, this one was a teenager. Same sack of mail, though. He said he and his brothers are coconuts about baseball and could not be happier with my support of the sport! As a sign of thanks, they suggested I dress up 'Hail to the Chief' the next time I attended a game. I thought it was a fantastic idea. Nora and I even used some of their lyrics!"

"Great. I'm sure they're laughing it up in a pool room right now," growled the Secret Service director.

"What was the boy's name?" asked Wickersham.

Taft had to think for a minute. "Groucho. Strange name for a youth. I think he comes from a family of Italian Jews."

"It's nice to know you have that voting bloc locked up," Wilkie scoffed as he lit a cigar.

"John, you should be enjoying this more than anyone!" Taft chided. "Teddy never took you out to the ball game, did he?"

"Colonel Roosevelt preferred football," Wilkie grumbled as the president shook hands with the athletes.

None of this political banter reached Norton. The overworked secretary groaned loudly as the president exchanged handshakes with Deacon McGuire and Loafer McAleer. Norton had no idea how he was going to keep such a huge appearance a secret, never mind the even worse disaster unfolding at the executive mansion. "Mr. President, may we *please* leave? We are urgently needed at the White House!"

"Go home? We just got here!—Oh, thank you!" The president caught a five-cent bag of peanuts lobbed at him from the stands. "Hey, can someone throw me a hot dog and a pop!"

"Will . . ." the attorney general urged.

"Oh, and an ice cream?"

"Norton's right," said Wickersham. "We need to leave. That military hardware in the air is supposed to be a national secret."

"Relax! Just say it's a hot-air balloon, or a weather experiment."

"Yeah, some sort of gasbag," Wilkie ragged.

"Mr. Wilkie, don't be cruel," Taft tut-tutted as he daintily flicked an empty peanut shell at the Secret Service chief's face.

"Mr. President, I agree with the attorney general. Expedience is advisable," advised Butt. "Also, please remember our conversation from earlier. It's Tuesday. Haven't we caused enough damage already?"

"All right, all right. This one's for you, Archie." Taft handed Norton his bag of peanuts and made a beeline to home plate, where a podium with fan flags had been hastily assembled. On his way, Taft shook hands and chatted with his home state's star player, Cy Young. "I hope I am not a hoodoo!" Taft joked as he lightheartedly punched the pitcher in his right shoulder. As the president took the podium, several teammates rushed to Cy's aid. The man was holding his right arm and doubled over in pain.

"Hello!" Taft greeted his overjoyed audience. Everyone in the stadium was cheering, eager to hear what their president had to say after such an extravagant entrance. "I must be going."

And on that note, Taft left.

Unprepared for the president's abrupt departure, the airship crew cranked a hurried "Hail to the Chief" on the Victrola as Taft punched Cy Young one last time on the shoulder. Taft's secretaries then whisked the president out of the park, leaving the stadium speechless and wondering what on Earth had just happened during the last several minutes.

"Good speech," said Robert, who had watched the spectacle unfold from the side lot. "My father always liked keeping things short."

"I'm flattered by the comparison, Mr. Lincoln. Too bad you couldn't join us."

Robert shook his head. "It's for your own safety, Mr. President. There is a certain fatality about presidential functions I attend."

"Too true, too true." Taft turned to Butt. "Is the car ready?"

"Yes, Mr. President."

"Very good. Let's skiddoo."

Outside National Park, White House chauffeur George Robinson leaned in full uniform against the president's forty-horsepower 1909 White Model M steam touring car. The emerald green, three-thousand-dollar auto sported brass fixtures, an open top, and a carmine leather interior as lush as any Airship One sofa. Its tall, barrel-chested custodian, while not the friendliest person in Washington, enjoyed the reputation of a daredevil behind the wheel.[8] He was the best driver in the War Department and a modern-day poet in the timeless art of profanity. With his hat tipped and arms folded, he looked like he had been waiting all day for someone to snap a picture of him in front of the fine vehicle.

"Good afternoon, Mr. President." Robinson saluted. "Welcome back."

"Hello, George. I'm afraid I have some bad news: You're fired."

The chauffeur took his termination without protest. "If you wanted to drive, Mr. President, all you had to do was ask nicely."

"Sorry, George. We don't have the time to play countess. I'm

---

8 "Taft's Daredevil Chauffeur," *New York Times*, 15 August 1909.

about to break every speed limit in this city, and I don't think your chauffeur's license can handle that kind of abuse."

"If you insist, Mr. President." Robinson kicked himself up from the car's running board and stepped aside. "Since we're being curt, Mr. President, you should know that your double is on a goddamn rampage through the mansion."

"How bad is it?" Robert asked as the chauffeur helped shove the enormous president into the driver's seat.

"Let me put it this way, Mr. Lincoln: I'm glad I got all the cars into the garage."

"And the horses?" asked Butt.

"I'm a chauffeur, not a squire, Captain." Robinson opened the side doors for Wilkie, Wickersham, and three Secret Service agents as he spoke. "Last I saw, the palfreys looked pretty spooked." Robinson turned to Taft. "I hope you're ready for war, Mr. President."

"Don't worry," Taft boasted. "I'm confident I can handle myself in a fight."

"I was referring to Madam President, Mr. President." Robinson slammed the car door, having wiped the wide smile from the president's face.

"Woah! Where do you think you're going?" Taft hollered as Norton approached the car.

The secretary froze. "Mr. President, I thought I was coming?"

"Oh, no, no, no. Mr. Lincoln's riding shotgun. You're flying home on the hydrogen helicopter. Same as you, Mr. Robinson, I'm sorry to say."

"No need to apologize, sir. You're the one I feel sorry for." The chauffeur stood at full attention. "Mr. President." Taft smirked as his chauffeur and Norton walked back to the airship.

"Archie." Taft addressed Captain Butt. "I want you to have the airship refueled and ready to depart by nightfall. You're taking Mr. Lincoln to Alaska on a scientific excursion. Pick up John Hays Hammond and meet us at the White House. Come in through the roof if you need to."

"Yes, Mr. President."

"And Archie"—Taft moved in close—"I want you to know it's not your fault that we floated in late. Just because you know both sides of the shield doesn't mean I get to use you as one."

The captain bowed his head. "Thank you, Mr. President."

"See you soon, Archie." Taft smiled. The captain marched back to his airship as the president blasted some steam from the auto. Its busy engine was hissing like a train at a station.

"That propels it," Robert pointed out.

"I know that!" Taft touted. "And this controls it!" The president sat proudly behind the steering wheel until he felt something sticking into his backside. He felt around with his hand and pulled up a pair of driving goggles. "Do you want these?" he offered.

"No thank you," said Robert. "I think my spectacles will suffice."

"Well, if you insist . . ." Taft put on the goggles and grinned brightly. "Hold on to your hats, gentlemen! It's a bumpy road to the White House!"

Taft stomped on the pedal and sent the car speeding, its driver's-side wheel gasping for air the whole ride.

Chapter VI

"So, What Do We Know About Aliens?"

The president shouted over the White Model M's screaming steam engine. The car was racing southwest down Vermont Avenue well over the speed limit for Washington, DC.

"Will, there's no need to shout!" Robert shouted over the whinnies of panicking horses. "Besides, are you sure you want to talk about this in the auto?"

"RELAX! I RIDE THIS THING ALL THE TIME! NO ONE IN THE BACK CAN HEAR US!"

In the backseat, the attorney general gave Wilkie a confused look. "I can hear everything," said Wickersham. The Secret Service chief responded by brushing his forefinger against his nose. Secret Service Agents Sloan, Jervis, and Wheeler nodded in agreement. Wilkie lit himself a new cigar as the eavesdropping began.

"LET'S START WITH THE OBVIOUS CANDIDATES, BOB. MARTIANS! DO THEY EXIST?"

Robert looked over his right shoulder, and then asked: "Do you mean empirically or hypothetically?"

"JUST TELL ME IF THERE ARE ANY LITTLE GREEN MEN IN ALASKA!"

The five men in the back shared uneasy glances with one another. Even Wilkie was caught by surprise. His cigar fell out of his mouth and onto his lap.

"I thought they were talking about foreigners," Wickersham whispered.

"So did I!" said Wilkie. He hurriedly brushed cigar ash from his crotch as the conversation in the front seats continued.

"Green-skinned Martians come from a story called 'The Green Boy from Hurrah.' It's children's literature," explained Robert. "There's nothing scientific about it."

Taft laughed heartily. "I THOUGHT YOU READ THOSE TYPES OF BOOKS ALL THE TIME!"

Robert watched the street with concern as pedestrians leaped away from the auto. "Some books make for better research than others. Jonathan Swift correctly predicted Mars had two moons in *Gulliver's Travels*."

"REALLY?"

"Yes. Phobos and Deimos. 'Fear' and 'Terror.'"

Lovely names, thought the president.

"Mr. President, the road!" the attorney general shouted.

"WOAH!" Taft stomped on his horn and swerved past an empty public school wagon. "HEY, LOBCOCK! SCHOOL'S OUT!" shouted the twenty-seventh president of the United States to a bewildered public school wagon driver.

"Will, would you slow down?" Robert pleaded. "The car's going twice as fast as the fastest racehorse in history!"

"HEY, FOR FORTY HORSEPOWER, I EXPECTED MORE FROM ITS MOTOR!"

"Horse!" screamed Wickersham.

"SORRY!" Taft narrowly threaded the auto through opposing carriages at R Street. "WHAT ABOUT H. G. WELLS? DID HE WRITE ANYTHING ABOUT MARTIANS THAT WE SHOULD TAKE SERIOUSLY?"

"Not really," said Robert. "He was using old data. Giovanni Schiaparelli started that whole Martian canal craze last century. Many astronomers believed it until better telescopes completely debunked the theory. I observe Mars regularly from my observatory. There are no Martian canals. Or at least none we can see from our planet."

"THAT'S TOO BAD!" Taft shouted. "I WAS ABOUT TO ASK YOU TO FLY TO ITALY WHEN YOU WERE DONE IN ALASKA!"

Robert dismissed this. "I couldn't interview Schiaparelli if I wanted to. He died two weeks ago on the Fourth of July."[9]

Taft stared at Robert, dumbfounded.

"Turn the wheel, you beanhead!" Wilkie yelled from the backseat. The steamer was veering into oncoming traffic at Iowa Circle.

"BEJESUS! HOLD ON!" Taft made a sharp right onto the sidewalk and into Iowa Circle's small park. The auto sped headlong toward a statue of Union General John A. Logan, prompting Taft to steer in a tight circle around the equestrian.

---

9 "Prof. G. V. Schiaparelli Dead," *New York Times,* 6 July 1910.

"Are you sure you don't want me to drive?" Robert offered.

"BOB, JUST POINT ME HOME AND EVERYTHING WILL BE BULLY!"

Robert reached into his pocket and pulled out a compass. It was spinning like a pinwheel. "That road will take us straight to the White House," he directed, pointing southwest.

"UH . . ." The tiny park and its twelve paths rushed past Taft like a merry-go-round. "WHICH ONE? THEY ALL LOOK THE SAME!"

"The one with the Washington Monument behind it."

"Just get us the hell out of here!" In the back, Wilkie was desperately trying to hold on to his boater hat. And his hair.

Taft aimed for the monument, but steered his wheel a little too late. The car tore through grass until it was out of the park, sputtering westward down Rhode Island Avenue.

"Enough of this." Wilkie shoved Agents Sloan and Jervis aside and stuck his head between Robert and Taft. "Mr. President, as the man most responsible for your life, I must report that you're on the verge of getting yourself killed!"

"COOL YOUR COALS, HOTHEAD!" Taft honked the horn until Wilkie returned to his seat. "SO, MARTIANS ARE COMPLETELY OUT OF THE PICTURE?" the president asked Mr. Lincoln.

Robert fell silent as he considered this.

"BOB?"

"No," he answered. "Not entirely. There are a few things that concern me about Mars once you add Alaska to the equation."

"LET'S HEAR 'EM! AND KEEP IT SIMPLE!"

"Evolution," began Robert. "Wells based a lot of *The War of the Worlds* on Darwin. In my research, I never found anything more compelling about life on Earth than how closely we resemble our planet. Seventy percent of Earth's surface is water. So is about seventy percent of the human body. Even large animals like elephants are seventy percent water."

Taft smiled at this, taking it as a nod to the Republican Party.

"If there is or ever was life on Mars, it had to adapt to an environment with freezing temperatures and much less water than we have on Earth."

"WHAT DOES THAT HAVE TO DO WITH ALASKA?"

"Mars doesn't have water. It has ice!"

"Watch the road . . ." Wilkie grumbled.

Taft zigzagged the steamer past a trolley and onto the north side of Scott Circle.

"Make a right at that fish wagon onto Sixteenth Street," said Robert.

"TOO LATE!" Taft accidently steered into a different fish wagon on Massachusetts Avenue, destroying it. Fortunately, no one was hurt.

"WILKIE! WHAT KIND OF WAGON WAS THAT?"

The Secret Service chief quickly studied the wreck behind them. "There's a big sign that says 'kipper.'"

"YES, THAT'S WHAT I SMELLED! HAVE SOMEONE FROM THE TREASURY REIMBURSE THAT MAN! ALSO, HAVE THEM BRING HOME SOME OF THAT FISH!"

A frustrated Wilkie reached into his jacket for his pad and a pencil.

"SO, BACK TO THE RED PLANET!"

Robert picked up where he left off. "We have known about the Martian polar ice caps for centuries. We know they grow and shrink at different seasons, just like ours. We know Mars has an axial tilt similar to Earth's. We even know the Martian day is approximately twenty-four hours long. If Martians, assuming they exist, need a cold environment with conditions similar to their own, Alaska would be a convenient location for them on Earth."

"GREAT! AND HOW DID THEY COME OVER?"

"Will, we're talking well beyond any reasonable—"

"JUST TELL ME HOW WE WOULD DO IT!"

After a moment's thought, Robert replied, "Newton's cannonball."

The president gave Robert another confused look.

"Dupont Circle," one of the men from the back seat called out.

Taft looped the car around the intersection and onto New Hampshire Avenue. "You should have taken Connecticut Avenue," Wilkie pestered, but Taft ignored him.

"It is theoretically possible to journey into outer space," Robert continued. "However, I suggest we lower our voices for the rest of the ride."

"OH!" Taft gasped. "Sorry! So, Newton's cannon . . ."

"Cannonball."

"Is there a big gun involved, or is this just something he made up to prove a point?"

"It's a bit of both, actually. The idea is if you fired a cannon high enough, you would be able to shoot something out of orbit. Jules Verne used it in *From the Earth to the Moon,* as did Georges Méliès in one of his moving picture shows. In 1903, a Russian scientist named Konstantin Tsiolkovsky dismissed the idea as unrealistic. He said it would be impossible to design a gun barrel long enough for it to work. However, that same year he determined space exploration could be accomplished using liquid-fueled rockets.[10] I have examined Tsiolkovsky's research, Will, and believe me: It is brilliant. Space exploration is inevitable, and I am convinced Tsiolkovsky's method will be what first puts a human out of orbit. But . . ."

"But what?" Taft and the five men in the back were listening closely.

"This"—Robert patted the timepiece in his right coat pocket—"changes everything. It proves there is a power source in Alaska that even the greatest scientific minds in the world don't know about. Rocketry is much more feasible than anything Isaac Newton or Jules Verne envisioned, but that's because rockets are within the means of modern technology. A spaceship built using the same mechanics as this pocket watch could travel for decades rather than minutes. It would be as if Newton's cannonball shot itself into space without any powder, or Tsiolkovsky's rockets without liquid fuel. That's how you make interplanetary travel possible. Turn here."

Taft, nearly forgetting he was behind the wheel, steered off the empty sidewalk and back onto Washington Square.

"I think you know the way from here," Robert offered.

"Oh, yes." Taft raced around George Washington's bronze equestrian and onto Pennsylvania Avenue. After traveling nearly four thousand miles from a pub in London, the president was less than one mile away from his home. "So, are you expecting to find some Martian equivalent to Newton's cannonball in Alaska?" Taft asked.

"Honestly, no. Not at all."

---

10 Konstantin E. Tsiolkovsky, "The Exploration of Cosmic Space by Means of Reaction Devices (Исследование мировых пространств реактивными приборами)," *The Science Review* 5 (1903).

"Why not?"

"You read that transmission we intercepted. Those 'gentlemen' said they were recovering bodies and materials, not spaceships."

"I believe you, Bob, but we're both lawyers. You know as well as I do that that ciphertext wouldn't hold up in court as evidence that these gents were talking about Alaska. For all we know, they were prospectors drilling oil, trying to recover dead workers and lost equipment."

"And attempting to murder Nikola Tesla?"

"That part is most unsettling, Bob, no doubt about that. Unfortunately, Dr. Tesla's little lightning machine left us without so much as a fingernail of his would-be assassin. I want to know who wanted Tesla dead as much as you do, but with no body we have no bread crumbs for you or the Justice Department to follow."

"I accept that," Robert acknowledged. "And I want you to know I respect the Justice Department's decision to investigate that strange matter in New York without my involvement. I just hope they don't find anything that prompts you or Wickersham to send in the cavalry with guns blazing. The fewer moving pieces there are to this puzzle, the easier it will be for us to solve."

"For *you* to solve!" Taft corrected. "Bob, you're more than welcome to play bloodhound in Alaska, but I have an appointment with my wife to keep! Speaking of which . . ." The president accelerated his roaring steamer straight for the White House.

"However," Robert continued, "I still can't figure out *why* Halley's comet figures into this, never mind *how*. There are mines and rigs throughout the country; only the Wrangell Mountains showed irregularities. If these 'gentlemen' found something foreign to Earth in Alaska, why wait until we passed through Halley's comet to extract it? If there is a connection between the two, how could anyone possibly have known about it?"

"Is it possible the Martians used the comet as a vehicle?" Taft asked. "It's supposed to be a big ball of ice, right? That sounds like something they could travel quite comfortably on if they prefer the cold."

Robert took off his glasses and cleaned them as the car neared Lafayette Square. "I think that would be extremely unlikely. There are plenty of comets out there, Will, and Halley's comet has been documented for millennia. We have Babylonian tablets, the Bayeux Tapestry, Renaissance paintings, and now the dying witticisms of Mark Twain as testament to it. If Martians went through the trouble of figuring out how to travel all the way to Earth, I doubt they would have abandoned their primary mode of transportation."

"What if it was meant to be a one-way trip?"

"What do you mean?"

"What if they never intended to leave Earth?"

Robert was about to laugh, but caught himself. "Do you mean like Ellis Island or Plymouth Rock?"

"Weren't they both buried under two miles of ice at one point?"

Taft and Robert shared a long, uncomfortable look with each other as they considered that maybe, just maybe, humanity evolved from an ancient ancestor far stranger and more disturbing than anything Charles Darwin could have imagined.

"Cow," said Wickersham.

Taft looked over his shoulder. "Cow?"

Wilkie drew his revolver. "Cow!"

Standing straight in the auto's path was a Holstein blissfully grazing the White House North Lawn.

"PAULINE!" Taft turned the steering wheel as far left as he could, narrowly sparing the life of the beloved White House cow, Miss Pauline Wayne. The experience left her panicking.

"WHAT THE HELL IS SHE DOING ON THE NORTH LAWN?" Taft shouted. "She usually grazes in the South Lawn."

"Mr. President, the brakes!" urged Wickersham.

"The breaks?"

The speeding steamer was on a collision course with Mrs. Taft's beautiful 1909 Pierce-Arrow 36 H.P. landaulet parked outside the White House North Portico.

"The brakes!" shouted Robert.

"Where are they?"

"There!" Robert pointed at a lever on Taft's side. "Pull that!"

Taft pulled the lever with all his strength, plucking it clean off the car like a dandelion. "It's broken!" he cried.

"You're supposed to squeeze the handle!" screamed Wilkie.

Taft tried squeezing it. "It isn't working!"

"God damn this day . . ." Wilkie swore. The Secret Service chief holstered his pistol and discarded his boater hat. "I'll get the big guy!" he shouted. Secret Service Agents Sloan, Jervis, and Wheeler rushed into action, helping Robert and Wickersham off the auto and onto the grass. Wilkie, meanwhile, seized Taft from behind in a mighty bear hug and, with *all* his strength, leaped out of the car with the president in his arms. Taft and his bodyguard tumbled onto the North Lawn, stopping just in time to see the White Model M obliterate Mrs. Taft's blue landaulet. As the Model M's boiler exploded, Wilkie buried Taft's face in the grass and used his body to shield the president. Once the explosions were over, Wilkie whistled. Agents Sloan, Jervis, and Wheeler helped their three protectees back onto their feet.

"Are you all right, Mr. President?" asked Wilkie, his mustard suit completely stained with grass and what he hoped was mud.

"Yes, I am, John," Taft exhaled. "Thank you." The president patted his savior on the shoulder and took a few steps toward the roaring fire consuming both autos. As Taft's blue eyes followed the growing cloud of smoke and steam in the air, he spied a figure looking down at him from the mansion's second-floor sitting room. The figure slipped back into the darkness of the White House and closed the curtains, causing Taft's heart to sink like a stone.

The president lowered his head and turned around. "Is everyone in one piece?" he asked. Aside from their ruined suits, the six men he had been riding with appeared unhurt. "Bob?" he asked Robert, who was anxiously checking his coat pockets. Once he found what he was looking for, Robert looked at Taft and nodded.

The distraught president breathed in relief and took one last look at the burning autos. "Sorry, fellas. I'm not a very good motorist," Taft confessed.

"We know," said Wilkie.

But, with more important matters to attend to, Taft dusted himself off and straightened his mustache. "Well," he chirped, "we didn't come here to roast marshmallows. Let's go inside and inspect the real damage."

The group walked up the stairs of the North Portico. There

was no doorman, so Taft knocked on its dark wooden doors. It was the first time he had ever done so.

The door creaked open ever so slightly—just far enough for someone to stick both barrels of a shotgun in the president's face.

Chapter VII

"Mr. President! Thank God You're Here."

White House chief usher Irwin H. Hoover lowered his Remington Model 1900 from the president's head.

"Hello, Ike. Nice haircut." Taft could not remember the last time he had seen the man so unkempt.

"I'm sorry, Mr. President. We have been under siege since midday. Please, come in." Mr. Hoover nervously opened the North Portico doors and just as quickly locked them behind Taft and his men. "Mr. President," Hoover bowed, "Mr. Lincoln, Mr. Wilkie, Mr. Wickersham, Agents Sloan, Wheeler, Jervis. Welcome to the White House."

The Entrance Hall of the White House was very much what you would expect from its exterior. It was opulent, spacious, and so stratospherically white that it looked like it was slathered with wedding cake icing. Its six Doric columns seemed two or four columns too many for a man of Taft's modesty. The hall's gold mirrors, though large and stately, were frequent, unfriendly reminders of how desperately the president needed more exercise. Far worse was the Entrance Hall's low-hanging chandelier. That obnoxious creation was imprisoned in an oversized gold lantern as punishment for its assault on good taste. Even the gold emblem in the center of the hall's marble floor troubled Taft. Whenever he crossed it, he feared the gold lantern above it would descend and trap him in the White House forever like a fly in a jar. It was hardly a welcoming experience for this president.

And lastly, Taft sighed as he observed the west wall, was John Singer Sargent's famed portrait of Theodore Roosevelt. There he stood proudly, silently, watching, waiting. Following your every move as if about to inquire what the hell you were doing in his mansion. He had the eyes of a hunter and the trigger finger to go with it. Within the portrait, his right hand gripped—almost groped—a round wooden newel as if about to trigger a booby trap right under your feet. Or perhaps open a secret passage to some underground lair. Or maybe blow up a bridge in some faraway country. The man's motives were as unknown as his plans for the 1912 election, but there he stood triumphant. Already back in the White House. Theodore Rex.

Taft twitched his mustache.

To his right were four valets dressed in fine livery. They were brandishing M1895 Lee Navy rifles in the Ushers' Room behind overturned furniture. To Taft's left, a small squadron of doormen, footmen, cooks, maids, and butlers guarded the Grand Staircase in a phalanx formation several chests deep. The militia was armed with carbines, Henry rifles, Smith & Wesson Model 3s, musketoons, rifle muskets, a blunderbuss, and a vast assortment of kitchen knives. Commanding them was White House custodian Arthur Brooks, a former officer in the DC National Guard. He had a Browning Auto-5 shotgun in his steady hands. Like the four ushers on Taft's right, Arthur Brooks was a man of color, something that upset quite a few Washingtonian snobs Nellie Taft could not possibly give a goddamn about. Mr. Brooks was Nellie's closest adviser and confidant at the White House, so seeing him so heavily armed was all Taft needed to know whom he was guarding upstairs.

"Good day, Mr. Brooks," said the president graciously.

"Mr. President." Brooks bowed. "How are you, sir?"

"Not too bad. I won the fight!"

"Congratulations, sir."

"Thank you kindly." Taft smiled. "How are things here?"

"Not well, Mr. President. Not well at all. The android's been out of control for at least five hours now. There are no injuries, but we got a lot of worried people upstairs."

"And my wife?"

"Mrs. Taft is with her sisters in the east sitting rooms. She is completely unhurt, sir, but I strongly recommend taking swift action down here before going upstairs."

Taft bit his lip and quickly surveyed the scene. "In that case, I think you'd better do the talking for me. Please go upstairs and tell my wife I've arrived. Also, please escort these fine men with you. I think the West Sitting Hall will do nicely for them."

"Right away, Mr. President. Gentlemen?" Robert and Wickersham stepped forward and the phalanx parted for them, but one stubborn Secret Service chief refused to budge. He stared at Taft in disbelief. "Are you nuts?" he asked.

"Mr. President," Taft corrected.

"Mr. President, are you nuts? There's no way I'm going upstairs. You nearly got us killed on the way over!"

"Mr. Wilkie, we both know there is no one more sacred to me than my wife and family. Please guard them with your life while I take care of things here."

"Mr. President," Wilkie seethed, taking a step forward.

"Upstairs, Wilkie. Now."

The Secret Service chief was boiling over with outrage. "I'll be back," he insisted.

"No, you won't," Taft replied as Wilkie stomped up the steps. "See to it he doesn't come down, Brooks. Unless I'm in a real pickle, of course!"

"As you wish, Mr. President." The custodian bowed and escorted Robert and Wickersham up the stairs.

Taft wiped some sweat from his forehead before calling, "Agent Sloan?"

"Mr. President," he replied quickly.

"Jimmy, I want you to round up whatever Secret Service agents we have in the mansion and bring them down here. Also, please bring Mr. Brooks along with you. Have him meet me with those valets whenever he's ready."

"Right away, sir." Sloan hurried up the stairs.

"Ike!"

Mr. Hoover scampered to Taft with his enormous gun still in hand. "Yes, Mr. President."

Taft started walking down the Entrance Hall with Hoover as Agents Jervis and Wheeler followed closely beside them. "Ordinarily, I'd speak to Mr. Brooks about this, but since he's a better bearer of bad news than you are, his services are more needed upstairs for the moment."

"Yes, Mr. President. I understand completely."

"Of course you do, Ike." Taft slapped the agitated usher on the shoulder so hard he nearly discharged his shotgun. "So, can you please explain what the holy hell happened while I was gone?"

"Mr. President," Ike said, trembling, "it's that accursed automaton again! Mrs. Taft had some of her friends over to play cards around lunchtime. All was peaceful, until . . ." Mr. Hoover tried to collect himself. "Mr. President, the creature's face started sliding off of its skull!"

"Yes, I know. It's been an Indian summer all year.[11] Why didn't you just turn on the air conditioner?"

"Mr. President, the air-conditioning does not work. It never works."

"Ah, yes," Taft remembered. It was one of many reasons why he preferred spending summer on the airship. "We've really got to do something about that."

"I am so sorry, sir. We had no choice but to put the android on ice in the Master Bath. However, the ice melted, sir, and then a few ice cubes—"

"It's all right, Ike," Taft interrupted. "You don't need to remind me just how personally I think Thomas Edison is a pain in my backside. Today is the last day you'll ever have to deal with my decoy. I'm here to retire it."

Mr. Hoover looked like he had just been given a new breath of life. "Oh, thank you so much, Mr. President!"

"It's no problem, Ike. I just need you to answer two big questions for me. Number one, where is the handsome bastard?"

"It's in the Blue Room, Mr. President."

---

11 "Record Heat in Boston," *New York Times*, 26 March 1910.

Taft stopped walking and looked at the double door in front of him. "He's in there?"

"Yes, Mr. President. Mrs. Taft and her guests were in the dining room when the automaton came down the stairs."

"Did he do anything?"

"Mr. President," said the usher, his voice fading, "please don't force me to relive the details. Just know that many of the ladies ran out of the mansion screaming. We were able to shoo the beast into the Blue Room with some brooms, but Mrs. Taft refused to abandon the White House. We had no choice but to stand guard until you returned."

"Why no soldiers or fire crew?"

"Mrs. Taft did not want to raise suspicions that the mansion is in use, sir. She is supposed to be on vacation with you, if you remember."[12]

"Ah! Very clever, that gal." The president winked. But as Taft looked down both ends of the crimson Cross Hall and then back to the phalanx, he added, "I don't understand, though. Why didn't Nellie just leave the building?"

Hoover was silent. He did not want to answer.

"Ike?"

"Because she did not want her reputation sullied, sir. When Dolley Madison fled the mansion, it was because the British were set to burn down the city. That was war, Mr. President. Not this strange new type of"—Hoover's eyes widened—"monstrosity!"

Taft raised his eyebrows and looked back at the two doors to the Blue Room. There was no damage or barricade, but he could hear the faint sound of piano keys mashing.

---

12 "Taft on Mayflower for Ten-Day Cruise," *New York Times,* 19 Jul 1910.

"Well, I guess that more than answers my first question," said Taft. "Question number two, what's for dinner?"

Mr. Hoover thought he misheard something over one of the chiming grandfather clocks. "Excuse me, Mr. President?"

"I bumped into a fish cart on my way over. It whetted my appetite for a little bit of whatever we have."

A confused Hoover slowly raised his arm and pointed off to the right. "There's a buffet in the State Dining Room, sir, but it's been sitting there all day."

"All right, we'll start there." Taft signaled Agents Jervis and Wheeler to lead the way to the vast room through the Cross Hall's lush curtains.

If John Singer Sargent's portrait of Theodore Roosevelt was a faithful rendering of the former president's likeness, the State Dining Room served just as well as a window into the active man's mind. The room's green rug and curtains may have resembled the Taft Oval Office, but the mounted menagerie overhead was all Roosevelt's doing. An entire zoo of dead animals, each one shot by the famous huntsman himself, encircled the room's wooden walls as if it were Noah's Ark gone terribly wrong. If these mounted bears, bucks, and bull moose still had working eyes, they might have observed the overturned chairs and playing cards scattered around the dining room's small central table. The banquet spread on the room's long north table, however, appeared perfectly edible to Taft, despite having been uncovered all afternoon on a hot summer day. The president daintily helped himself to the feast one little nibble at a time while Agents Jervis and Wheeler inspected the area. Both of their Colt Police Positive Special revolvers were out and up.

"Mr. President, both doors to the Red Room are open," said Jervis. "So is the south door to the Blue Room."

"That's fine," said Taft through a mouthful of smelts. "Just make sure the dining room is secure." Both agents sneaked into the Red Room while Taft moved down the buffet and helped himself to some peach salad.

"Mr. President?" asked a familiar voice.

"Yes?" Taft turned his head to see Attorney General Wicker-sham enter the room. "Georgie! What are you doing here?"

"Mr. President," he spoke curtly, "Agent Sloan and Mr. Brooks are in the hall with their men, awaiting orders."

"Can you tell them to wait a bit longer?" Taft asked as he sipped some persimmon beer.

"Mr. President," said Wickersham with restrained urgency, "I must insist that we secure the mansion before Archie arrives with the airship."

"Come, come now! Let's not be too picky," Taft said as he picked at some beef tenderloin and deviled almonds.

"Will, enough of this dillydally. John Wilkie is becoming very impatient."

"Ha!" Taft laughed, sending chewed bits of food flying. "He's always impatient."

"And I don't blame him one bit! This is no time to . . . What are you doing?"

The president's expert hands were at work. Taft took a cheese sandwich, placed six strips of bacon on it in a crosshatch, added a breaded salmon cutlet with some black pepper and lemon, ladled a generous amount of lobster bisque over the salmon, paused to pop a salted almond into his mouth, added six more strips of bacon and some lettuce, pressed the whole thing together with a second cheese sandwich, and then took a mighty bite. The president smiled with complete satisfaction.

"I thought you were supposed to be on a diet," chided Brooks as he entered the room.

"I am dieting!" Taft insisted. "I'm watching everything that I eat. See?" He held the sandwich so both men could see it, and then took an even larger bite out of it.

An unamused Wickersham waved in Agent Sloan from the hallway. He was followed by Secret Service Agents Bowen and Murphy from upstairs, Ike Hoover, and the four armed valets from earlier. "Mr. President, we're ready," said Brooks.

"All right, all right." Taft put his great sandwich on a plate and handed it to Wickersham. "Hold this for me, would you? I'll be right back." The president fluffed the bread crumbs from his mustache while the attorney general accepted the high-piled plate in disgust. Taft cracked his knuckles while the men around him readied their weapons. Every chamber was loaded, every grip tightened, and every heart pounding. Agents Jervis and Wheeler peeked in from the Red Room and signaled the president. It was time. Taft nodded, and the nine men slowly filed into the Red Room.

Only Ike Hoover remained in the State Dining Room with Wickersham, the former still nervously clutching his Remington Model 1900. The attorney general, knowing full well what was about to unfold, thrust the plate with the president's sandwich into the chief usher's hands and just as impatiently robbed the man of his shotgun. Wickersham marched out of the dining room and hurried up the Grand Staircase.

Hoover mindlessly discarded the plate's contents back onto the buffet table.

His eyes were fixed on the Red Room.

Chapter VIII

Taft vs. Taft

President Taft and his bodyguards cautiously crept into the Red Room to the monotonous din of mashed piano keys. The men moved quietly under the watchful eyes of John Adams, James Monroe, Martha Washington, and the Lansdowne portrait of George Washington hanging over the fireplace. This painting, which Dolley Madison famously rescued from British torches during the burning of Washington, was of particular interest to Arthur Brooks. Without speaking, he directed two valets to take the portrait and bring it upstairs. Taft did not notice this motion, and for good reason. Brooks was operating under the personal orders of Nellie Taft to mitigate whatever damage was awaiting the White House.

In front of Taft, Secret Service Agents Jervis and Wheeler peered into the Blue Room. The president could hear the drumming of piano keys grow louder with each step he took. Deep down, he hoped the sound was actually one of his Victrola discs skipping, and not that lovely piano the Baldwin Piano Company had generously given to Nellie. Once Agents Sloan, Bowen, and Murphy joined their two colleagues, the five huddled in discussion, nodded, and then slowly stepped into the parlor. From his angle, Taft could not see where the agents fanned out, but Agent Sloan was clearly framed in the doorway taking aim at a target. Seconds later, Agent Jervis opened the door on Taft's left from inside the Blue Room. Brooks moved into the room through this entrance with his two other valets. The men had fear in their eyes and quickly raised their weapons. Whatever everyone was aiming at, it was not in the direction of the Victrola. The president gulped.

With all eight men in a crescent and ready to fire, Agent Sloan turned his head and nodded to Taft. The president took a deep breath and squeezed through the Blue Room's tight doorway.

There are many reasons why the Blue Room is frequently praised as the most beautiful salon in the White House. It is the largest of the three parlors on the State Floor, has a distinct oval shape, and offers a stunning view of the South Lawn and the Washington Monument from its three windows. Such luxuries make the Blue Room a uniquely personal space in the White House to decorate, as demonstrated by Nellie Taft's decision to transform the parlor into a music room.[13] Music had always played an important role in Will and Nellie's life since that fateful garden party when a twenty-five-year-old Nellie Herron

---

13 "Music Room Plays a Large Part in White House Life," *New York Times,* 8 May 1910.

complimented a slightly overweight Yale graduate's singing. If those days were the Dickensian best of times for Will Taft, imagine the look on his face as he watched his exact double destroying his wife's beloved grand piano.

"Is it trying to play something?" Brooks winced as the automaton pounded the dying Baldwin. Its empire design and gold trimming were reduced to splinters under its attacker's brass fists.

"Actually, I think he's trying to sign my name," Taft responded. "It was the only thing he was ever good at."

Like so many bad ideas, the presidential automaton started off as a good one. How else could Nellie sign bills into law and outwit the press into thinking her husband was *not* out of the country for weeks at a time? An automaton was the best solution Secretary Norton's predecessor, Fred Carpenter, could come up with. Specifically, something resembling those remarkable eighteenth-century automatons built by Swiss watchmaker Pierre Jaquet-Droz and family. "These androids are over a hundred years old," Fred had told Taft, with a copy of *The New York Times* on the table.[14] "Imagine what Thomas Edison could build for us!" One year later, was it any surprise that this man no longer worked at the White House?

"Well," Taft clapped, "let's have a look-see-daisy, shall we?" Every armed man in the room lowered his weapon as Taft moseyed over to examine the android. "Let's see . . . hmm . . . no . . . Where is it . . . Aha! Here's the culprit!" The president lowered the android's trousers to reveal a corporate emblem stamped on its rear:

---

14 "Wonderful Automata That Have Survived More Than a Century," *New York Times*, 18 March 1906.

Edison Manufacturing Co.
Est. 1889
"Got any BRIGHT ideas?"

Taft turned around and pointed his thumb at the stamp. "If I ever see this man again, I swear to God I'm going to murder him with a lightbulb."

Aside from the droning piano, the room remained quiet.

"Mr. President, would you please resolve the matter with your decoy?" Brooks urged.

Taft grinned cheerfully. "Yes, yes! I'm getting there. I just need some help removing its pants. Dick? Jimmy?"

Secret Service Agents Jervis and Sloan holstered their pistols while Taft took off his jacket. Together, the three men pulled the android's slacks down to the room's tiger-skin rug.

"There we are!" said Taft proudly as he admired the specimen. Anatomically, the android looked no different from a doll under its clothes—except for the prominent exhaust vent in the automaton's backside. "Boys, I think you'll want to stay clear of this thing." Sloan and Jervis backed away from the android as the president addressed the assembled.

"Gentlemen!" Taft began as he held his suspenders. He carried himself like a third-grader about to give a book report he was particularly proud of. "As many of you know, the chief structural flaw in my clockwork counterpart here is and always has been its thermal exhaust port. I first discovered this after returning from a round of golf at the Chevy Chase Club with General Edwards, John Hays Hammond, and, naturally, Captain Butt. And before I continue, I must add that Mr. Hammond and I crushed our opponents in our little Yale versus Army reunion."

Aside from the president, not a single person in the room was moved by this feat.

"Anyway, we were informed of the malfunctioning android as we pulled in to the White House. According to Mrs. Jaffray and Maggie Rogers, the brass menace was in the laundry drying yard, frozen in place like the Tin Woodman. Since neither Mr. Hammond nor General Edwards had seen the machine yet, I decided to take advantage of the situation and asked my friends if they would like to meet it. It was such a beautiful day and the location so neatly concealed behind bedsheets that the gentlemen could not possibly say no. Ever vigilant, Captain Butt insisted that the valets bring our golf clubs—a wise precaution.

"After examining the machine with my chums, one of them— whose name I prefer not to mention—deduced that the villain was not a foreign object lodged in the android's exhaust port, but rather some internal water damage caused by its recent hosing and scrubbing. So, I asked Captain Butt for one of my woods and took a swing at the android right here"—Taft pointed at the Edison insignia—"and zounds! It worked like magic, just as I will demonstrate right now, you GODDAMN STUPID MACHINE!"

The president delivered a hard kick to the android's posterior. The machine emitted a deep rumble similar to the rev of an engine, but continued assaulting the piano. Surprised, Taft delivered a second, more surgical punt to its rump. This time, all the men in the room heard several gears fall into place. Convinced he could end this with one more kick, the president put all his weight into a third and final blow to the Edison emblem on the automaton's backside.

It worked.

Every coil and gear in the machine sprung into action, causing a tremendous explosion to shoot out its exhaust port like a cannon. "There it is!" Taft shouted as the force of the blast sent him backward. All three of the Blue Room's tall windows were shattered. The hairs on the parlor's tiger-skin rug were singed. Every valet and agent in the room was taken aback by the burst. Even the Victrola was shaken into readying a recording of Mozart's Symphony No. 25 in G Minor, K. 183, first movement.

As the smoke cleared, Taft regained his footing and hurried back to the automaton. The machine was motionless and the piano silent.

"What did I tell you! Zounds!" the president cheered to the coughing ushers and agents. "It worked just like magic! Hey, Brooks, if we ever do this onstage, you and I could put Houdini *and* Le Pétomane out of business!"

"That's fantastic, sir," replied the irritated custodian. "I'll ring the cleaners and the piano tuner immediately."

"Oh, but I'm just getting started," Taft boasted as he leaned against the piano. "For my next trick, I'll—urk!"

The automaton snapped its hand and seized Taft by the necktie just as the Victrola filled the Blue Room with Mozart.

"Mr. President! Mr. President!" The Secret Service agents rushed in. The two valets raised their rifles, but Brooks held them back with both arms.

"No shooting!" he ordered.

The prizefighter struggled helplessly as the android stood tall and slowly clicked its arm upward. Taft was forced up from the piano and onto the tips of his toes. Agents Sloan, Wheeler, and Jervis raced desperately to support Taft lest his neck snap under his weight. Despite their best efforts, there was little they could do to restore the president's airway. Taft was already turning as blue as the walls around him.

As Agents Bowen and Murphy tried fruitlessly to sever Taft's necktie, the automaton slowly turned its head like a ticking clock. Just as Hoover described, half the android's wax face was melted away and hideously distorted. Taft could see his own terrified face reflected in the android's lifeless doll eyes. With all his remaining strength, Taft reached out and clawed at the monster. His fingernails ripped off the android's left cheek, revealing a brass jaw and a grinning death's head of ivory teeth. The Mozart faded from Taft's ears. The whole world around him was vanishing.

But then, the Blue Room's north door was kicked open. "CLEAR!" a voice shouted. All five Secret Service agents hit the floor. A gunshot rang through the air and severed Taft's necktie, sending the president tumbling into the arms of the valets. As oxygen returned to Taft's lungs, he limply looked to his left. There, standing in the Blue Room's broken doorway, was Secret Service Chief Wilkie with a smoking gun in his hand and a thick cigar in his teeth. He glanced at Taft, but only for a split second. His eyes, mind, and pistol were aimed at the android.

"READY!" Wilkie shouted. Mr. Hoover and a phalanx of rifles assembled behind him.

"This way, Will!" Attorney General Wickersham rushed in from the Red Room and pulled Taft to safety.

Mozart's strings quickened. . . .

"FIRE!"

The Blue Room exploded in a symphony of gunfire.

"What the hell is going on here?" Taft hollered as he was dragged through the Red Room. "George! Did you see what happened?"

"I did!" Wickersham and two valets helped the president back onto his feet. "Has anything like that happened before?"

The Blue Room cackled with gunfire, killing the Victrola.

"Of course not!" Taft shouted. "I don't believe it. That thing tried to murder me! Here! In the White House! I've never heard of such—"

The conversation was interrupted by valets and Secret Service agents rushing into the Red Room. There was a deep thudding behind them that shook the paintings on the wall. Without saying a word, Agents Sloan, Wheeler, and Jervis seized Taft and forced him into the State Dining Room. Wickersham followed with Hoover's mighty shotgun gripped tightly in his hands.

In the dining hall, plaster fell from the ceiling and the chandelier shook with each terrible crash from the Red Room. The Secret Service agents made a wall in front of Taft as all the riflemen from Brooks's militia flooded in from the Cross Hall. Wilkie bustled in with them, fuming mad as he emptied his revolver's spent shells. Ammunition clips were tossed through the air and nearly every piece of furniture was overturned. In a matter of seconds, the State Dining Room was converted into a fortress.

Amidst the cacophony of their approaching attacker, Wickersham took off his glasses and turned nervously to Taft. "I think you need this more than I do." The attorney general handed his president the enormous Remington scattergun.

"Thanks, George," said Taft, albeit somewhat uneasily. He gripped the weapon like a cudgel while every other gun homed in on the Red Room.

There was a clang of metal against stone that caused the dining room's southeast wall to protrude. Seconds later, the automaton knocked through the Red Room's small fireplace and demolished the wall. The instant the creature was visible, every rifle and revolver in the room tore its fleshy exterior to pieces.

"How are we supposed to kill this thing?" shouted Brooks through the melee. The android was unaffected by his buckshot, and ammunition was running low for everyone.

"Hold your fire!" Taft shouted. The president pushed his Secret Service agents aside and squared shoulders with his adversary.

"Mr. President, stand down!" Wilkie barked. "That's an order!"

"I have not yet begun to fight!" Taft boomed.

The president gripped the shotgun with both hands and marched toward the brass menace. Once he was close enough to see the teeth in its gears, Taft uppercut the automaton with his gunstock. The shotgun exploded, breaking into two pieces and blasting a large hole through the ceiling. It was an unorthodox maneuver that nearly took down the chandelier, but Taft managed to knock the hulking android a step backward.

"WHAT THE HELL ARE YOU DOING?" Wilkie hollered across the room.

"I'm trying to knock it on its back!" Taft replied as he walloped his decoy a second time. "Assist me!" Brooks was the first fighter to volunteer. After discarding his spent shotgun, he picked up an overturned chair and charged into the beast.

"Everyone, back away!" Wilkie ordered. "You're in my line of fire!" The Secret Service chief's shouts were ignored. With the exception of his five agents, everyone in Brooks's home guard was beating the android side by side with their president.

A frustrated Wilkie holstered his firearm and looked at his agents. "Stay here and help them. I'll be right back." The Secret Service chief rushed through the door behind him to the Butler's

Pantry while his agents turned over the buffet table to use as a ram.

Wilkie moved through the pantry like a burglar, opening and slamming every cupboard around him in a determined search for the White House's liquor. He bit his cigar in frustration as the situation grew dim, thinking all the booze in the White House had been relocated to the airship. But then, just as the shouting and clattering in the dining hall became savage, Wilkie found the cupboard he was looking for. He rummaged through the mansion's liquor stores until he found a bottle of rum given to the Roosevelts from the Royal Canadian Navy. The harsh liquid was 150 proof. Wilkie ripped off its cork and poured some K C Baking Powder into the bottle, the whole time puffing a voluminous cloud of smoke. He then shook the bottle and plugged it with his handkerchief, using the chewed end of his cigar as a stopper. In a matter of seconds, his rum-soaked handkerchief ignited. Wilkie darted back into the dining room to see the buffet table split in half against the automaton. The machine seemed to weigh as much as a bronze statue.

Wilkie whistled. "Brooks! Move Wickersham and your men upstairs! All agents, stand back!"

A battered, sweating Taft spied the bottle in the Secret Service chief's hand. "Wilkie, whatever you've got there, now's not a good time."

The Secret Service chief had no time to respond. He hurled his lethal cocktail through the air and hit his target head-on. The android erupted in flames and half its torso burst open. The fire spread everywhere.

"John, are you mad?" Taft screamed. "You're going to burn down the whole mansion!"

Wilkie rushed to the president, shouting commands to every agent he passed on the way. "Mr. President, come with me!"

"The hell I am!" Taft yelled right in the man's face. "You're out of line, Wilkie!"

The Secret Service chief pointed angrily at the burning machine. "Just take a look at the thing! All its guts are exposed." Wilkie's five agents were taking targeted, timed shots at the android, staggering the advancing automaton with each slug. "My men can now shoot at its insides! In a few minutes, this beast will be dead."

"In a few minutes, we'll both be dead!" Taft shouted, grabbing the Secret Service chief by his jacket.

"Mr. President! Mr. Wilkie!" Sloan shouted through the encircling flames. The approaching android and its fire had both men surrounded. Sloan tried to fell the beast, but his gun clicked without firing. Every Police Positive Special in the room was empty.

Except Wilkie's.

Wilkie seized Taft by the collar and forced the president into the dining room's fireplace. As the android approached, the bodyguard spun around and raised his revolver. There were only three bullets left in its cylinder. Wilkie fired his first shot at the machine's chest, but the bullet passed harmlessly through it. He fired a second shot at its abdomen, blasting a long trail of brass gears and springs behind it. The machine slowed and seemed about to collapse, forcing Wilkie's third shot to accidentally hit the lurching automaton in the head. The bullet bounced upward and knocked the room's stuffed moose head off the wall. The trophy landed squarely on Wilkie, staggering the Secret Service chief until he fell over, unconscious.

"John!" the president shouted as the flaming android advanced. Without a thought for his own safety, Taft picked up his protector and stepped over the moose head through the fire around them. He thrust Wilkie into the arms of Agents Bowen and Murphy, ordering them to "Take him to safety!" As Wilkie was rushed out the door, Taft turned and watched with his three remaining agents as the skeletal automaton trudged through the roaring fire. The machine seemed unstoppable.

"What are your orders, sir?" asked Sloan.

Taft followed the smoke and flames to the chandelier overhead. "Give me a boost," he said.

"Mr. President?" asked Wheeler.

"The chandelier! Get me up there."

The three agents looked up at the chandelier and then back at Taft. "I don't think we can manage that, sir."

The president's mustache drooped. "Well then, steady that for me!" he ordered, pointing to an overturned table surrounded by burning playing cards. The agents brought the table to Taft as he planned his attack: He would leap off the table, swing on the chandelier, and then drop-kick the automaton onto its back, crippling it. Unfortunately, the president failed to take the gravity of his weight into consideration, never mind the huge hole he shot by the chandelier earlier. Taft jumped off the table and seized the chandelier, accidentally pulling it down along with a good chunk of the ceiling. Instead of felling the android, a rug and a chair and a chest of drawers from the overhead room fell onto Sloan, Jervis, and Wheeler. The agents were able to avoid them, but the fresh kindling trapped them in an impossible maze of fire.

Taft fell to the floor, winded and stunned. He was surrounded by flames with nothing between him and the automaton. As the clinking, screeching, droning monster approached, the president could do nothing but scurry backward on the floor like a scared child.

But then, as the android walked under the great hole in the ceiling, Taft could hear a deep rumbling above him. He looked up as an enormous bathtub was pushed through the hole, crushing the android and sending water to every corner of the dining hall. Nearly all the fires in the room were extinguished. Taft cautiously crawled toward his aggressor; its wheels were silent. The killer android was defeated.

"Are you all right, Mr. President?" someone called from above. Taft looked up to see Captain Butt and Robert Todd Lincoln staring down at him from what used to be the Master Dressing Room.

"Captain Butt!" Taft beamed. "Mr. Lincoln. I assume this was all your idea?"

Robert shook his head. "It was a team effort," he insisted.

"A Harvard-Yale effort!" said John Hays Hammond, sticking his head into the frame.

"Jack!" Taft smiled. "Thanks for joining us! I hope we're not inconveniencing you at the moment."

"Not at all, Will! It's a pleasure to be here."

"I'm glad to hear it. We need you," said Taft as he looked over the wreckage around him.

A few minutes later, President Taft and his ensemble—including a revitalized John Wilkie—were saluting their victory with cigars in the ruined remains of the State Dining Room.

"There is no way this automaton could have attacked you unless it was designed to do so," said Robert.

"I agree, Mr. President," observed Wilkie, whose head was bandaged under his boater. "That thing went straight for you the entire battle. I think you'll agree that this amounts to an assassination attempt."

"I'm afraid to say it, but I think you're both right," Taft acknowledged. "But who would want me killed? I'm this century's Falstaff."

"Mr. President." Brooks entered from the Cross Hall.

"Yes?" Taft turned around to see two women descend the Grand Staircase. They were wearing afternoon dresses and assisting a third lady behind them. She was led down the stairs, one lady to each arm, while her escorts wielded Winchester Model 1897 shotguns in their other hands. She was wearing a white evening gown with silver embroidery and a decorative, almost medieval green bodice wrapped tightly around her chest. She wore white gloves, pearl earrings with a matching pearl choker, and her brown hair was worn up like a geisha. At one point, her brown eyes glanced in the president's direction. Taft quickly discarded his cigar as she walked down the Cross Hall and through the blackened remains of the dining room's once emerald curtains.

There, in full regalia with two of her four sisters beside her, was Helen Louise Herron "Nellie" Taft. She was not smiling.

The gentlemen in the room lowered their cigars and politely bowed in reverence, but Taft panicked. Not knowing what to do, his eyes fell on a bottle of Heidsieck & Co. Monopole on the ground.

"Champagne?" Taft offered as he pulled the bottle from its lobster bisque bowl.

Nellie turned her head to inspect the damage done to the State Dining Room: the burnt carpet, the crushed furniture, the water-damaged wood floors, the enormous hole in the ceiling, the shattered chandelier, the ruined Red Room fireplace, the overturned banquet, the broken windows, the spent bullet casings, the innumerable bullet holes, the upstairs bathtub that was downstairs for some reason, the felled automaton, and the burning curtains Mr. Hoover and some butlers were desperately trying to control with seltzer bottles.

She looked over this mess and then back at her husband.

"I need a beer," she responded.

Chapter IX

"Madam President."

Mr. Lincoln."

Robert respectfully excused himself from the room so he could return to the airship hovering over the White House. He was followed closely by Captain Butt and John Hays Hammond while Brooks escorted Wickersham and Wilkie out of the mansion. Nellie was determined to have a word with her husband. Alone.

"Nellie . . ." Taft started.

"Downstairs," she ordered.

The location shifted from the dining room to the White House Kitchen for privacy. And for a tall pint of porter for Nellie. She was on her second glass and third cigarette by the time her husband was done rambling about bad weather, Halley's comet, gold pocket watches, Alaska, little green men, defective car brakes, and malfunctioning automatons. He ran out of breath several times in his desperate defense, but Nellie did not interrupt him. Not even when the brazen remains of the android came crashing down through the charred dining room floor. It landed in the downstairs hallway, shaking the ash from Nellie's cigarette.

As always, her restraint remained nothing short of remarkable.

"You have done more damage to this poor house than anyone since the British."

"You have to believe me, Nellie, it was an assassination attempt!"

"How could it be an assassination attempt if you triggered it?"

"I don't know! Because . . ." Taft's eyes moved over the innumerable pots and pans hanging over the table and the neat row of knives laid out in front of Nellie—including a cake knife. Taft never liked being down here for arguments. It made him equally nervous and hungry. "Because Wilkie said so!" he remembered.

Nellie's gloved hand tightened its grip on her cigarette holder. "John Wilkie? You realize every room in this mansion stinks of burnt hair because of John Wilkie."

"Oh, come now! You hated those silly trophies more than anyone in the city."

"Not enough to set them ablaze in the dining room of *the White House*." Nellie's voice quivered like a bowstring as she spoke those three words. "This has gone on long enough, Will. John Wilkie is the loosest cannon in Washington. He cannot be trusted and must be discharged."

Taft drank despondently from his empty champagne glass. He had finished the whole bottle of Monopole about halfway into his defense. "I can't in good faith fire someone who saved my life twice in one day. Both times were due to my errors. My faults. And Nellie . . ." Taft paused. "We cannot spare him. He fights!"

Nellie focused intently on her husband. Above all his other qualities, she knew that her husband was just. "In that case, he can stay. But I still don't like or trust him."

Taft chuckled. "Nellie, you never trusted him."

"Wilkie is not a trustworthy man, Will. You knew this before you even met him. He's a tabloid journalist whose life is shrouded in mystery, and we've been seeing a lot less of him since 'the Colonel' returned from Africa.[15] Does that not seem suspicious to you?" Nellie blew a long snake of smoke as if to wrap up her case with a question mark–shaped ribbon.

Taft didn't see where she was going with this. "What?"

"I think he's a spy working for Teddy Roosevelt."

Her husband laughed. "Nellie, you think everyone is a spy for Teddy Roosevelt!"

"Not everyone. Just those who are clearly more interested in seeing Teddy elected to a third term than you elected to two."

"Teddy does not have every baseball fan in the country in his corner!" Taft touted. "Besides, his allies are not as cancerous as you claim."

"What about Alice?" Alice Roosevelt Longworth, or "Princess Alice," as the newspapers called her, was Theodore Roosevelt's eldest daughter and hated Nellie with a passion. The feeling was mutual.

---

15 "Mr. Roosevelt's Return," *New York Times,* 18 June 1910.

Taft shrugged. "What about her?"

Nellie's eyes widened. "She buried a Voodoo idol in the South Lawn the day we moved in!"[16]

"So? Nothing came of it. Right?"

Nellie took a long, angry drag from her cigarette. It did not take her husband long to realize his blunder from the pained look in her eyes. They spoke of a whole year's worth of suffering. "I am so sorry," he said.

At that moment, Brooks walked into the room. "Mr. President. Madam President."

"What's the damage report, Brooks?" Nellie asked. She was referring to the automaton's recent fall through the floor.

"Madam, the Hayes china has been completely destroyed."

Both Will and Nellie turned their heads in surprise. "It's gone?" she asked.

"Crushed beyond repair, madam."

Nellie looked back at her husband. Her entire face changed. "That will be all, Brooks. Thank you."

"Madam President. Mr. President." He bowed on his way out the door.

Nellie could not believe it, and neither could her husband. "That's good news," Nellie whispered across the table.

"I know!" Taft replied. In one of Captain Butt's many, *many* letters to his sister, he described the Hayes china "as ugly as it is possible for china to be." Having them destroyed by the android was a breath of fresh air for the president.

---

16 Alice Roosevelt Longworth, *Crowded Hours* (New York: Charles Scribner's Sons, 1933), 158.

"You said it was Archie's idea to crush the automaton with the bathtub. You're absolutely sure?" Nellie pressed.

"Yes. I think I'm going to promote him to major."

"Do it," she affirmed.

Taft grinned with delight while Nellie finished her beer. Aside from the ruined mansion, things suddenly seemed a bit calmer in the White House Kitchen. But only briefly. "If this was an attempt on your life," Nellie started, "it means the mansion is no longer safe. You cannot spend the night here, Will. I won't allow it."

Taft's face twisted with worry. "But Nellie—"

She locked eyes with her husband. "I won't allow it. Not until Wilkie and Wickersham have this matter thoroughly investigated."

"Why George?" Taft asked. "He's busy enough investigating the strange case of Dr. Tesla and the disappearing assassin."

"Unlike Mr. Wilkie, I trust Mr. Wickersham with my life. Have the two pay Thomas Edison a visit on George's way to New York. I want them to sweat everything they can out of Edison about this monster he sold us. He has been a very bad wizard."

"With gusto." Taft smiled.

"There's more," Nellie added without returning the smile. "There is no way we can go on vacation with the mansion in such disrepair. Fortunately, the press is expecting us to be away for the next week and a half. That provides us some cover. You will accompany Mr. Lincoln to Alaska while I take care of things here."

"You want me to leave you?" Taft asked in disbelief.

"We need to stay separate."

The president could barely speak. "Is this because I was late?" he asked, devastated.

"No, Will. I am saying this because it is what needs to be done."

Taft inched closer to Nellie, saying shyly, "Nellie, we were supposed to go on vacation together. I wanted us to be together. You and me. For your health."

Nellie set down her glass and placed her cigarette holder across her lap. "Will, you know how it aches me whenever we are apart. You have all my letters. We shared the same grief every minute we have ever been apart. That is why you must respect me when I say that, for my health, I need you to stay away from me these next couple of days."

Just like that, Nellie Taft rendered powerless the single most powerful man in the western hemisphere. Taft hung his head, feeling every ounce of failure in his three-hundred-fifty-pound body. "I understand." The president set his glass down and began his quiet march out of the kitchen.

"Will . . ."

Taft turned around.

"I know that I am very cross with you, but I love you just the same."

Taft's whiskers curled. "My dearest Nellie . . ."

The first couple shared a darling embrace.

"Now listen," Nellie said, getting straight to business. "You have less than ten days to solve this riddle up north. Mr. Lincoln is a man of science, just like his father was. If his concerns turn out to be unfounded, we can put this whole matter of Martians and pocket watches behind us. However, if he can gather scientific proof that there are or ever were 'visitors' to this planet, your administration could use it to quash the brewing scandal in Alaska once and for all. You would win more than reelection, Will. You could be remembered as one of the greatest presidents in history."

Taft snickered. "Well, for all the fortune and glory that would bring us, you know I'd rather be chief justice than as wealthy as a roomful of robber barons."

Nellie paused. The slight smile on her face faded.

"Nellie, what is it?"

"Nothing too important," she said. "You just reminded me of something unpleasant I forgot to tell you. J. P. Morgan stopped by the house in Beverly while you were away."

"J. P. Morgan?" Taft grimaced. "What does he want?"

"I don't know! I didn't meet with him. The man is a revolting human being. All I know is that he showed up in his motorboat the day before we left. His men said he wanted to speak with you in private. There were no reporters or cameras."

Taft twitched his mustache. "He probably wants to give me more uninvited advice on how the Sherman Antitrust Act does not apply to him or his friends. Mark my words, Nellie: I will not have him bully me the way he bullied Teddy three years ago. Nobody is above the law in this country. If he thinks otherwise, you and I can redecorate the dining room with the heads of the animals from Upton Sinclair's type of jungle! Just like this!" Taft seized his Monopole bottle and shattered it against the table-top. He then stabbed his shard through the air, shouting, "Take that, Standard Oil! Take that, U.S. Steel!"

Nellie stood back and smiled. She loved moments like these.

Moments when her husband, acting entirely on his own, looked and sounded like the president she always knew he could be. "Kiss me," she required.

Taft discarded his weapon and effortlessly picked up his wife. The presidential couple kissed passionately as Will carried Nellie across the White House Kitchen floor. Within her husband's embrace, Nellie felt lighter than air.

Chapter X

Up in the Air

That's quite a view, isn't it?" Taft remarked to his friends. The moonlit twilight of the evening painted a breathtaking panorama of the National Mall from Airship One's Oval Office.

The vast landscape was particularly striking for John Hays Hammond, who, like most people, had never seen the Washington Monument with the full expanse of the Potomac behind it. He rubbed the back of his nearly egg-bald head in disbelief. "I don't know what to say," he observed. "It's dazzling."

"Beautiful sights, plenty of food . . ." Taft helped himself to some of the amuse-bouche on his desk. "Gentlemen, we should do this more often!"

"Will, if you don't mind my asking . . ." Robert approached with a glass of amontillado in his hand. "What do you plan on doing during this trip?"

"That's a good question." Taft tapped his champagne glass

as he thought. With the exception of the three Secret Service agents—and Miss Knox—posted outside the office's four doors, there were no staffers or secretaries in the zeppelin's West Wing. Administratively, Airship One was operating with a skeleton crew. "Honestly, I don't know. Maybe hit some golf balls into the mountains? See what happens?"

Robert and John glanced nervously at each other. "I think that could trigger an avalanche," Hammond cautioned.

Taft stopped tapping. "Oh! Well, in that case, I guess I'll just drink some hot cocoa and catch up on my reading."

"Anything in particular?" asked Robert.

"Not really. The cleaners threw out my funny papers." Taft's eyes moved across the miraculously uncluttered office, eventually falling on Robert's well-thumbed copy of *Tom Swift and His Airship* on one of the room's leather sofas. "How about that? Any chance I can borrow your book when you're done?"

Robert looked at the book's brightly colored dust jacket and smirked coyly. "Sorry, Will. I brought that for research."

"What? You're borrowing my airship! Why can't I borrow yours?" Taft teased.

"Wait a minute," John backtracked, "you've got hot cocoa in there?" He pointed his glass of vermouth toward the president's remarkable cabinet.

Taft smiled proudly. "It's got chocolate liqueur, if that wets your whistle!"

The Surprise cabinet meeting was interrupted by a knock at the door.

"Come in!" Taft laughed as he reached for another delightful amuse-bouche. Captain Butt walked in through Miss Knox's door. "Archie! I hope you're here to join our little summit."

"I'm sorry, sir. I've come to report that the airship is ready to depart."

"What's our flight path?" asked Robert.

"We travel northwest through Canada. The land should be uninhabited once we clear the Great Lakes, so we can fly during daylight. The whole trip should take less than forty-eight hours."

"You're sure this time?" Taft prodded. His whiskers curled playfully.

The upright officer fell victim to the president's infectious simper. "Yes." Captain Butt smiled back at his friend.

"Very good, Archie. Have the cooks prepare supper immediately. We'll be expecting you at our table."

"As you wish, Mr. President."

Taft finished his champagne and the remaining appetizers on his desk. "So, who's hungry?" he asked as he rubbed his hands together eagerly.

Five bowls of terrapin soup, four roast canvasback ducks, three different types of desserts, two bottles of champagne, and quite a few laughs later . . .

"So I told them, 'Hey! Can the number seven train stop here for a large party?' And when it arrived, I jumped on the train and said, 'You can go ahead; I am the large party!'"

The four men laughed heartily in Airship One's elegant dining room.

"Has Will always been like this?" Robert asked John across the lavishly dressed table.

"Oh, yes. He hasn't change a bit since his Yale days."

"My bathroom scale disagrees!" Taft said to more merriment.

"Seriously." John snickered. "I was two years ahead of Will, but he was always quite popular. 'Big Lub' was his nickname. He was our champion wrestler."

"Heavyweight," Taft emphasized, slapping his stomach.

"He was also salutatorian, a member of Psi Upsilon, Skull and Bones—"

"That's like the Porcellian Club," Taft clarified for Robert, "only better!"

Robert set down his coffee cup and accepted this Ivy League banter with a smile. "Tell me, Will. If Skull and Bones recruits only the best and brightest young minds, how come you got to join but John didn't?"

Captain Butt raised his eyebrows. These were fighting words.

"It was a technicality," Taft assured. "Jack went to Yale's Sheffield School, which has a completely different student body with separate secret societies. Besides, judging from how much a man like Jack earns compared to being president of the United States, I don't think he's complaining."

"I'm not," John bashfully validated.

"Trust me," Taft continued, "my father cofounded Skull and Bones, and three of my brothers are Bonesmen. If I went to Sheff, there's no way even I could have gotten into the Tomb."

"Actually," John corrected, "that's not quite the case anymore. At least not since I started teaching at Yale."

"Oh, *really?*" sneered the proud Bonesman. "And why would that be, wise guy?"

John sipped his coffee nonchalantly.

"Mr. Hammond . . ." Robert's ears piqued with curiosity. "What do you know?"

A Cheshire cat's grin spread across John Hays Hammond's

face. "It's a bit of an alumni secret, but some of my undergraduates at the Sheffield School figured out how to snoop on all of Yale's secret societies, including the Skull and Bones tomb. I considered telling Dean Chittenden, but the students weren't violating any laws or damaging any property. Besides, I must say I was quite impressed by their discovery! It was far more interesting than the interior of the Tomb."

"Ha! You and all your engineer bookworms couldn't break into our broom closet!" Taft challenged.

John thought for a minute. "Was the broom closet to the left or right of Yorick? I forget. There are so many doors in that dusty old place."

The president's smile disappeared.

"Yorick?" asked Butt.

"It's the name of their skull," John smirked. "And Will, as one Yale man to another, I must ask: Could you and your Bonesmen have possibly picked a less original name?"

Robert's eyes shifted between both Elis. "Will?"

"All right, enough of this," Taft grumbled. "I didn't invite you two on this airship so we could play twenty questions. Mr. Lincoln, please explain to Mr. Hammond and the captain why you are taking us on this unexpected trip to Alaska."

"Thank you very much, Mr. President." Robert pushed his coffee aside and adjusted his spectacles. "Gentlemen. Earlier this year, I was asked to chair an executive inquiry on the recent reappearance of Halley's comet. This decision was made by the president"—Taft nodded—"based on spectroscopic data collected by the Yerkes Observatory, the Harvard Observatory, and my personal observations in Manchester, Vermont. Our concern was nothing short of a credible threat to all life on Earth."

"You're talking about Professor Flammarion and his cyanogen scare," John entered.

"Yes."

"Mr. President, why wasn't I told we were investigating this?" Captain Butt asked with concern.

"Because the investigation wasn't official, Archie," replied Taft. "Robert was working strictly off the books, same as you do every time you man the helm of this zeppelin."

Or as Miss Knox was as she listened to this conversation from behind the dining room door.

Her notebook was open and her pencil was moving.

A clock chimed.

Chapter XI

[Written in Shorthand]

LINCOLN: CAPTAIN [BUTT], I CAN ASSURE YOU THAT OUR INVESTIGATION WAS STRICTLY SCIENTIFIC. ALTHOUGH THE MILITARY DID ASSIST US WITH OUR RESEARCH, MY TEAM DELIBERATELY OPERATED OUTSIDE OF THE GOVERNMENT FOR THE SAKE OF ANONYMITY.

BUTT: I RESPECT THAT, MR. LINCOLN, BUT SURELY A THREAT OF THIS MAGNITUDE—

TAFT: ARCHIE, IF IT HONESTLY LOOKED LIKE THE WORLD WAS GOING TO END, YOU WOULD HAVE BEEN THE FIRST PERSON I'D ASK TO DO SOMETHING ABOUT IT. BELIEVE ME.

BUTT: BUT—

TAFT: NO BUTS. JUST KEEP DRINKING YOUR WATER AND LET THE GOOD MAN CONTINUE. [LAUGHTER.]

BUTT: VERY WELL. MY APOLOGIES, MR. PRESIDENT.

TAFT: THAT WON'T BE NECESSARY. MR. LINCOLN?

LINCOLN: THANK YOU. WITH THE HELP OF SIR ROBERT BALL FROM THE CAMBRIDGE OBSERVATORY, WE CONCLUDED THAT THE APOCALYPTIC SCENARIOS OUTLINED BY PRO-FESSOR CAMILLE FLAMMARION OF THE JUVISY OBSERVA-TORY WERE UNSUBSTANTIATED. NEVERTHELESS, AS A PRECAUTION I ASKED ANY AND ALL AVAILABLE OUTLETS THROUGHOUT THE COUNTRY TO MONITOR THEIR SKIES THE NIGHT WE WERE EXPECTED TO PASS THROUGH THE COMET. TOGETHER WITH INFORMATION PROVIDED BY [BRITISH AMBASSADOR TO THE UNITED STATES] JAMES BRYCE, I WAS ABLE TO COMPARE ALL OUR FINDINGS WITH THOSE FROM SIMILAR OUTPOSTS THROUGHOUT THE BRITISH EMPIRE.

TAFT: WAIT A MINUTE. YOU WERE MONITORING THE SKIES AROUND THE ENTIRE WORLD?

LINCOLN: YES. BRIEFLY.

TAFT: YOU NEVER TOLD ME THAT!

LINCOLN: IT WAS AN ACT OF AMITY BETWEEN OUR TWO NA-TIONS. I DID NOT THINK YOU WOULD MIND.

BUTT: IN MR. LINCOLN'S DEFENSE, AMBASSADOR BRYCE IS A VERY KIND MAN. HE HAS BEEN WORKING HARD TO IMPROVE ANGLO-AMERICAN RELATIONS DUE TO THE GROWING POSSIBILITY OF WAR IN EUROPE.

TAFT: WELL, IT'S NICE TO KNOW WE CAN COUNT ON HIM FOR THESE TYPES OF FAVORS! ANYWAY, PLEASE CONTINUE.

LINCOLN: ACCORDING TO OUR FINDINGS, NOTHING APPEARED OUT OF THE ORDINARY ANYWHERE ON THE PLANET, EXCEPT IN ALASKA. EYEWITNESSES FROM THE U.S. SIGNAL CORPS ALONG THE ALL-AMERICAN ROUTE FROM WILLOW CREEK TO THE TANANA RIVER REPORTED SOME SORT OF ATMOSPHERIC PHENOMENON EMANATING FROM THE WRANGELL MOUNTAINS. THE DISPLAY STARTED AT SUNSET, MAY 18: THE PRECISE MOMENT EARTH PASSED THROUGH THE TAIL OF THE COMET. WE EVEN RECEIVED SIMILAR SIGHTINGS DAYS LATER FROM A DETACHMENT OF THE ROYAL NORTHWEST MOUNTED POLICE OPERATING IN THE YUKON TERRITORY.

HAMMOND: WHAT DID THEY SEE?

LINCOLN: BLUE LIGHT. A SPECTACULAR, INCANDESCENT BLUE LIGHT LOOMING OVER THE MOUNTAINS LIKE A CLOUD.

BUTT: HOW DO YOU KNOW THIS WASN'T THE DEADLY GAS?

LINCOLN: BECAUSE CYANOGEN IS COLORLESS, CAPTAIN. AND EVEN IF THIS DISPLAY WAS SOME SORT OF LIGHT

REFRACTION, IT STILL WOULD NOT HAVE APPEARED BLUE.

HAMMOND: IS THERE ANY CHANCE THIS WAS AN AURORA?

LINCOLN: THERE IS ABSOLUTELY NO WAY THIS WAS AURORA BOREALIS. AURORAS ARE USUALLY GREEN, AND NO OTHER AURORAS WERE REPORTED ANYWHERE IN THE REGION. FURTHERMORE, WE KNOW FOR A FACT THAT THIS BIZARRE DISPLAY WAS SUSTAINED, OBSERVABLE FOR SEVERAL DAYS UNTIL IT WAS CARRIED OFF BY THE WIND. THAT'S HOW WE WERE ABLE TO TRACE ITS POINT OF ORIGIN BACK TO THE WRANGELL MOUNTAINS. NOT THE KENNECOTT MINES IN PARTICULAR, BUT SOMEWHERE VERY CLOSE TO IT.

HAMMOND: HOW CLOSE?

LINCOLN: I'D SAY NO FARTHER THAN FIVE OR SIX MILES FROM THE MINES. MAYBE LESS.

HAMMOND: AND THERE WAS NOTHING LIKE THIS ANYWHERE ELSE IN THE WORLD?

LINCOLN: NOTHING EVEN REMOTELY RESEMBLING IT. ACCORDING TO ONE OF OUR WITNESSES IN ALASKA, THE SKIES RESEMBLED AN IMPRESSIONIST PAINTING.

HAMMOND: I MUST SAY THAT IS MOST PECULIAR, MR. LINCOLN. MOST PECULIAR INDEED.

TAFT: YES, I DON'T UNDERSTAND HALF OF IT MYSELF. FOR-
TUNATELY, THAT'S WHY WE BROUGHT YOU ONBOARD,
JACK! YOU WERE THE GUGGENHEIMS'S CHIEF ENGINEER
FOR YEARS, SO PLEASE TELL US: WHAT MAKES THE WRAN-
GELL MOUNTAINS SO [EXPLETIVE] SPECIAL?

HAMMOND: WELL, I CAN TELL YOU IT'S ONE OF THE BEST
PLACES IN THE WORLD TO MINE COPPER. THE ENTIRE
MOUNTAIN RANGE IS DOTTED WITH VOLCANOES, WHICH
TURNED IT INTO A TREASURE TROVE OF PRECIOUS MIN-
ERALS. COPPER WAS FIRST DISCOVERED THERE SHORTLY
AFTER THE KLONDIKE GOLD RUSH, BUT THE MOUNTAINS
WERE TOO REMOTE FOR ANYONE TO THOROUGHLY MINE
THEM. NOT EVEN THE GUGGENHEIMS COULD AFFORD
TO MOVE A MOUNTAIN OF ORE ACROSS 200 MILES OF ICE
JUST TO SHIP IT ANOTHER 2,000 MILES TO TACOMA. THE
COST OF THE NECESSARY RAILROADS ALONE EXCEEDED
$25 MILLION. ONLY J. P. MORGAN HAD THE CAPITAL TO
MAKE EVERYTHING FUNCTION, AND SINCE HE HAD JUST
FORMED THE IMM [INTERNATIONAL MERCANTILE MA-
RINE CO.], HE WAS EAGER FOR ANY EXCUSE TO EXPAND
HIS SHIPPING EMPIRE. THERE WAS ALMOST NO OTHER
WAY OUT OF ALASKA THAN THROUGH HIM. THE GUG-
GENHEIMS APPROACHED MORGAN IN 1903, AND I WAS
HIRED A YEAR LATER AS THEIR GENERAL MANAGER AND
MINING CONSULTANT.

TAFT: I STILL CAN'T BELIEVE MORGAN WAS COAXED INTO
DOING ANYTHING WITH THE GUGGENHEIMS.

HAMMOND: WHY IS THAT?

TAFT: ARE YOU KIDDING? J. P. MORGAN IS SO ANTI-SEMITIC THAT YOU'D THINK HE WAS RUNNING FOR TSAR.

[PAUSE.]

TAFT: WHAT?

LINCOLN: JOHN, WHAT CAN YOU TELL US ABOUT THE KEN-NECOTT MINES?

HAMMOND: IN WHAT REGARD?

LINCOLN: DID YOU FIND ANYTHING UNUSUAL THERE ONCE THE GUGGENHEIMS STARTED DIGGING?

HAMMOND: ROBERT, FROM A MINING STANDPOINT, EVERY-THING ABOUT THE WRANGELL MOUNTAINS IS MIRA-CULOUS! I WAS HANDED ORE SAMPLES TAKEN FROM ITS SURFACE THAT WERE OVER 70% COPPER, INCLUDING SOME BEARING BITS OF GOLD AND SILVER AS WELL. WORKING ON THIS PROJECT WAS LIKE BEING HIRED TO EXCAVATE KING SOLOMON'S MINES!

TAFT: IF THAT'S THE CASE, WHY DID YOU QUIT?

HAMMOND: TO BE COMPLETELY HONEST, AFTER WORKING WITH THE GUGGENHEIMS FOR FOUR YEARS, I BEGAN TO SEE AND HEAR THINGS I DID NOT LIKE. SOME STARTED

OFF AS JUST RUMORS, BUT OTHERS BECAME TOO REAL
AND PRONOUNCED FOR ME TO IGNORE.

LINCOLN: SUCH AS?

HAMMOND: WELL, JUST OUT OF MY OWN EXPERIENCE,
THE GUGGENHEIMS WERE NOT VERY PLEASANT TO WORK
WITH. THE PAY WAS EXCELLENT AND I ENJOYED BEING
ABLE TO CONTINUE TEACHING AT YALE, BUT MY EMPLOY-
ERS DID NOT HAVE MUCH RESPECT FOR MY METHODS. I
EXPLORED EVERY OPTION TO MINE THOSE MOUNTAINS
AS QUICKLY AND PROFITABLY AS POSSIBLE, BUT I WAS
CONSTANTLY TOLD TO DIG DEEPER, EVEN PAST THE
VEINS OF COPPER IN THE MOUNTAIN. I DON'T KNOW
WHY THE GUGGENHEIMS WANTED TO DO THIS, ESPE-
CIALLY SINCE THEY DID NOT BEHAVE SO ERRATICALLY
AT ANY OF THEIR OTHER SITES THROUGHOUT THE
COUNTRY. I'M GUESSING MORGAN WAS PUSHING THEM
TO ACHIEVE UNREALISTIC RESULTS. PERHAPS HE WAS
HOPING WE WOULD FIND A VOLCANIC PIPE WHERE WE
COULD MINE DIAMONDS JUST LIKE THE AUSTRALIANS IN
THE '90S. ALL I KNOW IS THIS MEDDLING UNNECESSARILY
ADDED YEARS TO THE PROJECT AND EXPOSED MANY OF
MY WORKERS TO SERIOUS HAZARDS.

LINCOLN: WHAT KIND OF HAZARDS?

HAMMOND: I HAVE ONE EXAMPLE THAT PERFECTLY UNDER-
SCORES THE CONSEQUENCE OF HAVING TOO MANY
COOKS IN THE KITCHEN.

TAFT: I'M LISTENING.

HAMMOND: DURING MY LAST YEAR WITH THE GUGGEN-
HEIMS, THEY BROUGHT IN SOME SORT OF OUTSIDE CON-
SULTANT TO ASSESS A PART OF THE MOUNTAINS I HAD
PREVIOUSLY DEEMED UNSAFE. A FEW WEEKS LATER,
I LEARNED MY OBJECTIONS IN ALASKA WENT COM-
PLETELY IGNORED. MY MINERS WERE PUT BACK TO
WORK IN THE AREA WHILE I WAS VISITING ANOTHER
SITE IN UTAH. AS I FEARED, THE DIGGING DISRUPTED A
HOT SPRING THAT FLOODED THE ENTIRE MINESHAFT
WITH STEAM. SEVERAL MEN DIED AND MANY OTHERS
WERE INCAPACITATED. I ISSUED A COMPLAINT ONLY TO
RECEIVE A REPLY THAT THIS SPECIALIST WOULD SERVE
AS MY SURROGATE IN ALASKA WHENEVER I WAS AWAY. I
REFUSED TO COMPLY AND SHORTLY AFTER QUIT MY
COMMISSION.

BUTT: THIS "SPECIALIST" THE GUGGENHEIMS BROUGHT IN.
WHAT WAS HIS NAME?

HAMMOND: I DON'T KNOW. I NEVER MET HIM IN PERSON
AND WE NEVER SPOKE OVER THE WIRES. HOWEVER,
I KNOW THAT HE WAS NEVER AN OFFICIAL EMPLOYEE OF
THE GUGGENHEIMS, OTHERWISE I WOULD HAVE FIRED
HIM. AS I SAID, HE WAS AN OUTSIDE CONSULTANT HIRED
BY THE MORGAN-GUGGENHEIM SYNDICATE AS A WHOLE.

LINCOLN: DID THE MINERS DISCOVER ANYTHING STRANGE
WHEN THEY BREACHED THE HOT SPRING? ANYTHING

THAT COULD HAVE CAUSED THE ATMOSPHERIC DISPLAYS OBSERVED ON MAY 18 AND AFTERWARD?

HAMMOND: NOT AT ALL. THERE WAS NOTHING IN THAT GROUND BUT A LEAD CAVERN AND AN UNDERGROUND RIVER. IT WAS A COMPLETE WASTE OF HUMAN LIFE, AND I SAW TO IT THAT THE FAMILIES OF ALL THE FALLEN MINERS RECEIVED PAYMENTS AT MY OWN EXPENSE.

TAFT: JOHN, IS THERE ANYTHING ELSE YOU CAN TELL US ABOUT THE MINES OR THE MOUNTAINS THAT MIGHT EXPLAIN THESE STRANGE OCCURRENCES BOB MONITORED?

HAMMOND: ALAS, I HAVE TOLD YOU EVERYTHING I CAN THINK OF. I WISH I COULD BE MORE HELP, BUT PLEASE REMEMBER THAT I WAS GENERAL MANAGER FOR EVERY MINE THE GUGGENHEIMS OWNED. I SPENT VERY LITTLE TIME AT THE KENNECOTT SITE COMPARED TO THE REST OF THE COUNTRY.

BUTT: YOU MENTIONED SOMETHING ABOUT RUMORS. WHAT WERE THEY?

[PAUSE.]

TAFT: JACK? YOU ALL RIGHT?

HAMMOND: WHENEVER YOU WORK FOR AN ENTERPRISE AS ENORMOUS AS THE GUGGENHEIMS OR THE HOUSE OF

MORGAN, IT IS INEVITABLE THAT YOU WILL FIND YOUR-
SELF AMONG CLIENTELE YOU WOULD OTHERWISE PREFER
TO AVOID. THIS CONSULTANT THE SYNDICATE BROUGHT
IN BEFORE MY DEPARTURE WAS ONE OF THESE PEOPLE,
BUT THERE WAS ONE NAME I HEARD MENTIONED PREVI-
OUSLY THAT NEARLY MADE ME QUIT ON THE SPOT.

BUTT: WHO WAS IT?

HAMMOND: KING LEOPOLD II.

[NOTE. ADDED JULY 20, 1910, 3:22 A.M.

LEOPOLD II, KING OF THE BELGIANS. BORN TO KING LEOPOLD I
ON APRIL 9, 1835. COUSIN TO QUEEN VICTORIA, PRINCE ALBERT,
TSAR NICHOLAS II, AND OTHERS.

ASCENDS TO THE THRONE DECEMBER 17, 1865.

ORGANIZES THE INTERNATIONAL AFRICAN SOCIETY IN 1876 FOR
HUMANITARIAN EFFORTS IN CENTRAL AFRICA.

FOUNDS THE INTERNATIONAL ASSOCIATION OF THE CONGO ON
NOVEMBER 17, 1879.

LOBBIES THE U.S. GOVERNMENT FROM 1883–84 FOR INTERNA-
TIONAL RECOGNITION. THE UNITED STATES BECOMES THE
FIRST COUNTRY TO FORMALLY RECOGNIZE KING LEOPOLD
II'S CLAIM TO THE CONGO ON APRIL 22, 1884.

THE BERLIN ACT ON THE CONGO, SIGNED FEBRUARY 26, 1885, LEGITIMIZES LEOPOLD'S CLAIMS TO THE INTERNATIONAL ASSOCIATION OF THE CONGO. BY ROYAL DECREE, LEOPOLD RENAMES HIS HOLDINGS THE CONGO FREE STATE ON MAY 29, 1885.

GEORGE WASHINGTON WILLIAMS, A CIVIL WAR VETERAN AND NEGRO HISTORIAN, WRITES "AN OPEN LETTER TO HIS SERENE MAJESTY LÉOPOLD II, KING OF THE BELGIANS AND SOVEREIGN OF THE INDEPENDENT STATE OF CONGO" ON JULY 18, 1890. THE LETTER DETAILS EXTENSIVE ABUSES, KIDNAPPINGS, AND MURDERS COMMITTED BY LEOPOLD'S FORCES IN THE CONGO FREE STATE.

THE NEW YORK TIMES PUBLISHES A FRONT-PAGE ARTICLE ON "COL. WILLIAMS' CHARGES" ON APRIL 14, 1891.

GEORGE WASHINGTON WILLIAMS DIES AUGUST 2, 1891, IN BLACKPOOL, ENGLAND, AT AGE 41.

JOSEPH CONRAD PUBLISHES HEART OF DARKNESS IN 1899 BASED ON FIRSTHAND EXPERIENCES IN THE CONGO FREE STATE.

THE BRITISH GOVERNMENT INVESTIGATES ALLEGED VIOLATIONS OF THE BERLIN AGREEMENT IN 1903.

THE CASEMENT REPORT ON ATROCITIES IN THE CONGO IS PUBLISHED IN 1904.

MARK TWAIN PUBLISHES KING LEOPOLD'S SOLILOQUY *IN 1905. REPORTS OF WIDESPREAD ABUSES IN THE CONGO FREE STATE ESCALATE.*

"KING LEOPOLD'S AMAZING ATTEMPT TO INFLUENCE OUR CONGRESS EXPOSED" IS PUBLISHED IN NEW YORK AMERICAN *ON DECEMBER 10, 1906. PUBLIC OUTRAGE MOUNTS OVER PHOTOGRAPHS OF ATROCITIES IN THE CONGO AND BELGIAN ATTEMPTS TO INFILTRATE THE U.S. GOVERNMENT.*

LEOPOLD ASSUMES ABSOLUTE RULE OVER THE BELGIAN CONGO ON NOVEMBER 15, 1908.

SIR ARTHUR CONAN DOYLE WRITES THE CRIME OF THE CONGO *IN 1909.*

KING LEOPOLD II DIES DECEMBER 17, 1909.

UNOFFICIAL ESTIMATE OF DEATHS IN THE CONGO DUE TO BELGIAN RULE: 10 MILLION.

CONCLUSION: ACCORDING TO A PERSONAL INVESTIGATION INTO MR. HAMMOND'S CLAIMS, J. P. MORGAN AND THE GUGGENHEIMS WERE LIKELY SOLICITED AT SOME POINT FROM 1905–06 AS PART OF KING LEOPOLD II'S ATTEMPT TO MAINTAIN SUPPORT WITHIN THE U.S. GOVERNMENT. WHETHER MR. MORGAN OR ANY MEMBER OF THE GUGGENHEIMS AGREED TO ENTER INTO SOME SORT OF PARTNERSHIP WITH LEOPOLD BEFORE HIS DEATH REMAINS BOTH INDISCERNIBLE AT THIS TIME AND APPARENTLY IRRELEVANT TO THE

U.S. SECRET SERVICE'S INVESTIGATION INTO THE ATTEMPT ON PRESIDENT TAFT'S LIFE.

HOWEVER, THERE IS A POTENTIAL LINK BETWEEN THE MORGAN-GUGGENHEIM SYNDICATE'S ACTIVITIES IN ALASKA AND THE ENCRYPTED TRANSMISSION RECEIVED ON AIRSHIP ONE PRIOR TO THE ATTEMPT ON NIKOLA TESLA'S LIFE. THE "GENTLEMAN FROM BOMA" IN THE COMMUNICATION WAS LIKELY A REFERENCE TO BOMA, THE FORMER CAPITAL OF THE CONGO FREE STATE AND THE PRESENT CAPITAL OF THE BELGIAN CONGO. IT IS SUSPICIOUS THAT SUCH A LITTLE-KNOWN CITY WOULD BE FEATURED SO PROMINENTLY IN TWO SEPARATE INVESTIGATIONS. UNFORTUNATELY, ANY CONNECTIONS BETWEEN THESE EVENTS AND THE RECENT ATTACK AGAINST THE PRESIDENT REMAIN TENUOUS AT BEST.

IN SHORT, THERE IS NOT ENOUGH EVIDENCE TO WARRANT AN OFFICIAL U.S. SECRET SERVICE INVESTIGATION INTO ANY MEMBER OF THE MORGAN-GUGGENHEIM SYNDICATE IN RESPONSE TO THE ATTEMPT ON PRESIDENT TAFT'S LIFE. HOWEVER, IF ANY ADDITIONAL INFORMATION SURFACES FOLLOWING YOUR MEETING WITH THOMAS EDISON, I AM HAPPY TO VOLUNTEER MYSELF FOR AN "UNOFFICIAL" INVESTIGATION INTO THE SYNDICATE'S ACTIVITIES.

-K

P.S. STILL NO MENTION OF THAT MYSTERIOUS POCKET WATCH.]

Chapter XII

"Taxi!"

Secret Service Chief John E. Wilkie shouted over the packed mob of horses, cars, and pedestrians from the south corner of Wall Street and Nassau. It was lunchtime in New York on Friday, July 22, and Wilkie had more than 2.3 million people to move through on Manhattan Island alone. J. P. Morgan was not at his Wall Street office, and any chance of an impromptu meeting at his uptown branch hinged on how quickly Wilkie could get there. He did not want to be told Morgan was out to lunch. And to make matters worse, Wilkie was down to his last cigar.

Fortunately, he knew he could be counted among the best-dressed men in the city in his red and white striped suit, matching vest with red bowtie, freshly starched collar, and white boater hat as he hollered "Taxi!" a second time.

"I thought you knew your way around the city," said Attorney

General Wickersham as he walked down the steps of the stately Drexel Building.

"What are you going to do? Indict me for perjury?"

Wickersham discarded his spent cigarette. "I don't know, John. This surprise visit of yours is turning into a wild-goose chase."

"Maybe so, but the minute I get my hands on that goose, he's cooked." Wilkie whistled. "Hey, you! Get over here!"

A French Darracq taxicab pulled up to the curb. Its friendly looking driver was dressed like a West Point cadet. "Good afternoon, gentlemen."

"Skip the foreplay, Frank. Can you take us to the Morgan Library? It's on East Thirty-sixth Street between Madison and Park."

"Sorry, sir. I don't operate north of Fourteenth Street."

"You do now." The Secret Service chief flipped a ten-dollar gold eagle into the driver's hand as he and Wickersham stepped into the red taxi. The cabbie bit the coin, pocketed it, and away they sped.

"I still don't understand why you want me to come," said Wickersham as the cab made a right at Trinity Church onto Broadway. "My investigation into the Tesla matter is over."

"It's over because you found nothing," Wilkie huffed through his cigar.

Wickersham furrowed his brow. "John, we didn't find anything at Tesla's lab because there was nothing to find! The crazy wizard electrified his assassin out of existence. I'm happy to side with the police and have this ruled as self-defense, but the question of who wanted to kill Tesla and for what reason is completely unsolvable."

"But that's all the reason in the world to stick around a bit longer, don't you think?" Wilkie removed his cigar and looked the attorney general in the eyes. "George, has it not dawned on you that this has been a rather unusual week? Your Justice Department is investigating the single strangest attempted murder since the Chicago World's Fair. The Secret Service and the War Department are examining the remains of a killer automaton that nearly destroyed the White House. And William Howard Taft, a man we both know couldn't solve his way out of a hat, is suddenly looking for Martians in Alaska after one conversation with Robert Todd Lincoln. I'm not saying that I like this odd turn the twentieth century is taking, but it is certainly a lot more interesting than what you and I have been doing for the past year and a half. If you want to go back to arresting ice-cream cones, I won't stop you. Hell, I'll even have Frank here drop you off at the nearest playground. Otherwise, I suggest you sit back and keep me company for the next hour or two. When we're finished, I'll buy you lunch at Delmonico's. Does that sound like a square deal?"

Wickersham thought this over as their cab passed City Hall. Outside the window, it was a particularly nice day to be in New York. "All right, John. We'll try things your way. What's your plan?"

The Secret Service chief treated his companion to a yellowed, tobacco-stained grin. "Good choice, my friend! Simply put, we're going to sit down and have a nice, friendly chat with Mr. Morgan. Since you and I spoke with Thomas Edison yesterday, it'll make sense that the two of us would want to have a word with the big cheese himself."

"I don't know, John. Yesterday was a pretty embarrassing day

in my career. I don't want to repeat it with one of the most powerful men on the planet."

"Really?" Wilkie chirped. "I kind of enjoyed it!"

"John, you left Thomas Edison in tears for no other reason
than your own amusement."

"That's not true," Wilkie corrected. "Dr. Tesla thought it was
funny as hell."

"Maybe so, but I'm convinced Edison had nothing to do with
the attack on the president."

"As am I! I knew he wasn't smart enough to construct the
automaton. The War Department told me the combined technical might of the U.S. military could not have built that machine.
I'm thinking whoever wanted to kill Taft brought in some help
from overseas."

"So why waste our time pulling the house of Morgan into this?
Do you honestly think he wanted to kill the president of the
United States?"

"Even if he didn't, Morgan may know something about Edison's
records that even Edison doesn't. Morgan's his financial agent,
for Christ's sake!"

"Spoken like a true Treasury agent," said Wickersham, already
dreading the paperwork.

"Think about it, George. Why else was the android a complete failure at everything except trying to rip the president's head
off? Why else are its guts loaded with springs and wheels you
can't even find in America? Why else did it weigh several hundred
pounds more than it was supposed to? For all we know, Morgan
had the automaton built by international anarchists simply because he knew they have a lousy trade union."

Wickersham shook his head. "I don't know, John. It sounds

to me like you're somehow convinced J. P. Morgan was in the center of all this."

Wilkie smiled devilishly. This was precisely the opening he was looking for. "George, what if I told you that one of my operatives uncovered information potentially linking your Tesla investigation, my Edison inquiry, and President Taft's little green manhunt in Alaska to none other than J. P. Morgan himself?"

"I'll believe it when I see it," said Wickersham as he looked out the window. The cab was crossing Canal Street when the attorney general heard the sound of paper rustling. He looked down to see Miss Knox's report on King Leopold II lying flat on his lap. "What is this?"

"Take your time." Wilkie smiled as he patiently smoked his cigar.

The attorney general read through the brief and then stared at the Secret Service chief, aghast. "There's been a breakthrough in the Nikola Tesla transmission?"

"Potentially. It looks like Mr. Hammond has proven himself more useful than any of us could have imagined. After reading what he knows, I'm amazed he's still alive."

"John, where did you get this information?"

"Honestly," Wilkie laughed, coughing on a cloud of smoke, "it came to me in a dream!"

"Be serious."

"I am being serious! I went to sleep Tuesday night, woke up bright and early the next morning, and there it was!"

"John," Wickersham said sternly, holding the document between the two men, "where did you get this?"

Wilkie narrowed his eyes and brushed his finger against his nose.

The attorney general looked back at the note in disbelief. "If J. P. Morgan was in any way involved in the attack on Tesla, even peripherally, that would connect him to the attack on the president *and* the investigation in Alaska."

"Yes, and wouldn't that be the luck of Barry Lyndon! The Morgan-Guggenheim syndicate wrapping all our cases in a neat little package . . ."

"John, that would point to conspiracy."

"Well," Wilkie puffed with assurance, "that's the milk in the coconut, isn't it?"

Wickersham still could not believe it: the Morgan-Guggenheim syndicate plotting against the United States? But to what extent? And for what purpose? Who else was involved? The possibilities were endless and the attorney general was speechless.

"So here's what I'm thinking," began Wilkie. "If this 'Gentleman from Boma' is just a code name for some grizzled prospector or a goddamn nihilist, that'll very quickly be the last anybody in Washington hears of you or me. We need more information to tie the syndicate to all three cases, which is why you and I are going to speak with Mr. Morgan today. I want you to look that fat bastard in the eyes and then tell me who you think is crazy: me, him, or the two of us on a bicycle. Either way, I have no choice but to trust your judgment on this. If there is a conspiracy, you're the person who will have to prosecute it. I'm the shield of the presidency, but you're the sword."

"John," Wickersham exhaled, "we have both taken oaths to defend the Constitution against all enemies. If our nation is under attack right now, I don't want to prosecute its conspirators. I want to annihilate them."

"That'll work, too," Wilkie shrugged, returning to his stogie.

However, as Wickersham reexamined the document, something stood out to him. "What's this little note at the end?"

Confused, Wilkie took the paper and looked it over. "Ah, yes. Do you remember that device Mr. Lincoln talked about during our little joyride with the president? The one he said contained a power that rivaled all existing science?"

"Of course. He said it could be used for interplanetary travel."

"Yes, well . . . Whatever it is, I think it's somehow related to that pocket watch he always carries around but never wears. He guarded it closely in a coat pocket the entire time we were in London. I didn't know what he had in there at first, but one of my agents saw him stuff a gold pocket watch in the same pocket when Norton burst into the Oval Office with the Tesla transmission. I even caught Robert checking it after the president nearly killed us in his auto. I'm convinced that trinket is what persuaded Taft to throw his entire weight into the Alaska investigation. Figuratively, of course."

"What do you think it is?"

Wilkie did not want to embarrass himself by saying "time machine," so instead he answered, "I don't know. Whatever it is, I just hope we don't see it used as a weapon against us in the future."

An uncomfortable silence filled the red cab.

"Hey, John," said Wickersham. "A thought occurred to me. Suppose the president and Robert have been approaching their investigation the wrong way?"

"What do you mean?"

"Suppose this device Robert has isn't alien to this planet at all. But rather, it's something foreign to *us* because it has not been invented yet. Like something from so far into the future that it was able to bring someone backward in time."

Wilkie looked a long time at the attorney general. "Don't be ridiculous." The two men sat quietly as their taxi slowed in approach of Union Square. Looking to change the subject, Wilkie took a final puff from his cigar and asked, "Did you know Abe Lincoln's funeral train traveled down this road?"

"Is that right?"

"Yup. His body lay in state at City Hall before they moved it up Broadway. I think it went to Albany after that."

Wickersham was surprised to hear this. "Well, I stand corrected."

"About what?"

"What I said earlier. It sounds like you do know your way around the city!"

Wickersham awaited a reply, but there was none.

"John?"

Again, no response. Instead, Wilkie looked out his window as if to deliberately ignore the man sitting next to him.

The attorney general, thinking he somehow offended Wilkie, tried to repair the conversation by revealing something he had never shared with anyone. "I actually saw Lincoln's funeral train when I was a boy."

Wilkie turned his head. "Really?"

"Yes, in Philadelphia. I had been living in the city with my grandparents since my father served in the war." Wickersham, overcome with the memory, exhaled heavily. "I was too young to remember my mother's death, but not Father Abraham's. At times, I can't even think about it without returning to that moment when the whole city was in mourning." Wickersham, sensing some camaraderie returning to his companion, asked, "What about you? Do you remember where you were when it happened?"

The Secret Service chief hesitated for a moment, and then threw his cigar stub out the window. "It doesn't matter." As the taxi entered Union Square, Wilkie took one last look at the building to his left as the cab turned right. His eyes moved from a second-floor window to the equestrian statue of George Washington in the park to a sad-looking paperboy, until . . .

"What's a space toilet?" Wickersham asked.

Wilkie drew his revolver. "Where?"

"There!" The attorney general pointed at a sign on the tallest building behind the Union Square Savings Bank.

For a split second, Wilkie and Wickersham assumed the absolute worst: that Robert Todd Lincoln's pocket watch was indeed a time machine and that history had been rewritten without anyone knowing. But as Wilkie's eyes focused on the display, he slowly returned to his seat and gave his companion a look of profound disappointment.

"It says 'space to-let,' George."

"Oh."

The two men sat silently for the rest of their trip.

"Here we are, gentlemen," said the driver, stopping in front of the library on Thirty-sixth Street.

Wilkie checked his watch. "Very good. Thanks for the ride, Frank."

"It's James, sir."

"Whatever."

Wilkie and Wickersham stepped out of the taxi and let their eyes take in the great library.

"You might want to put that away," said Wickersham.

"Oh . . . Sorry."

The Secret Service chief holstered his pistol.

Chapter XIII

The House of Morgan

I feel like we're in Rome," said Wickersham.

"Yeah, and J. P. Morgan's the pope."

The two men walked up nine stone steps flanked by twin lionesses guarding the imperial entrance of J. P. Morgan's private library. Designed by Charles Follen McKim, the pillared palace was a marble masterpiece of Classical Revival, capturing all the vices and virtues of antiquity in its white exterior. It was money. It was power. It was empire. It was awe. And above all else, it was J. P. Morgan's.

"No knockers?" Wickersham observed under the building's Palladian arch.

"When in Rome," Wilkie shrugged. The Secret Service chief slipped on some brass knuckles he always carried and gave the library's bronze doors a good pounding, leaving several dents behind as a souvenir. Less than a minute later, Wickersham and

Wilkie heard the sound of a key turning. The right-hand door opened inward, revealing Belle da Costa Greene, J. P. Morgan's legendary confidant and librarian.

Born in Washington, DC, under a different name and background, Belle da Costa Greene was twenty-six years old in 1910 — i.e., she was actually thirty. A former employee of the Princeton University Library, Belle was an expert in illuminated manuscripts, rare books, and the timeless practice of presentation. "Just because I am a librarian," she once boasted, "doesn't mean I have to dress like one." She didn't. For this sunny afternoon, she was wearing a silk calling gown that left no secret about her fine figure underneath. Her skin was olive, her hair dark, and her dress a radiant Hooker's green.

"Hello, gentlemen," she greeted them.

Wilkie looked her up and down. "Hello, lady." The Secret Service chief flashed his silver badge and black commission book, making it explicitly clear that he did not ride halfway across Manhattan just to admire her wardrobe. "My name is John Wilkie, United States Treasury. Chief of Secret Service Division. The gentleman with me is George Wickersham, attorney general of the United States. I believe you are expecting us."

"Yes, we are." Belle smiled. "Please come in. And wipe your feet."

The two men removed their hats and walked into the building, one of them making sure to wipe his feet against the library's beautiful marble floor.

"If you gentlemen would please wait here, I will tell Mr. Morgan of your arrival."

"Certainly," said Wickersham, who compensated for his partner's churlish attitude with kindness.

Miss Greene bowed deeply and moved in a curvy line to J. P. Morgan's study, temporarily leaving Wilkie and Wickersham in the building's regal rotunda.

The duo's previous allusions to the Vatican were apt. Within the library, the two stood amidst a forest of lapis lazuli columns supporting a museum of frescoes, mosaics, and reliefs modeled after the finest works of Raphael and Pinturicchio. The figures surrounding the rotunda's octagonal oculus painted perhaps the most intimate portrait of J. P. Morgan's ambitions for his library. There, situated like deities above the men, were female personifications of Religion, Philosophy, Art, and Science in flowing robes. Their presence strongly echoed Raphael's frescoed ceiling at the Stanza della Segnatura, which similarly served as the private library for Pope Julius II. By constructing such an equally grandiose library in Manhattan, it was hard to view J. P. Morgan as anything other than il Papa Terribile's spiritual successor to the Americas.

"I can see why Mr. Morgan spends so much time in here," said Wickersham as he glimpsed the library's vast holdings in its East Room.

"So do I," said the Secret Service chief as he glanced at Miss Greene's shapely rear in the West Room. After a few grumbles from her employer, she gracefully sashayed back to the library's two visitors.

"Mr. Morgan will see you now."

"Thanks, missy. Would you please lead the way?"

"Certainly, Mr. Wilkie. Please follow me."

The Secret Service chief winked at his companion as they followed Belle da Costa Greene's swaying hips into J. P. Morgan's private study.

"Mr. Morgan?" asked Wilkie.

"Gentlemen," he spoke.

J. P. Morgan rose from his vast desk to receive John Wilkie and George Wickersham in his lavish study. The room's red silk walls were patterned after the coat of arms of the Chigi, a Sienese banking family whose crest of a star looming over a mountain formation made Wilkie think about Robert Todd Lincoln's recent interest in Alaska. A vast collection of paintings from Italian and Northern Renaissance masters lined the room, as well as decorative shelves of rare books from all over the world. The study's stained-glass windows came from Swiss churches and monasteries dating back to the fifteenth century, and some of the sculptures atop the bookshelves were carved by artisans nearly five thousand years old. To Wilkie's left, he spied a solid steel vault where he imagined Morgan kept either his most prized possessions or his darkest secrets—maybe both. Even the study's coffered wooden ceiling was antique, taken from an Italian palace and refitted all the way across the Atlantic. It was one of the most beautiful rooms on the planet containing perhaps the greatest collection of art and literature in U.S. history, and its current purpose: background art to amuse its owner while he played solitaire at his desk.

And then there was Morgan.

Only Wilkie had the courage to shake the man's hand first. In addition to being a tall, imposing figure despite his old age, his face looked like it could have doubled as a battering ram. The tycoon's thick, dark mustache stretched all the way to his jaw like the tusks of an ill-tempered walrus. His broad, bald forehead and sparse white hairs only made his dark eyebrows even more prominent. And to quote one of his photographers, to look into his glaring, hazel eyes "was a little like confronting the headlights of an express train." But his most prominent feature, and the one that compelled everyone who met him to avert their eyes as much as possible, was his nose. His enormous, bulbous, crimson nose was completely deformed with rhinophyma to the point that it more closely resembled an enema ball. From a distance, it made J. P. Morgan look lit up with alcohol, but up close? Let's just say that neither Wilkie nor Wickersham had ever seen a proboscis monkey in such a fine suit before.

"We appreciate you meeting with us," said the attorney general.

"Yes, well . . ." J. P. Morgan sized up the Secret Service chief with disapproval. "It's not every day someone brings a gun to my Wall Street office." His voice was deep, unpleasant, and about as welcoming as a dog's growl.

"Don't worry, Mr. Morgan. We're only here to rob you of your time." Wilkie smiled.

"Yes, about that. I'm afraid I don't have much time to spare, because—"

"Oh, are we interrupting you?" The flip investigator glanced at the playing cards on Morgan's desk. And just like that, the lights of the freight train bore down on John Wilkie.

"Is there anything else I can do for you?" asked Belle.

"No, Miss Greene," said Morgan. "That will be all." Belle politely excused herself and returned to her office, leaving Wilkie and Wickersham alone with the king of Wall Street. "Have a seat," their unfriendly host offered.

Wickersham settled on a red Renaissance-style sofa to Morgan's left while Wilkie helped himself to a decorative chair closer to the windows. As the Secret Service chief crossed his legs and made himself comfortable, he noticed a gilt-tooled leather box on Morgan's desk. And next to it: a smoking cigar on an ashtray supported by four small sphinxes.

Wilkie had to whistle when J. P. Morgan picked up the thick, black beast. "That is one mighty fine Havana you have there," he observed.

"Yes it is," Morgan confirmed.

"I wouldn't suppose you have one of those Hercules' clubs for me?" Wilkie hinted, eyeballing the tobacco treasure chest.

"I wouldn't suppose so either," rebuked Morgan, blowing a thick cloud of smoke.

Wilkie grinned. "You know, the sooner you give me and my colleague what we want, the sooner we can leave you to . . . whatever it is you and your little librarian actually do here."

J. P. Morgan's eyes glowered like a raging bull's. Never before had he been so grossly insulted within the sanctity of his study. He wanted nothing more than to seize Wilkie by the throat and throw him into the room's massive fireplace. However, since Attorney General Wickersham was the man who would be deciding the fate of the entire house of Morgan in the coming months, there was little Morgan could do but acquiesce to their requests. He opened the leather box and rotated it for Wilkie. Triumphant, the Secret Service chief sprang out of his chair and selected an eight-inch Meridiana Kohinoor, which he carefully cut with the puukko knife strapped to his belt. He also tossed a cigar to Wickersham and stuffed a generous handful into his pocket.

"Those cost a lot more than two for a nickel," Morgan growled.

"I'll have the Treasury send you a dime," said Wilkie. He returned to his seat and struck a match against his collar, puffing a tall plume of smoke that touched the study's antique ceiling. "That," he judged, "is one damn fine cigar."

Morgan angrily slammed the tobacco chest shut. "Let's get down to business."

"Yes, let's." Wilkie turned his chair to face Morgan, tearing a bit of the study's antique carpet in the process. "First things first, Pierpont: Why did you visit the president's summer home in Beverly?"

With the exception of his bright red nose, J. P. Morgan's face somewhat lightened. "Is that what this is about?"

"Partially," said Wickersham.

Pierpont raised his eyebrows. "Well, in that case, I had hoped to meet with President Taft to offer my support in the upcoming election."

"Presidential or congressional?"

"The presidential race, naturally."

Wilkie narrowed his eyes. "You took a boat all the way from New York to say that?"

"No," Morgan clarified. "I was in the area aboard my yacht, *Corsair.*"

"And you have witnesses?"

"Of course," he answered grumpily. "Including two Secret Service agents stationed there. Do I need to elaborate any further?"

Wilkie, who had little interest in this meeting and merely asked about it to put Morgan temporarily at ease, was nevertheless compelled to ask—

"Why do you support him?" asked Wickersham.

The attorney general beat him to it.

"Well, now that Theodore Roosevelt is back in the country, he is almost certain to challenge President Taft to the Republican nomination. I would much rather see Taft elected to a second term than Teddy elected to a third," Morgan said plainly.

Wilkie's cigar was burning, as was his curiosity. "You're no fan of Colonel Roosevelt?" he probed. "After all he's done for you?"

"What do you mean by that?"

"Well, this is where it happened, isn't it?" Wilkie outstretched his arms. "Here in this room, three years ago, you and your Wall Street friends were able to come up with the solution to the economic panic they helped create. All it required was their complicity and an overnight ride to Washington so President Roosevelt would bless your acquisition of the Tennessee Coal, Iron and Railroad Company less than an hour before the markets opened. I'd say that's a pretty big favor considering the Sherman Antitrust Act. Wouldn't you say, George?"

Wickersham, whose Justice Department was currently suing Standard Oil and preparing for an even longer war against J. P. Morgan's vast empire, politely replied, "I'm more interested in what you have to say, Mr. Morgan."

J. P. Morgan nodded to his legal adversary, accepting the opportunity. "Much obliged. I'd say that a man always has two reasons for doing something: a good reason and the real reason. In '07, President Roosevelt had only the best reasons to accept my proposal for how to save the economy. I know this because I offered him only the best possible solution to the crisis. However, the real reason he accepted my help was because he did not have a choice. I knew he did not like the agreement despite it being precisely what the nation needed, and for that I consider it a blemish on his character."

"You know a lot about character?" asked Wilkie.

"Character is the most precious resource there is," Morgan boomed. "It cannot be bought or manufactured; it simply is."

"Ah, but by implication, that means you should be very happy to see us," said Wilkie.

"And why should that be?"

"Because the 'real reason' we are talking to you right now is also a damn good reason: it's our job."

Morgan's eyes shifted between both men before directing his response to Wickersham. "The real reason you are speaking with me and intruding upon my most private property is because I, much like Roosevelt, do not have a choice. However, if you believe that you are here with good purpose despite me having committed no offense, then I believe your character is even more flawed than Theodore's. As far as I am concerned, the presence of both of you in this library is a tyranny."

As J. P. Morgan's gaze pierced through Wickersham, the attorney general glanced at Wilkie. Behind his hand and glowing cigar, the Secret Service chief was smiling.

They had him.

"Since you are such a good judge of character," Wilkie started, "what can you tell us about your suspicious relationship with Thomas Edison and the Edison Manufacturing Company?"

Morgan looked like his face had transformed into a ticking time bomb. "What is that supposed to mean?"

Wilkie scooted to the edge of his seat. "Jay—"

"Don't call me Jay."

"Jay, Mr. Edison was approached in '09 by then-Secretary Carpenter to construct an important piece of equipment for the U.S. government. At the same time, you personally praised Edison's abilities in a private communication to President Taft."

"I did no such thing!" Morgan shouted.

"Yes, you did. I've seen the telegrams. They were among the

many sweet songs of praise you sent the president shortly after his inauguration. Since this equipment Edison constructed is currently under investigation by the U.S. Secret Service, I am afraid you must provide the Treasury with all necessary financial records—"

"I will not comply!"

"*Including shipping manifests,*" Wilkie stressed, "so that we can clear this business partner you know so well of any culpability in an attempt on the president's life."

J. P. Morgan was furious. His face was so boiled over with anger that his nose turned dark purple. Choking with rage, he turned to Attorney General Wickersham. "You cannot possibly condone this schoolyard rambunctiousness. This is criminal idiocy!"

"Mr. Morgan," Wickersham said in a calm, controlled tone, "I am the chief law enforcer of the United States. We are not asking for your assistance or your opinion on these matters. We are telling you that you will provide us with the information we need to conduct our investigation."

Morgan emitted a deep grunt that shot smoke through his nostrils. "Gentlemen," he glared, "this conversation is over. If you have any further questions, address them to my attorneys and not me at my library. Or at my office. Or in my home. You are not welcome here, and it is time for you to leave. Do I make myself clear?"

"As plain as," Wilkie paused, "that . . . thing on your face."

The ash fell from J. P. Morgan's cigar.

"That went well," said Wilkie, proudly puffing his Meridiana Kohinoor. The bronze doors behind him slammed closed and locked.

"I'm glad you think so, John, because I'm afraid we are no closer to linking Morgan to the attack on Dr. Tesla."

"I figured as much," Wilkie puffed. "With your permission, I'd like the Secret Service to assume authority over the Tesla affair in the interest of gathering information potentially connecting it to the attack on the president."

"It's yours," said Wickersham as the two reached the sidewalk and made a right toward Fifth Avenue. "Unfortunately, I think it's going to be a while before you get the records you need out of Morgan. He'll stonewall us until the day he dies if he has to."

"Yeah, about that. George, do you think Secretary MacVeagh would object to me employing some experimental methods as part of my investigation?"

"You're not going to kill Morgan, are you?"

"No, but I am thinking of sending a secret agent to monitor the house of Morgan personally."

"You want to penetrate his fortress?" Wickersham laughed. "I don't think any man could pull off that feat."

"I know. That's why I'm sending a woman."

Wickersham stopped walking. "You're talking about Miss Knox."

"Well, naturally."

"Miss Knox is your secret—"

"Shh-shut up!" hushed Wilkie. "Why else do you think I hired her? Kate Warne proved invaluable to Allan Pinkerton. I'm confident that my little angel will perform just as admirably."

"You crazy Chicagoans," Wickersham said, shaking his head. "John, this is a bad idea."

"Can you think of a better one? You saw that nice toffer

Morgan has working for him. The man clearly has an affinity for pretty faces. If Miss Knox can use her looks and smarts to get a job at J. P. Morgan's head office, we'll be up to our armpits in confidential paperwork come Christmas."

"John, I'm more concerned about her safety. I mean, she's Philander Knox's niece."

"Relax!" Wilkie said smugly. "If Morgan so much as pinches her bottom, she'll castrate him with a letter opener. I know she's the shortest person in whatever room she's in, but she's also the deadliest. The young lady is well trained in Bartitsu, judo, jujutsu, fencing . . . hell, I've even boxed with her! You just wait and see, George. She'll be the perfect concealed weapon for the Secret Service on this case."

"Well, can we at least discuss this over lunch?"

"Sure. Delmonico's is just a few blocks from here. In the meantime, let me buy you some ice cream."

"Are they gone?"

"Yes, Pierpont."

J. P. Morgan stepped back from his window and took a puff from his disappearing cigar. "Good. Call the wire operators. Tell them we need an emergency meeting."

"Right away, sir." Belle hurried out of the study while Morgan returned to his desk. He took a pad and paper and wrote:

ALIENS

And then, after some consideration:

```
A L I E N S
A  a  b  c  d  e  f
L  g  h  i  j  k  l
I  m  n  o  p  q  r
E  s  t  u  v  w  x
N  y  z  1  2  3  4
S  5  6  7  8  9  0
```

He set the note aside and resumed his solitaire. A few minutes later, he reached for a new Meridiana Kohinoor only to discover that his leather cigar box was empty. John Wilkie had taken every single one of J. P. Morgan's hand-rolled Havanas.

The king of Wall Street threw the empty tobacco chest across the room and swore angrily.

Chapter XIV

"BULL—!"

Captain Butt looked up from the ticker tape. "That's all it says, sir."

Robert Todd Lincoln and John Hays Hammond shared a look of mutual puzzlement. President Taft, who knew the wireless room was not built for a man of his size, preferred to stand in the doorway. He teased his mustache as he contemplated the message.

"Is this some type of code word?" Taft asked the captain.

"No, sir." The transmission was Wilkie's report on his recent meeting with J. P. Morgan. His entire report. Mr. Hammond, who was not entirely used to John Wilkie's curtness, could not help snickering.

"Robert, may I have a word with you?" Taft walked back to the Oval Office before his friend could respond. It was the first time the president had ever given Robert an order.

"I'm sorry I could not be more helpful," Hammond confided.

"It's all right," said Robert. "Just take today's samples back to the laboratory. I'll meet you there as soon as I can."

"Of course." John picked up a tote full of vials and was about to walk out the door, but Robert caught him.

"John!" Lincoln picked up a sealed jar on the table containing two tiny metallic fragments. "*Please* do not forget these! Keep them on your person at all times. Never leave them unattended."

"Oh! I'm so sorry." John accepted the precious container, but his tired eyes were full of grief. "You know I can't give you a definite report on these until we're back in the States, right?"

"I know. Take all the time you need." Robert nodded to Captain Butt and then hurried out the door.

"Robert . . ."

The last son of Lincoln turned around.

"It could be many months," John added.

Robert, standing alone in the corridor with his coat wrinkled and mud speckled on his boots, bowed his head in reply. He was prepared to accept whatever fate was awaiting him in the Oval Office.

It had not been a good week for anyone on the airship.

"Why won't you tell John about the pocket watch?"

"We have already discussed this. You know I cannot."

"Bob, do you realize how severely you've crippled this entire adventure with your secrecy?"

"Will, I do not have a choice!"

It was Saturday in Alaska, sunset, and for the third day in a row there was nothing unusual on the ground or in the skies above the

Wrangell Mountains. For Captain Butt at the helm, the landscapes were scenic but not surreal. There were countless clouds and stars to behold, but no spectacular streaks of blue light. For Robert and John, the airship's modest laboratory became a headquarters filled with snow, earth, air, and ice collected throughout the region. Unfortunately, the zeppelin lacked the necessary equipment to test these samples thoroughly. There had been no grand discoveries. No surprises. No little green men from Mars.

Although the president had prepared for this scenario by saying and doing very little the entire trip, something he did not anticipate nor know how to handle was the mounting crisis over Robert Todd Lincoln's pocket watch. When Robert first revealed this mysterious timepiece to Taft, he did not expect the president to tell anyone about it. Not Captain Butt, not John, and most certainly not Nellie. One week later, tensions were brewing between the two men over who should know about the device, transforming the Oval Office on Airship One into a floating room full of arguments.

"Bob, you could tell Archie was insulted we did not include him in your initial investigation. Why keep him in the dark all over again?"

"Mr. President, we both know whose decision it was to exclude him from the Halley's comet affair."

"Yes, we do," Taft said sternly, "and while I do not agree with everything Nellie tells me, I accept her decisions. All the same, you need to accept that we would probably not be here right now if I did not tell her about your pocket watch."

"Will, you had already offered me the airship by that point."

Taft slammed his hand against his table. "But not before that goddamn automaton tried to murder me in the White House!"

Robert shook his head and took a long drink from his tumbler. The two had been rehashing the same argument all week, only from rotating parts of the office and with slightly different vocabulary. Robert glanced into his nearly empty glass of scotch and ice, wanting nothing short of a silver bullet to end this discussion once and for all. He looked at the Surprise cabinet, which presented one option. "Do you have any more of that comet vintage?" he asked. "The 1858?"

The president's mood lifted. "I might. Let me check." Taft walked over to the cabinet and flipped through its shelves. After a thorough search, his mustache drooped a bit. "No. There's a bottle of '61, but it's not on ice. Besides, I think we should avoid a Civil War year."

The room brightened a bit thanks to the president's attempt at humor.

"Too bad," said Robert. "I think the '58 would have cleared our heads. My father saw that comet the night before his third debate with Stephen Douglas."

"Really?" Taft smiled. "Did it help him?"

Robert rubbed his short, thick beard. "I think seeing the comet lifted his spirits going into the debate. My father was in an unfriendly part of Illinois that day. I imagine he took the comet as a sign of better things to come."

"In that case, I suggest we do the same with this elixir." Taft popped the cork off a bottle of 1811 Veuve Clicquot, which he had been saving in the event that John and Robert made a major discovery. Since there appeared to be none in sight and the president considered the current situation an emergency, he poured two tall glasses of the bubbly stuff and handed one to his friend. "With malice toward none!" Taft toasted, lifting his glass high.

"With charity for all," Robert followed.

The two clinked their glasses and drank down the comet.

"Thanks, Bob." Taft belched. "I needed that."

"I think we both did." With peace restored, the two friends were finally able to talk out their differences. Robert went first. "You have to understand, Will. If I am wrong about Alaska just as I was about Halley's comet, I do not want to disgrace my family name by having brought my father's assassination into this. I have worked so hard for so long to preserve his memory, and I must not tarnish it during these last few years of my life." Robert looked up at Taft. "Please respect that."

Taft leaned with one hand against the Roosevelt desk. "Bob, you will always have my deepest respect and admiration, but you need to be more open with those who are here to help you. Archie gossips like a magpie, I'll give you that, but I think Jack has a right to know the real reason why we brought him three thousand miles from home."

"I gave him two samples from the watch's power source," assured Robert. "He should be able to determine everything he needs to know about its mechanics from them."

"I don't think that's enough, Bob. I think we need to bring in a new brain to figure out where the watch was built."

"Why is that?"

Taft looked this way and that, as if someone was listening. "Suppose you're right about the phenomenon you monitored here, but wrong about where the pocket watch comes from. 'Made in America' could refer to anywhere in the Western Hemisphere. I know your reasons for suspecting Alaska, but how many of the world's greatest clockmakers ever lived in this icebox?"

"I will admit that I sometimes ask the same question."

Taft thought for a moment. "Let me see it again."

Robert set his champagne glass on the Roosevelt desk and handed Taft the folded handkerchief from his pocket. The president unwrapped it and, once again, carefully studied the mysterious object's even more mysterious message:

Сдѣлано

въ

Америкѣ

"I wish I knew the Russian for 'curiouser and curiouser,'" said Taft. He looked the watch over and weighed it in his hand. "Is there anything special about this stone?" he asked, pointing at the fob.

Robert wrinkled his eyebrows. "The quartz?"

"Yeah. You said whatever powers this watch is the most unusual thing about it, but what about its fob? Did this rock come from Alaska, or America, or . . . well, did it even come from this planet?"

"Gold-bearing quartz is rare, but not impossible to find," said Robert. "The forty-niners mined plenty of it during the California Gold Rush."

"Is there any gold-bearing quartz in Alaska?"

"There might be. I will ask John. However, I doubt the Russians would have sold us Alaska if they knew there was gold here."

Taft took one last look at the engraving before snapping the watch shut. "This doesn't make any sense to me. The more you tell me about this timepiece, the more it sounds like it did not come from Alaska." Taft wrapped the watch in Robert's handkerchief and handed it back to its owner.

"It is possible," Robert reluctantly admitted. "And for that reason, I am willing to accept that this watch is no longer a matter of national security."

Taft looked concerned, as if his words were somehow pushing Robert away from him. "But there are still so many unanswered questions about the mountains and the mines!"

"I agree, but there is the distinct possibility—no, the likelihood—that this pocket watch has absolutely nothing to do with them. John and I collected our materials and he will run the necessary tests on them at Yale, but as for this mystery"—Robert patted the pocket watch in his coat—"I do not want to burden the government with my problems for one minute more."

"Bob . . ." Taft implored. "Helping you find all the answers to your father's murder is not a burden. Please, I only want to help you more!"

"I am the most qualified person in the country to investigate this," Robert affirmed. "I have my father's papers and was able to find the pocket watch in the first place. If I am lucky, there may be something in my archives that eluded me."

Taft bit his lip, empathizing. "Well, for whatever it's worth, it's probably better off that you will be far away from me these next few months. Nellie is meeting with George Wickersham as we speak. If they choose to go to war with J. P. Morgan, he is going to fight against my administration with every ounce of his strength."

"Really? The government is finally going to break up U.S. Steel?"

"Possibly," Taft acknowledged. "And I think a mutual friend of ours is not going to be all too happy about that."

"Which one?" asked Robert.

The president lowered his head and groaned loudly. "Politics makes me sick."

Chapter XV

Theodore Rex

My dear sister:

The meeting between the President and Colonel Roosevelt is over, and none, not even any of us who are with him, are much the wiser as to what actually happened. They lunched at Mr. White's, and then, at the Colonel's suggestion, he and the President were left alone, with Jimmy Sloan on guard at the door. Even Griscom and Norton were excluded, and whatever passed between them remains a secret between them—up to the present time. When I arrived, after lunching with Stokes and Mrs. Griscom, they were still locked in the dining room. Jimmy told me that no person had been with them and added:

"The Colonel is too foxy a guy to let any of these chumps hear what he says."

. . . Such is politics as seen from the inside, dear Clara. Aren't you glad that Lewis is in the wholesale cotton business?

> With love,
> *Archie.*[17]

Taft sat comfortably at the head of the dining room table, munching salted almonds and sipping coffee while the former president quickly closed the curtains across the room. It was an overcast and unpleasant day, but old Big Lub could not complain. Spending a September afternoon in New Haven was a trip down memory lane for the Yale graduate. Besides, he did not just ride a motorboat across Long Island Sound from Oyster Bay, battling gale-force winds, six-foot waves, and probably a few great white sharks along the way. Why didn't TR just take the train? Such is the strenuous life, Taft supposed.

The perceptive president could not help admiring his predecessor as he moved. He had the body of a football player, the speed of a boxer, the eyes of an archer, the mustache of a bodybuilder, and the determination of an Olympic athlete. He circled the room like a general once the curtains were closed, checking every door and lock until he finally settled in his chair. The former president sat upright, took a loud gulp from his enormous coffee cup, and nodded with approval. The coffee, just as requested, was strong enough to take the balls off a bull.

"Mr. President," he addressed.

---

17 Archibald Willingham Butt, letter to Clara Butt, 20 September 1910, *Taft and Roosevelt: The Intimate Letters of Archie Butt, Military Aide,* Vol. II, 518–522.

"Colonel," Taft responded.

The former president smirked. "I appreciate you calling me that."

"I must admit," Taft said, blushing, "when I hear someone say 'Mr. President,' I sometimes look around expecting to see you in the room!"

The former president grinned brightly, displaying both rows of his white, cartoonish, almost impossibly straight teeth. "Since we're on the subject"—Roosevelt's smile faded—"that scurrilous secretary of yours called me 'Teddy' earlier."

"Who, Norton?"

"Yes," hissed Roosevelt. "That one."

Taft raised his eyebrows in disappointment. "We've been having problems with him as well. I don't think he'll be staying with us much longer."

"Good. I despise that nickname. It's such an outrageous impertinence." Roosevelt looked to his side and narrowed his eyes as if to stare down some unseen foe. "I should have smote that damn bear."

Taft, sensing this subject could go on for a while, decided to redirect the conversation. "I suppose it is the New York situation you want to discuss."

Roosevelt locked his blue eyes on his blue-eyed successor. "Yes, Mr. President."

"Very well." Taft pushed aside his bowl of almonds and folded his hands, but then pulled the almonds back and threw a few in his mouth. "Colonel"—Taft chewed—"after several months of investigating, the Justice Department and I agree there is a conspiracy afoot in the house of Morgan."

"J. P. Morgan?" Roosevelt snorted. "What's that goldbricker up to this time?"

"We honestly don't know, but we have very good reason to suspect it is related to his recent partnership with the Guggenheims."

"What? Their copper mining?"

"Yes. In Alaska."

"I see . . ." he spoke softly.

Roosevelt stared intently at the president, tapping his finger against his temple. It was his unspoken way of getting in Taft's head about several issues the latter did not want to discuss: the deteriorating situation with Interior Secretary Ballinger, the widening rift within the Republican Party, and, perhaps most pressing of all, whether or not these two men would face each other as rivals in the 1912 election. Just thinking about these festering political ulcers made Taft's stomach turn.

Fortunately, the larger president's insides emitted a long, low rumble, breaking Roosevelt's concentration. Taft tapped his fist against his chest. "Excuse me. Anyway, the Justice Department has been investigating J. P. Morgan with the help of the Secret Service—"

"The Secret Service?" Roosevelt interrupted. "Why are they involved in this?"

"Let me get to that," Taft responded impatiently. "We think the Morgan-Guggenheim syndicate and their Alaskan activities are linked to a recent attack on Nikola Tesla and a separate but clearly premeditated attempt to kill me."

Roosevelt removed his eyeglasses in disbelief. "Will, what happened?"

"It's a long story, Theodore. I—"

"Did you speak with Wilkie?" pressed Roosevelt. "You must speak with Chief Wilkie!"

"Colonel, I just said we're working with the Secret Service on this. *Of course* I've spoken to Wilkie."

"Why isn't he here now?" Roosevelt demanded, raising his volume.

"Please forget about Wilkie. He's in Washington working on some unrelated case."

"Unrelated!" Roosevelt shouted, rising to his feet. "What could be more important than an attempt against the president's life? Mr. President, this is a dangerous oversight and I insist that John Wilkie be fired!"

"Mr. Presi— . . . Colonel, I'm begging you—"

"I insist!"

"God damn it, will you *please* let me finish speaking!"

The former president, who looked like he was about to dive across the table, contained his excitement and returned to his seat.

"Colonel, you know that unrelated case I said John Wilkie is working on? It took the Secret Service *three years* of investigating before they made an arrest.[18] I can't wait three years on this. In three years I could be out of office, or worse. Since there is no way we can learn the full extent of this conspiracy in order to prosecute it, Attorney General Wickersham"—and Nellie, Taft omitted—"devised a plan that should sabotage our enemies in every inch of this country."

"Bully for you!" Roosevelt congratulated. "What's your strategy, my friend?"

Taft finished his remaining coffee and snacks. "The Justice Department is going to file antitrust suits against J. P. Morgan's entire financial empire: U.S. Steel, International Harvester, the

---

18 "Three Years' Vigil by Secret Service," *Washington Times,* 18 September 1910, 1, 11.

whole ball of wax. The whole house of Morgan will be shattered beyond repair, crippling its clandestine efforts. And then, when the time is right, Congress will officially investigate Morgan and his Wall Street allies to see how deep this treachery goes."

Roosevelt was speechless. Never in their time together had he seen Taft so decisive. So ambitious. So bully. But at the same time, so much more aggressive on a subject that could very well decide both of their legacies. "You're going to file more antitrust suits in two years than I did in two terms of office," the former president said with a faint hint of jealousy.

"Am I?" Taft scratched his head.

"Mr. President . . ." fumed Roosevelt. "You don't even realize the history you're making!"

Taft, not knowing what to make of the former president's strange behavior, continued reading the remarks Nellie prepared for him on his cuff. "My friend, I believe what Morgan did to you during the panic of '07 was nothing short of blackmail: a plot engineered by his cabal to prevent you from thwarting their schemes sooner. If I expose them, these conspirators will come after me with every weapon they have. I don't think I can win this fight alone." Taft folded his hands and leaned forward for a better look at the writing. "I need your help. You and I are the nation's only living presidents. If we aim to defeat our foes once and for all, we must do it together. Colonel, will you help me defend this country by testifying against J. P. Morgan before Congress?" Taft artfully adjusted his cuff and awaited his friend's response.

Roosevelt was furious. He did not need to ask Taft how large a part his wife played in this performance. Every single line in his sorry speech had Nellie's fingerprints all over it. It all worked perfectly. Her husband would go down in history as one of the greatest presidents of all time, eclipsing his predecessor as a true champion of the common man. Taft would be elected to a second term, and maybe even a third, should Nellie desire it. And Roosevelt? He would be reduced to a helpless victim in front of the entire country. It would be Roosevelt, not Taft, who would testify to Congress about his inability to contain this crisis and his capitulation to J. P. Morgan in 1907. The very name Roosevelt would be stained and humiliated. The legacy he had built for his children would be shattered. And worst of all—for Roosevelt, at least—any possibility of challenging Taft for the Republican nomination in 1912 would be lost.

But on the other hand, there was this foul conspiracy.

Roosevelt had to think fast.

"Mr. President," he started.

"Yes?" Taft waited.

"With all my heart and soul, I pledge you my word to do everything I can."

Taft exhaled. "That is a relief to hear, my friend!"

Roosevelt's mood changed like a storm flag in a hurricane. "What do you mean by that?"

"By what?"

"Were you not expecting me to do my duty for my country?"

Taft's eyes filled with worry. "No, Colonel! Not at all!"

Roosevelt stood up. "You admit it! How dare you throw such accusations at me!"

"No, that's not what I meant! You must believe me! Teddy," the president pleaded, "I feel nothing but love for you!"

The former president's eyes narrowed. "Teddy?" he seethed.

Hours later . . .

NELLIE

HOW DID IT GO?

TAFT

NOT WELL AT ALL.

NELLIE

?

TAFT

IF YOU WERE TO REMOVE ROOSEVELT'S SKULL, YOU WOULD FIND "1912" WRITTEN ON HIS BRAIN.

Minutes passed with no response from Nellie in the White House.

TAFT

NELLIE?

NELLIE

YOU KNOW THAT SOFA MRS. ROOSEVELT IS ALWAYS ASKING ABOUT? THE ONE SHE WAS NOT ALLOWED TO TAKE WITH HER WHEN THEY MOVED OUT?

TAFT

YES. WE TALKED ABOUT GIVING IT BACK TO THEM THIS CHRISTMAS. WHY DO YOU ASK?

NELLIE

I JUST HAD BROOKS DESTROY IT WITH AN AX.

TAFT

!

NELLIE

I HATE THE ROOSEVELTS.

Chapter XVI

Pirouette

"Going Christmas shopping with the president is such a lark!" sang Captain Butt. He led Miss Knox by the arm through New York's Central Park on a snowy, busy, delightfully Christmassy afternoon. "You would be surprised how few people recognize him during our shopping tours. Those who do are always happy to raise their hats and say 'Merry Christmas' as we pass. Even the inebriates! Oh, and the president is such a generous gift giver. It's like the people elected Santa Claus! Every single employee at the White House is guaranteed a turkey—no exceptions. He also gave me such lovely books last Christmas. I should know because I picked them myself, but they were just what I wanted: the *Memoirs* of Cellini and the *Life* of Whistler. I highly recommend both books, although I must warn you that Cellini's *Memoirs* is quite risqué. He was a very naughty man."

"I think I can handle it," chimed Miss Knox, whose face was hidden from onlookers in her mink scarf and dark fur hat.

"We shouldn't be having such conversations. Please forgive me! It's so uncouth," the captain fussed. "And to think my poor, dear mother hoped for me to join the clergy!"

Miss Knox rolled her eyes. Despite the captain's ability to cover virtually every aspect of fine art, interior decorating, ladies' fashion, and gossip in the same breath, he always found a way to weave whatever he was talking about back to his beloved mother. Naturally, Miss Knox did not have much to add to Captain Butt's frequent reminiscences about the departed old lady, or his artist friend and housemate Francis Davis Millet, or how lovely Mrs. Taft looked in certain dresses and hairstyles, or how much he enjoyed wearing his officer's cape in the wintertime, or how dreadful the Hayes china truly was, or how friendly the squirrels in Washington are if you feed them regularly, or how his home with Mr. Millet boasts, quite simply, "the nicest bathroom in the world."

"Also, I apologize for saying this again, but it would be an insult to honesty if I did not compliment how thick and lovely your hair is. I wish I could write my sister about it! I don't know how you wear it so well."

"I use a rat," said Miss Knox.

"So that's your secret!"

"Archie . . ."

"Oh, I'm such a winter fool! We're here!"

The stealthy Secret Service agent and her plainclothed bodyguard arrived at the park's ice-skating pond. The frozen lake was thickly crowded with families, newlyweds, young couples, and endless, endless schoolchildren skating in a thick mob. The location was not Miss Knox's choosing, but it was an excellent place for her meeting.

"Is there anything else I can do for you?" asked Archie.

"Would you hold your arm out?" Miss Knox quickly attached her skates to her shoes while the captain supported her.

"Now, I'll be right here if you need anything."

"I know. Thank you, Archie."

"And you know what to look for?"

"I do. Thanks again, Archie."

"And you have your weapons?"

"Of course!" Miss Knox never left her apartment without them.

"Well . . ." Captain Butt could hardly contain his excitement. "Good luck!" The two embraced, partially to make it look genuine and partially because it was genuine.

"If anything happens to me—" she whispered into Archie's ear.

"Oh, don't speak that way!" he chided. "No harm will befall you, not while I'm here! Just focus on your meeting and I will focus on your safety." The two parted, and Miss Knox stood by herself on the ice. "You remind me of my mother," the captain sighed.

Miss Knox smiled and skated into the crowd. Captain Butt stood erect and honed his eyes on the young agent, knowing full well that her life was in his hands. He reached for his sword as he watched, but nearly panicked when he could not find it. He forgot he was in plainclothes. By the time he looked back at the pond, the young woman he was guarding had completely disappeared into the throng of ice skaters.

Miss Knox's small stature somewhat limited her vision, but it did not take her long to find what she was looking for. Above the mob, she spotted a thin string of smoke wafting in the air like spider's silk. Miss Knox followed it to its source: John Wilkie, gliding across the ice in a figure eight with a thick cigar in his mouth. He was dressed in black from head to toe, almost like a priest or a reverend, which amused Miss Knox. Crowned in a black top hat, it was the perfect disguise for a man of his character.

Miss Knox skated right up to him. "Chief Wilkie?" she asked. The incognito investigator skid behind the young agent and gently led her off by the waist. Together, the two slid toward a brass band playing Christmas carols loud enough to drown out every syllable of their conversation.

"How are you, darling?" The Secret Service chief smiled. It had been months since their last meeting, but Wilkie's teeth were as stained as always.

"I am well," she replied. "Captain Butt and I encountered no hostiles on our way over."

"Very good," said Wilkie. "And how's the captain's mother?"

Miss Knox's eyes widened. "My God . . ."

Her boss could not have been more satisfied with her response. "We need to put him in touch with Dr. Freud, don't we?" Wilkie teased.

"It's adorable, really, but I don't know how much more of this I can take!"

"Trust me, you're doing a service to every single man on the airship. The less they hear about the late, great Mrs. Butt, the better it will be for everyone."

"This isn't part of my assignment, is it?"

"Of course not! I just consider it a happy accident. Not that anyone will ever thank us for it," said Wilkie, puffing his cigar.

"Is that why they call it the Secret Service?" Miss Knox smiled.

"Don't be fresh, young lady." Wilkie flicked away his cigar so the two skaters could talk more intimately. "Tell me about your new employer."

Miss Knox skated in a circle, scanning their surroundings as she spoke. "I only met Mr. Morgan once at the Wall Street office. He was very pleased to meet me, but we have not spoken since."

"The less you see of that man, the better. Also, how is your alias holding up?"

"Quite well. Nobody suspects me, since they needed someone proficient in foreign languages."

"Good. What kind of work do they have you doing?"

"Secretarial work. Mostly international transactions."

"Do any of their activities seem suspicious to you?"

"From the work I'm given, no. I have not come across anything related to Alaska or the Congo, or any illegal activities the Treasury can convict Mr. Morgan of. On paper, the man is clean."

"Clean?" A frustrated Secret Service chief grimaced. "What about Belle da Costa Greene? Have you met her yet?"

"Yes. Several times. Twice at the library and two other times at parties."

"What do you think of her?"

"I don't like her," Miss Knox said bluntly.

"I expected that. Is it for personal reasons, or professional?"

"Professional. She's a brilliant woman, but what Miss Greene does behind closed doors is her business, and I mean *her business*. She thinks I'm after J. P. Morgan for his money. Because of her, there's no way I'll be able to visit the library again. She thinks I'm encroaching on her territory."

Wilkie was not happy to hear this. For nearly a minute, the couple slid across the ice without saying a word. "So, is this the end of your investigation?"

"Not at all. Belle and I had a confrontation last time we met that ended quite embarrassingly for her. In exchange for my silence, she offered to have me transferred with her full recommendation to wherever I liked in Morgan's companies—provided I stay far away from her, of course."

"Oh? Are you going to take her up on this?"

"I already have, Mr. Wilkie. I apologize for not discussing this with you sooner, but I needed to act quickly."

The Secret Service chief was surprised. "Well, are you going to tell me where you're going, or am I supposed to guess?"

Miss Knox moved in as if to kiss Wilkie on his cheek. Just as the brass band started playing "Christmas on the Sea," a little-known Long Island carol, she whispered, "The IMM."

Wilkie's eyes lit up, and not just because of the music. "What are you after?" he asked.

Miss Knox spoke quickly. "Morgan invested millions in the International Mercantile Marine Company, but it's all a loss. Countless ships in his fleet are going unused while these enormous 'Olympic' liners the White Star Line is constructing could potentially steer the IMM to ruin.[19] Morgan doesn't seem like the kind of person who would act so recklessly on such a massive undertaking. Something suspicious is going on in the IMM, and whatever it is, there is no paper trail for me to follow."

"No trail would suggest Morgan's hiding something," Wilkie weighed, "or nothing. Are you certain it's the former?"

"I don't think it is the latter, Mr. Wilkie. The overseas construction of the president's automaton, the mining operations in

---

19 "Olympic, World's Biggest Ship, Huge Floating Hotel," *New York Times,* 30 October 1910.

Alaska, and the Nikola Tesla transmission all point toward some sort of extensive operation involving shipping. It may not be enough to implicate J. P. Morgan as the 'Gentleman from New York,' but it could explain the apparently irrational behavior of the IMM. They're planning something big, Mr. Wilkie, and I think the only way we can uncover it is by delving deeper into the company."

"That could be dangerous work," Wilkie cautioned. "If you believe the IMM is a front for some massive illegal operation, you're going to have a lot more to worry about on the high seas than pirates."

"I know. That's why I modified some records at J. P. Morgan and Company to give myself a new name and identity."

"Again? Your current one is just a few months old! Besides, I thought you liked the name 'Rose.'"

"I took care of everything, Mr. Wilkie. The IMM already has me listed as an employee under my new identity. The necessary paperwork is in your pocket."

The Secret Service chief furrowed his brow and looked down at his black coat. He patted one of his supposedly empty pockets and could feel paper inside it. "How did you do that?" he demanded.

"Do what?"

"Nobody can sneak up on me like that. Not you, not Houdini!"

"Is that a problem?"

"No, not at all! In fact, I've never been more proud of you!"

Miss Knox laughed and bowed her head.

Wilkie extended his hand. "May I?" The two skaters waltzed across the ice to the brass band's Christmas tunes like a father dancing with his daughter on her wedding day. Although there were no cameras to preserve the memory, both Wilkie and Miss Knox knew this might be their last moment together. "Will you at least be spending Christmas with your family?" he asked.

"No. I leave the city tomorrow. I already explained everything to my parents. They understand my line of work."

The Secret Service chief was misty eyed, but it was probably because of the cold. Probably. "Well, don't forget to write."

"I'll contact you the moment there's a new development."

Wilkie smiled. "I was referring to your parents, but— Oh! You just reminded me! I'm sorry I did not tell you this when it happened, but Robert Todd Lincoln is off the Alaska case."

"He is?"

"Yes. He's been in exile in his mansion since he failed to bring anything new to the investigation."

"I don't see why the president would do that."

"He didn't. It was Mr. Lincoln's decision, and frankly . . ." Wilkie paused to light a new cigar. He offered one to Miss Knox, but she declined. "Frankly, I think Mr. Lincoln is making a big mistake by sitting this out. There's no way we would have known about this activity in Alaska had it not been for him, even if we intercepted the Tesla transmission." Wilkie blew a thick, frustrated cloud of smoke. "And I'd give anything to know how his pocket watch is tied in to this."

"Has the president made any mention of the pocket watch to you?"

"No. Whatever Robert told him about the timepiece, he hasn't shared it with anyone. And it's not like I can approach either of them for more information about something I'm not supposed to know about." Wilkie puffed his cigar in deep thought, at which point he spied a worried Captain Butt watching the skaters. "Anyway, you should go back to your bodyguard. Have a very merry Christmas." The chief bowed, removing his top hat.

"Thank you, Mr. Wilkie. And a happy new year to you."

"Well, here's hoping." The Secret Service chief stuck his cigar in his mouth and disappeared into the crowd while Miss Knox skated back to her escort. The captain looked mortified.

"Are you all right?" Butt stammered. "That took much longer than I was expecting!" He continued voicing concerns with his arm extended so Miss Knox could take off her skates.

As she considered how this might be her last evening with the captain, Miss Knox decided to make it as pleasant as possible for him. "Can you tell me more about your mother?" she asked.

The captain's eyes brightened. "Oh! What would you like to know?"

"Everything," she emphasized, looping her arm around the tall officer's.

"Well," he began proudly, "as I'm sure you gathered, she wasn't born Mrs. Butt."

The two walked off together into the snow-covered park. They were both smiling.

A clock chimed.

Chapter XVII

Reunion

B ob?" inquired a familiar voice.

Robert Todd Lincoln stepped away from his window beneath the North Portico. He was smoking a cigar and had been staring at a carriage outside. "I'm coming," he murmured.

Robert moved across the smoke-filled bedroom in a drowsy, almost dreamlike state. After enduring two of the most decisive weeks of the Civil War alongside General Grant, the twenty-one-year-old Union Army captain could barely stand. He saw American cities reduced to ruins and Virginia meadows transformed into killing fields. He had witnessed the ravages of war and the beatitudes of peace. He had not bathed or even changed out of his uniform for weeks, could barely think straight, and went so long without sleeping that the soft bed next to him seemed like a distant, foreign object.

Robert opened his bedroom door to find his well-dressed father looming behind it. He was wearing his greatcoat and had his stovepipe hat in his hand.

He smiled warmly at his son. "We're going to the theater, Bob. Don't you want to go?" Abraham had a sparkle in his eyes and a hopeful hint in his voice.

Robert shook his head. "Not tonight. If it's just the same to you, Father, I'd a whole lot rather turn in early. I haven't been sleeping well these last couple days."

"Oh . . ." his father voiced with concern. "Is it anything serious?"

"I don't think so. I have some medicine for it."

"Oh, good. That means I can come in." Abraham scurried into the room before his son could close the door on him.

"Father . . ." his son groaned wearily.

"May I sit down?" Before Robert could explain how exhausted he was, his father had already taken off his greatcoat, folded it, and set it on his son's bed. Abraham moved with such eagerness that the coat appeared to get caught on something. After a quick tug, a small object fell onto his shoe and rolled over to Robert.

"You dropped this," said the son, picking up a blue sleeve button with a gold "L" initial.

"Oh, thank you." Abraham took the button and stuffed it into his pocket with disinterest as he made himself comfortable beside his greatcoat and hat.

Robert, thinking his father was behaving erratically, asked, "Are you well?"

"Oh, I'm fine," his father assured him. "I was just hoping you and I could have a talk before I departed, since you won't be joining us this evening."

"But there's a carriage waiting outside," said Robert, pointing toward the window with his cigar. "It's been there for a long time."

"It can wait," said Abraham, lifting his hand. "Bob, I'm sorry to interrupt you and even sorrier to leave your mother waiting like this, but the thing is . . . I'm in the most unusual quandary. This coat the Brooks Brothers made for me is just so goddamn inspirational!" he laughed heartily. "Every time I put it on, the more philosophical part of my being is treated to something I must show you. Look!"

Abraham opened his coat across his son's bed as if unfolding a map. Stitched into the coat's silky silver lining was a large, out-stretched eagle bearing a ribbon with writing on it.

Abraham ran his long fingers under the words. "It reads, 'One Country, One Destiny.' I first noticed this just before I delivered my second inaugural. Ever since then, I've made an effort to reflect on this image whenever I put the coat on. Now, I've always known about the bird and its message, but these"—Abraham pointed to the four Union shields surrounding the eagle—"are completely new to me! I spotted them for the first time just a few minutes ago. At first, they made me think about the nation and the four-score, some-odd years since our founding, but Bob, these shields mean something even more important to me that I must share with you."

Robert, completely lost as to where his father was going with this, looked down at the eagle and then back up with confusion. "What am I looking for?" he asked.

Like a teacher pointing to a passage in a schoolbook, Abraham directed his son to all four Union shields, moving clockwise. "This is me . . . your mother . . . your brother . . . and you." Abraham emphasized this last shield beneath the eagle's right wing. "Bob, with Willie and Eddie gone, we are now a family of four. As painful and torturous as that is, I accept it. However, just like our country, we must not let this bond be broken. No matter how much you and I disagreed these past four years, we need to unite. We need to heal and move forward, stronger, as a family."

Robert, though moved by his father's words, was still racked with disappointment and guilt. And, deep down, shame. Shame that he did not serve his country the way he wanted to during the war.

Robert wanted to make peace with his father, but he was not ready to.

Abraham sensed his son's frustration and dug deeper into the subject. "Bob, do you remember when I called upon you to help me resolve the cabinet crisis? The one between Mr. Chase and Mr. Seward?"

Robert's tired eyes awakened a bit. "I don't think I was much help at all." He laughed.

"Bob," his father pressed, "I called upon you for your view of my conduct. Not merely for my guidance, but as a compass for you to carry in case you ever find yourself lost, as I was. Do you remember what kind of lesson I said it would be?"

Robert struggled to remember. "You said it was a lesson on morality, I think."

Abraham shook his head. "No, Bob. I said it was a lesson on Machiavelli."

Any clarity or understanding faded from Robert's face. He looked a whole lot more than a little bit lost.

Abraham smiled and leaned forward a bit. In a soft, clear voice, the father retold the story. "When Mr. Chase sowed his seeds of discord after the disaster at Fredericksburg, I knew he aimed to rally the Radical Republicans against Mr. Seward and myself so he could run unopposed for the presidency. I couldn't blame him. I felt like I was in a worse place than hell after Fredericksburg. However, even then I maintained that every man must skin his own skunk in this business. Mr. Chase, on the other hand, whipped those radicals into such a frenzy over how we conducted our cabinet meetings that Mr. Seward felt compelled to resign. Naturally, this put me in quite a bind. I needed both men in my cabinet, but I no longer knew if Mr. Chase could be trusted. How could I retain both their services while guaranteeing Mr. Chase's loyalty? That's the part of the story where Mr. Machiavelli came in." Abraham smiled.

"Bob, Machiavelli believed that if you are unsure about a secretary or minister, you should examine where his loyalties lie: to you or himself. In this case, I subjected Mr. Chase to the most humiliating examination since the Galileo affair. I summoned my cabinet—sans Mr. Seward, of course—along with Mr. Chase's congressional allies so they could personally see the lies in his charges. I explained how my cabinet had always been open, committed to unity, and then called on each one of my secretaries to express whether this was so. When the question eventually fell to Mr. Chase, he knew he had to choose his loyalty carefully. He chose me, which was wise, since at that point the radicals realized their once-trusted ally was out of manure to sell them. Senator Trumbell was furious!" Abraham laughed. "He said, 'Somebody has lied like hell!' 'Not tonight,' I responded. For the first time in a good while, Mr. Chase had spoken the truth.

"Naturally, the tables turned against Mr. Chase so quickly that—the poor devil—*he* offered to resign! But I wouldn't accept it. When he handed me his resignation the next morning, I seized it and laughed to Mr. Welles: 'This cuts the Gordian knot!' The crisis was over and I reunited my men. Mr. Chase went back to his job, Mr. Seward to his, and I was able to ride the next two years with a pumpkin in each end of my bag." The president grinned.

A tired Robert ran his fingers through his dark hair. "I remember that night," he said. "You asked me to lay out writing materials for you. So you could pen your request that Mr. Chase remain in the cabinet."

"That's correct. Right over there, I believe." Abraham pointed to a lonely-looking writing desk in the room. Robert could picture his father's phantom at work over it, redeeming the man he would eventually make the nation's next chief justice.

Robert blinked back to his senses. "What does the coat have to do with all this?"

With these words, Abraham stood tall and looked at his son with sincere, repenting eyes. "Bob, I know I stood in the way of how you wanted to live your own life. I know you wanted to serve in the Army, not as an officer, but as a soldier fighting alongside your fellow countrymen. My decision to stand against you strained our relationship throughout this whole war, and I am so sorry, but you must believe me when I say that I never doubted your loyalties. Mr. Chase's loyalties were only to himself, and I fixed that. But Bob, you must not deny yourself the valor you demonstrated by standing up to your family so you could defend your country during its hour of need. That was the greatest sacrifice you could make in this fight, Bob, and you made it again and again. But the war is over. It's time for the two of us to make peace so that our family can emerge from this war united, and so you and I can properly face the greater challenge ahead."

The president's son was silent. And listening.

His father started pacing the room. "Bob, winning a war will never be as important as winning the peace. You saw with your own eyes the brotherhood this nation is capable of when General Lee and General Grant sat down at Appomattox. Their peace is *the* peace we must strive for: unity. It is the bond that has guided us through every war and struggle since our independence. But reconstruction will be our greatest challenge, Bob. It is a test we cannot fail, lest the darker angels of our nature descend upon us again. I will do everything in my power to unite this land once more, but it cannot end with me. It will take more than one president, and possibly more than one Lincoln."

Robert was mystified by his father's choice of words. "What do you mean by that?"

Abraham grinned brightly and clasped his son by the shoulders. "Bob, you have already made me prouder than any father could hope for. Not even John Adams could boast that John Quincy witnessed the surrender at Yorktown. So please, get some rest. Do just what you feel most like, but please let us continue this conversation tomorrow. After a good night's sleep, I want you to tell me what your plan is for our nation. Our destiny."

Robert Todd Lincoln had never felt more understood by his father. For so long he felt coddled, denied the opportunity to decide his own future. At last, at long last, he felt truly at peace with his father. He felt ready, and welcome, to serve his nation the way he had always wanted to. "I look forward to it with all my heart," he replied.

Abraham smiled and patted his son on the cheek. "All right, my boy. Well, I don't want to keep your mother waiting." Abraham picked up his coat and opened it wide, treating both father and son to one last look at the eagle inside. The president put on his coat, adjusted the ruffled gloves in his left coat pocket, and took his hat.

"Good night." He smiled to Robert.

"Good night, Father."

Abraham walked out of the room and shut the door.

Chapter XVIII

Wide Awake

B ob?" inquired a familiar, fainter voice.

A sixty-seven-year-old Robert Todd Lincoln opened his heavily-lidded eyes.

"Are you coming to bed tonight?" asked Mary Harlan, Robert's wife.

Robert sat up in his wooden chair and stretched. "In a moment, dear. I have some work I need to finish."

An introvert herself, Mary rarely interrupted her husband during his frequent sleepless nights. Poring over papers and studying the stars until sunrise was the norm at Hildene, their Manchester mansion. However, tonight was different. "You know we have to leave for Washington tomorrow," she reminded him.

"I know. Just let me put everything away."

"That would take all summer," Mary teased as her blue eyes ran over Robert's crowded, cluttered library.

"Just my desk, then." He smiled sleepily. "And then I'm yours. I promise."

Mary kissed her husband and left him to his work.

Robert put on his spectacles and raised his head. The brass clock on his mantelpiece showed it was well past midnight. The gold pocket watch on his desk, however, remained frozen at a different hour. Robert closed the silent timepiece and slipped it into his pocket.

Within his scarlet library, seven steamer trunks formed a fortress around Robert's desk. Prepared by Charles Sweet, Robert's Chicago secretary, the chests contained every correspondence, letter, and note then-Captain Robert T. Lincoln packed in Washington nearly fifty years ago. It was a treasure trove of history and one of the greatest private archives in the world: the presidential papers of Abraham Lincoln.

Among the many files scattered across Robert's desk was an open folder. It was marked "A" for "assassination" by his father's own hand. The file contained just a fraction of the more than ten thousand death threats his father received in his first term, not counting the innumerable jars of poisoned fruit sent to him by Southerners before his inauguration. Since Abraham never took any of these threats seriously, Robert imagined that Secretary of War Edwin M. Stanton or Allan Pinkerton had urged his father to collect them for further investigation. He never could understand why his father was so convinced no one would ever harm him. It was a fatal mistake, thought Robert. He closed the folder and stowed it in its trunk, dejected that its contents brought him no closer to solving the mysteries of his enigmatic pocket watch.

Also on Robert's desk was an open book with a clipping from

the Washington *Evening Star* in it. Dated April 14, 1894, the article featured the personal account of Detective James A. McDevitt of the Washington Metropolitan Police during the earliest hours of the manhunt for John Wilkes Booth and his accomplices. The clipping retold the search for Lewis Powell "Payne," the madman who nearly murdered Secretary of State William H. Seward, his son Frederick, and many others the night of the assassination:

TRAGIC MEMORIES

Some Interesting Reminiscences of a Thrilling Night.

WHY BOOTH WAS NOT SOON CAPTURED

Detective McDevitt's Recollections Following the Assassination.

MR. AL. DAGGETT'S STORY

Interests.

Written for The Evening Star . . .

A Hint Given.

"The crowd acted very well, indeed. They received my speech in good faith and made way for us thereafter, as we came and went with our witnesses. I was out on one of these scouting expeditions when I met a man whose face seemed very familiar. He was evidently an actor whom I had seen on the stage, and the impression left on my mind was that it was John McCullough, the afterward famous tragedian. I do not want to speak positively on this point, for I have never ascertained whether McCullough was in Washington at that time or not. At any rate, the man stopped me, called me by name and gave me this startling hint:

"'If you want to find out all about this desperate business, keep an eye on Mrs. Surrratt's house in H street.'

"Mark you, this was the first intimation given or received by any one as to where the plot was hatched. I acted on it without delay. With some other detectives I visited Mrs. Surratt's house and searched it; we then turned it over to the military to watch, and it was they who captured Payne as he was returning to the house . . . "[20]

Robert knew the eventual arrest of Booth's coconspirators hinged on this crucial tip Detective McDevitt received from John McCullough so shortly after the assassination. There was just one problem with the detective's account of that evening: the book Robert kept the clipping in. It was the Army's official

---

[20] "Tragic Memories," *Evening Star,* 14 April 1894.

transcript of the trial for the conspirators, and one of its passages was circled:

> Mr. Ewing, with the consent of the Judge
> Advocate, offered as evidence of the same
> validity, as if the same fact were testified to by
> Mr. John McCullough, the actor, on the stand,
> the following telegraphic dispatch:

> MONTREAL, June 2, 1865.
> *To John T. Ford, National Hotel:*
> I left Washington on Monday evening, March
> 26th, and have not been there since. You can have
> my testimony before American Consul here, if
> requisite.
> JOHN McCULLOUGH.[21]

Robert had spent the last month trying to figure out how McCullough—or anyone, for that matter—could have provided the government with such intimate details about Booth's coconspirators when McCullough was supposedly in Canada that evening. Detective McDevitt was at the Surratt house with three other detectives less than three hours after the assassination: a fantastic feat. Almost too fantastic to be taken seriously. After researching the subject, Robert began to wonder if Detective McDevitt's unknown source even existed. Was it possible the War Department or the Pinkertons were

---

21 Benn Pitman, ed., *The Assassination of President Lincoln and the Trial of the Conspirators,* United States Army, Military Commission (Lincoln's assassins): 1865, 243.

monitoring John Surratt, a spy and member of the Confederate secret service, just days before the assassination? That might explain why the government was convinced so early on that Surratt was involved in the plot against William and Frederick Seward, who Robert believed were the most likely candidates to have given his father the mysterious pocket watch on his desk.

Unfortunately, a letter beneath the timepiece put an untimely end to the investigation.

CHICAGO-JUNE-12-1911

MR. R. T. LINCOLN
MANCHESTER, BENNINGTON CO., VERMONT
DEAR SIR,
    I AM IN RECEIPT OF YOURS OF MAY 2ND ASKING
THAT I WRITE ABOUT ANY SURVELANCE MY FATHER
AND/OR THE PINKERTON NATIONAL DETECTIVE
AGENCY CONDUCTED ON THE SURRATT BOARDINGHOUSE
PRIOR TO YOUR FATHER'S MURDER. AS SUCH, DO NOT
WRITE ME AGAIN.
                    VERY TRULY YOURS,
                    W.A.PINKERTON
P.S. EDWIN M. STANTON KILLED MY FATHER AND
PROBABLY YOURS AS WELL.

Robert, who wept with Stanton every morning for more than ten days after the assassination, knew he was a wholly honorable man. After closing his book, Robert crumpled Pinkerton's letter and tossed it onto a growing pile in his fireplace.

Much more important to Robert were his letters from John Hays Hammond about the samples they had collected in Alaska.

Unfortunately, they amounted to little more than an entire year of false hopes and dead ends.

One by one, Robert collected them into their folder.

August 4, 1910.

My dear Mr. Lincoln:-

I am writing to let you know I have arrived in New Haven. I am sorry I could not write you sooner, but I had to host a conference at my home in Gloucester. I hope my tardiness did not distress you.

Unfortunately, quite a few of my colleagues are on vacation, but I should be able to run some preliminary tests on our specimens starting tomorrow. Naturally, I will be operating under the utmost secrecy. No one will know where these samples came from or the purpose of my experiments. If anyone asks, I will tell them I am testing the university's laboratory equipment in preparation for the upcoming school year.

As for those "other" samples you gave me, I have already subjected them to numerous chemical tests. The results are the same as on the airship: lead (Pb).

Are you certain these samples came from the "power source" of that artifact you described? I've never heard of a machine that ran off lead and cannot fathom how such an invention could work. If you were to show me this device, perhaps it would aid me in my research. Until then, I respect your privacy.

With best wishes,

Sincerely yours,
John Hays Hammond

August 10, 1910.

My dear Mr. Lincoln:-

Some news!

The top layers of several soil samples from Alaska were slightly more radioactive than their lower layers. This suggests the atmosphere above the

Wrangell Mountains was radioactive in the weeks and months before we arrived. Possibly because of the planet's recent interaction with Halley's comet!

I also analyzed the dust coating some of our rocks, earth, and ice samples and boiled them down into mineral salts. They displayed a <u>deep blue</u> band when measured with a spectroscope, which suggests an unusually high amount of cesium (Cs) in the region.

Could this have caused that mysterious "blue light" over the mountains?

Either way, I believe the high level of radiation on and around the Wrangell Mountains is related to, if not caused by, these surprising amounts of cesium we collected.

I suggest you ask some of your international friends if they detected high levels of cesium in their atmospheres when we passed through the comet's tail. It would be the best use of both our time since I have to travel in the coming months.

Good luck,

Very sincerely yours,
John Hays Hammond

October 3, 1910

Dear Mr. Lincoln:

It is a pleasure to hear from you again.

Yes, I still have the air samples I collected in May. I examined them as you requested but did not detect any cesium.

Is it possible this radioactive phenomenon you described is emanating from outside the Earth's atmosphere? I had a piece published in Physikalische Zeitschrift *last month about my experience measuring radiation atop the Eiffel Tower. Please read it, because I believe it may explain the fantastic displays you monitored as a rare, but natural occurrence originating from the heavens.*

However, I must confess that the high levels of cesium you detected is alarming. The element is quite explosive in elemental form.

Godspeed on your endeavor.

> My deepest blessings,
> Fr. Theodor Wulf, S.J.

December 6, 1910.

Dear Mr. Lincoln:-

As you've probably read in the papers, I will be going to Russia this winter to discuss mining operations in European Russia with the tsar.

Is there anything you would like me to ask them about Alaska?

> Sincerely yours,
> John Hays Hammond

December 17, 1910.

My dear Mr. Lincoln:-

That is a most unusual request, but I will do as you ask. Consider it a Christmas present.

Seasons greeting,

> Very sincerely yours,
> John Hays Hammond

December 29, 1910.

Mr. Lincoln:-

My meeting with the tsar ended yesterday.

Would you mind explaining why I had to make a fool of myself by asking his Majesty about Russian watchmakers in Alaska during the American Civil War? His aides laughed about it for days at my expense.

> Yours,
> John Hays Hammond

Zurich. 2.II.11.

Dear Sir:-

Thank you for your compliments on my writing about the link between critical opalescence and Rayleigh scattering. I am hopeful it will settle the dispute since time immemorial over why the sky as we know it is blue.

Unfortunately, I remain at a disadvantage to explain this atmospheric occurrence you described since it does not read like anything found in nature. The report you shared from Yale University involved cesium detected in soil, ice, etc. However, there is little evidence to suggest this cesium came from Halley's comet due to our most recent understanding of the comet's composition.

I must concur with the Yale scientists that this phenomenon somehow originated from our planet. How and why, however, remains a mystery to me.

I would like to continue this correspondence, but I am afraid it must wait. I am starting a new position in Prague and must prepare myself. Please accept my apologies.

Sincerely yours,

Albert Einstein

P.S. These designs you included for a pocket watch are elegant, but fanciful. Do the laws of thermodynamics no longer apply to clocks? If only I had known, I would have become a watchmaker!

April 8, 1911.

My dear Mr. Lincoln:-

I must regretfully report that my colleagues at the Sheffield School, the Kent and Sloan Laboratories, and the Peabody Museum have determined yet again that those samples from your "artifact" are lead and nothing but lead.

I apologize if their findings are unsatisfactory, but they have run just about every chemical test known to science on your specimens.

Yale is growing suspicious about my activities, so I am afraid we can no longer use university equipment for our research. However, I think we should consider the matter closed: your artifact does not work because it cannot work. It is scientifically impossible.

How can any device run on lead?

Very sincerely yours,

John Hays Hammond

P.S. I am including a newspaper article on some recent developments in Alaska. It looks like the Morgans and the Guggenheims have finally started moving copper out of their mines.

The clipping, which arrived with John's letter on Good Friday, was particularly damning for Robert. It brought him closer than ever to acknowledging that the entire expedition to Alaska had been a folly: "Lincoln's folly" if the papers ever got wind of it.

ALASKA COPPER COMING.

**First Shipment Made by the
Guggenheims from the Bonanza.**
Special to The New York Times.

TACOMA, Wash., April 2.—The first ore shipment to the Tacoma smelter from the world-famous Bonanza copper mine, 200 miles from Cordova, will leave the mine next Thursday. The day will be celebrated as "copper day" at Cordova and along the railroad. The shipment of 2,000 tons of picked ore has been insured for $250,000. Beginning May 1, two cargo steamships will be operated between Tacoma and Cordova, bringing Bonanza ores to the smelter here. The Superintendent of the Bonanza mine last Fall made the announcement that returns from the initial shipment to the Tacoma smelter would amaze the mining world, and it is confidently believed this promise will be fulfilled . . .[22]

Robert closed this folder and threw it into the fireplace as well.

However, there were some papers on Robert's desk that survived the evening. One folder chronicled the war Attorney General Wickersham was currently waging against U.S. Steel.

STEEL TRUST INQUIRY
ORDERED BY HOUSE

Authorizes Committee to Ascertain if It Has Violated the Anti-Trust Law.

TO BARE ITS RAMIFICATIONS

Seeks Light on Its Relations with Other Steel Concerns and with Railroad and Financial Interests.

Special to The New York Times.

---

22 "Alaska Copper Coming," *New York Times*, 3 April 1911.

WASHINGTON, May 16.—The House to-day passed the Stanley resolution for the investigation of the Steel Trust. This is the third investigation authorized by the House this session, the first being the Sugar Trust and the second the Post Office Department . . .[23]

CARNEGIE IN STEEL INQUIRY.

House Committee to Call Him on Tuesday—Wickersham to Testify.
Special to The New York Times.

WASHINGTON, May 20.—The Steel investigation will start off next Monday in full blast. The special committee has had several sessions this week, and to-day decided to call Andrew Carnegie, Attorney General Wickersham, and Herbert Knox Smith, Commissioner of Corporations. The committee will have a conference on Monday with Mr. Wickersham and Mr. Smith to draw up a programme for the conduct of the investigation . . .[24]

---

23 "Steel Trust Inquiry Ordered By House," *New York Times,* 17 May 1911.
24 "Carnegie in Steel Inquiry," *New York Times,* 21 May 1911.

GATES TELLS HOW
STEEL CORPORATION
ACQUIRED CONTROL.

Tells Probers That Morgan,
Schwab, and Himself
Evolved Scheme.

John W. Gates, of New York, went on the witness stand before a select committee of the House today and told of the manner in which the United States Steel Corporation was organized and the motives which prompted that organization.

J. Pierpont Morgan, Charles Schwab, and Gates were the three men who evolved the scheme whereby Andrew Carnegie was eliminated as a factor in the steel industry and that this scheme was worked out at an all-night conference in the home of Mr. Morgan . . .[25]

ROOSEVELT CALLED
IN STEEL INQUIRY

Will Be Asked to Tell What He
Knows About Tennessee Coal
and Iron Purchase.

---

[25] "Gates Tells How Steel Corporation Acquired Control," *Washington Times*, 27 May 1911.

DUE TO GATES'S TESTIMONY

Colonel's Version as Explained When President in a Letter to Bona- parte Was Contradicted.

WASHINGTON, May 29.—Theodore Roose- velt is desired as a witness before the special "Steel Trust" Investigating Committee of the House. A request has been sent to Col. Roosevelt to appear and tell what he knows about the taking over of the Tennessee Coal and Iron Company by the United States Steel Corporation . . .[26]

PROBE OF STEEL TRUST NOW SEEMS CERTAIN

Information from Reliable Source Has It That Department of Justice Will Next Move Against U.S. Steel Corporation—Report Almost Finished.

It is apparent now that the Department of Justice is seriously considering the possibility of moving against the United States Steel Corporation as a combination in violation of the Sherman anti-trust law . . .[27]

---

26 "Roosevelt Called In Steel Inquiry," *New York Times*, 29 May 1911.
27 "Probe of Steel Trust Now Seems Certain," *Washington Herald*, 7 June 1911.

STEEL TRUST HEADS
FACE CRIMINAL TRIAL

Evidence Gathered by Bureau of
Corporations Now Available
for Prosecution.

FREIGHT RATES AN ISSUE

Chairman Stanley Draws Attention to
Charges Over Lines Owned by Steel
Corporation—Gary in Washington.

Special to The New York Times.

WASHINGTON, June 6.—It was learned to-day that the Administration has been keeping close watch on the doings of the United States Steel Corporation for a long time . . .[28]

URGED TO CALL MORGAN.

Steel Committee, However, Believes
It Can Make a Case Without Him.
Special to The New York Times.

WASHINGTON, June 10.—There is much speculation in Washington as to whether the

---

28 "Steel Trust Heads Face Criminal Trial," *New York Times*, 7 June 1911.

Stanley Committee that is investigating the
Steel Trust will subpoena J. Pierpont Morgan as
a witness. Chairman Stanley has received many
letters urging him to call Mr. Morgan, but he
has given no intimation as to what he has in
mind . . .[29]

Robert closed this file and placed it in a desk drawer. However, before he turned off the large lamp on his desk, he decided to leaf through a remaining folder that followed some of his friends' exploits throughout the year.

TAFT AND NORTON
WILL SOON PART

President's Secretary Will Take
Up Private Business in Chicago
When He Retires.

SHAKEUP AT WHITE HOUSE

Bill Before Senate to Reorganize Its
Force—Norton Said to Have Aspired
to Treasury Portfolio.

Special to The New York Times.

---

29 "Urged to Call Morgan," *New York Times,* 11 June 1911.

WASHINGTON, Jan. 20.—After less than a year's service, Charles D. Norton, Secretary to the President, will shortly retire and his successor has already been chosen. This much is made known tonight in a statement from the White House in which it has specifically refused to divulge who the successor would be . . .[30]

"WE ARE GETTING BETTER EVERY YEAR"
—CHIEF WILKIE.

Head of U. S. Secret Service believes that the average individual is upright. Read of it in
NEXT SUNDAY'S TIMES[31]

President's Aide Now Maj. Butt.

———————

WASHINGTON,   March   24.—Capt. Archibald W. Butt, President Taft's military aid, and who served in a like capacity with President Roosevelt, to-day became a full-fledged Major in the army. Capt. Butt passed his examination some time ago, but his commission was not ready to be signed by the President until to-day . . .[32]

———————

30 "Taft and Norton Will Soon Part," *New York Times,* 21 January 1911.
31 "We Are Getting Better Every Year," *New York Times,* 24 January 1911.
32 "President's Aide Now Maj. Butt," *New York Times,* 25 March 1911.

HAMMOND QUIT YALE SCHOOL

**Follows Prof. Huntoon in Resigning
From Sheffield Scientific Faculty.**
Special to The New York Times.

NEW HAVEN, Conn., May 31.—The trouble
in the Faculty of the Sheffield Scientific School,
Yale, which recently resulted in the resignation
of Prof. Louis D. Huntoon, has been followed by
the withdrawal of John Hays Hammond from the
Faculty and the consequent loss of his financial
support . . .

Mr. Hammond is en route to England, where
he will represent America at the coronation of
George V.[33]

ROOSEVELT TO AID
TAFT IN 1912 FIGHT?

**President Is So Assured by a
Friend Formerly Connected with
Both Administrations.**

THEY MEET IN BALTIMORE

---

33 "Hammond Quit Yale School," *New York Times,* 1 June 1911.

**And Have a Cordial Ten-Minute
Interview—Ex-President is Invited
To White House on Friday.**

THE COLONEL SAYS HE HASN'T SAID SO.

Col. Theodore Roosevelt, who arrived on the 12:50 o'clock train from Baltimore this morning, was informed at the Pennsylvania Station by a *Times* reporter of the report that a mutual friend of Col. Roosevelt and President Taft had given the latter assurance that the Colonel would not be a candidate for the Presidency in the next election, but would leave Mr. Taft a free field. The Colonel refused to comment on the statement other than to say with a smile:

"You know I never give interviews." Then he added: "But any statement purporting to come from me to the effect you have just mentioned is an unqualified falsehood."

And, closing his jaws with a snap just before opening them again with a smile, he jumped into a taxicab and drove away . . .[34]

---

34 "Roosevelt to Aid Taft in 1912 Fight?" *New York Times,* 7 June 1911.

THE TAFTS TO CELEBRATE
THEIR SILVER WEDDING
JUNE 19

**Second Such Event to be Observed
in the White House, and Mrs.
Taft, Then Miss Herron, Was
Present at the Previous
Occasion.**

THERE is to be an interesting gathering of the Taft clan at the White House June 19.

The Herrons, representing the root and branch of the family tree of Mrs. Taft, will assemble there with representatives of the Tafts.

The occasion is the twenty-fifth anniversary of the marriage of William Taft and Miss Helen Herron of Cincinnati. There is to be a silver wedding at the White House . . .[35]

This last article was the reason Mary Harlan Lincoln had reminded her husband about their upcoming trip. As Robert closed the folder, he glanced at a nearby invitation calligraphed in copperplate script.

*The President and Mrs. Taft
request the pleasure of the company of
Mr. and Mrs. Lincoln
at*

---

35 "The Tafts to Celebrate Their Silver Wedding June 19," *New York Times*, 11 June 1911.

*The White House
on Monday evening, June the nineteenth
at nine o'clock*
Dancing   *1886–1911*

Just like the presidential seal atop the invitation, the years in its corner were embossed with silver. Robert left the invitation centered on his desk so he would not forget it in the morning.

Finally, it was time for the last son of Lincoln to go to bed.

Robert turned off the lights in his library and walked down the hall to find his wife already asleep in her husband's large white bed. Robert sighed with disappointment as yet another attempt at a romantic rendezvous was ruined. Not wanting to disturb her, Robert sneaked through the darkened room to his closet for one final, crucial step in his nightly routine. With his back to the window, Robert moved a bag of golf clubs aside and opened a white door inside the closet to reveal a small steel safe. He quickly unlocked it and deposited his pocket watch, fob, and chain on a silk handkerchief next to a paper bundle marked "MTL Insanity File." They were his mother's insanity papers, quietly locked away from the world, as she was.

Robert closed the safe and resigned himself to yet another evening with no new information about his father's murder. Or the pocket watch. Or Alaska. His head was throbbing with questions he feared would never be answered in his lifetime, but there was nothing he could do about them. Not tonight, anyway. He changed out of his suit and staggered back into his room, where he sat upright on his bed beside his sleeping wife.

However, as Robert was about to lie down, something turned his head. It was as if a long-forgotten memory was whispered into his ear.

Twenty-one-year-old Robert Todd Lincoln sat upright in his bed. He had long ago finished his cigar and was ready for sleep. It had been more than two hours since his father left for Ford's Theatre, and Robert had passed most of the time chatting with his friend John Hay, the presidential secretary down the hall.

However, as Robert reached for his sleep medicine, he saw something glimmer out of the corner of his left eye. Within the ruffled covers of his bed was a rather magnificent gold pocket watch.

Robert pulled at the shining timepiece by its chain and flipped its lid open. The watch's busy dial showed that it was several minutes past 10:30 P.M. It did not look like one of his father's timepieces, and its bizarre inscription was unlike anything Robert had ever seen in the White House. Thinking it belonged to one of the room's prior occupants, perhaps an ambassador, Robert folded the watch in a handkerchief and walked down the hall. There, in his father's darkened, vacant office, he placed the ticking timepiece on the president's desk.

Robert walked back to his room and sat down on his bed. Outside, he could hear the clatter of horses approaching the White House. Thinking it was someone who had arrived too late to catch his father, Robert reached for the bottle and spoon on his nightstand. He was about to pour his medicine when he heard footsteps rush through the hallway.

Thomas F. Pendel, one of the White House ushers, threw open Robert's door. "Captain Lincoln! The President is shot—the President is shot!"

First the spoon, then the bottle fell from Robert's hand. Its black liquid gurgled like an open wound onto the carpet.

In his darkened room at Hildene, Robert's mind raced and his eyes widened. He leaped out of his bed and rushed to his safe, which he threw open as quickly as his fingers could move.

For the first time in half a century, Robert Todd Lincoln was wide awake.

Chapter XIX

"Till death do us part, my dear."

I t'll take a lot more than that," avowed Nellie.

With these whispered words, the president and Mrs. Taft emerged arm in arm from the Red Room to the cheers of more than five thousand friends, family, and guests on the South Lawn.

The Tafts' silver wedding anniversary was the fairy-tale ending to a journey without precedent in American history. Birthed from the first lady's first visit to the White House for the Hayeses' silver wedding, Nellie's subsequent celebration was a lifetime in the making. Times changed, presidents changed, the century changed. But Nellie? She was the same sixteen-year-old girl she had always been. Only this time, the president of the United States was leading her down the steps of their shimmering castle.

Never before had the White House looked so majestic. The entire mansion was illuminated with innumerable lights. Hundreds of red paper lanterns filled the trees as if to evoke the thousands of cherry blossoms Nellie recently secured for the city. A great flashing American flag hung from the South Portico. The mansion's grand fountain shimmered with a prism of colors. Huge searchlights flooded every edge of the South Lawn with light. And in the distance, the Washington Monument was lit like a beacon for the whole world to see. If Nikola Tesla should be credited as the man who invented the twentieth century, Nellie Taft had effectively conquered it this midsummer's eve.

"That's quite a sight," observed Secret Service Chief Wilkie. He was standing beneath an elm tree with the years "1886–1911" displayed in white lights above him. "Every single eye in the city is fixed on the president, but not ours. We're spying from the rooftops with snipers who can shoot a toothpick in half. We're lurking in the shadows ready to pounce like a panther with a spring in its step. We're the sorry sons of bitches who make silly shindigs like these run like a Swiss watch. We are the unblinking eye that watches over this nation, and we never sleep. We are the United States Secret Service.

"Gentlemen," he puffed as he paced back and forth, "we didn't come for the food or the booze or the women this evening. We came for the deadbeats, the lowlifes, the scum of society. I want you to know everyone in that crowd right down to who's sleeping with whom. If anyone waves so much as a handkerchief that looks suspicious, I want you to shoot him full of more holes than the Spanish navy. I will not allow two assassinations in less than ten years. You should be wearing your suits prepared to take no fewer than three bullets in them. . . ."

"Mr. Wilkie, who are you talking to?" asked Bob Taft, the president's twenty-one-year-old son.

The young man broke Wilkie's concentration. "Never interrupt a man while he's working," he snapped.

"Wilkie?" asked the president in white tie and tails.

"Hmm?" He looked up.

"What the hell are you doing?"

Wilkie looked behind him to find two confused cooks and a cow in the distance. All the agents he was prepping had already formed a receiving line for the president and first lady. "Just securing the area, Mr. President."

"Why don't you secure someplace else?" Nellie huffed, swatting the chief's stinking cigar smoke.

"As you wish, Madam President." Wilkie bowed.

"Just shuffle off," Taft shooed. "And watch your language around the children."

So shuffle he did.

There was a vast cast of suspects for Wilkie to study as he meandered through the richly dressed mob: ambassadors, baronesses, senators, governors, congressmen, religious figures, and plenty of other high-society types the Secret Service chief did not trust any further than he could spit. However, he did tip his hat to Mrs. Wickersham, whose husband was out of town for the evening, and to the secretary of state and Mrs. Knox on his way to the best-dressed man at the party.

"Major Butt," Wilkie greeted, slinking alongside the dashing officer.

"Chief Wilkie," the uniformed man acknowledged. "How goes security?" he asked under his breath.

"Oh, I'm pleased as Punch," Wilkie puffed. "I have eighty policemen outside the south fence and enough detectives on hand to catch the Invisible Man if he tried to sneak in. I imagine every burglar in town is having a field day tonight." He took a swig from a flask of explosive scotch he had brought in case any killer automatons crashed the party. "And how about yourself?"

"All is well," the major whispered. "I increased the aides for the president and Mrs. Taft to twelve. They should provide adequate protection as well as a sufficient honor guard."

"Yes, I can see that. However, I'm more interested in how many soldiers we have on hand in case we need to destroy the mansion again."

The officer shot Wilkie a disapproving glare, but Wilkie responded with a wink and a smoke ring. "A company of engineers is patrolling the grounds," the major reported. "Captain Hubert L. Wigmore and Second Lieutenant Richard Park are commanding."

Wilkie waited for more, but was surprised to hear there was none. "That's it? What are a merry band of engineers going to do if we're under attack? Whitewash Aunt Polly's fence?"

"Mr. Wilkie, I can assure you that this mansion is as unassailable as the moon. Even the storm clouds ran for cover this evening." The major was quite proud of this last feat. Professor Moore of the Weather Bureau predicted "one chance in a hundred of having a garden party tonight." Coupled with Nellie Taft's surprise recovery from a second lapse of illness, the evening appeared to be nothing short of a miracle. The only potential problem was the noticeable nonattendance of the former president and Mrs. Roosevelt. However, Wilkie understood their absence better than most people at the party.

"Well, that all sounds dandy," the smoking man continued, "but what are your engineers and honor guard going to do if some lunatic shows up without an invitation?" The Secret Service chief had Leon Czolgosz in mind as he asked this. The anarchist assassinated President McKinley in a reception line much like the one moving toward the Tafts.

"Mr. Wilkie," assured the major, "nothing sinister will befall us because the only way in or out of these grounds is past *your* guards at the gates. I have no doubt your men are mustard."

"Are you kidding?" Wilkie snickered. "My boys were breast-fed on the stuff!"

With these words, a commotion drew Major Butt and Chief Wilkie's attention to the east entrance. Both men could hear shouting and saw several policemen racing toward the gate.

"Speak of the devil," Wilkie hissed. "Stay here, Archie. Let me mop up this mess." The Secret Service chief pocketed his flask and slipped through the garden party as silently as a snake. Not even the Roosevelt children noticed him. However, "Princess Alice" Roosevelt Longworth did turn her head and smile when she heard him cursing.

"What the hell's going on here?" Wilkie hollered when he arrived on the scene. Agent Sloan and several detectives were wrestling a man to the ground. "Sloan! Report!"

"We got a real schmuck here!" shouted Sloan as he examined the wallet of the man pinned under his knee. He tossed the leather billfold to Wilkie, who caught it and flipped it open. He found a card inside that matched several scattered across the ground.

George B. Schmucker
Consul of the United States to Mexico City

"Stand him up," Wilkie ordered. Agent Sloan and his agents forced the man to his feet while two policemen clamped him in handcuffs. Wilkie stood with arms akimbo and took a good look at the man: His hair and suit were a mess, his face unshaven, and the Secret Service chief did not like the crazy look in his eyes.

"If you want my opinion, Mr. Schmucker, I'd say you're a bag full of nuts."

"I'm a diplomat!" the man resisted. "I must speak with the president! Take my card! It is urgent!"

"Mr. Wilkie, this chump was discharged weeks ago due to mental illness," explained Sloan.

"Who are you, his mother?" Wilkie spoke through his cigar. "Just tell me what kind of pistol this crackpot is packing."

"We searched him, sir," said Secret Service Agent Bowen. "He doesn't have any weapons on him."

"Nothing?"

"Just the wallet," Sloan confirmed as a police wagon pulled up.

Wilkie glowered at the miscreant and shook his head with disapproval. "You're no killer," he surmised. "You're just a waste of my goddamn time, and time is money to Treasury agents." Wilkie jammed the wallet into the madman's mouth and shoved him toward the lawmen. "Get him out of here!" he barked.

Policemen assembled on the vagrant while Wilkie treaded back to the mansion with Agent Sloan. "I don't want to come here again for this," said Wilkie, carrying Mr. Schmucker's card. "No one gets in or out without an invitation or a badge. The next time someone pulls out a card, I want you to pull out your gun. Think you can remember all that?"

"Like the *Maine*, sir."

Wilkie smiled. "You're a scholar, Sloan. Now, if you'll please excuse me . . ." The Secret Service director took a long drag from his stogie. "I need to use the can."

Wilkie left Sloan and moseyed over to the East Wing: a wide white building that closely resembled a Greek temple. The chief plodded past its Doric pillars and through its glass doors on his way to the Police Room, which was conveniently located next to the East Wing's lavatory.

"Who called this in?" asked Wilkie, tossing Mr. Schmucker's card to the lone officer on duty.

"Welcome to the White House," said the policeman behind an issue of *The Saturday Evening Post*. A lovely lady surrounded by white flowers graced the magazine cover.

"Hey!" The chief snatched the magazine from the young lolly-gagger.

"Chief Wilkie!" the policeman blurted.

"Oh, I'm sorry, darling. Did I interrupt you at work?"

"No, sir!"

"Good! Then tell me who called in the Black Maria arresting that loon at the east entrance."

The officer stared blankly. "Can't say that I know, Mr. Wilkie. No requests for a police car came from me."

Wilkie angrily snapped his terrible teeth together. "All right, then. That means the van was one of ours. Ring some real cops and tell them to send that wagon back to the mansion as soon as they drop off their mental patient. Think you can handle such an important job?" asked Wilkie, pointing the rolled-up magazine in the policeman's face.

"Yes, sir," the officer replied nervously.

"Good. If anyone inquires, I'll be in the head office for the next few minutes."

Wilkie tossed the magazine in the wastebasket on his way out the door. However, before he got to the men's room, a familiar voice stopped him.

"John!"

The Secret Service chief turned around and raised his eyebrows. "Mr. Lincoln! You're looking unusually awake this evening."

Robert, who had not slept a wink the previous night, had no time for Wilkie's sarcasm. "John, I need to have a word with the president."

"I'm sorry to say it," Wilkie said, smirking, "but you're the second person to tell me that in as many minutes. Why don't you ask Archie? He'd probably be happy as a clam to help."

Robert glanced over his shoulder toward the coatroom before continuing. "There are too many people around the major. I would prefer it if you took care of this personally."

"Is it an emergency?"

"No, John, it isn't. I just don't want any reporters to get wind of this. Can you arrange for the president to meet with me, alone, tonight?"

Wilkie narrowed his eyes and looked the last living son of Abraham Lincoln down and up. "All right, I'll take care of it. Be in the Yellow Oval Room around 1:00 A.M. The party should be winding down by then."

Robert's tired eyes brightened. "John, consider me in your debt!"

Wilkie smirked and offered his hand. "Just a handshake. That's all I ask."

Robert graciously accepted. "Thank you, John."

"No, thank *you*," chimed Wilkie.

Just as he suspected, the mysterious lump in Robert's jacket pocket was not caused by his hand.

The Secret Service chief spun around and whistled his way into the men's room.

The idyllic garden party, which Major Butt would later describe as the most brilliant function ever held in the White House, refused to die down. When Taft received a note at 1:00 A.M. asking if the Engineers Band should play "Home Sweet Home," he refused. He demanded more ragtime, more dancing, and "more champagne!" to the delight of all in attendance. The East Room was filled with dancers. The scent of wedding cake still wafted in the State Dining Room. The entire South Lawn was sloshed with sparkling wine and spirits from the glasses of thousands of entertained guests. As far as Taft was concerned, there was plenty of party left in the White House. Even after he took Nellie to bed and the two shared a private embrace, he went back downstairs to continue hosting in her stead. From the windows of the Yellow Oval Room, it appeared Robert was in for another sleepless night. Minute after minute, cigar after cigar, he paced the room impatiently as he waited for Taft.

Finally, at 2:00 A.M., the band was out of breath. The lights dimmed, the guests applauded, and the president gave his final good-byes. When the last guest left the grounds, Taft rose from his chair and walked with Major Butt back to the White House. As they approached the South Portico, the soldier made a motion toward the Yellow Oval Room. The president looked up and saw Robert staring at him from a window.

The last son of Lincoln smiled. Wilkie had come through for him after all.

"So, another job well done?" asked Agent Wheeler. All the off-duty Secret Service agents were joining Wilkie for cigars outside the East Wing.

"Well, the president still has a pulse," their boss boasted, "so I'd say that's worth at least a huzzah."

"Huzzah!" The agents laughed.

"Mr. Wilkie?" interrupted the policeman Wilkie had scolded earlier. "That gentleman you asked about is being moved to Washington Asylum Hospital."[36]

Without acknowledgment, the Secret Service chief slowly turned his back on the officer. "Well, that's a disappointment," Wilkie observed. The saddened policeman sulked back into the building.

"That nut was as cracked as the Liberty Bell," said Sloan. "A trip to the lunatic asylum will do him well."

"Maybe so," said Wilkie, "but I don't like taking policemen off guard duty just so they can fit some joker in a new straitjacket."

"Nobody was taken off guard duty," corrected Agent Joseph E. Murphy.

"What are you, on opium?" Wilkie laughed. "I saw it happen with my own eyes!"

"No, he's right, sir," said Sloan. "A wagon full of cops arrived right after you left us. Their timing was perfect. We were never short a man the entire evening."

Wilkie, thinking for a minute, asked with his cigar between

---

36 "Arrest at White House," *New York Times*, 20 June 1911.

his fingers, "Are you absolutely sure it wasn't the same Black Maria that took the vagrant?"

"Positively. Why do you ask?"

"Because I know for certain that nobody put in a call for an extra wagon."

"Bob!" The president greeted his aging friend with open arms. "It's so good to see you again. I was afraid you and Mary left before Nellie and I could thank you for your gift!"

"Think nothing of it." Robert smiled. "Also, congratulations to you and Nellie."

Taft, still amazed by the anniversary present, continued, "Bob, the machine is ingenious! You simply must tell me how you built it!"

Robert raised his hand, insisting, "It can wait."

"Hey, Officer Darling. What time did you—"

Wilkie walked into the Police Room to find the same officer reading the same crumpled magazine as before.

"You lummox!" the chief shouted as he snatched the lovely lady a second time.

"So the watch did belong to your father," spoke a seated President Taft.

"Yes, Will. There's no denying it anymore. It slipped out of his pocket in my room right before he left for Ford's Theatre. That's why he had the fob with him."

"And you saw the watch. You held it. You saw its strange inscription?"

"I did. Only seconds before I was notified about the assassination," Robert sighed.

Wilkie sprinted through the darkened White House while his agents fanned in all directions.

"Archie!"

In front of them, the major emerged from the Blue Room with Arthur Brooks.

"Why is your pistol drawn, Mr. Wilkie?"

"Major," the chief panted in the bloodred Cross Hall. "Our security has been compromised!"

"Well, considering everything that happened," Taft spoke with sincerity, "I think it's a miracle you remember that much."

"A miracle?" Robert gasped with widened eyes. "Will, do you have any idea how miraculous it is that we are even able to share this conversation? If everything had gone according to plan; if I had been with my father that evening . . ."

The major unsheathed his sword and drew his pistol. "Protect the president!"

"If General Grant had come to Ford's Theatre, as he was offered . . ."

———

"Alert the military!" Major Butt shouted. "Someone wire the Washington barracks! Send men here immediately!"

"During simultaneous attacks against Secretary Seward, his son Frederick, and the intended assassination of the vice president . . ."

"I want this place locked like the Panama Canal!" Wilkie ordered. "Sweep every room for thugs and bombs. Brooks! Bring out the guns!"

". . . every single one of us could have been murdered, the pocket watch might have been stolen, and worst of all, I don't think the Constitution would have survived the evening."

"Upstairs! They're upstairs!"

The president turned his head. "Did you hear that?"

Footsteps filled the hallway. The table lamp next to Robert was trembling. "What's going on?"

At that moment, Major Butt charged through the doors with more than a dozen Secret Service agents behind him. After a panicked look at the president, he shouted, "Secure the first family!"

Taft leapt to his feet. "Archie! What is this?"

"Security breach, Mr. President! We need to evacuate the mansion." Secret Service agents swarmed into the room and secured every window.

"How bad is it?" Robert asked.

The major's jaw clenched. "I think we need to get airborne."

"Mr. President!" Wilkie ran into the room with a cigar in his mouth and a gun in his hand. "Where the hell are your kids?"

"You keep away from my children!" ordered Nellie Taft, shoving her way past Wilkie. She was wearing a flowing black evening robe and was followed closely by guards.

"Madam President, this is urgent!" Wilkie continued.

"They should be upstairs on the Sleeping Porch. I already sent my sister Jennie to find them."

"Nellie, are you all right?" The president took his wife into his arms.

"I'm fine, Will. Could someone please explain what's going on?"

Wilkie, knowing he had to choose his words carefully, reported: "As many as ten men disguised as police officers slipped through security when the party began. They were clever. They caused a diversion at the east entrance while we guarded you on the South Lawn. This was a well-planned, coordinated operation. We have to assume the worst."

"Why did they choose tonight?" Nellie glowered angrily. "We have family here. Children!"

Wilkie fidgeted his cigar nervously. "Best guess: to cause as much mayhem as possible." The Secret Service chief lowered his gaze and quickly scanned the sitting room. He whistled to his men. "This space is safe! Search every other room in the mansion."

"How long must we stay here?" asked Robert, his mind awash with bad memories.

Wilkie: "Until Archie's boys ready the zeppelin."

"How long will that take?" asked the president.

"They're moving as fast as they can," said Major Butt as he closed the window curtains.

"You'd better start your stopwatch, Mr. Lincoln," said Wilkie to a stunned Robert.

But then: "*Chief Wilkie!*" shouted an agent from the hallway.

"Excuse me a moment." The chief darted out of the room, leaving the presidential couple and Robert surrounded in a busy hive of men with guns.

After an agonizing minute of silence, Agent Sloan entered the Yellow Oval Room. He had a look of death on his face.

"Jimmy, what is it?"

"Mr. President, you'd better take a look at this."

Taft tightened his wife's hand. "I'm not leaving you," he vowed.

"Good, because I'm not sitting here." A determined Mrs. Taft led her husband out the door.

"Nellie, wait!" He scampered after her.

Chapter XX

The Family Plot

"Where's my sister?" Nellie fumed. "Brooks, please go upstairs immediately. I want my children brought down here."

"Yes, Madam President."

Family member after family member from the Tafts and Herrons was hurried down the Center Hall, some of them barefoot upon the hall's white rugs.

"Mama, Papa, what is this?" asked an alarmed Helen Taft.

"Helen, find your brothers and stay together!" her mother instructed.

"What is this confusion, child?" an impossibly old Delia C. Torrey asked her nephew.

"It's nothing, Aunt Delia," Taft placated. "Just a late-night parlor game."

"Oh . . . in the White House? That sounds delightful. . . ."

"Yes. Boys?" The president directed Agents Wheeler and Jervis to escort the ancient lady to the West Sitting Hall. It was as far away as possible from the trouble brewing in the Treaty Room.

Chief Wilkie emerged from the study through a wall of armed men. He was smoking like a chimney and his eyes moved like a cat's. "Take Mr. Lincoln to the West Sitting Hall, Sloan. I want two men on him."

"Right away, sir."

"What? Why me?" Robert resisted.

"It's for your own protection," Wilkie promised as the man was dragged off.

The Secret Service chief's eyes then shifted back and forth between the Tafts. "Mr. President, Madam President: I'm afraid only one of you can enter this room."

"What!" Taft gasped. "Why?"

"If whatever's in here is a bomb, we're going to need one of you on hand to brief the vice president due to the . . . constitutional peculiarities of your copresidency."

The presidential couple was outraged. "This is madness!" Taft shouted. "How dare you say that on such a sacred day!"

"Mr. President," Wilkie growled, "there's nothing sacred about what's on the other side of these doors."

"Mr. Wilkie, if the situation is dire, let me go in," Major Butt volunteered.

"You're not going anywhere, Archie," the chief dictated. "If someone dies tonight, the country's going to need you more than ever."

"John, this is a democracy, not a dictatorship. I am ordering you to stand aside!" Taft thundered.

"I cannot allow that, Mr. President."

"God damn it!" Butt shouted. "The president just gave you an order!"

"I'm trying to protect his life!"

The situation collapsed into a shouting match that ended only when Nellie Taft stepped forward. She said, in a low, controlled tone, "Enough of this. Major, help Mr. Brooks take a head count of the household. Mr. Wilkie, allow my husband through these doors while I observe through the doorway."

A concerned Taft turned to his wife. Although he was always ready to die for her, he was not prepared to say good-bye to her. Not on this evening. "Nellie, I—"

The first lady threw her arms around her husband and kissed him on the lips. "I won't be out of your sight. Now, go!"

"That's good enough for me," said Wilkie. He snapped his fingers and the Secret Service agents opened the doors to the Treaty Room. As Taft peered into the room, Wilkie searched through his jacket and produced his flask. "Take this," he offered the president.

Taft seized the flask and guzzled it. "Thanks, Wilkie," he replied.

"I meant wear it over your heart. It's bulletproof," the chief instructed.

"Oh . . ." Taft did just as he was told and nodded.

"All right," Wilkie told his agents. "We're moving in." One by one, the United States Secret Service joined their chief in the president's study.

The White House Treaty Room was a setting of enormous consequence to the Taft presidency. As the site of Spain's recent peace treaty following the Spanish-American War, the room had transformed the United States into a world power, eventually sending both Taft and Roosevelt to the presidency. Théobald Chartran's painting of this historic moment hung on the room's west wall, and it resonated deeply with the Secret Service agents present due to President McKinley's prominence in the picture. In this painting at this moment, the slain McKinley appeared to be looking down on some of the same agents who failed to protect him ten years ago—Chief John E. Wilkie in particular. It was a room of great victories and devastating defeats, and it was not chosen for this evening by accident.

It was impossible for Taft to enter the Treaty Room without being bombarded by old memories. Some of the president's most cherished Yale memorabilia filled the space. Wrestling trophies lined his bookcases, as did law books he had been using since his college days. The walls were covered with photographs of old friends and family, some of them long gone. The study was not the airship or the Oval Office, nor the Morgan Library or Robert Todd Lincoln's Hildene. Taft's entire life was in this room, and stepping into it was like walking into his heart. Such was the site of the most inhumane desecration to befall the White House since its burning.

"Dear lord . . ." said the president.

Atop the Resolute desk, a gift of goodwill to the president and people of the United States, was a skull. A shimmering, silver-plated human skull. Grinning. Reflecting the horrified look of every man in the room.

Using his saffron handkerchief, Wilkie took a piece of paper off the desk. "This was under it." He showed the president.

The note, in immaculate handwriting, read:

Mr. President:

You have 48 hours. Otherwise, the next skull in our collection will be Robert's.

> Regards,
>
> The Gentleman from Brussels

The blood drained from Taft's face as he read the note. "They're after Lincoln?" he asked.

Wilkie shook his head. "I don't think so."

"Then who—" Taft's face froze and his heart stopped. "No. NO!"

"Will? What are you looking at?" asked Nellie through the doorway.

The president spun in panic. "Don't come in here!" he yelled.

Nellie saw the silver skull. "My God . . ."

A bloodcurdling scream rang through the hallway. Nellie saw her tearful sister Jennie racing toward her with Major Butt and Arthur Brooks. "Bob is nowhere in the mansion!" Jennie sobbed. "They took him, Nellie! They took your boy!"

Nellie slowly turned her head and stared helplessly at her husband. She tried to speak, but there was no breath left in her.

"NELLIE!" Taft screamed as she fainted.

Fortunately, Major Butt rushed in and caught Nellie just before her head hit the floor.

Chapter XXI

The Skull

How could this have happened?

Taft sobbed helplessly at his wife's bedside, just as he had for so much of his presidency. Any thought of moving Nellie from the mansion was now completely out of the question. Helen and Charlie wept with their parents, desperately longing to be reunited with their older brother. The grieving households of Taft and Herron were powerless to comfort the first family. Hundreds of men in uniform combed the White House for clues, but there were none to find. Chief Wilkie burned through the early morning hours shouting orders. Major Butt put every base in the nation on high alert. Gunboats patrolled the Potomac and closed the Chesapeake Bay. In secret, a stunned cabinet prepared for a Constitutional crisis. The president of the United States had been brought to his knees.

For Robert Todd Lincoln, the once blissful evening had transformed into a living nightmare of his father's murder. Once again, there was little he could say or do to repair the ruined world around him. He stared vacantly from the open window of the Closet Hall: the slender corridor where his father delivered his last public address. Robert did not know what to make of the horrific situation. From his vantage, the nation's future appeared as frozen as the lifeless pocket watch in his hand.

Then there was a knock, and Robert pocketed the timepiece. "Come in," he said in a pained, scratchy voice.

Chief Wilkie entered the tiny room, closing its doors behind him. "Hello, Bob. I just wanted to check in. How you feeling?"

"Weak, useless," said a wounded Robert Todd Lincoln. "There are no words of mine that can alleviate this family's loss." He turned his head to face the chief. "I want to help, but I don't know what I can do."

Wilkie stepped forward, illuminating the darkened hallway with every breath through his cigar. "Care for a smoke?" he offered, producing a Meridiana Selecto from his jacket.

Robert raised an eyebrow, tempted by the fine Havana. "Thank you," he accepted.

"Just so you know," said Wilkie, lighting Robert's cigar, "your wife is safe and sound. Archie has two men guarding her at the Willard."

"I appreciate that." Robert exhaled. "Mary and I were together during my father's assassination. It's terrible to subject her to this all over again."

"You can rest assured she's taken care of. That is, assuming you rest at all."

"I'm accustomed to evening hours." He sighed. "I just wish they were more productive."

Wilkie, sensing his opportunity, moved closer. "Bob, I know you and the president like to keep your work private. I respect that. When you took your little Alaskan excursion, I didn't mind." Wilkie innocently pursed his lips for a second. "However, I need to ask if there was anything you and the president discussed tonight that could be related to his son's disappearance."

Robert removed his glasses and pinched the aching bridge of his nose. "No, there wasn't. Our talk was completely unrelated."

"You're sure of this?"

"Positive," he said, slipping his spectacles back on.

"Sure enough to risk Bob Taft's life?" Wilkie pressed.

Robert turned his exhausted eyes to the chief. "John, as a national authority on the subject, I can assure you that my father's assassination had absolutely nothing to do with the events of this evening."

There were two rapid knocks on the door. "Chief Wilkie?" a voice inquired.

"What do you want?" the chief snapped.

Secret Service Agent Frank Burke peeked through the doors. "Sir, we found something."

Wilkie raised his eyebrows and Robert turned his head.

"Well, aren't you the son of a bitch I've been waiting for all evening!" Wilkie grinned at the agent.

Major Butt whisked the emotionally crippled president back into the Treaty Room.

"What is it, John?" Taft asked wearily.

The president saw Chief Wilkie, Robert Todd Lincoln, and Arthur Brooks huddled around the silver skull. There was a toolbox on the Resolute desk and Wilkie was seated in the president's chair. He was carefully examining the skull with the blade of his puukko knife.

"John . . ." Taft winced. "What are you doing to that thing?"

"It's definitely not a bomb," Wilkie puffed as he worked. "If it was, it would be heavier, even with its silver plating. We also didn't find any explosives when we examined its, uh . . ."

"Its foramen magnum," Robert explained to the president. "The large opening in the occipital bone where the spinal cord extends."

"What he said," Wilkie confirmed. "However, while this poor bonehead is as brainless as the Prohibition movement, it looks like he has one or two secrets worth sharing. There's something foreign lodged in here that we can't extract. Also, this skull sports a feature quite unusual to the normal noggin."

"What is it?" asked Taft.

"There're hinges on this thing," said Wilkie, tapping the skull with his knife.

The president's eyes widened. "Hinges!"

"Yup. Just like a jack-in-the-box. Its top lid was sealed shut, but Mr. Brooks and I were able to jimmy it without difficulty."

"Have you opened it?"

"We're about to. You want to watch?" Wilkie smirked.

The president stared nervously at the shining skull. "May I . . . examine it?" he asked uneasily.

"Be my guest," said Wilkie. "There're no fingerprints on it, and I think its former owner would have been delighted to meet the president in the White House."

Taft stepped forward and, with a hesitant hand, lifted the skull from the Resolute desk. As he studied it closely, his eyes awoke with recognition.

"Mr. Brooks, please notify Mrs. Taft about our progress."

"Yes, Mr. President." Nellie's aide left the room.

"You're sure this thing's not explosive?" Taft asked the chief.

"Mr. President, I just spent the last few minutes hitting it with a hammer."

Satisfied, the president rubbed his fingers together and dug his thumbnail into its lid. It wouldn't open, so Taft knocked the skull against his desk a couple of times.

"What'd I tell you?" Wilkie smiled. "That son of a bitch is adamantine!"

When at last the lid lifted, President Taft felt inside and removed a folded piece of paper from the skull. He flattened the document across the Resolute desk as Robert, Wilkie, and Major Butt huddled around to read it.

Mr. President:

You will enter the Skull and Bones tomb on Wednesday, June 21, at 10:00 P.M. You will come alone with no escort, no Secret Service, and no military within twenty miles of New Haven.

If you fail to appear at the appointed time, you will never see your son again. If you alert Yale University about your meeting, every single person on its campus will be killed. If you make any attempt to interfere with our arrangements by force, every single inhabitant in New Haven will die.

Please do not underestimate the forces you are up against. They are in possession of a weapon more powerful than anything the world has seen. It is far beyond your comprehension.

Yours most respectfully,
The Gentleman from Paris

"What kind of a ransom note is this?" asked the president, trembling. "They're not requesting anything!"

The four men exchanged uneasy looks across the Resolute desk.

"They're asking for you," said Wilkie. "And I'm pretty sure they're not inviting you over for tea."

"Mr. President," began the major, "whoever's behind this villainy knew you would be at Yale on Wednesday. They planned their attack to coincide with your silver wedding and Commencement Day at the school. This dastardly plot must have been months in the making."

"Years," Wilkie corrected.

Taft rubbed his face with an unsteady hand. "They could have killed us all tonight. Half the government. My whole family. Everyone I've ever known."

"On that subject, Mr. President, you know this fella, don't you?" Wilkie pointed his puukko to the silver skull

"I do," Taft nodded. "That's the skull from the Skull and Bones tomb."

"That's *the* skull?" asked Robert. "The one John told us about?"

"Yes. Yorick. We used him as a ballot box. I've never seen him in silver, though. That must be some kind of sick joke."

"You mind explaining whose skull it was before your Bonesmen acquired it?" asked Wilkie.

"I don't know! It was there before I was born! It was probably stolen from the medical school."

"Mr. President, no more bull. What goes on inside that tomb?" Chief Wilkie demanded.

"John, I can assure you it's nothing but a private club for Yale chums. Nothing important goes on in there. It's a crowded, cluttered building piled high with antiques, dust, and rubbish! I have no idea why they would want to meet me there."

"Your father was cofounder," began Robert. "And you said yourself several of your brothers are members. As are Secretaries MacVeagh and Stimson."

"Yes. And so is Bob. My poor son . . ." Taft lamented. "What's your point?"

"It sounds to me like these villains are trying to get inside your head," said Wilkie, snapping the skull shut with his knife. "I suggest we get into theirs."

"John, this isn't a game of checkers. They have my son! I'd resign the presidency right now if it would bring him back!"

"Will, don't say that," said Robert.

"I'll say whatever I damn well want, Bob! I never wanted this job! You know it! Everyone knows it!"

"Will," Robert's voice deepened, "the presidency is too precious to surrender like a chess pawn."

"Bob, they have my son. MY SON!" Taft pounded the desk, shaking the skull. "My wife is weeping in her bed! My entire family has been crippled! I'd rather be assassinated on the spot than see any further harm befall those I love!"

Robert took off his glasses. "Mr. President," he said in a clear voice, "you still have a pulse. You still breathe air. You are still *very* much alive, so do not trivialize the consequence of your death! You have been dealt a terrible blow, but believe me, my father came close to defeat countless times throughout the war. I saw with my own eyes moments when this nation hinged on how much pain one man can endure. My father forfeited everything for this country just so you and every president to follow would have a United States to govern. You owe him your allegiance to this office!"

Taft, whose mounting anger was held back only by his exhaustion, replied, "Bob, your father was the greatest man to ever assume the presidency. Maybe even the greatest American there ever was. I cannot be his equal. I am not his equal."

"You don't need to be," a woman's voice spoke from the doorway.

The president turned to see his wife, supported by Arthur Books. "Nellie!" Taft rushed to her. "Are you unhurt?"

"Only physically," she said, reeling as she spoke. "Will, these are the most painful hours of my life, but if I can stand them, so can you. We cannot allow the country to fall victim to this malice. No parent in the nation should suffer what we are going through right now. You must engage our enemies. You will meet them as they requested, find out who they are and what they're plotting. And then, once you have rescued our son, you will make sure these villains never leave that tomb alive."

"Nellie . . ." The first couple embraced. "What if I cannot stop them? What if I fail?"

"You won't," she assured. "You're a fighter."

Nellie's words, like a bell, awoke the prizefighter in her husband. Renewed, restored, resurrected, Taft lifted his wife off the ground and kissed her with the same passion they had shared for twenty-five years. Everyone else in the room looked away until they were finished.

As Taft gently returned Nellie to her feet, he nodded to Brooks with gratitude. The aide returned in kind and, together, the three charged into the Treaty Room.

"Archie!" Taft hollered. "How long will it take for you to plan an attack on Yale campus?"

"I—"

"Speak, damn you!" Taft ordered.

Although this interruption was completely unnecessary, it snapped the major into unexplored heights of attention. "I can have one ready within twenty-four hours. It will have to be a nighttime raid, of course."

"Oh? And how are you going to sneak your soldiers in without anyone noticing?" Wilkie put to the major. "It's Commencement Day. Our enemies could have a thousand armed men on that campus without any of us knowing. Besides, the president's going to be naked in that tomb without my agents—no offense," he acknowledged to Nellie. "Whoever these villains are, they'll be more prepared than Boy Scouts for an attack. Be it by land or by sea."

But not from the air, Taft realized. "Archie," said the president with glistening eyes, "use the zeppelin!"

Every face in the room froze except Nellie's. Intrigued, she raised an eyebrow. "Mr. Lincoln, how serviceable would Airship One be in combat?" she asked.

Robert was perplexed with this request, but after a thought: "Very well, actually. Bullets should pass through it quite harmlessly. It was built with defense in mind, but we could have the War Department refit it for assault. In fact . . ." A revived Robert looked straight at Major Butt. "The zeppelin is ideally suited for a nighttime raid. It's silent, fast, and steady."

Wilkie's eyes lit up like gasoline. "Major, if you stationed sharpshooters on the zeppelin with searchlights, you'd be able to open fire on any enemy as if it was raining bullets!"

"That's mustard, Wilkie! Archie, who can you put up there?" asked Taft.

The major rapped his fingers against his saber's hilt, but then gripped it tightly. "We'll use cavalrymen. Crack-shots. The kind who can shoot the neck off a bottle at full gallop."

"Send in the Rough Riders!" shouted Wilkie, grinning his yellow teeth.

Everyone in the room looked at the Secret Service chief as if he were wearing the silver skull as a hat.

"Are you daft, man?" asked Taft.

"The Rough Riders were disbanded in 1898," said the major. "They no longer exist."

"We could reassemble them!" Wilkie continued. "I have no doubt Colonel Roosevelt will proudly join them on the battlefield."

"No," Nellie Taft said sternly. "No Roosevelts."

The chief shut his mouth.

However, as Nellie reflected on the use of cavalry, she turned to her aide and asked, "Who were those other riders who fought so well at San Juan Hill? The ones the papers didn't write about?" Because they were Negro units, Nellie did not need to explain.

"The Buffalo Soldiers," Brooks responded.

"Yes, the Ninth and Tenth Cavalry Regiments," Major Butt clarified. "I'm afraid we cannot use them. They're stationed too far out west to bring them by train."

"What about the West Point detachment?" Brooks countered.

The Georgia major looked Brooks in his brown eyes without smiling. "What about them?"

"There's a detachment of one hundred of the Ninth Cavalry's best riders stationed at the academy as instructors. The airship could pick them up en route to New Haven," Brooks proposed to the president.

"I know the Ninth Cavalry," said Taft, "and I know them to be good men. Archie, can these soldiers rescue my son?"

Major Butt, after mulling over some of his personal prejudices, buried them and responded, "Yes, Mr. President. They can, they will."

The president smiled. "Good. Let's use them."

"Hold on just a minute," Wilkie interrupted. "Even if Archie and his air cavalry ride in there like Galahad, they could end up as dead as Don Quixote if this superweapon these madmen are threatening New Haven with exists."

"Mr. Lincoln, is such a device possible?" asked Nellie.

Robert, holding on to his father's pocket watch in his coat, replied, "Undoubtedly."

"Undoubtedly? Well, that sounds easy enough to identify," Wilkie seethed with sarcasm. "How the hell are my men supposed to disable a weapon when we don't even know what it looks like?"

"I'll come with you," Robert pledged.

Taft's eyes wrinkled. "Bob? Are you sure you want to do this?"

"Mr. President, recent events have made me uniquely prepared for this mission. Please, let me help you."

The president checked with his wife, and she nodded. "All right. Welcome back to the Army, Captain Lincoln. If your uniform no longer fits, believe me, I empathize!" The president did not need to pat his ample stomach, but he did anyway.

"Thank you, sir, but I think my civilian suit and rank will service me just fine."

"As you wish," said Taft. "Now there's only one more matter we need to discuss." The president rummaged through a stack of mail on his desk until he came to a Yale brochure he was sent for Commencement Day. He unfolded its map atop his desk and tapped his finger on the Skull and Bones tomb. "What's our plan once I get in there?"

"Once *we* get in there, you mean."

The president looked up at Wilkie. "What was that, John?"

"Mr. President, there's no way in heaven, hell, or Washington you're going inside that tomb without the Secret Service."

"John, you saw the terms in that letter. We have no choice," Taft conceded. "If we're to get any information out of these villains, we need to make them think they have me beaten."

"We can do more than that," Nellie added. "Will, I want you to continue with our plans for a second party at the mansion tomorrow. One that's open to the public. We must not let anything appear out of the ordinary."

"Are you mad?" snapped Wilkie.

"Don't speak to my wife like that," Taft reprimanded.

"I'm sorry, Mr. President, but we must be realistic! Do you have any idea how difficult it's going to be to provide adequate security after what happened today?"

"I have no doubt it will be taxing," Nellie continued. "That's why you must do it. We need to make our enemies think it would be impossible for my husband to sabotage their meeting."

"Madam President," Wilkie stressed, "I am sorry, but this is too dangerous. For all we know, this could all be a trick to assassinate the president during Yale's commencement."

"If they wanted my husband dead, they would have killed him hours ago. Also, at no point in that letter did they threaten his life. I believe they need my husband alive."

"Well, so does the United States!" Wilkie insisted.

"Excuse me," Robert interrupted, "but I think I know a way we can ensure Secret Service protection within the Skull and Bones tomb."

———

HAMMOND

WILL! THE MAJOR BRIEFED ME ON EVERYTHING. I AM SPEECHLESS. HOW CAN I HELP?

TAFT

JACK, HOW DID YOUR STUDENTS EAVESDROP ON SKULL AND BONES MEETINGS?

HAMMOND

WHAT?

TAFT

LAST YEAR, YOU SAID SOME STUDENTS FIGURED OUT HOW TO SNOOP ON ALL OF YALE'S SECRET SOCIETIES. HOW DID THEY DO THIS?

HAMMOND

DO YOU HAVE A MAP OF THE UNIVERSITY IN FRONT OF YOU?

TAFT

YES, WE HAVE SEVERAL.

HAMMOND

GOOD. THE FIRST THING YOU NEED TO DO IS ENTER
THE STEAM DEPARTMENT. IT IS THE SMALL BUILDING
TO THE WEST OF THE PEABODY MUSEUM. . . .

Chapter XXII

Commencement

June 20, 1911, went precisely as Nellie Taft planned. While the president greeted guests at the White House with the best fake smile of his career, his wife was upstairs quietly managing one of the most daring military operations in history. Major Butt was in frequent communication with the United States Military Academy at West Point, briefing its Ninth Cavalry soldiers on their upcoming mission. Robert Todd Lincoln was hard at work with the War Department modifying Airship One. Chief Wilkie patrolled the White House grounds with more than a thousand soldiers and every Secret Service agent in the city, pausing only once to check on Washington Asylum Hospital's newest mental patient. Unfortunately, the lunatic ex-consul did not know anything about Yale University, silver skulls, or pocket watches. At sunset, Attorney General Wickersham was summoned to the White House along with Vice President James

S. Sherman and Secretary of War Henry L. Stimson, who agreed to remain in Washington in the event of disaster.

And lastly, when chauffeur George Robinson was briefed on the role he might have to play in the upcoming operation, he laughed, said "I was raised on steam!" and went straight back to work in the White House garage.

June 21 was Commencement Day.

Just as Wilkie predicted, President Taft squirmed throughout Yale's two hundred tenth commencement, feeling unusually vulnerable. Whether this had anything to do with the split in his trousers, we will never know. Fortunately, the president was wearing his academic robe that afternoon. There were numerous moments throughout the ceremony when Taft's eyes nervously moved across the many windows and rooftops surrounding him. Whether someone was pointing a rifle at him or not, the president knew he was being watched. He even suffered a lack of appetite during the alumni luncheon as he pondered the possible civilian casualties. However, when Yale President Arthur Hadley offhandedly mentioned that the campus should be deserted by nightfall, Taft relaxed a bit and requested some dessert. If this was to be his last meal, he wanted it to be something sweet.

As sundown approached and the university cleared, the president of the United States went on a final walk through Yale campus before relieving his men. Taft's dedicated Secret Service agents regretfully abandoned their president at Yale's Old Campus and boarded the evening train for New York City. Exposed and completely alone save for the silver skull his agents left with him, Taft sat on a bench between Chittenden Hall and the Art

School as he composed himself. He closed his eyes, filled his lungs with crisp New England air, and waited. For the first time since this horror began, old Big Lub felt relaxed.

Then, the clock towers and churches throughout New Haven tolled ten. Taft opened his eyes and rose from the bench, walking northwest with Yorick in his hands. He looked this way and that along High Street and, after glancing just a second into the night sky, crossed the road. In front of him was the tall brownstone Egypto-Doric fortress better known throughout the university as Skull and Bones Hall. The Tomb.

The president passed under the Tomb's vaulted entrance and knocked on its tall doors. The left door opened outward. After waiting patiently with Yorick, the puzzled president leaned forward and asked, "Hello?" There was some murmuring, and then the other door opened. Taft smiled. He had grown quite wider since his Yale days.

Four tall men in military garb walked outside and surrounded Taft. "Mr. President?" one of them asked.

"Yes?"

The four men forced Taft into the Tomb. Once its large doors slammed shut, the villains proceeded to pound the daylights out of the president.

Chapter XXIII

"He's in."

Several hundred feet in the air above New Haven, a wireless radio operator sent an encrypted message to the West Wing of the White House.

AIRSHIP ONE

HE'S IN.

Seconds later, the West Wing aboard Airship One received a reply.

WHITE HOUSE

COMMENCE.

The operator looked out the door and gave a thumbs-up to Major Butt, whose summer uniform included an eye patch this evening. The major nodded and threw open the double doors behind him, plodding through its darkened corridor until he reached the airship's main deck. The vast expanse was devoid of light, but all the major had to do was switch his patch from one eye to the other to see clearly. Staring back at him was Chief Wilkie, Robert Todd Lincoln, over a dozen Secret Service agents, and all one hundred soldiers from the Ninth Cavalry's West Point detachment. The Buffalo Soldiers carried 1903 Model Springfield rifles specially modified with Maxim silencers. The Secret Service agents had their trusty Colt Police Positive Specials holstered. Major Butt wore his M1911 and Army officer's sword on his belt. And Robert Todd Lincoln was armed with his wits and a gold pocket watch.

Major Butt gave the order: "It's time."

The New Haven raid of 1911 sprang into action.

Twenty soldiers from the Ninth Cavalry dropped ropes from Airship One and descended upon Yale as quietly as leaves in a summer breeze. Their primary targets were the Steam Department and Boiler House in the center of Library, York, Elm, and High Streets. Sixteen men raced toward the buildings while the remaining four provided security for the Secret Service agents sliding down after them. Robert Todd Lincoln and a delighted Chief Wilkie were the last men to jump, the former securely strapped to the latter as if he were a knapsack. Wilkie smiled on their way down, thinking Mr. Lincoln was afraid of heights. In truth, Robert was more concerned about his most important contribution to the operation: Airship One. As the two slid down the line, Robert forced himself to look upward. The titanic zeppelin, which Captain Wigmore's engineers had spent a whole day repainting black, appeared completely invisible in the evening sky. Robert's eyes widened with awe. His confidence was renewed.

Once the two hit the ground and separated, Wilkie quickly surveyed the scene. Satisfied, the Secret Service chief lit himself a cigar. The men above him saw this signal and raised their ropes while sharpshooters filled every window on the zeppelin. Airship One assumed guard duty while Wilkie deployed his men. "Sloan, Wheeler, Jervis: I want you looking after Mr. Lincoln like he's your mother's mother. The rest of you: Work your way into Herrick Hall and get a good look at the Kent and Sloane Laboratories. If there're any bad eggs around the Tomb, they're probably nesting in those buildings. Keep your heads down, mind your flashlights, and for the love of Roosevelt, keep quiet. If so much as a duck farts, this whole operation could play out worse than Little Bighorn. Is that understood?"

The men nodded.

"Good boys." He grinned. "Now, make your parents proud you went to Yale."

The agents disappeared into the night while Wilkie looked over at Sloan, Wheeler, Jervis, and Robert. "This is a nice school," their ringleader observed. "I always wanted to go to clown college. If the five of us stick together like the Ringling Brothers, we might make it out of this circus alive." Wilkie drew his pistol and puffed a large cloud of smoke. "Let's go."

The five hurried to the Boiler House, which the Ninth Cavalry had already moved in and out of. "What's the good word?" the chief asked Sergeant William H. Hazel.

"The Boiler House is secured, but it looks like there may be enemies inside the Steam Department."

"How can you tell?" asked Wilkie. The building appeared dark and there was no smoke coming from its chimney.

"We found some footprints around the Boiler House that all lead to the Steam Department. Also, we found this." The sergeant handed Wilkie a bullet cartridge. "There's a whole case of these in the Boiler House."

Wilkie took out his flashlight and studied the shell. It was a 7.65mm Belgian Mauser cartridge with "F N" stamped on its base. "Fabrique Nationale," he read.

"Whoever these men are," said the sergeant, "they ain't American."

As Wilkie mulled this, a gunman on the top floor of the nearby Peabody Museum set the iron sights of his Belgian Mauser on the American with the flashlight.

Chapter XXIV

The Tomb

Within this dusty, stuffy, and soundproof piece of Yale history, the twenty-seventh president of the United States was getting pummeled within an inch of his sorry life.

Actually, not really.

Being six foot two and three hundred fifty pounds provides a man with a unique advantage when it comes to absorbing punches. Since Taft walked into this ambush blessed with a thick layer of muscle under his blubbery armor, the only thing he hoped to avoid was getting hit in the head. Naturally, this applied as much to the silver skull he carried as to his own.

Also working to the president's advantage was that these four thugs were mercenaries, not boxers. The men tired so quickly that, to Taft, the whole affair might as well have taken place underwater. He even cracked one of the men's hands by moving his head to dodge a punch, forcing the thug to painfully land his knuckles against a stone wall. Taft knew he could probably kill these men in less than a minute, but he would not. He could not. He needed to take their abuse and smile at every insult they hurled at him. He had to buy all the time he could so that maybe, just maybe, he could walk out of this tomb a bit wiser about their plot against America.

Unfortunately, near the tail end of this melee, one of the bullies punched Taft below the belt. The president dropped the silver skull and keeled over, instinctively crying, "Foul!"

These villains fought dirty. And to make matters worse, they were just getting started on poor Taft.

Just as John Hays Hammond described to Robert Todd Lincoln on the airship, the most remarkable thing about Skull and Bones Hall is how unremarkable it looks on the inside. Despite having doubled in size since Taft's Yale days, the Tomb in 1911 more closely resembled an antique shop after the great San Francisco earthquake. A vast forest of doors lined its halls, each one leading to a closet filled with an assortment of unsorted junk. The whole building was overflowing with decaying books, old trinkets, rusted military antiques, dusty furniture, and countless curiosities stolen from rival fraternities. Such was the vast treasure horde of Skull and Bones and the greatest secret of the society: its lack of any particularly meaningful secrets.

That is, until recently.

Why was this location chosen for this unexpected meeting? Its purpose became evident once the four thugs dragged the battered president into the dining hall. Surrounding the great hall were group photographs of many Bonesmen of yore, including a young Will Taft and three of his brothers. However, far more outstanding were the two paintings hanging across from each other at the dining table's midpoint. The president smiled smugly as the brutes forced him into the chair with William Huntington Russell behind it. Russell was one of the cofounders of Skull and Bones and a man whom Taft admired. He was one of the founders of the Republican Party and a personal friend of John Brown; he founded the Connecticut militia, served as their general during the Civil War, and died defending birds from cruel boys in a park just a stone's throw from the Tomb.

However, as Taft looked at the wall across the table, his smile disappeared. Hanging in front of him in full view was a portrait of Skull and Bones's other cofounder. A man who served as secretary of war and then attorney general for President Ulysses S. Grant: something Taft was quite proud of. The man was also the first U.S. official to confront tsarist Russia on its horrendous treatment of Jews, some of whom he personally helped immigrate to America. Both the president and Mrs. Taft were quite proud of this as well.

Looking down at the president with the eyes he always loved was Alphonso Taft. His father.

Wilkie was right, Taft realized. These men were trying to get inside his head, and they were doing a good job at it.

After rooting through Yorick, one of the four brutes slammed the silver skull on the table. Against its reflective surface, Taft saw his own unhappy face.

Chapter XXV

The Secret Passage

W hat are you doing, Wilkie?" Major Butt brooded from the airship. The Secret Service chief was distracting every portside sniper with his flashlight.

"Sir!" called one of the sharpshooters. "The museum! Fourth-floor window!"

The major turned his binoculars to the Peabody Museum, where he saw a rifleman aiming at Robert and Wilkie.

The officer spun around and blew his whistle.

Three powerful searchlights blinded the gunman at the window. As he shielded his eyes, the sharpshooters aboard Airship One opened fire. Wilkie's agents and the Ninth Calvary on the ground turned to see six well-aimed bullets tear through the man. As he fell backward, dead, the sniper's Mauser tumbled out the window.

Wilkie's cigar fell from his mouth. "Duck!" he shouted, pulling Robert Todd Lincoln onto the grass.

The Mauser hit the ground and discharged, shattering a window at Pierson Hall. The noisy gunshot echoed throughout all corners of Yale campus. Faster than Wilkie could curse about it, a column of armed men rushed out of the Steam Department. Gunmen filled the windows of Pierson Hall along York Street, the Peabody Museum along Elm and High Streets, and the two laboratories Wilkie was concerned about on Library Street. None of these men were with the Ninth Cavalry.

Wilkie and his rescue team were surrounded and completely exposed.

But then, every single searchlight aboard Airship One switched on, shining thick pillars of light on the hostiles as if the night sky had exploded. As the enemies stared skyward, aghast, Wilkie and his men raised their weapons.

Just before they pulled their triggers, the airship emitted a mighty roar. It sounded like Gabriel's horn on Judgment Day with a hint of tuba to it.

BRRRRRRRAAAAAWWWWRWRRRMRMRMMRM-RMMMMM!

All the enemies around the Steam Department fell lifelessly, as did many snipers in the surrounding buildings. Airship One's booming foghorn not only distracted every villain on the battlefield, it artfully obscured the gunfire that cut them down.

"INSIDE!" Wilkie screamed, leading the charge through their fallen enemies.

Secret Service agents and the soldiers with the Ninth Cavalry

stormed the Steam Department, killing the few remaining gunmen inside it. As the warriors emptied their weapons and took
defensive positions within the building, Wilkie and his agents
raced to its basement.

"See anything that can destroy a city?" Wilkie threw to Robert as they hustled.

"No."

"Do you think it's all a bluff?"

"No!"

"Any idea where the president's son is?"

"Jesus Christ, John. I don't know!"

Wilkie sneered at these responses. "Mr. Lincoln, we're going
to need some good news and fast if we're to make it out of this
meat grinder!"

"Mr. Wilkie!" hollered Agent Barker from the basement. He
pointed the chief to a large metal door covered with chipped yellow paint.

"There it is," said Robert.

"Best news I've heard all day!" Wilkie grinned.

The Secret Service agents gave their chief the light and space
he needed to pick the lock. However, as Wilkie worked, something about the basement's earthen floor troubled Robert.

"Someone's been here."

The men looked down to see fresh footprints in the soil where
Wilkie had not stepped. One set of the footprints disappeared
under the door.

"They know about the steam tunnels?" asked Wilkie with
alarm.

A worried Robert Todd Lincoln rubbed his beard. All of a
sudden, their well-thought-out plan appeared poised for disaster.

"John, this is the only viable passage into the Tomb. The only other option is to besiege the building with the president still inside it."

As Wilkie pondered this, the monotonous din of Airship One's epic foghorn shook the building.

The chief lit a fresh cigar. "Flashlights, gentlemen! We're going underground."

Wilkie raised his pistol and kicked open the door to Yale University's vast labyrinth of steam tunnels.

Chapter XXVI

The Gentleman

A bandaged hand adjusted the silver skull on the table so that it was staring straight at the injured president. Taft followed the man's arm to see the angry thug whose hand he broke earlier. He was also the same villain who felled the president with a low blow.

"I'll have you know that such behavior is most unsportsman-like," chided a fat-lipped and bruised Taft.

The thug responded by slapping the president across the face.

The dining table at Skull and Bones Hall stretched about ten feet in both directions from where Taft sat at its middle. Although the president was not bound, he was in no position to escape. On the opposite side of the table, the thug with the bandaged hand joined his three companions. The four men flanked the painting of Alphonso Taft with shotguns aimed at the president.

As Taft looked them over, a grandfather clock beside the bandaged thug tolled 10:15 P.M. Moments later, Taft could hear the faint sound of footsteps approaching. A door beside his father's portrait opened, and a gray figure emerged through its darkened portal. ·

A tall, thin man about Robert Todd Lincoln's age, maybe older, entered the dining hall with a cane and took a seat across from the president. He was bald with sparse white hairs and a feathery Van Dyke beard. He had a scaly neck, sunken eyes, and a prominent nose that pointed outward like a beak. Never before had Taft seen a man more closely resemble a vulture. Or more specifically, a vulture in a gray suit hovering above a silver skull. The president glared at this man he had every reason in the world to hate, but for all his anger, he could not help glancing at the portrait of his father hanging over him. The man in the gray suit noticed this and grinned as if he had been waiting all day to see this happen.

Still smiling and without breaking eye contact, the man reached into his jacket and produced a black box with gold lettering on it. The writing was in French. The stranger opened the box and gently placed it beside the silver skull.

"Chocolates?" he offered.

Taft winced. The man's voice was uncomfortably overfriendly, as if he was trying to win the confidence of a child for purposes unknown.

"What are they?" Taft asked, thinking the treats might be poisoned.

The man's eyes widened. "They're . . . *delicious,* Mr. President! Please, try some!" The stranger picked up a chocolate and bit into it with his pinkie raised.

Taft strained his eyes and ears in a vain attempt to decipher the man before him. He spoke in a strange, indiscernible accent that rendered his place of origin a mystery. The president detected a slight French accent as well as a hint of Russian, but the man looked like he could be Greek or Turkish. Where did he come from? His every pore oozed maliciousness, and yet he presented himself in a way Taft imagined any culture would find sophisticated. Charismatic, even. The president was beginning to feel that he was not speaking to a kidnapper, but to a seasoned dignitary. The man was an ambassador, but to whom? To whose flag did he owe allegiance? Did he even have a flag?

Or was he a gentleman without a country?

A frustrated Taft stared at the chocolates and then back to the man across the table. His opponent's eyes glowed eagerly as he discerned the president's conflict. However, once Taft remembered something Nellie mentioned earlier, he picked up a chocolate and studied it. It looked and smelled delicious. Quite delicious.

Taft bit into it, and . . .

Almonds!

Whether it was cyanide or not, Taft figured it would take a lot more than one dose to kill him. He finished his chocolate and helped himself to another.

The gentlemen smiled proudly. "I am pleased to see I have so *overwhelmingly* earned your trust, Mr. President."

"Actually," Taft said, chewing, "my wife figured that if you wanted me dead, you would have done it a while ago."

The gentleman continued smiling, but for a moment it seemed forced. "Yes. Your wife is most perceptive, Mr. President." Once again, Taft shifted in his seat. The gentleman enunciated every word with too much saliva in his mouth. "How is she?"

Taft scowled. "She wants her son back. As do I."

The gentleman licked his white teeth as he heard this. "Did she enjoy the anniversary gift?" He motioned toward the skull.

Taft's gaze intensified with anger.

"I must confess, Mr. President, I was not expecting you to bring it. However, now that it is here, I think it makes the perfect centerpiece for our discussion."

"Enough talk, you skinny buzzard. Who the hell are you?"

The delighted gentleman folded his hands as if he was watching an infant take his first steps. "Since you have blessed me with your confidence, Mr. President, it is my pleasure to introduce myself and the purpose of this meeting. My name is Basil Zaharoff, and I am here to facilitate a peaceful transaction between the United States government and parties that must not be named." He sat back and smiled.

"Where is my son?"

"Mr. President, before we get to the matter of—"

Taft rose to his feet. His large belly forced the table forward. *"Where is my son?"*

The four gunmen raised their shotguns to Taft's face while the gentleman waited patiently. "Mr. President, I can assure you with full confidence that your son is safe. The young man is unharmed; he is in this building, and nothing would make me happier than to have the two of you reunited."

"Let me see him," Taft demanded.

The gentleman pressed his hands to his lips as if in prayer. "Mr. President, I must insist that we continue this conversation seated." Two gunmen hurried over and shoved Taft back into his chair. "For the sake of decorum, of course." As the gentleman spoke these words, the thug with the bandaged hand smacked the president upside the head.

"You don't know the meaning of the word, you stupid nincompoop!" Taft growled.

"Mr. President, I am a master of many languages."

"Good. Then answer me in plain English: Where is my son?"

The gentleman signaled one of his guards to fetch something from another room. "Mr. President, as a legal man, I trust you are mentally fit to act as your own attorney?"

Taft's brow furrowed. "What?"

"Are you of sound mind? Is your brain fully functional?"

Taft's eyes were aflame with fury. "Oh, I can think of a number of things I'd like to do to you right now!"

"Good," said the unaffected gentleman. "Because I included an insanity clause."

A mystified Taft looked to the man's left and saw a gunman return with a briefcase. The thug opened it for the gentleman, who carefully emptied its contents.

"Where is my son?" Taft insisted.

"Just a moment, Mr. President."

Taft leaped back to his feet. "WHERE IS MY SON?"

The gunmen forced the president back down while Basil removed a piece of paper from the suitcase. "Here!" he offered eagerly, extending the document across the table.

Surrounded by primed shotguns, Taft seized the parchment angrily. As he looked it over, the blood in his veins went cold.

"What is this?" he whispered breathlessly.

The document was covered with rust-colored writing.

"What is this!"

"Mr. President," said the gentleman, grinning, "that document *is* your son!"

It was an executive order written in blood.

Taft roared like a wounded animal and reached across the table, but the gunmen held him back. The enraged president attacked one of them with a throat strike, but the thug with the bandaged hand knocked the president in the groin with the butt of his shotgun.

Taft collapsed into his chair while the gunmen rushed around the table to guard their master. "Mr. President, I am nothing more than a messenger," said the gentleman. "I come bearing gifts of peace and the wisdom of honest words. If you want your son back, you must sign that document."

"I'll kill you with my bare hands!" Taft foamed, writhing in pain.

"Mr. President . . ." The gentleman disapprovingly shook his head. "Your hands are capable of so much more than that. My employer is a great harvester of hands, and to save your son, you must use yours. You will use your executive powers to abolish the U.S. Constitution. You will abolish the U.S. Congress and the judiciary. You will dissolve the union between the states. You will disband the U.S. military. And then, you will resign your office, as will all your secretaries and ministers."

"Never!" Taft snarled.

"Mr. President, you must comply."

"You'll never get away with this! Even if you gutted the whole goddamn government, Teddy Roosevelt would take my place! You know he would!"

This proposal caught Basil Zaharoff by surprise. His employers had not considered it. "Then he will be executed," said the gentleman. "Along with all his children."

"You inhuman monster . . ."

"I am quite human, Mr. President."

"Tell me my son is alive right now!"

"Mr. President," laughed the gentleman, "only you have that power. Your son is here! On this campus! You can be reunited with him tonight if you only put a pen to that parchment."

The guards placed an inkwell and an ivory pen in front of Taft. As the president's hopeless eyes fell upon them, he realized the inkwell was filled with red liquid and the ivory pen was a finger bone.

"Who are you working for?" Taft insisted. Tears were streaming down his face.

"Mr. President, you must respect their privacy."

"Is it Morgan? Guggenheim? Tell me!"

"Mr. President," the gentleman said with a smirk, "I can assure you that neither Mr. Morgan nor Mr. Guggenheim know anything about this."

Taft gasped. Not Morgan? Not the Guggenheims? "Then who?" he demanded. "Who are you working for?"

"Mr. President, please. I am trying to spare your life."

Chapter XXVII

The Universe of Battle

Several stories beneath the battle for Yale campus, Robert Todd Lincoln, Chief Wilkie, and sixteen Secret Service agents raced through the university's underground network of steam tunnels. It was a dark, humid place illuminated only by flashlights and wide enough for only two men at a time. It seemed to stretch on forever, and the agents had no blueprints to work with. Fortunately, John Hays Hammond and some of the bravest undergraduates in Yale history had been able to discover which passage led to the Skull and Bones tomb years ago. It was how Wilkie and his men planned to rescue their president without anyone on the surface knowing, and Robert Todd Lincoln was their guide.

"Which way, Bob?" asked the Secret Service chief at a crossing.

"Hold here!" called Robert, forcing the men to stop. Scattered across this central hub were hundreds of capsule-shaped objects that glistened like amber under the men's flashlights.

"What the devil?" asked Wilkie. "Did someone try to Hansel-and-Gretel his way through this place?"

"John, step away!" Robert shouted. He was terrified of the effect Wilkie's cigar might have on the objects. As he crouched and put on some white kid gloves, Robert asked, "Can you give me your knife?" Using Wilkie's puukko, Robert studied the capsules while the chief and his agents watched impatiently.

"Mr. Lincoln, whatever they are, I'm sure we can hopscotch our way through this."

Robert's attention was elsewhere. The objects were the same shape and size as medicine capsules, only with a sickly color like brown mustard. Robert considered cutting one of them in half until he spotted specks of dirt sticking to their underside. He then noticed a waxy sheen left behind on his gloves and knife.

Robert froze.

"Enough of this," huffed Wilkie. "Mr. Lincoln, I'm stepping through."

"John," Robert choked out, "this is the superweapon."

Shocked, Wilkie shined his trembling flashlight on the capsules and backed away slowly. "What are these, Mr. Lincoln?"

"They're time-dissolving capsules," spoke Robert. "Tablets coated with a material that reacts instantly to air. In a matter of time, the coating will dissolve and expose whatever material is inside. If they contain what I think they do, the explosion would surge through the steam tunnels, killing all of us. I don't believe it." He gasped. "They found a way to turn the whole university into a weapon."

As the men stared speechlessly at one another, Robert whipped out a handkerchief and started collecting the yellow capsules.

"What are you doing!" hollered Wilkie. "Are you trying to get us killed?"

"No, I'm trying to save us all! I can neutralize the reaction by putting the capsules into a desiccator. The Kent Laboratory should have plenty of them."

"That laboratory is a fortress! You'll get killed from three directions if you try to enter it."

"The Peabody Museum, then." Robert stopped working and looked up at the confused men around him. "Don't just stand there. Help me!"

"You heard the man!" Wilkie ordered. One by one, the agents closest to Robert took off their coats and crouched down. "Sorry, Jimmy, but you'll have to surrender your hat." The chief took Agent Sloan's boater hat, wiped the sweat from it, and threw it into the ring for the men to put their capsules into.

"Gloves! Gloves!" cautioned Robert.

"Mr. Wilkie!" shouted Agent Barker from afar. "We can't get close enough!"

"I know!" Wilkie grumbled. The chief chewed his cigar and came to a decision. "Bowen, Murphy: You two are going to the Skull and Bones tomb with me. Here, give me that dynamite. . . . The rest of you, help Mr. Lincoln with his cleanup and escort him wherever he needs to go."

"Aye, chief," they answered.

Robert looked up from the ground. "John, are you sure you'll be able to rescue the president with only two agents?"

"Are you mad, man? I'm going, too!" Wilkie shouted, pointing his gun to his own heart.

"John, do you even know how to get to the Tomb?"

After an embarrassingly long silence, Wilkie responded, "Well, are you going to tell me or not?"

Back on the surface, the Steam Department building was under siege. Although Airship One continued to rain death from above, the twenty Buffalo Soldiers on the ground continued their valiant defense against relentless opposition.

One of these brave warriors was James "Bell Bottom Jack" Jackson.

"Soldier!" shouted Robert Todd Lincoln.

Sergeant Jackson turned around to see fifteen men race up the staircase. "What is it, Mr. Lincoln?"

"We need to get into the Peabody Museum," he panted. "Can your men cover us?"

"Whoa . . . Mr. Lincoln, you don't want to go there. That place is a hornet's nest! The president's son is in there."

Robert nearly dropped the bundle of capsules he was carrying. "They found him?"

"Where is he?" asked Agent Sloan, whose boater had never looked so filthy.

"He's tied up in the basement. One of our men saw him through the windows when we tried to flank the museum. We couldn't get to him, but we've notified the major. He's already dropping men to take the building." Robert and his bodyguards looked out the window to see twenty, maybe thirty soldiers descending onto the museum.

"Mr. Lincoln!"

Agents Sloan and Wheeler pulled Robert away from the window just as two bullets whizzed past his head.

"If you need to get in there, it's not going to be pretty," warned Sergeant Jackson. "A race through those doors will be like charging Fort Wagner."

"What about the Kent Laboratory?" asked Wheeler.

"We can't help you there. My men are needed to cover the major's assault. Just wait a few minutes, and the museum will be ours."

"Sergeant, we have no time! We found the weapon of the enemy." Robert lifted his bundle. "The museum is the only place we can neutralize it."

After thinking this over, Sergeant Jackson blew a brass whistle. Soldiers stationed throughout the building rushed toward him while he signaled Airship One with his flashlight. "If that's the case, you're coming with us, Mr. Lincoln."

Robert and the Secret Service agents nodded and waited.

And waited.

And then . . .

BRRRRRRRAAAAAWWWWRWRRRMRMRMMRM-RMMMMM!

The enemy gunfire stopped. The Buffalo Soldiers charged out of the building with Robert Todd Lincoln surrounded by Secret Service agents behind them. More soldiers slid down lines onto the museum like spiders.

BRRRRRRRAAAAAWWWWRWRRRMRMRMMRM-RMMMMM!

The charging cavalrymen opened fire while the soldiers on the roof broke through the museum's windows. Airship One flashed its searchlights through the building, exposing its terrified occupants to sharpshooter fire.

BRRRRRRRAAAAAWWWWRWRRRMRMRMMRM-RMMMMM!

The Ninth Cavalry reached and breached the museum's main entrance, destroying its barricades with the butts of their rifles. As Robert rushed into the building alongside his protectors, his heart slowed to a near stop. He was completely unprepared for the awful yet awe-inspiring universe of battle being waged inside the Peabody Museum.

Robert watched in stunned silence as the Buffalo Soldiers operated on the museum like gifted surgeons. Every single shot was perfectly timed to Airship One's mighty horn. Crystals and precious metals glittered with gunfire. The soldiers took positions behind mineral displays and dinosaur bones with clockwork precision. Four men opened fire from behind the skeleton of an ancient sea turtle more than thirteen feet high. Some enemies were shot through rows and rows of glass cases. Others were ambushed by Buffalo Soldiers hidden behind massive brontosaurus bones. One villain was shot in front of a claosaurus display, splattering his blood all over the broken lizard. Another enemy suffered the indignity of being crushed by a giant octopus suspended above him. Room by room, floor by floor, the battle moved through the building while Robert Todd Lincoln and the Secret Service raced to the basement. They had a superweapon to disarm and the president's eldest son to rescue.

But who would be downstairs waiting for them? Would it be a bound and gagged Bob Taft, or would it be the cruel gunmen who abducted him?

It was both.

Chapter XXVIII

Skull and Bones

A deep rumble shook Skull and Bones Hall, wiping the smile from Basil's face. *"C'était quoi ça?"* he asked his henchmen.

Realizing that help had come at last, Taft regained his senses and let his blood cool. He leaned back in his wooden chair and innocently tapped his chest with his fist. "Excuse me," he added, hoping to pass the recent rumble as indigestion.

It did not work.

Unnerved, Basil stood up and whispered to the guard with the bandaged hand. As the gunman left the room, the anxious gentleman glanced at the grandfather clock in the dining hall. He compared its time to the magnificent pocket watch on his waistcoat.

Taft's eyes focused like binoculars on the silver timepiece. "That's a very interesting pocket watch you've got there."

"Yes, it is," Basil said impatiently.

"You mind telling me where you got it?"

"Mr. President, we already gave your wife an anniversary present," snapped the gentleman. "Clearly, it did not make a strong enough impression. Next time, I will simply suggest some more arsenic."

The entire world around William Howard Taft slowed and dimmed. "What did you say?" he whispered.

Basil scowled. "How did a simpleton like yourself ever get elected president? While I am impressed you felled our android and discovered our experiment in Alaska, I attribute that more to our failings than to your mental faculties."

"What did you say about my wife?" Taft repeated slowly and clearly.

"Mr. President," a bullying Basil smirked, "do you think it was coincidence that your wife fell ill so soon into your tenure? Your Secret Service chief discovered the bomb we planted at the White House for your inauguration.[37] We had no choice but to change our tactics once you assumed the presidency."

"What did you do to my wife?"

An amused Basil Zaharoff grinned menacingly and swaggered between the silver skull and the portrait of Taft's father. "Mr. President, your nation should not have stepped upon the world's stage so unprepared to play the greatest game. Kingdoms and countries are commodities where I come from. All my employers did was challenge you to a friendly game of chess. And in my experience, when facing an opponent who does not know how to play, you simply rob him of his queen."

---

37 Archibald Willingham Butt, letter to Clara Butt, 27 February 1910, *Taft and Roosevelt: The Intimate Letters of Archie Butt, Military Aide*, Vol. I, 291–292.

Taft twitched his mustache, and then he attacked.

The president shoved the dining table forward with both hands, knocking Basil and two of his guards to the floor. As the third thug raised his shotgun, Taft seized the silver skull and lobbed it at the man as if it were opening day at National Park. The shining orb hit the gunman like a cannonball to the face, sending him crashing into the grandfather clock behind him. Both the man and the clock fell silent. Taft then leaped across the table for Zaharoff, but the coward fled through the great hall's double doors. The two gunmen on the ground scurried to their feet and aimed their weapons, but Taft got the drop on them. He landed heavily against both men, forcing them back to the ground. While crushing one of the thugs under his weight, Taft seized the other by the throat and smashed his head against the table like a glass bottle. The gunman's neck snapped instantly.

It was at this point that the guard with the bandaged hand hurried back into the room. As Taft looked up at him amidst his broken enemies, the gunman gasped out, "*Mon dieu!*" The president rushed at the man, carrying one of his fallen adversaries as a shield. The assassin raised his shotgun and fired, but his former colleague absorbed the blast. Panicking, the gunman fired a second time. Taft's human shield exploded like a piñata, spraying the president with human gore but not nearly enough buckshot to stop him. The blood-covered president seized the gunman before he could fire again, snapped his wrist, and then lifted him off the ground by his crotch.

On the other side of the double doors, Basil listened fearfully as the gunman's screams raised in a sickening crescendo. Taft, having just subjected his nemesis with the bandaged hand to the dreaded "Skull and Bones," hurled his opponent through the doors, knocking them both open. Basil backed away in horror as the blood-splattered president stared down his adversary with determined, Yale blue eyes.

Taft lunged at Basil, but the villain rushed into a closet and slammed it shut just as the president reached its doorknob. Locked! Enraged, Taft punched the door repeatedly, trying to break it open with such intensity that he did not notice Secret Service Agents Bowen and Murphy as they rushed into the Tomb. They were just as stunned by the carnage inside its halls as their chief when he arrived.

"Jesus Christ . . ." said Wilkie, looking over the heroic mess Taft had made of his enemies. "What the hell happened in here?"

"The door!" Taft pleaded, completely oblivious to the buckshot lodged in his hip. "Someone open the door!"

Wilkie walked to the president and unloaded his revolver at the closet, destroying its lock and likely killing anyone inside it. "That should do it," he assured, chomping on his cigar as the president ripped the door off its hinges.

Alas, there was nothing inside the closet but mounds of garbage and a revolving bookcase that disappeared into a darkened tunnel. Basil Zaharoff had escaped.

"No!" Taft cried. He tried squeezing inside the narrow passage, but it was impossible. "Someone get in there!" Taft ordered.

"Mr. President, are you hurt?" asked Wilkie. The president was covered with blood.

"No! I'm fine," Taft insisted.

"Good." Wilkie and his agents seized the president and forced him out of the building.

"What are you doing?" Taft resisted. "That man! We need to capture him!"

"Mr. President, we're getting you out of here. The superweapon is real! Bob found it in the tunnels."

"He did?" asked Taft, stunned. "What was it?"

"I don't know! Whatever it is, Mr. Lincoln has it taken care of."

"What about my son!"

"Mr. President, no matter where he is, *you're* leaving! Boys!"

Wilkie's agents forced the Tomb's heavy doors open and raced with the president into the epic battle outside. The Peabody Museum was secured and Airship One had just evacuated the last of the soldiers there. However, there was still heavy fire coming from the Kent Laboratory, forcing Wilkie and his agents to push the president back against the Tomb's front doors.

"What happened?" gasped Taft. "This was supposed to be a covert mission!"

"It was," said Wilkie, reloading his revolver, "but things got louder than a—"

"Will! John!" The men looked across the street to see Robert Todd Lincoln and his three bodyguards racing toward the Tomb.

"Bob!" called the president. "How did you get here?"

"We took the tunnels. Will, your son is safe! He was in the basement of the museum!"

"My boy . . ." Taft's eyes watered. "Is he all right?"

"Yes! He's completely unhurt! He's already aboard the zeppelin."

"What about the weapon?" asked Wilkie.

"We took care of it! It's neutralized and aboard the airship.

However, there may be more capsules in the tunnels. We had no time to search them all. We need to leave!"

"Can we go the way you came?"

"Trust me, chief. You don't want to take the route we did." Agent Sloan had been shot through the hand and Agent Wheeler was bleeding from his arm and shoulder.

"They're getting desperate," said Robert, whose jacket was frayed by bullets. "They're converging on the Tomb from all over the campus."

"Are there any buildings the zeppelin can pick us up from?"

"Not anymore," said Wheeler.

"All right, all right! I'll just signal Archie to drop some ropes."

"That won't work," Taft corrected. "I can't climb ropes."

Wilkie took a long puff from his cigar. "I guess we'll have to opt for plan B then." The chief looked up at the enormous zeppelin and blew a whistle. After a small light flashed from its communications room, Wilkie signaled the airship in Morse code using his flashlight.

"Major Butt?"

"Yes, sergeant."

"We just received a signal from Chief Wilkie. The president is safe at the Tomb, but we cannot extract him. He's requesting we use plan B."

Under different circumstances, Major Butt would have cringed after hearing this. However, since his zeppelin was leaking hydrogen and each passing second meant life or death for the president, he had no time for anything but action.

"Very well." He turned to his crew in the airship's bridge and gave the order: "Plan B!"

Airship One changed its course and quickly moved toward Grove Street Cemetery. As it descended, the skipper used its mighty horn to send a message loud and clear throughout New Haven:

"__ . . ."

Chapter XXIX

"That's my cue."

George Robinson put on his driving goggles and raced the president's 1909 Pierce-Arrow limousine to the Skull and Bones tomb. Just like the massive airship in the distance, the fine auto had been recently repainted black.

Several gunmen opened fire at Robinson as he came barreling down High Street, but the driver had no reason to be afraid. Not only had the president's car been fitted with bulletproof glass and armor plating, but its driver had been personally assured by Attorney General Wickersham that no policemen would pull him over for speeding. That was all Robinson needed to unleash the daredevil inside him.

The car raced through Chapel Street and screeched to a stop in front of Skull and Bones Hall. As he honked his horn, Airship One used its searchlights to dazzle the remaining riflemen, distracting them from the auto.

"Time to fly, Mr. President!" Robinson shouted through the melee.

"Right on time." Wilkie smiled. The Secret Service agents rushed Taft and Robert inside the limousine and shielded them with their bodies while Wilkie climbed into the passenger seat. "Move!" he ordered, and the car accelerated toward Grove Street Cemetery.

In the backseat, Taft had three agents on top of him. "I can't breathe back here!" he shouted to Robert, who could not even speak. Agents Jervis and Wheeler had Mr. Lincoln pressed against his car seat so tightly that he could not keep his hand on his father's pocket watch. Throughout the ride, he flailed his right arm desperately.

"Shotgun!" Wilkie shouted. Agent Sloan handed his boss a shotgun from the backseat. As Robinson raced the auto toward the zeppelin, Wilkie opened fire on every gunman he could see. Once his last cartridge was spent, Wilkie tossed the weapon from the car and shouted, "Machine gun!"

As Bowen and Murphy handed Wilkie his heavy Colt "potato digger" from the backseat, the remaining gunmen throughout Yale rushed to the enormous Egyptian gateway of Grove Street Cemetery. Since it was no longer safe for the Ninth Cavalry to fire from the descending zeppelin, their jubilant enemies thought they had the airship beaten. However, the truth was that Wilkie could not have been happier to see so many adversaries converging at the end of High Street. He chomped on his cigar and blasted away with his machine gun, reaping a bountiful harvest of condemned men for the graveyard. Almost all the villains fell when Robinson sped through the sandstone arch into the cemetery. Airship One was nearly touching the ground, and the daredevil behind the wheel knew he had to time things perfectly.

But then, just as the auto was about to race up the zeppelin's cargo ramp, a gunman behind a tombstone fired a single shot at Chief Wilkie. The bullet went straight for Wilkie's heart, and bounced off his armored flask. The precaution saved his life but unfortunately sent him sideways into Robinson, causing the driver to lose control. The startled chauffeur knew that if he crashed his car, the fires would engulf Airship One, killing everyone.

Fortunately, Robinson managed to safely skid a few feet away from the zeppelin. Its cargo hatch was still open, but the whole airship was slowly ascending.

"INSIDE!" screamed Wilkie.

The Secret Service agents leaped out of the car and rushed the president up the ramp. However, the airship rose so quickly that the remaining men had no choice but to jump aboard. Robert Todd Lincoln in particular was so winded that he had to be pulled up the ramp. Once he was helped back onto his feet, it appeared that everyone was on the airship safely: the president; Mr. Lincoln; Chief Wilkie; Secret Service Agents Sloan, Wheeler, Jervis, Bowen, and Murphy; and a relieved George Robinson.

But then, Robert felt inside his pocket to find only a handkerchief. He looked down and watched in horror as his father's pocket watch slid down the ramp. As the airship shot skyward, the timepiece disappeared over the edge and into darkness.

The pocket watch was gone.

Fortunately, Wilkie dove across the floor and caught the timepiece just as it slipped off the edge, nearly taking the chief with it.

"Can someone help me!" he shouted with half his body out of

the airship. Wilkie watched in terror as, with these words, his lit cigar tumbled over Grove Street Cemetery.

The Secret Service agents grabbed their man by his legs while President Taft personally pulled his bodyguard back onboard Airship One by his belt. His hat was missing and his thinning hair was a mess, but Chief Wilkie was alive.

And holding a magnificent pocket watch, its lid open for the world to see.

The chief swaggered over to a disbelieving Robert Todd Lincoln and handed him the golden timepiece.

"I believe this is yours, Mr. Lincoln."

Robert was reunited with his father's pocket watch and, seconds later, an overjoyed President Taft embraced his rescued son.

The New Haven raid of 1911 was a success.

Chapter XXX

The Pullman Conference

June 23, 1911.

The President arose early this morning in spite of the fact that he did not arrive here from New Haven until after midnight, but he slept well on the train. I did not get down to breakfast until late, and I found him in a most uncommunicative mood. I knew that something had happened since last night to upset his equilibrium. It was not long for me to find out . . .[38]

Shortly after the spectacular nighttime battle was over, Major Butt steered a battle-damaged Airship One back to West Point. Although there had been many injuries, not a single member of the academy's triumphant Ninth Cavalry was killed. The

---

38 Archibald Willingham Butt, diary, 23 June 1911, *Taft and Roosevelt: The Intimate Letters of Archie Butt, Military Aide*, Vol. II, 684.

battle, as Taft described it, was a "splendid little victory" for everyone except Professor Moore of the Weather Bureau. That unfortunate fellow spent the next several days deflecting criticism about the "freak summer squall" he failed to predict hitting New Haven Harbor. As for the extensive damage done to Yale campus, the whole affair was resolved quickly thanks to a generous endowment from the Tafts and a surprise donation of nearly a hundred cadavers to the Yale School of Medicine.

Basil Zaharoff, however, remained missing, leaving nothing behind but his briefcase and its mysterious contents. For the entire day, state and federal investigators scoured every yard of Yale campus, every crevice of its steam tunnels, and every darkened corner of Skull and Bones Hall for any clue that might bring them closer to the madman.

The president, meanwhile, reunited with his son, and boarded Robert Todd Lincoln's private train for New York while Major Butt stayed behind to repair the zeppelin. When Taft pulled into the city that afternoon without reporters or fanfare, an incognito Nellie was waiting for him alongside Attorney General Wickersham. Together, the three paid a visit to J. P. Morgan at his library while Wilkie waited outside his study smoking a fresh Meridiana Kohinoor.

That evening, as Major Butt piloted Airship One back to Washington, President Taft departed New York more frustrated than he had ever been in his presidency. Aboard Mr. Lincoln's luxurious Pullman Palace train car, the president had a late-night meeting with his closest aides.

Also, at Nellie's insistence, the president had a terrible secret to share.

"Poisoned!" gasped an outraged Arthur Brooks.

A heartbroken Taft nodded heavily. "Yes. Arsenic, I am so sorry to say." The somber president firmly held his wife's hand as he said this.

"Is there any way this could've come from someone on the White House staff?" Wilkie put to Brooks.

"Absolutely not! Mr. President, Madam President, we have known each other for many years. I can personally assure you that nobody employed at the mansion would ever harm you."

"John, this treachery may not even have occurred in the White House," noted Robert. "With the president and madam president's many travels, there is no telling where this cruel act occurred."

"Could the automaton have done this?" Wilkie suggested with his eyes afire. "Brooks, has that thing ever been allowed near the first lady's food?"

"Please don't call me that," Nellie interrupted. The car fell silent as the first lady took a long breath from her new silver cigarette holder. "I never cared for that term," she puffed.

"Sorry. Madam President," the Secret Service chief corrected.

"According to my husband," she continued, "these conspirators who tried to kill or incapacitate me are the same villains who tried to bomb the White House before we moved in. Mr. Wilkie, who could these people be?"

"Ask George! He'll tell you it's J. P. Morgan and his Guggenheim cronies!"

"John, there is simply not enough evidence to convict them!" fumed Wickersham. "Also, your whole idea of Morgan being in the center of this no longer makes any sense. If our entire government were dismantled as this 'gentleman' intended, Morgan would have just as much to lose in the ensuing panic as anyone.

Besides, I was at Yale *three days* ago to speak at their law school.[39] If our enemies wanted to thwart the government's lawsuit against U.S. Steel, they would have assassinated me. That's a lot easier than abducting the president's son from the White House while simultaneously holding New Haven hostage, wouldn't you say?"

"On that subject, is there anything you were able to learn about this weapon of theirs?" the president asked Mr. Lincoln.

"A little bit. The capsules contained radioactive samples of cesium hydroxide, a chemical compound that reacts violently to water. I think our enemies planned to turn on the university's boilers to trigger them. If they did, the steam would have caused an explosion that would have destroyed several buildings at the university. However, far more dangerous would be the deadly clouds this would have released. Cesium hydroxide is so corrosive that it can eat through glass. If Zaharoff planned to release it as an aerosol, it would have been like covering half of New Haven in lye. Its effects on the population would have been catastrophic."

"Could this material have come from the Morgan-Guggenheim mines in Alaska?

"Possibly. Many of the samples Mr. Hammond and I collected contained radioactive cesium. However, I still don't see why anyone would have gone through the trouble of mining cesium in the Wrangell Mountains when there are plenty of deposits around the world they could have used. I think it has something to do with the radioactive nature of the cesium they found, since the cesium hydroxide used at Yale was radioactive as well. Either way, we should definitely speak to John about this."

---

39 "Wickersham at Yale," *New York Times,* 20 June 1911.

"Oh!" The president sat up so quickly he accidently spilled champagne on himself. "That reminds me! Bob, did you or John see any strange experiments when we were in Alaska?"

"Experiments?" asked a puzzled Robert.

"I don't know. . . ." Taft dabbed the champagne from his suit with Nellie's help. "When I was in the Tomb with that vulture, he said we stumbled upon some kind of experiment in Alaska. Do you know what he was talking about?"

"Will, you know we didn't see anything even remotely resembling that. In fact, I'm surprised he even knew we went to Alaska."

"Could he have been referring to the Tesla transmission?" asked Wilkie. "They said something about recovering bodies, didn't they?"

"That seems probable, but . . ." Robert thought for a moment, and then came to a shocking realization. "Dear lord . . . Will, it was the comet!"

Taft and Nellie looked up from the president's shirt. "You're telling me this was comet vintage?"

Robert jumped out of his seat. "Not the champagne, the experiment! Zaharoff was referring to Halley's comet! The conspirators knew their weapon was an aerosol, so they tested it in Alaska when we passed through the comet to mask its effects! It was a perfect ruse. A once-in-a-lifetime opportunity to test a weapon so terrible that it could potentially destroy an entire city!"

"You knew all this?" asked Wilkie through a cloud of smoke. "You knew a weapon like this was possible?"

"Of course not! I was more concerned about the comet's cyanogen, same as everyone else that year."

"Well then, why did you even go to Alaska? How were you able to accidentally find a secret experiment in the middle of nowhere?"

"I had an unfair advantage, Mr. Wilkie." Robert took out his pocket watch and handed it to the chief. "This watch belonged to my father. I suspected it came from Alaska due to its Russian inscription and thought it might be connected to an atmospheric phenomenon observed over the Wrangell Mountains when we passed through the comet. I was wrong, and possibly on both counts. However, it nevertheless provided us with valuable foreknowledge on the weapon our enemies are using. The blue clouds my contacts observed above the mountains were caused by aerosols of cesium. Likely the same kind that would have destroyed New Haven."

"So, you're saying we can call off the search for little green men in Alaska." Wilkie smirked.

Taft raised his hand. "That was my blunder," he confessed. "Between what Robert told me about the pocket watch and the strange matter with Dr. Tesla, I thought the Morgan-Guggenheim syndicate stumbled upon something in Alaska that was not of this planet. The red planet was a red herring of my own invention." He sulked.

"Our invention," Robert acknowledged.

"Well, even a broken clock is right twice a day." Wilkie snapped the timepiece shut and returned it to its owner. "Mr. Lincoln, you said during our little joyride through Washington that this watch has potentially fantastic powers. If it came from Alaska, is it possible our enemies are harnessing something similar?"

"I don't see how," said Robert. "Even if they assembled all the components this watch is made of, I can't imagine how they built it. This pocket watch is unlike any machine in history. It violates the very principles of thermodynamics."

"Actually," Taft interjected, "I saw Zaharoff sporting a timepiece just like that one. Only his was silver."

There was a pause.

"Well, that's a load off," Chief Wilkie said sarcastically. "Hey, George, I think we finally have something we can nab J. P. Morgan for: conspiring to violate the laws of science."

The attorney general shook his head.

"Mr. President . . ." Robert was trying not to laugh. "I am pretty sure you are mistaken. Superficially, there's nothing special about this watch."

"Just hear me out," said Taft. "His watch had no keyhole; I did not see him wind it once. . . ."

It was evident to everyone in the room who was not a Taft that the president was wasting their time.

". . . And his watch had the number four written 'I-V' in Roman numerals instead of four I's, just like on yours."

Robert went rigid. He flipped open his timepiece to see its Roman numerals depicted precisely as the president described. It was a rarity for clocks made in the nineteenth century. "You're absolutely sure this man wore the same watch?" he asked, alarmed.

"Bob . . ." Taft leaned forward. "I walked into that tomb prepared to murder this villain with the same skull he sent my wife on our anniversary. I did not simply speak with him. I hunted him. I studied how he moved, breathed, and ate for anything I could use to end his life as quickly as possible. So, to answer your question: Yes, he did wear the same watch. Only his timepiece worked."

"My husband is very observant," confirmed Nellie. The first couple smiled at each other and shared a quick kiss.

"Well, bully for you!" Wilkie brimmed with confidence. "So please tell me, Mr. President: What does your killer instinct say the lot of us should do now?"

The president thought long and hard about this. He threw a salted almond in his mouth, chewed it, and then threw another one in. And then another. Finally, after thinking of everything he could, he turned to his most trusted adviser and asked, "What should we do, Nellie?"

Nellie sucked on her cigarette and looked over the waiting men in the room. "Do you have any beer on this train, Mr. Lincoln?"

"Unfortunately, no."

"Damn." With her legs crossed and arms folded, Nellie slowly assembled the next course of action. "What do we know about the enemy combatants at Yale?" she asked Wickersham.

"Not much," he replied with disappointment. "There were no survivors to interrogate. All we have to work with are what the Marshals found on them."

"What types of weapons did they use?" she put to Wilkie.

"Belgian Mausers armed with 7.65mm ammunition. In fact . . ." The chief rummaged through his jacket pocket. "I have one of their bullets. Here." He tossed the cartridge to Brooks. "If you examine its headstamp, you'll see that it was not manufactured in the U.S."

As Brooks looked over the cartridge, the attorney general asked, "Why would someone smuggle bullets into the country they could have easily purchased here?"

"Probably an army whose rifles were already loaded when they arrived," Brooks appraised.

"Exactly," said Wilkie. "Madam President, your son's kidnapping and last night's incursion in New Haven were most likely carried out by a foreign military secretly operating in the U.S."

"Are there any armies besides Belgium that use these weapons?" asked Nellie.

"Only Argentina," replied Brooks. "Can anyone think of a reason the Belgian government would be waging a clandestine war against the United States?"

"I don't think our enemies are working for any government," said Wilkie. "Even if their henchmen had military equipment and training, it sure as hell did not come through in their methods. Kidnapping the president's son, holding a city hostage, and"—the chief bowed his head with respect—"poisoning the head of state's spouse; I'd say that's a crook game to be playing."

"Such cruelty was not out of character for King Leopold II." Nellie glowered. "He deceived the whole world with his vile intentions for the Congo Free State. For all the pomp of the White House, my husband and our children are still but one family. Leopold and his merciless agents slew millions of families in the Congo."

A deathly silence fell over the train car.

"Well, can we stop splitting hairs and agree that these henchmen were soldiers from the Belgian Congo?" asked Wilkie. "They used Belgian rifles armed with Belgian ammunition, and they couldn't fight a pitched battle to save their own lives. With Leopold dead, I imagine he has a whole private army in Africa that is suddenly out of work. Perhaps someone gave them two weeks' notice before putting them on a steamer bound for New Haven Harbor. Mr. President, Mr. Lincoln, you remember those 'gentlemen' from the Tesla transmission. One of them was from Belgium and another from Congo. The writing's on the goddamn wall!"

"Could this man you met in the Tomb have been one of these gentlemen?" asked Robert.

Taft shook his head. "Not those two. When we met, he offered me chocolate." He looked to Wilkie. "French chocolate."

The chief raised his eyebrows and took a great puff from his cigar. "The Gentleman from Paris, I presume."

Taft nodded. "Most likely. But there's more to that. Bob, I think Zaharoff was the specialist Jack told us about. The one who took over in Alaska after he quit. I think he's the emissary in the group. If we capture him, he should be able to implicate everyone in the conspiracy."

"What are you proposing?" asked Wilkie.

Taft looked back to Nellie, but she did not want to answer. She was too afraid to. Wilkie was right, Taft realized. The writing was on the wall.

Or, more specifically, printed out on telegraph tape in a different part of the train.

There was a knock on the door from an adjoining car.

"Come in," said the president.

Agent Jervis entered the opulent train car. Behind him, Taft could see his son eating a hearty meal with four Secret Service agents surrounding him. "How's everything with my boy, Jervis?"

"Mr. President, this just arrived from the U.S. Marshals at Yale. They say it's urgent."

The agent handed Taft a piece of paper:

NEW HAVEN CONN 1127P JUN 22 1911

URGENT! URGENT! URGENT!

MR. PRESIDENT:

MAJOR BREAKTHROUGH. DEAD BUTTERFLY FOUND IN BASIL ZAHAROFF'S BRIEFCASE. ACRAEA LUALABAE ACCORDING TO YALE PROFESSORS. DID NOT COME FROM UNIVERSITY. NATIVE ONLY TO CONGO. NAME TAKEN FROM LUALABA RIVER.

SIDNEY E. HAWLEY US MARSHAL

"It's a good thing you have a wireless telegraph on this train," Agent Jervis said to Robert Todd Lincoln. However, Robert did not hear this. Everyone was focused on Taft, whose face was turning white with each sentence he read.

"Mr. President?" asked Jervis.

Taft's hands were shaking.

Wilkie leaped out of this chair. "Mr. President!" Together with Agent Jervis and all the men in the room, the Secret Service chief assisted the faint president back into his seat.

"Will, what's wrong?" asked an alarmed Nellie.

Taft stared almost deliriously over the faces in the train car until his eyes eventually fell on Robert. "What time is it in England right now?"

"Will, what are you talking about?" asked Lincoln.

"What's got him all riled up?" Wilkie helped himself to the page in the president's hand, but Nellie snatched it and handed it to Brooks.

"Just tell me the time in London."

Stupefied, Robert glanced at his pocket watch, but then remembered it did not work. "It should be early morning there. Why?"

"Just curious," Taft said wearily. "Once we're in Washington, we'll need to get Joseph Conrad on the telegraph." The president looked to his wife and held her small hand. "Nellie, I am so sorry, but we need to change our tactics. The White House is no longer safe. Our children are no longer safe. You are no longer safe. I can no longer sit here waiting until our enemies strike again. It is time I engaged these villains no matter where they are hiding."

An unshakable Nellie tightened her grip. "I will take the children into hiding. The military will protect us." She turned her head. "Mr. Wilkie, while we are under guard, I want you to interview every possible lead we have in this case. After that, you will go to Europe and meet with your secret agent. We need her now more than ever."

The Secret Service chief coughed out a cloud of smoke. "You know about her?" he gasped.

"Mr. Wilkie, Miss Knox works for me. She always has."

The Secret Service chief went stiff, his only movement the string of smoke from his cigar.

Nellie looked back into her husband's worried eyes. "Do what you must," she instructed.

The president nodded and turned to the assembled. "We must go to the Congo."

Chapter XXXI

The Airship Logbook
of Major Archibald W. Butt

August 11, 1911.

We departed Washington, D.C., shortly after nightfall. Our crew consists of the usual hands plus one troop of cavalry from the New Haven operation. Their commanding officer is Captain Charles Young, who was reassigned from Fort D. A. Russell for this mission at the special request of the President. The Captain is also serving as my second-in-command, and I have spent the last few weeks preparing him for the task.

As of this hour, Mr. Lincoln is our only passenger.

There was a serious risk of thunderstorms shortly after we left the city, but Mr. Lincoln assured me the zeppelin could withstand a lightning strike. Nevertheless, I brought the airship to 17,000 feet as a precaution. Thanks to the full moon, we were able to steer through the storm as if the clouds were icebergs.

We just passed New York City on our way to Beverly, where the President is waiting for us.

August 12, 1911.

We arrived at Beverly just before five o'clock. It was still dark and the skies were clear, but I did spot some rainclouds lingering in the west.

After the President bid adieu to Mrs. Taft, he boarded the airship with Sloan, Wheeler, and Jervis of the U.S. Secret Service. The President looked exhausted and I imagine he did not sleep a wink all evening. When I inquired about Mr. Wilkie's absence, Sloan reported the chief was on assignment in San Francisco and would not be joining us.

We departed at daybreak, leaving Mrs. Taft and the first family in the care of nearly one thousand soldiers and sailors patrolling the summer cottage. The family is to be relocated to Fort Banks at the first sign of danger, which I am outwardly confident but secretly hopeful will not happen.

From Beverly, we turned east for Casablanca. And from there, the Belgian Congo.

August 13, 1911.

Egad! What an incredible day!

It all started over breakfast with the President and Mr. Lincoln. We were about halfway across the Atlantic and Captain Young was piloting.

The conversation started with the President renewing his gratitude for the immeasurably thoughtful present Mr. and Mrs. Lincoln gave to the Tafts for their silver wedding. The gift, a truly remarkable and uncanny device, is a freestanding viewing machine similar to a Mutoscope, only far more luxurious than any I had ever seen. Its cabinet was built out of polished mahogany that was rich with engravings and appropriately adorned with silver. When its silver hand-crank is turned, its viewer is treated to a moving picture of the President and Mrs. Taft dancing at their inaugural ball in a seamless, uninterrupted loop.

Had Mr. Lincoln stopped here, he would have won the hearts of the Tafts and their entire family for the rest of their lives. But instead,

Mr. Lincoln chose to push his creative energies to levels more befitting Leonardo da Vinci. The viewing machine also has a Victrola built into it, which is simultaneously operated by the hand-crank. The result is nothing short of one of the most heavenly images I have ever beheld: the President and Mrs. Taft, immortalized in black and white on one of the happiest days of their lives, dancing for eternity to the theme from Mozart's Piano Sonata No. 11 in A major, K. 331, first movement.

Stunning. Simply stunning. If only my mother could have seen this!

After this brief thank-you, the conversation shifted to the more pressing issues awaiting us in the Congo. In addition to the diplomatic crises we could trigger by engaging in hostile actions overseas, there was still the delicate matter of how to hold our international adversaries responsible for their crimes. The President expressed regret over our failure to capture any prisoners for questioning during the New Haven operation, to which I replied that quite a few enemy deaths were revealed to be due to suicide. The President thought about this and asked if there were any nonlethal alternatives to the weapons currently used on the battlefield. I said there were none. He then asked if some could be developed, to which I replied that such an effort, while noble, would run counter to the increasingly industrial nature warfare has been taking.

Mr. Lincoln, however, did not offer an opinion. He simply excused himself and rushed to his workshop, pausing only for the copy of Tom Swift and His Electric Rifle *he left on the table. Hours later, one of our wireless operators reported that Mr. Lincoln had been flooding the radio room with messages all day to and from Nikola Tesla in New York, and that some of their correspondence included phototelegraph images. I went to Mr. Lincoln's workshop to discuss this only to find the door locked and my knocks drowned out by what sounded like classical music. Beethoven's Symphony No. 9, second movement, I believe. Concerned, I went at once to the Oval Office and gave a full report to the President, but he only leaned back in his chair and said: "Let him alone. When Bob gets this way, it's usually for the best of everyone."*

The President was correct.

That evening, I was summoned to the Oval Office for one of the President's private salons. I arrived to find the delighted chief executive sharing a bottle of red wine with Mr. Lincoln. I also noticed one of the soldiers' Browning Auto-5 shotguns resting on the President's desk. When I asked what this was about, the President directed me to a sheet of paper underneath the weapon. It showed designs for a working, patentable invention Mr. Lincoln and Dr. Tesla developed over the telegraph and which Mr. Lincoln built that afternoon using equipment found on the airship.

I am including a facsimile of Dr. Tesla's designs for this remarkable "electric rifle," as well as Mr. Lincoln's description of how the device works:

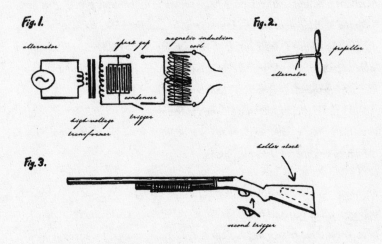

"Dr. Tesla's electric rifle transfers an electric 'bullet' by shooting two wires from the barrel of the shotgun. The projectile itself is a hollow wax bullet containing a spool of wire that uncoils when fired. The wires are separated by insulated coating except at its pointed tip, where two exposed

*needles deliver a debilitating but nonlethal jolt of electricity. The high
voltage is generated using the common form of circuitry for electric sparks
(Fig. 1). To power the device, a modest electric current was obtained from
an alternator attached to one of the airship's propeller shafts (Fig. 2). This
current enters a small transformer that is attached to the Tesla coil in
Fig. 1 to generate the required voltage. A common condenser stores
the transformer current to be fed into the Tesla induction coil. A rifle
trigger (Fig. 3) is used to both shoot the electric bullet and electrify the Tesla
coil by completing the electric circuit. For ease of use, this secondary trigger
can be added alongside the shotgun's existing trigger. Not only does this
allow the electric rifle to operate almost identically to any rifle, but its
wooden stock can be hollowed out to store the necessary equipment to
power it.*

*"Unfortunately, only a single electric bullet can be shot from the rifle
without a reload, which would be a long and cumbersome process this early
into the development stage. However, if fired correctly at a range commensu-
rate to the length of wire inside the bullet, Dr. Tesla's electric rifle should be
able to successfully electrocute an enemy into submission without killing or
destroying them." —Robert T. Lincoln.*

As I said earlier, stunning. Simply stunning.

*But I must go now and try to get some rest. We are expected to arrive in
Morocco within the next few hours.*

August 14, 1911.

We are in Africa.

*Airship One landed in Casablanca at about 3:55 a.m. local time. We
encountered no difficulties and all necessary arrangements were made
by Fred Carpenter, the President's former secretary and now U.S. envoy
to Morocco.*

Mr. Carpenter had some news for us: Mr. Wilkie finished his assignment in San Francisco. The chief met "Colonel" Henry I. Kowalsky, an attorney who briefly worked as a lobbyist for King Leopold II before he exposed the king and his atrocities to the New York American. Mr. Wilkie said Mr. Kowalsky did not have anything particularly useful to share and even fell asleep several times in their meeting, including one time when the two men were crossing a busy street. I can only imagine how frustrating Mr. Wilkie must have found Mr. Kowalsky's narcolepsy during such a time-sensitive moment for our nation.

Nevertheless, Mr. Wilkie was able to take two things from his meeting, both of them potentially bad for us. It appears Leopold had a secret plan for the Congo in the event that his crimes were exposed, and it involved reaping vast amounts of natural resources before the international community could stop him. Unfortunately, it is far too late to curtail this operation since it has already been in motion for nearly a decade. Even worse, Wilkie learned there is no way we can ever know the full extent of this program due to Leopold having burned the entire archives of the Congo Free State in 1908.

In short, we are racing headlong into a conspiracy nearly a decade in the making, spanned across three continents, and involving nothing short of a diabolical aim known only to Leopold II of Belgium, deceased.

August 15, 1911.

A sad day.

We left Casablanca shortly after midnight and spent the entire day crossing the Sahara.

All seemed well until I was on my way to lunch with the President and Mr. Lincoln only to be handed some unhappy news: Major Henry Rathbone has died.

Below is the official report from Hanover, Germany:

"Major Rathbone, who was military aid to President
Lincoln and who, in attempting to defend him on the
night President Lincoln was assassinated, received a
stab wound from John Wilkes Booth, died yesterday
in Hildesheim Asylum for the Criminal Insane. He
was incarcerated for the murder of his wife."[40]

Understandably, the three of us immediately lost our appetite.

*How could anyone have tortured themselves over the murder of
President Lincoln more than Major Rathbone? I can think of no other, not
even Mr. Robert Lincoln. No man in uniform was closer to President
Lincoln that evening, and although he was badly injured, Major Rathbone
never forgave himself for failing to prevent the unfortunate course John
Wilkes Booth charted for our history.*

*It deeply disturbs me to imagine how I, or Mr. Robert Lincoln, or
anyone would have fared if we had been in Major Rathbone's place in that
theater. Would we have suffered the same sorry fate as he did? Would our
fiancée have been as doomed as the blood-splattered Miss Clara Harris that
evening? I sincerely hope and pray not, for after twenty years of madness the
retired Colonel Rathbone brutally murdered his wife with a knife and a
pistol only two days before Christmas. He then turned the knife on himself
and had to be subdued by police, claiming a "stranger" committed the
murder. It was nothing short of a miracle that the couple's children were
not slain.*

*Of all the horrors of this episode, I was always most bothered by how
Rathbone, in his madness, chose a knife and a pistol as his foul instruments:
the same arms John Wilkes Booth carried into Ford's Theatre. Is it possible*

---

40 "Major Rathbone Dies," *New York Times,* 16 August 1911.

Rathbone was driven mad like Macbeth by the visage of these terrible
weapons? Or worse, that after twenty long years of torture, the late Major
Rathbone had finally lost the war in his mind against that American savage
from Ford's Theatre. Back from the dead. For his wife.

But I must stop now. Listening too closely to these echoes from history
will only drive me mad as well. My president is alive and needs my help.
Also, on a day like today, so does Mr. Robert Lincoln. After Captain Young
relieved me for the evening, I found Mr. Lincoln by himself in the main
dining hall. He was standing at attention with his hands behind his back
and his eyes honed on the enormous eagle engraved in wood on the hall's
central wall.

Then again, I do not know if he was focusing on the eagle or the words
written in gold beneath it: "Una natio fatum unum," the ship's motto.
Either way, I have no doubt his mind was absorbed on the grim reminder
we received today about his father's assassination.

August 16, 1911.

We have a serious problem.

The airship is stopped about two hundred miles southwest of Cameroon.
We could be in Boma this evening, but we just learned that our arrangements
for safe passage into the city have collapsed.

Our plan was to enter Boma by boat, which Mr. Wilkie's special agent
secured with the help of two contacts in the Congo Reform Association
known as "Tiger" and "Bulldog." However, we are now told by our contacts
that their associates in Boma have abandoned us. Their reason: fear of the
"King of Beasts," which Tiger and Bulldog explained was a code name for
King Leopold. It sounds like news of Leopold's death has not reached certain
parts of the Belgian Congo. Perhaps deliberately.

Thus, King Leopold's ghost has dealt a severe blow to our mission, since we are left with no viable entry into the city. Fortunately, these associates in Boma know nothing about our mission other than the involvement of Tiger and Bulldog, who are both based in Europe. However, this is little consolation after crossing a desert and an ocean only to be forced to a halt so close to our final destination.

Morale is steady for now, but it could take a turn for the worse pretty quickly.

August 17, 1911.

Still nothing. I have decided to keep the airship at its current position over the Gulf of Guinea. There is a very real possibility that we may have to turn back, and if we must, I need to conserve fuel.

Mr. Wilkie's special agent, Miss Knox, is in talks with Tiger and Bulldog to find an alternate route into Congo that will not interfere with our manhunt for Basil Zaharoff or the "Gentleman from Boma." No other news to report.

Captain Young is doing a fantastic job maintaining morale among the crew. Better than I could have hoped for. While I admit I was skeptical about his addition to the airship, his impeccable conduct has earned him my full confidence.

August 18, 1911.

Still no movement beyond the Gulf of Guinea, but there has been an unusual development over the wireless.

According to Miss Knox, Tiger and Bulldog have offered to put us in touch with a third person known as "the Colossus." The President was outraged when he heard this and threatened to turn back, but Mrs. Taft convinced him otherwise. Apparently, the Colossus wants to examine the butterfly found in Basil Zaharoff's briefcase to determine whether or not we even need to enter Boma to fulfill our mission.

This is most peculiar, but apparently Miss Knox knows something about the Colossus that she is willing to risk her credibility and, I am sorry to say, her career over.

Morale is steady. Again, thanks in large part to Captain Young's stewardship.

August 19, 1911.

We are moving again.

Mr. Lincoln completed his conversation with the Colossus over the telegraph, during which he answered numerous odd questions about the butterfly. He even conducted what appeared to be some sort of chemical test in the wireless room at one point.

The Colossus believes the butterfly found in Basil Zaharoff's briefcase was not a keepsake, but rather a stray insect that flew in there to its death. This means Zaharoff must have been in the native region to this butterfly, the Lualaba River, and recently. Maybe even immediately before the operation in New Haven. The Colossus deduced this because the butterfly was found in the same part of the briefcase where the President said the blood-covered parchment was pulled from. This might also explain why the executive order was written in blood despite there being no injury to the President's son: the parchment came from the Congo as well.

After discussing these findings in a private conference, the President decided that we should bypass Boma altogether and journey directly toward the Lualaba in the heart of the Congo.

We are now flying east-southeast into Africa and are expected to cross into the Congo under the cover of darkness.

August 20, 1911.

The Congo—First Day.

We have officially entered the graveyard that King Leopold's ghost continues to haunt.

We crossed into the Belgian Congo at about four o'clock in the morning. Once we spotted the Congo River in the moonlight, we needed only follow it southeast until we reached the Lualaba River at noon.

It must have rained before we arrived because the vast jungle was cloaked in mist. Flying low at about forty m.p.h., the Lualaba led us on a steady course due south. Captain Young had sixty soldiers on watch with binoculars, but neither they nor I could see through the haze. At 1:30 that afternoon, the President said "enough" and I brought the zeppelin to a halt about one hundred and twenty miles down the river.

During our pause, Mr. Lincoln asked if he could use the observation car to take some air samples. I complied, and Mr. Lincoln braved the extreme heat and humidity to collect whatever he needed from outside the airship. However, before reentering, he spotted what looked like an abandoned station several miles ahead of us. A Corporal Williams confirmed this, so we turned our engines back on and moved down the river to the building. I then descended the airship as low as I could and dropped sixteen men to investigate with Captain Young commanding.

The men did not return until sundown.

According to Captain Young, the abandoned building was a telegraph station whose sole occupant was found dead inside. He was dressed in a Belgian military uniform and had been shot in the back of the head while seated, apparently at work. The body was significantly decayed and the Captain believes it had been exposed for a year. His assessment seems corroborated by a logbook he found underneath the sprawled body. Although covered with dried blood, the book shows that the station's last transmission occurred in the early hours of July 16, 1910: the same date and time as the Tesla transmission. No date of termination was written.

Alarmed by this find, I gave Captain Young and his men the rest of the night off. The Captain declined, preferring to work at the bridge for his evening shift, but the soldiers graciously accepted.

It appears Dr. Tesla was correct when he said there was a mass murder following the transmission he intercepted. Everyone working at the relay stations carrying the message must have been killed. However, assuming J. P. Morgan is indeed the "Gentleman from New York," why would he want to have Nikola Tesla murdered? Morgan was one of Dr. Tesla's most generous financiers at one point. Furthermore, if the Belgians are involved in this conspiracy, why would they kill one of their own soldiers at this station?

Is it possible Mr. Morgan and Mr. Guggenheim made a deal with the devil that we are only beginning to see the full consequence of? If so, what could they possibly have in store for the country worse than what nearly happened at New Haven?

August 21, 1911.

The Congo—Second Day.

Who are these madmen?

The mists cleared this morning and we continued our expedition along the Lualaba River. Before we moved, the President and I asked Mr. Lincoln why he was taking air samples. He said he was testing for cesium in the atmosphere, but found none.

However, that afternoon we stumbled upon something even more disturbing than what we found inside the abandoned telegraph station. There was a vast expanse of jungle, maybe two miles wide, maybe more, that had been completely eradicated of any sign of life. There were no trees, no birds, no animals, no grass. Nothing. Just a lifeless expanse as barren as the Sahara we crossed earlier.

I considered landing the airship in the area, but Mr. Lincoln advised against it. Instead, he asked me to take us skyward to varying altitudes while he took additional air samples. Hours later, Mr. Lincoln asked the President and myself to join him in his laboratory, where he showed us the bright blue band in his spectroscope caused by large amounts of cesium. He added that the cesium, just like the cesium hydroxide our enemies tried to use at New Haven, was radioactive, and that the radiation appeared to jump the closer we moved to the ground. The President asked Mr. Lincoln if such high levels of radiation are dangerous, to which the latter replied he was not sure. He cited Mme. Marie Curie's prolonged exposure to radiation and relative good health as a sign of the contrary. However, he added that our enemies' reliance on heavily radioactive cesium hydroxide is most unusual. He said far more research will be needed to come to a conclusion about the full effects of radiation exposure. However, he said that it seems pretty clear that this vast field of desolation was caused by the same weapon Basil Zaharoff threatened New Haven with.

As such, it appears our enemies were not bluffing. They do possess a weapon capable of not only destroying the population of an entire city, but all surrounding plant and animal life as well. New Haven, beautiful New Haven, was nearly wiped off the map of Connecticut, along with every bird in its skies, every leaf on its trees, and every one of the city's more than 100,000 souls.

Tonight is my evening at the helm, but Captain Young offered to work my shift while I rest. I am most indebted to this man. He has outclassed me on this mission.

August 22, 1911.

  The Congo—Third Day.

  Horror.

  Joseph Conrad was right. The devil is in these jungles. The devil is walking the Earth as a man.

  I saw him.

  We continued down the Lualaba until eleven o'clock this morning, when Sgt. Hazel spotted what appeared to be some sort of private estate.

The house was located several hundred yards from a small dock on the river, but otherwise appeared completely isolated within the jungle.

Since we saw no signs of danger and were nearing the end of the Lualaba, the President insisted that whatever was down in that building was something he wanted to see for himself. I advised the President against this, but he overruled me, insisting that if he did not do something soon, "I might as well not have come." I agreed to the President's request, but only if I personally escorted him to the premises. He accepted, and I descended the airship along the river so that we could approach the dock by ladder.

Before we left the airship, some very serious decisions had to be made about what to do if either the President or Airship One came under fire. We were too far inland for our wireless telegraph to work, and any damage sustained by the zeppelin could make any attempt to leave the jungle impossible. After a heated argument in the Oval Office, the President insisted that only a handful of soldiers should accompany him to the building while the remaining men provided cover from the airship. He also insisted that two of his three Secret Service agents protect Mr. Lincoln and not himself. This angered Mr. Lincoln to the point that he insisted he would not leave the zeppelin, but the President was adamant: "You're coming, Bob." The President then sat at his desk and wrote several letters to be delivered to Mrs. Taft, the Vice President, the Attorney General, and the Secretary of War in case of catastrophe. With this last act, the President exited the airship with Mr. Lincoln, Agents Sloan, Wheeler, Jervis, myself, and sixteen soldiers. Captain Young repositioned the airship above the building as we walked toward it.

The heat hit us like a wall, worse than anything the President said he experienced in the Philippines.

We passed through the trees along a path that appeared to be paved with cobbles, but Mr. Lincoln was the first to notice that the shape and size of these "rocks" resembled human clavicles. One of them cracked under the President's boot, and Mr. Lincoln and I backed away in disgust. The President had crushed the exposed top of a partially buried skull. The entire path to the villa was paved with human bones.

However, there was something far more terrible waiting for us at the building. When our first soldiers emerged through the wilderness, one of them lowered his rifle while the other said, "My God . . ." Human skulls surrounded the doorway to the eerily derelict homestead. "What is this place?" asked Sloan, to which we had no response. The President looked more horrified than I had ever seen him in his life, but nevertheless, he clenched his fists and marched forward, surrounded by bodyguards in the shade of the airship.

I volunteered to personally inspect the building with ten soldiers while those remaining guarded the President and Mr. Lincoln, but the President overruled this. He said it would be best if we all entered the building together, to which I reluctantly agreed. I then signaled Captain Young in the airship with a flag, and he signaled back that we would be covered. With my sword and pistol drawn, I led the way into the abandoned villa, past its skulls, and through its front door.

I had no idea what was waiting for us inside that building. I don't think any of us were prepared. When I charged inside with the President and his protectors, who amongst us was expecting there to be music? At first we thought it was a woman screaming, but we were wrong. It was a soprano singing Schubert's "Gretchen am Spinnrade": a swirling, dizzying song that only made our pulses quicken. We raced past vases, paintings, sheet music, and an expansive butterfly collection that stretched across every wall in the building until we at last found the source of the music: a Victor phonograph with a large black horn.

A butterfly flapped past the phonograph's spinning disk and across the face of the thin, mustached man seated next to it.

"Don't move!" I shouted to the figure. The soldiers raised their weapons and surrounded him, but the man did not blink or flinch.

The President shoved past his Secret Service agents. "Let me see him."

"Stand up!" I ordered, but the man was unresponsive. He just stared ahead with a vacant look in his eyes. However, I could see the man was alive. His head had a slight sway to it. I soon realized that it was because he was listening not to me, but to the music.

The President pushed me aside and took a good look at the seated man. He then put his hands on his hips and asked, "Is this your house?"

At last, the thin man moved, slowly lifting his head upward. He had a strange unevenness to his movement, almost like a doll or a puppet. But as he looked at the President's face, one could see the life return to him. "Mr. President!" He smiled.

The President scowled at the man. "Search every single room in the house," he said to me. "I want evidence linking this man to New Haven. Maps, papers . . . anything."

"Soldiers!" I instructed. The men filed out, but I had two soldiers stay behind to guard the door.

"You too, Archie," said the President.

"Me?" I asked, surprised.

"I want to have a word with him," he said in a firm tone.

I obeyed his wish and joined the soldiers in their search. As I walked out of the room, I could hear the President say, "Look around, Bob."

For nearly an hour, my men and I searched the premises. We emptied desks and dresser drawers, finding nothing but summer garments, music compositions, and page after page of poetry. I must say I was struck by the man's impressive collection of classic texts and fine wines. The home was everything one would expect of a gentleman: neat, proper, and completely devoid of business. There was nothing useful to be found and, to everyone's shock, nobody else in the building.

I returned downstairs to find the President seated closely to the man, leaning forward in his chair and having what sounded like a most unusual disagreement:

"You don't understand. We would never hurt you. The United States is a friend of ours," the man said in a faint voice.

"You don't know anything about America or what we stand for."

"You stand for Leopold! You always have!"

"Your king was a heartless madman."

"Mr. President, you and I were friends before we even knew each other. Your president, the great Chester Arthur, made the Belgian Congo possible."

"Leopold's agents deceived him. Just like they deceived the whole world."

"Mr. President, we no longer live in secrecy. The truth has freed us! At last, we can embrace each other as friends. As brothers! If only . . ."

Agents Sloan and Wheeler seized the man mid-lurch and forced him back into his seat.

I had no wish to interrupt the President, so instead I walked over to Mr. Lincoln. He was standing by himself looking out the room's lone window, clutching a long, white paintbrush in his fist. My eyes moved across the countless butterflies framed on the wall and the few fluttering through the air. An orange one perched on an easel by the window looked identical to the butterfly that brought us here. There was no doubt in my mind: Basil Zaharoff had been in this house, and possibly in this very room. But why?

One thing that unsettled me about the paintings in the estate was how they all portrayed the same image: smiling children chasing butterflies beside a garden with a picket fence. The artist, whom I gathered was the man we found listening to Schubert, had an unusual way of painting children. Their smiles were too broad. It almost looked like they were missing lips.

"What madness is this?" I asked Robert Todd Lincoln.

"Leon Rom," Mr. Lincoln replied.

"Who?"

He snapped the paintbrush. "Kurtz."

The President, who heard the crack, turned his head. "What is it, Bob?" he asked.

Mr. Lincoln did not reply.

"Bob?"

Curious about what had Mr. Lincoln so distracted, I looked out the window to see the same field depicted in so many paintings throughout the house. However, the white picket fence around the garden was made out of arms. Human arms. No larger than a child's

Butterflies were resting on their fingertip bones.

I covered my mouth while a startled Mr. Lincoln jumped backward. I looked over to see the poor man wiping his hands frantically. I moved to his aid only to step on the paintbrush he dropped, crushing it beneath my boot. I was horrified to discover, just as Mr. Lincoln had, that the paintbrush he snapped was made out of bone. We backed away in disgust and accidentally bumped into the President, who had been standing behind us with the most profound sadness in his face. He stared speechlessly out the window, just as we had, while Faust's Gretchen continued at her spinning wheel on the phonograph disk.

The President turned around in a fury. "Everyone out of the building! Archie, get us airborne! Once we're high enough, I want you to bomb this hellish place off the map!"

"What about this schmuck?" asked Sloan, referring to Leon Rom.

"He's staying RIGHT THERE!" Taft spit with rage. "EVERYONE OUT! NOW!"

And so, like that, we left the Gentleman from Boma to his music. We hurried out of the villa and I signaled Captain Young with my red flag, indicating that we had to leave immediately. Just as we planned, he descended the airship until it was nearly touching the trees and dropped its *ladders. Once we were onboard, I rushed straight for the bridge and told the surprised Captain to send all men to their bombing stations.*

We climbed to an altitude of 1,000 feet, at which point I gave the order to drop four 100-pound bombs of high explosives on the building. All four bombs hit their target, obliterating the sinister place out of existence. Once the fires died and our mission was complete, I turned the airship around so we could begin the long journey back to Washington. A tall plume of black smoke lingered behind us like a storm cloud until it at last slipped beneath the horizon.

I did not speak to the President nor Mr. Lincoln for the rest of the evening. However, as I walked to the wireless room, I could hear something emanating from the Oval Office. It was Mozart, sweet Mozart, coming from that lovely machine Mr. Lincoln built for the Tafts to remind them of happier moments. The President clearly needed it now.

Alone in the corridor, I collapsed to my knees and wept.

Chapter XXXII

"Ye Olde Cock Tavern."

"... Honestly, how do the Brits come up with these names? Do they just look out the window and name the first thing they see?"

"Wilkie, please just stop talking," begged Robert Todd Lincoln.

"I'm just saying that if God's so determined to have us killed in a pub, I would've much rather preferred dying at the Bucket of Blood."

Wilkie sucked anxiously at his cigar as he spied from the third-floor windows of the tall, narrow tavern. Airship One was cloaked safely behind a white veil of snowfall. More than a dozen U.S. Secret Service agents were patrolling the sidewalks of Fleet Street. Columns of British sharpshooters were perched along the London rooftops. Ambassador Bryce had been a great friend to provide so much security for the day's meeting, even though there was still no sign of "the Colossus." Frustrated, the Secret

Service chief took another swig from his nearly empty flask of explosive scotch.

There were three men seated at the wooden table behind Wilkie. Among them was Major Butt, who had not quite been the same since his encounter with the Gentleman from Boma. The officer sat upright, stiff as a board, with a tall glass of cold water in front of him. Across the table was Robert Todd Lincoln, who poured himself what must have been his fourth cup of tea. And seated between both men was President Taft, who had a frothy pint of ale and a platter of beer-battered fish and chips in front of him. However, even when faced with a house special so appetizing, he could not touch his food.

Taft had plenty of things to be worried about at the moment. His wife and children remained under military protection. Two assassins nearly blew up his train as he crisscrossed the country last autumn.[41] Theodore Roosevelt appeared all but certain to challenge Taft to the Republican nomination, effectively ending his presidency. And after six months of hunting, Wilkie's agents were no closer to capturing Basil Zaharoff than they were after they found the butterfly in his briefcase.

But for the moment, the president's chief concern was the leather harness he was strapped to. Its rope extended out the window behind him and disappeared up to the zeppelin.

"I can't eat like this," Taft said, irked. "I feel like a worm on a hook. That's no way to enjoy fish and chips."

"I'm sorry, Mr. President, but after your experiences at Yale and the Congo, Mrs. Taft insisted that we come up with a speedier method of getting you aboard the airship."

---

41 "Dynamite Mines Menaced Taft," *New York Times,* 17 October 1911.

"What's wrong with the ladder?"

"The airship's too high for the ladder. And if I may speak freely . . ." The chief tapped his ash out the window. "You don't climb very fast."

The president squirmed under his leather restraints. "Untie me, Wilkie. This unpleasant contraption is as batty as your Indian rope trick."[42]

Wilkie scratched his mustache. "I think that's a good name for it! What do you think, Mr. Lincoln?"

"Don't talk to me. I had nothing to do with this inane invention."

"Enough of this!" said Taft. "If there is an attack, I refuse to have the airship reel me in like a cod. The American people deserve more from their president." The prizefighter detached the metal hook from his harness and ripped its leather straps off. "Finally!" he breathed. Taft stretched his back and then immediately went to work on his meal.

"So much for plan B." Wilkie shrugged, holstering his weapon. "Any other bright ideas?"

"I have an opinion to share."

"Oh?" munched the president. "And what would that be, Bob?"

Robert set down his teacup and wiped the droplets from his beard. "Don't you think it would be wiser if we knew more about this 'Colossus' before meeting with him? We don't even know his real name."

"*You* don't know his real name," the chief corrected.

---

42 John E. Wilkie ("F. S. Ellmore," pseudonym), "It Is Only Hypnotism," *Chicago Daily Tribune,* 9 August 1890.

"But neither do you!" Robert protested. "Nor Major Butt, nor the president!"

"Miss Knox knows the Colossus quite well, and that's good enough for me," observed Wilkie. "And honestly, I'm more concerned for their safety than ours at the moment."

"Are they both coming tonight?"

"Just the Colossus," replied Wilkie.

Robert removed his spectacles and rubbed his forehead with worry. "Do we at least know what this person looks like?"

"Of course! He's tall, athletic, has blue eyes, fair hair, and supposedly sports a champion mustache."

"I like him already!" Taft smiled from his plate.

"You sure Miss Knox wasn't describing her ideal husband?" nagged Agent Sloan.

"Don't speak about a fellow agent that way," Wilkie rebuked. "None of you would have made it into Congo without her hard work."

"I'm sorry, Chief Wilkie."

"Don't be sorry. Be outside the door from now on."

A dispirited Sloan bowed his head. "Yes, sir."

"Oh! And would you mind placing a small order downstairs?" asked Taft.

"Not at all, Mr. President. What would you like?"

"Some tartar sauce and some lemon. And a Welsh rabbit."

"Certainly, Mr. President. Anything else?"

"Another pot of tea, please," spoke Robert. "Darjeeling."

"As you wish, sir. Major?"

Major Butt shook his head, so Agent Sloan looked to Wilkie.

"And two hard-boiled eggs," the chief added. "And tell them to be snappy about it."

"Right away, chief."

Sloan closed the door and his footsteps disappeared down the staircase, leaving the four men on the fourth level of Ye Olde Cock Tavern.

And so they waited.

And waited . . .

And waited until the skies darkened and London's streetlights turned on. The impatient Secret Service chief looked down both ends of Fleet Street, but there was no Colossus in sight. Wilkie took one last puff from his cigar and then flicked it outside. It fell forlornly to the sidewalk until it was snuffed out by snowflakes. "He's not coming." He sighed.

"Could Miss Knox have failed us?" asked Robert.

"I don't know, but I sure as hell hope she's all right."

Major Butt had a terrible thought for a second, but then shook his head. "She's fine."

Wilkie turned from the window just as Agent Sloan opened the door.

"What is it?" he asked.

"Just this chump," said Sloan. The agent held the door open for a server carrying a tray with their order.

Wilkie looked out the window one more time, and then resigned himself to defeat. "You have hard-boiled eggs there?" he asked.

"To be perfectly honest, my good sir, I don't know! I imagine they could be soft-boiled," said a warm voice in a cheery Scottish accent.

All four men looked up to see a snow-covered stranger with broad shoulders, blue eyes, and one spectacular mustache.

Chapter XXXIII

The Colossus

Wilkie raised an eyebrow and smirked slyly. "If I knew *you* were coming, I would have brought my copy of *A Study in Scarlet*."

Major Butt and Robert Todd Lincoln were speechless.

"Sir Arthur!" gasped Taft. "You work here?"

"Well, not regularly, Mr. President!" A merry Sir Arthur Conan Doyle laughed. "I am sorry I'm late, but I was delayed by the snow. Oh! Thank you!" Major Butt relieved the knight of his burdens and assisted him to his seat. "You see, I did not want to attract any attention by taking the streets, so I entered the building by means of the Temple Church passage. Once I was inside, why, I saw a poor fellow trying to carry this tray up that darkened staircase, to which I asked: If someone doesn't help him, then what's come of this country? So, I volunteered to carry the tray, a gentleman up the stairs opened the door, and here I am! Humbly your servant . . . for the time being, at least!" Doyle grinned.

His cheerful eyes and playfully selfless demeanor brought smiles to every face at the table. President Taft was particularly impressed by the man's strong build and wide mustache. "We appreciate your assistance on this matter, Sir Arthur."

"Please, Mr. President, call me Arthur!"

"And what about 'Colossus'?" Taft teased as he twisted lemon over his Welsh rabbit.

The deputy lieutenant–author–doctor–poet–playwright–athlete–humanitarian–dog owner smiled bashfully. "Yes, that's a nickname my friend Mr. Barrie calls me. We have a cricket team called the Allahakbarries. All very good chaps. However"—his tone shifted—"I can assure you that my more recent use of that alias is due to the seriousness of the matter at hand. Mr. Casement and Mr. Morel, whom I believe you know as 'Bulldog' and 'Tiger,' operated with the same secrecy when they exposed King Leopold's crimes in the Congo."

The president scooted to the edge of his seat. "You know why we went there?"

"Yes. Violet told me everything."

"Excuse me?" asked Robert.

Arthur looked stunned. As if he had just committed a dreadful mistake. "Violet Jessop! The young lady working for you! Is she not one of your agents?"

All eyes turned to Wilkie, who had a fresh cigar in his mouth. "I'm sorry to say this, Mr. President, but Miss Knox no longer works for me. Her name is Violet Jessop and she's been working for the White Star Line since 1910."

The president knew there was not a shred of truth to this. "No, she hasn't!"

"Exactly!" Wilkie lit a match, filling his eyeglasses with flame. After he lit his cigar, he brushed his finger against the side of his nose.

"How much did she tell you?" asked Taft, turning back to the Colossus.

"Well, aside from what I now *assume* was her real name, just about everything."

"Everything?" asked Robert.

"I believe so, Mr. Lincoln. She even briefed me about your timely dilemma! I understand you carry a most unusual pocket watch."

"Yes, I do."

The author's whiskers twitched. "May I see it?"

Robert Todd Lincoln looked at the four faces staring at him with curiosity. Deep down, he hoped and prayed that Sir Arthur Conan Doyle could put this American mystery to rest where it began: in a pub in London. Robert reached into his coat and pulled out a thick handkerchief, which he unfolded across the table. Its magnificent gold contents remained as captivating and mystifying as always.

Sir Arthur produced a pipe and began to pack it with tobacco. "Has it always been like that?" he asked Robert.

"Been like what?"

"Closed." Doyle smiled as he lit his pipe.

"Oh!" Robert carefully opened the timepiece and set it down on the handkerchief, revealing its silent dial and mysterious inscription for the author:

Сдѣлано

въ

Америкѣ

Doyle started puffing his pipe and gently picked up the timepiece. His careful hands and sharpened eyes ran over the silent device as if the doctor was examining a patient. "Ah, so you're an *American,* are you?" he playfully spoke to the timepiece. He then followed its gold chain to its shimming watch fob, which appeared to interest him greatly.

"You've examined its works, correct?" he asked Mr. Lincoln.

"Yes, I have."

"And what did you find?" The doctor puffed his pipe like a tugboat.

"It's paradoxical," Robert tried to explain. "On a whole, the watch is very much what you would expect, but it does not require any external kinetic force of any kind. The watch somehow winds *and* powers itself. The closest thing it has to a power source is a small cylinder of what numerous tests proved to be lead. The cylinder had copper strands embedded in it, possibly as heat sinks. When I cut into the cylinder, I also found a second, smaller gold cylinder inside it containing water. I don't know how, but somehow this lead-cased gold cylinder powered the device in a safe deposit box without interruption for decades. Maybe even since the time of my father's assassination until recently."

Doyle raised his eyebrows. "Nearly fifty years of continuous, uninterrupted movement without any external force whatsoever?" He puffed and puffed. "That is most curious."

"I know. The watch seems to violate the first law of thermo-dynamics, but I swear to you I saw it working the night my father was killed. It's an impossible invention."

"I agree. Too impossible, which would suggest there is some-thing about this watch which is not what we think," observed Doyle. "You said there is a gold vial inside surrounded by lead, correct?"

"Yes."

"You are absolutely sure it is lead?"

"*Yes,*" Robert stressed. "I ran extensive tests on the device, as did Yale University. They assured me that the samples I gave them were lead."

"Samples?" asked Doyle, surprised. "You never showed them the watch?"

"No. I . . ." Robert looked down at the timepiece for a moment with sadness. "I could not let the public know about the discovery. I'm approaching old age, Arthur, and I have worked so hard to maintain my father's good name. I did not want anyone to think that my father's assassination was driving me mad, as it did my mother or Henry Rathbone. I had to maintain some anonymity."

The patient Arthur listened attentively. "I completely under-stand and respect your decision," he replied. "And if I may say so, I can think of no president more worthy of his son's devotion than your father." Robert smiled, as did President Taft, while Sir Arthur Conan Doyle examined the watch's cauterized rim. "Is this watch completely airtight?"

"Yes, it is. Just as I found it."

"Ingenious." Within Sir Arthur Conan Doyle's mind, a vast array of wheels and locks suddenly fell into place. "Mr. Lincoln, would you please pass the tea?"

Taft, realizing their apparent error in etiquette, said, "I'm sorry. Where are our manners? Major, please pour the man a cup of tea."

"No, no. That won't be necessary," Doyle corrected. "Just the teapot, please."

Wilkie's cigar drooped in his mouth. "You plan on drinking that stuff straight out of the pot?"

Robert ignored this and offered the teapot to Arthur. "Careful. It's hot."

"Good! That will help."

The four Americans watched in horror as Sir Arthur Conan Doyle dropped the prized pocket watch into the steaming teapot.

"What are you doing!" screamed Lincoln.

"What kind of mad tea party is this?" barked Wilkie.

"Mr. Doyle, Mr. Lincoln is a good friend of ours! Explain yourself!" shouted Taft, pointing at the knight with a chip.

"Please be patient, gentlemen," Doyle urged politely. "You heard Mr. Lincoln say the watch is sealed, which means I am doing no damage to its internal works." The Colossus then folded his great hands and said, "Mr. Lincoln, your father was approached by Russian minister Eduard de Stoeckl to negotiate the sale of Alaska after the American Civil War. Correct?"

Robert grimaced at the teapot where his father's pocket watch was submerged. Nevertheless, he replied, "Not officially. The first offer from the Russians came during the Buchanan administration; they said no. The second came in 1867, two years after the war was over."

"And during this time, the Russians were, shall we say, quite friendly to the United States."

"Yes," said Robert. "They were our closest European allies

during the war. After the Crimean War, they sought to use us as a political counterweight to the British Empire."

"And during the Civil War, I think it is safe to say that the sale of Alaska was always in the back of their mind?"

Robert nodded. "Yes. They were clearly waiting for a Union victory and actively worked toward one. I imagine the only reason they didn't approach us immediately after the war was out of respect for my father's murder."

The Colossus paused for a moment out of reverence. "Mr. Lincoln, based on your personal knowledge, how would you describe the relationship between the American secretary of state and the Russian ambassador to the United States during the war?"

Robert, thinking back to William H. Seward, a man he knew well and one of his father's closest advisers, replied, "William Seward and Eduard de Stoeckl were very close friends. In fact, I would describe them as ideally suited for building a lasting relationship between the United States and the Russian Empire."

Sir Arthur smiled. "As would I," he said. He then lifted the simmering pocket watch from the pot by its chain. The Colossus carefully set the timepiece on Robert's handkerchief and flipped its lid open.

The magnificent pocket watch was ticking.

The four Americans stared speechlessly at Sir Arthur Conan Doyle. It was as if they had just witnessed a magic trick. Robert quickly picked up the wet timepiece and stared at it in disbelief. It was alive. It was moving. It was back from the dead.

"Is this how you English always take tea?" asked Wilkie.

"I am a Scotsman of Irish descent," Arthur corrected. "But to answer your question: No. Not all of them."

"Arthur," asked the president, whose old chair was creaking, "how did you fix Bob's pocket watch with a teapot?"

"Well," said the smiling Scot, "there are only two ways this watch could work based on Mr. Lincoln's description of it. Since the timepiece was clearly never meant to be wound, I opted for a more practical power source: heat. Gold is an excellent heat conductor. The watch's gold casing, while quite lovely, is part of the reason why it's working right now."

"You're telling me Abraham Lincoln had to dip that thing every day into his morning coffee?" Wilkie scoffed.

"Not at all. I have no doubt the watch worked splendidly in its own time. I am merely illustrating that the device's original power source has clearly expired."

Robert looked up from the timepiece. "You know what powers this?"

"I do." Doyle nodded. "What you are holding is a steam-powered pocket watch that runs on uranium. It's the only explanation for the lead surrounding the water-filled gold vial inside it. It's also the reason why your watch ran without interruption for so long. According to Ernest Rutherford's recent research on radiation, the uranium in this pocket watch slowly decayed over time until it became a completely new element. And there is another gentleman, an American. I believe his name is Bolt-wood—"

"Bertram Boltwood." Robert gasped as he realized how the pocket watch worked.

"Yes! The same year Rutherford published his theories on half-life periods, Mr. Boltwood determined that lead is the final decay product of uranium. As such, you are correct, Mr. Lincoln. You always were: This pocket watch is impossible. It cannot work in its present form because it is no longer the same device it was forty-five years ago!"

With these words, Taft's wooden chair collapsed under his weight. The president landed hard on the floor while a large piece of his chair pulled down on the harness beside him. Its line yanked it through the window and into the air at great speed until the contraption disappeared into the airship.

"Mr. President! Are you injured?" Major Butt and Chief Wilkie rushed to help him.

"I'm all right, I'm all right!" said Taft as he climbed back onto his feet.

Agent Sloan ran into the room. "Is everything all right, Mr. President? I heard an explosion."

"It's no trouble," Taft assured him. "False alarm."

Wilkie looked out the window up to the airship and whistled. "I guess it's a good thing you weren't wearing that harness. The Indian rope trick worked like a charm!"

Robert, meanwhile, continued his conversation as if nothing had happened. "How could the Russians have built a machine so technologically advanced nearly fifty years ago? And why would they give such a device to my father?"

"That, I'm afraid, is a question we may never be able to answer," confessed Doyle. "However, I do have a theory based on the most likely explanation for the timepiece's design, its strange message, and the circumstances in which you found it. Firstly, I believe this pocket watch was a gift from someone in the Russian government to resume negotiations for the sale of Alaska. Perhaps it came from Tsar Alexander II, but I'd say it more likely came from Russian minister de Stoeckl as a gift for your father."

"Why?" asked Robert. "Why such a strange gift?"

"Because the technical ingenuity behind this machine is only one of its surprises! Mr. Lincoln, I believe de Stoeckl used this watch to facilitate the sale of Alaska to the United States by revealing to your father that its lands contained gold! That is why the watch says 'Made in America,' which I am sure you gathered is in reference to Russian America. In this case, it is a literal truth. The watch's gold came from Alaska. Its magnificent sample of gold-bearing quartz came from Alaska. And I believe the uranium which once powered it came from Alaska as well."

"That can't be," said Taft as he dusted himself off. "If de Stoeckl knew there was gold in Alaska, why didn't he tell the Russian government? There's no way they would have let him sell the land otherwise."

"I agree," said Doyle. "I think there are several explanations why de Stoeckl chose to reveal this to President Lincoln, and they are quite sensible. One reason could have been to avoid a war with the British, who almost certainly would have invaded Alaska if they knew there was gold there. The empire could easily have claimed the deposits just as they did during the recent crisis in Venezuela. Not only would Russia have been powerless to fend off such an attack, but the loss of their gold fields would have made Russian America even less valuable. However, I believe Ambassador de Stoeckl could have just as well revealed this secret to President Lincoln so he could sell the land quickly, especially after the enormous financial expense of the Civil War. De Stoeckl was in very poor health when he resigned as ambassador two years later. But thanks to the generous reward he received from Alexander II for completing the sale, he was able to live another *twenty years,* eventually retiring in Paris. As a physician, I would say that's a rather remarkable medical recovery! Perhaps one made possible only because he was able to sell Alaska, which, if I am not mistaken, was something Secretary of State Seward was ridiculed for!"

"Yes, he was." Wilkie smirked. "Seward's Folly. Everyone thought it was hilarious until it led to a gold rush."

"Precisely," said Doyle. "Because of this pocket watch, Secretary Seward knew there was gold in those lands."

Robert thought about this. He had no doubt Secretary Seward would have been enthusiastic to purchase Alaska if he had this information, as would his father. The gold would have provided the country with much-needed funds to finance reconstruction and, if his father had lived, compensation for emancipated slaves in the South. He also knew that pocket watches were his father's preferred choice of gift, and a device such as this one would have been graciously accepted. For Ambassador de Stoeckl, it would have been an artful means of persuasion. All the same, such a revelation about Alaska would have immediately become a national secret and something the War Department would have desperately kept hidden from the collapsing Confederacy.

However, there was still something that did not make sense to Robert. "But why uranium?" he asked Doyle. "This could have been an ordinary watch. Why invent something so spectacular? In fact, how could anyone at the time even know that uranium could be used to power machinery?"

For a moment, Sir Arthur Conan Doyle appeared stumped. "That is a very good question, Mr. Lincoln." The author sat back in his chair and returned to his pipe. "Well, there is one possibility. It's faint, but it does enjoy my full confidence because it is part of a most important chapter in my life.

"During my youth, when I was still a medical student, I had the unique opportunity to serve as doctor aboard a whaler, the

Hope. It was a fascinating experience and very dangerous work. However, I have no doubt that the physical health I enjoyed throughout my whole life has been affected by it! The air is most pleasant in the extreme northern latitudes."[43]

"I know *exactly* what you are talking about." Taft smiled before resuming his meal.

"Thank you, Mr. President. It was a remarkable experience, but I am embarrassed to say that it also gave me intimate knowledge about what it's like to fall into freezing water! This happened so frequently that my captain came to call me 'the Great Northern Diver.' It was both terrifying and humiliating, but since I was the ship's doctor, I took the experience as an opportunity to learn whatever I could about how to treat hypothermia. After one particularly bad fall into the Arctic, a sailor told me he had heard of a people native to North America who use certain rocks for medicinal purposes, namely heat. After researching the subject, I learned that such stones do exist and are most likely uranium, which I imagine would be prized by indigenous fishermen and hunters in freezing climates."

"Such as Alaska?" asked Wilkie.

Doyle put his pipe in his mouth. "I imagine it would be somewhere you Americans have been finding uranium in the fifty years hence."

"Bob, could the Russians have found all the material they needed for this in the Wrangell Mountains?" asked the president.

Robert went over the innumerable maps and logs he had amassed in his head the past two years. "The gold and copper

---

43 Arthur Conan Doyle, *Dangerous Work: Diary of an Arctic Adventure* (Chicago: University Of Chicago Press, 2012).

could have easily come from the Morgan-Guggenheim mines. And Hammond said his men struck a lead cavern in the mountains."

"That's a recipe for tremendous amounts of uranium," Doyle added.

"And the gold-bearing quartz?" Taft continued. "You said it's quite rare. Has there been any found near the Wrangell Mountains?"

Robert set his eyes on the brilliant watch fob.

"Bob?"

"Yes, there has. Hammond said gold-bearing quartz was discovered at Willow Creek in 1906. It's located at the foothills of the mountain." Robert looked to every man as he spoke: *"Everything* necessary to make this watch could have come from the Wrangell Mountains."

This seemed to satisfy Taft. He celebrated by lifting his glass. "Well, I guess the mystery about your father's pocket watch has been solved! Congratulations! Now, is there anyone here who can explain how Basil Zaharoff got his hands on one as well?"

Sir Arthur Conan Doyle's brow furrowed. "Your enemy has a pocket watch just like this?"

"Yes. I saw it," said the president. "It's identical to Mr. Lincoln's in every way, only silver."

Arthur anxiously rapped his fingers against the table. "That is most interesting, Mr. President. Most interesting."

"Why?" asked Taft.

"Because silver conducts heat even better than gold. In fact . . . Please excuse me for a moment."

Doyle stood up and began to pace the room, puffing his pipe.

The Colossus appeared to be in deep thought while the president looked at the men around him.

"Archie, what did I say?" Taft whispered.

"I don't know, sir."

"Take your sweet time, sir knight," said Wilkie as he unshelled a hard-boiled egg.

"Arthur?" asked Robert. "Is something wrong?"

The Colossus spun around, his eyes alight with realization. "Mr. President, my dear sirs: Picture, if you will, a gentleman who came across a pocket watch just like this through purely unintentional, but nevertheless completely legal circumstances. He could have found it in a safe, just like Mr. Lincoln did. Or perhaps he purchased its patent. He may have even acquired the store where it was built, containing its designs as well as a prototype. My point is that no matter how he acquired this timepiece, the president of the United States is saying that this gentleman is Basil Zaharoff: the villain you encountered in New Haven. He is a man who has amassed an incalculable fortune by mating weapons with machines, and this pocket watch just might be the first machine in history to harness the radioactive power of uranium. A device such as this could be used as the basis for a most powerful weapon."

"This weapon exists," said Major Butt. "We encountered it at Yale and saw the full extent of its destructive power in the Congo. It is quite lethal. Powerful enough to kill all plant and animal life in an enormous radius."

Sir Arthur Conan Doyle's pipe began to shake in his mouth. "Mr. Lincoln. How much radioactive material do you think was mined from the Morgan-Guggenheim sites in Alaska?"

"There's really no way of knowing," replied Robert. "If this lead cavern the miners found contained uranium, they could have mined all of it out of the mountains by now."

"And this cesium hydroxide your enemies threatened New Haven with. It was meant to be transmitted using steam. Correct?"

"Yes, it was. Their plan was to use Yale University's steam tunnels to release it as an aerosol."

"How expansive are these tunnels? What would it take for them to be mobile?"

Robert's eyes widened. "Arthur, I don't think such a weapon could ever be moved. If someone were to duplicate what we encountered at Yale, this weapon would have to be the size of . . . I don't know. At least three city blocks!"

"Arthur," Taft interrupted. "Why are you asking us this?"

The Colossus meditated for a moment. "Mr. Wilkie, what is the shipping company your secret agent is currently working for? The one she suspects our enemies have been using for the bulk of their activities?"

"The White Star Line," said the chief.

"And where is she at the moment?"

"Belfast."

Sir Arthur Conan Doyle went pale. "Do any of you gentlemen have a copy of this transmission your agent told me you received from Nikola Tesla?"

Wilkie snapped his fingers and pointed to Major Butt, who was guarding a briefcase under the table containing copies of everything the president was prepared to discuss with the Colossus. The major handed a copy of the transmission to Doyle, who carefully looked it over.

GENTLEMAN FROM BRUSSELS
PARIS? WILL THIS INTERFERE WITH YOUR OPERA-
TIONS AT BELFAST?

GENTLEMAN FROM PARIS
NOT AT ALL. WE ARE CURRENTLY AHEAD OF
SCHEDULE.

GENTLEMAN FROM BRUSSELS
VERY WELL. I WILL WORK WITH BOMA TO FACILITATE
YOUR DELIVERY. WE WILL BE WAITING FOR YOU.

"Could I trouble one of you sirs for a pen and paper?"

"Why?" asked the president.

"Because our enemies will have everything they need in Belfast to make this weapon mobile, which appears to have been their
intention from the beginning. My friends," observed Sir Arthur
Conan Doyle, "I am sorry to say this, but I think the United
Kingdom is currently being held hostage, and the United States
is on the verge of an attack of titanic proportions."

Chapter XXXIV

April 14, 1912

MGY TO MWL

SHUT UP! SHUT UP! I AM BUSY . . .

R adio officer Cyril Evans turned nervously to his captain, Stanley Lord, in the crowded Marconi Room of the SS *Californian*. "That was their last reply, sir."

Captain Lord, who had been on duty for seventeen hours that day, could not have been more distressed with this report.

"Shall I reply using the MSG prefix?" asked Evans.

"No, don't bother. Monitor all their transmissions to Newfoundland, but otherwise send nothing more."

"Aye, Captain." Evans dutifully marked down the time in his logbook as 11:04 P.M.

Captain Lord dabbed the sweat from his face even though it was freezing outside. He turned around and shook his head at

Arthur Brooks, who was patiently waiting on the deck in his old National Guard coat.

Brooks bowed his head in response and walked over to the port side of the bow. There was a small cluster of people there guarded by a thick wall of soldiers. Brooks passed through these men to find Attorney General Wickersham engaged in a hushed conversation with Brigadier General Clarence Edwards, Secretary of War Stimson, and British Ambassador James Bryce. Behind these men, Nellie Taft was flanked by two of her sisters, both of whom were armed with shotguns.

Considering the circumstances, Mrs. Taft looked quite regal in her large Merry Widow hat.

"We heard back from the ship," Brooks reported. "They're not stopping."

Nellie looked away from the cold waters. "You're sure?"

"Positive," replied Brooks.

If Nellie sighed, her sadness was masked by the determination on her face. "Commence the attack."

"Yes, Madam President."

Brooks reported back to the radio room while Nellie set her binoculars once more to the southern horizon.

As she stared into the distance, it never occurred to Nellie or Brooks or anyone onboard the *Californian* that the *Titanic*'s Marconi operator, Jack Phillips, was already dead.

In the First Class Lounge of the RMS *Titanic,* Archie Butt was playing cards with some of the steamship's wealthiest passengers. He was wearing his full uniform and appeared to be enjoying himself: He was winning. He had also just returned from a luxurious dinner party and was developing an affinity for the lounge's lovely Louis XV style. And lastly, seated beside him was the masterful Francis Davis Millet, a gentle man Butt affectionately described in his letters as "my artist friend who lives with me."

The two were very good friends.

Archie had just won a hand with a pair of aces and eights, all black, when a stewardess approached the table and placed a tall glass of water in front of the officer. Archie, who did not request this, looked up to see a woman with luscious, voluminous hair and blue-gray eyes staring back at him.

A clock chimed.

Miss Knox walked out of the lounge for the promenade deck while Archie took one last look at Francis, who knew what was coming. The two nodded to each other, and Archie excused himself while Millet continued to entertain the ladies and gentlemen at the table. As Archie walked out of the room, he threw his officer's cape over his shoulders and once more became Major Butt.

When the uniformed major reached the stern of the ship, Miss Knox was already waiting for him. She was standing next to a black rope that appeared to disappear into space. There was a strong steel hook hanging from the end of it.

The officer dutifully unbuttoned his jacket. "When did they arrive?" he asked quickly.

"Less than five minutes ago. They dropped Mrs. Taft and the observers on a ship about five to six miles north-northwest from here. The SS *Californian*."

"Are they White Star Line?"

"No. Leyland Line. It's owned by the IMM, but the ship and crew can be trusted."

"Good for us," said Major Butt. His jacket was open, revealing a leather harness beneath it.

"Also, there's something you should know. Archie, two people tried to kill me in my room last night."

The major's face filled with worry. "My God . . . Were you hurt?"

"Of course not! I disposed of them easily. But Archie, there's something wrong with the crew. Each day, I recognize fewer of them. It's almost as if they're disappearing, replaced by people I've never seen or worked with before."

"That's odd. Does Captain Smith know about this?"

"No. The entire chain of command is intact. However, I know for sure that several hundred crewmen are completely unaccounted for at the moment. Maybe even more than half of them."

"That could be a problem," said the major as he hooked the line to his harness. "A big problem. And our targets?"

"They're all here." Miss Knox assisted the officer with his straps. "I know they said J. P. Morgan did not board, but I found a trunk containing a set of his clothing and . . . something else. Some sort of strange equipment I've never seen before."

The major raised an eyebrow. "Well, I'll make sure to notify Mr. Lincoln." Fastened safely in his harness, the soldier breathed heavily and gave Miss Knox a long look. "You have your weapons?"

"Yes, major."

"Do you have any questions?"

"No, major."

"All right." Archie looked into the night sky. Just as he hoped, there was only darkness above them.

"Please make sure Francis leaves safely."

"I will, major."

Major Butt smiled softly, and Miss Knox smiled back. It was always so adorable, she thought, to see him so proud in his cape.

But then the soldier turned skyward and to the matter at hand. He pulled on his rope and disappeared like a bat into the dark night above.

It was 11:40 P.M., *Titanic* time.

Chapter XXXV

"Welcome aboard."

M r. President." The major saluted.

President Taft, Robert Todd Lincoln, and a smoking Chief Wilkie were surrounded by a wall of Secret Service agents and more than one hundred of the best soldiers in the United States military. Although comprised primarily of the Ninth Cavalry, this was a special unit assembled after more than a month of intensive training and planning. They were men of every race, background, and belief. They were the soldiers, sailors, and U.S. Marines chosen to commandeer the *Titanic*. And above all else, they were sons, brothers, fathers, husbands, countrymen, and Americans.

Taft looked over the soldiers, every one of them awaiting his order. "You can go now."

"Go!" shouted Captain Young.

In a military maneuver as carefully choreographed as a symphony, the soldiers leaped out of the zeppelin and descended upon the *Titanic* from black ropes. Major Butt and Captain Young saluted each other and parted ways: the former to the bridge and the latter to the sharpshooters on the promenade. After Wilkie and his Secret Service agents slid down their lines, Taft turned to Robert Todd Lincoln, who was holding the electric rifle he and Dr. Tesla designed.

"You know the drill, Bob. Once the passengers are off safely, come down and help me put this ship out of commission."

"Yes, Mr. President." Robert extended his hand, exposing the gold pocket watch he was wearing beneath his thick winter coat.

Taft shook his friend's hand, smiled, and then slid down his special extra-thick rope. The president hit the deck with a "*Ha-ha!*" as if he had just swung in on a chandelier.

Chapter XXXVI

"What the bloody hell is this?"

"You First Officer Murdoch?"

"Yes, I am!"

"Smashing." Wilkie smirked as he took out his badge. "I'm John Wilkie, United States Treasury. Chief of Secret Service Division. I need you to step back and surrender this ship."

"Bollocks!" Murdoch barked back.

"Don't worry. We're not taking it for free." Wilkie put his badge in his coat and then produced something else. "Here. Have a cigar." The outraged lieutenant looked down at the offering and immediately smacked it out of the chief's hand.

"What's the situation, Wilkie?" asked Taft as he entered the bridge. He left Agent Sloan behind him to guard the door.

First Officer Murdoch looked at the enormous president with the same shock as if he had just seen an iceberg. "You're the American!" he gasped. "The president!"

"Yes, I am. I need you to summon Captain Smith to the bridge."

"What is this mutiny?" a voice shouted. "Who are you?" The fur-clad president turned around to see Captain Edward James Smith, the white-bearded captain of the *Titanic,* standing beside Agent Sloan. His collar was undone and he was not wearing his jacket. The captain was shivering, possibly due to the cold, but the president assumed it could just as well be out of anger. Or fear.

"Captain Smith," said Taft, extending his hand. "I am William Howard Taft, president of the United States, but you may call me Will."

The stunned captain shook the president's hand feebly. "What's going on here? How did you board this ship?"

"From a flying machine. Captain Smith . . ." The president walked with the captain into the bridge. "I'm afraid I have some bad news: Your ship contains a terrible weapon that could potentially kill everyone in and around New York Harbor. I have a letter here signed by the prime minister, Secretary of State Knox, Ambassador James Bryce, and myself authorizing that you turn command of this vessel over to the United States military. We will unload passengers onto two steamships that are racing here as we speak, arrest those we deem criminal, and then scuttle the ship. I am sorry, sir," Taft sighed, "but we may need to sink the *Titanic.*"

Captain Smith's sad eyes were watering. They looked to First Officer Murdoch and then helplessly at the ship's wheel.

"Captain?" asked the president.

A low gasp came from Captain Smith's lips.

"What the hell?" asked Wilkie as he looked out the window. There was shouting and gunfire outside.

Airship One blasted its horn, awaking everyone on the *Titanic.*

"What's going on out there?" Taft thundered.

Captain Smith collapsed to the floor with a throwing knife in his back.

Wilkie drew his pistol. "Who the devil—!" Two columns of armed men came charging into the bridge, overwhelming its hapless defenders. Wilkie fired four shots at the thugs, killing four men, but there were far too many for his six-chambered revolver. The brutes overpowered Taft's bodyguard and pinned him to the floor with two rifles pressed against his chest.

"No!" Taft shouted as more men rushed onto the bridge. Agents Sloan, Wheeler, Jervis, and the remaining officers on the *Titanic* surrounded the president, but they did not shoot their pistols. They were surrounded by Belgian Mausers aimed for the president's head.

Outside of the bridge, the president's men could hear screaming.

And then, thumping. A deep, ominous din that shook the floor beneath them.

Two men walked into the bridge. One was J. P. Morgan, who, oddly, was not wearing a coat and appeared to move somewhat rigidly. The other was a tall, impossibly thin man wearing a black suit and sporting a short white beard. He'd had it trimmed since his cruel reign as king of the Belgians.

"Leopold . . ." sneered the president.

Chapter XXXVII

Midnight

Y ou're not dead at all," Taft surmised. "Your state funeral was an elaborate hoax."

"It was not that elaborate," said the once-King Leopold II in a deep, ancient voice. "My coffin was spit upon by my own countrymen as it was carried through Brussels. My own kin abandoned me in disgrace. If I had enough bullets, I would have killed every one of them myself."

A livid president shook his head at the villain. "After what you did to the Congo, I should not be surprised."

"Yes, Mr. Rom has a unique passion for his work. He always has."

"Leon Rom is dead. My airship crew killed him."

Leopold smirked. "Good. That means I don't need to take care of him as well."

As Leopold said this, an entire army of stowaways flooded the decks of the *Titanic*. The sporadic shooting outside the bridge exploded into full war.

The president's men were outnumbered.

Aboard Airship One, Major Butt blasted the zeppelin's mighty horn a third time. But alas, it appeared Basil Zaharoff knew his Homer. The enemy soldiers storming the *Titanic* were wearing earplugs to protect against sirens.

"Who are these people?" shouted Corporal Winnie "Mike" Williams.

The major studied their clothing through his binoculars. "Pirates," he said. "Southeast Asian. There must be hundreds of them on the ship."

"Major!" cried Captain Young. "The enemies have the president surrounded!"

Major Butt turned his attention to the dire situation in the bridge. "Take us down to fifty feet!" he ordered. "Get us along the port side!" The major looked to Captain Young. "We can't use our sirens. Have the sharpshooters fire at will."

"Aye, sir!" Captain Young hurried back to the airship's main deck, where Robert Todd Lincoln was waiting for him. "I think you better stay in your cabin," said the captain.

Robert did not agree or disagree. Instead, he looked out the windows of the zeppelin and made calculations.

By the time Captain Young was done directing his soldiers, he turned around to see that Robert had already jumped off the airship with his rifle and a RK-1 knapsack parachute.

The president glared at J. P. Morgan while his agents were robbed of their pistols. "Where's Benjamin Guggenheim?" Taft asked Leopold.

"Packed neatly in four cases floating in the Atlantic," the former king smiled.

Taft turned to J. P. Morgan in disgust. "Conspiring against your own conspirators? I should have expected as much from you."

Morgan did not respond.

"Speak, damn you!"

"Rest assured, Mr. President, your Americans did not knowingly break any laws. They thought we were trying to monopolize a special type of uranium found only in Alaska and Congo. We told them it could be used to make a new type of weapon. We just never explained that this weapon would be used against their country."

"So that's what you and Zaharoff were smuggling all over the world."

"Yes," replied Leopold. "The material is extremely dangerous. Fortunately, we had no shortage of servants."

Taft's mind turned to the bones surrounding Leon Rom's garden. "How could you do this?" he growled at J. P. Morgan, staring straight into his soulless eyes. "How could you sell out America for this madman? Why?" He looked back at King Leopold. "Why!"

"Because crowns and thrones no longer carry the same weight," boomed the baritone Leopold. "Not in this century. There is nothing left for us kings except money. Fortunately, Mr. Zaharoff is so resourceful that he found a way to monopolize what will be the twentieth century's greatest commodity: war. When we arrive in New York, I will return to the Congo on a boat hours later. It will be the last you or anyone sees of your country. The *Titanic* will remain in New York Harbor, converting seawater into a lethal gas that will pollute your lands indefinitely. It cannot be shut off. It *will* not be shut off. New York will be destroyed, and then Philadelphia, and then Washington. In a matter of time, your entire east coast will be as dead as the moon."

The officers and agents huddled around President Taft shared his horror. "Why us?" Taft gasped breathlessly. "Why America?"

Leopold scowled and took a step forward. "Because your nation *ruined* my whole operation in Congo. I had the blessings of the world's governments, including yours, until an American soldier named George Washington Williams trespassed into my lands and exposed everything. After him came the British, and then the backstabber Kowalsky, and then Twain, all your newspapers . . . No more! You will pay for this offence with the lives of your citizens. With the United States crippled, the world will plunge into war. It is a powder keg that has been building for centuries. America will be the spark. Once all the monarchies that deserted me destroy themselves in the fighting, Mr. Zaharoff and I will approach the world as the sole vendors of the most powerful material ever discovered. We will be the true powers of this planet for the rest of the century. And when I die, my young wife and our offspring shall inherit the world."

"Your wife," said Wilkie from the floor, "is a harlot!"

Leopold raised his eyebrows. "And the president's wife is an invalid." He smiled at Taft.

The president had to be restrained by his agents, much to Leopold's amusement.

But then, a great searchlight flooded the bridge. Agents Sloan, Wheeler, and Jervis pulled the president to the floor while the whole room erupted with gunfire. Airship One's sharpshooters gunned down Leopold's men through the windows. Wilkie took out his puukko knife and stabbed one of his captors in the leg. First Officer Murdoch drew his officer's pistol and fired at Leopold, killing two of his bodyguards and blasting one of the king's ears off. For his heroism, the young officer was shot to death.

Horrified by his injury, Leopold abandoned the bridge with his men and fled into the steel maze that was the RMS *Titanic*. A maddened Taft charged after him while Secret Service agents picked up their guns and joined in the chase.

As the fighting spread rapidly throughout the steamship, Wilkie propped himself up in the bridge to examine the leaking bullet hole in his chest.

Chapter XXXVIII

"Bob . . ."

... $\mathbf{T}$he Secret Service chief coughed.
"John!" Robert set down his rifle and helped the stricken Chief Wilkie to his feet. "Are you hurt?"

"Nah, it's all right." Wilkie plucked a lead slug from his battle-damaged flask, causing the last of his whiskey to leak out like a wound. "I can't believe those Prohibitionists say this stuff'll kill you. It's saved my life twice!"

"You may not be so lucky next time." There was a war brewing outside for control of the *Titanic*. "John, where's the president?"

"Through there." Wilkie pointed his bloodied knife to the starboard-side door. "I think they're inside the ship. I've got to go after him. Would you mind watching that ugly fella for me?" he asked, motioning toward J. P. Morgan.

Robert was speechless. As was Mr. Morgan.

"Bob?"

The chief looked to Morgan, whose hideous nose had been shot off during the gunfight. He was neither bleeding nor breathing. The bone under his flesh appeared as brass as the bridge telegraph beside him.

Wilkie picked up his pistol and fired two shots at Morgan. The bullets bounced harmlessly off his skull.

The automaton took a heavy step forward, crushing the rifle of a fallen soldier as if it were paper.

"LEOPOLD!" bellowed Taft through the crowded *Titanic*. The maddened president chased the king like a bloodhound through the ship's chaotic First Class corridors.

Thomas Andrews, the ship's designer, hurried out of his cabin. "What is this?" he asked. King Leopold's agents shot him dead, splattering his insides against the white hallway. Panic gripped every passenger in the corridor.

"Sir, we can't open fire without hitting the passengers!" Sloan shouted. With so few White Star Line employees alive to manage the crisis, every hall in the vast ship had plunged into anarchy.

"I know! Stand back, men! Let me after him!" Taft tried to shove his way through the mob, but to no avail.

"Unhand me, fat person!" shouted J. Bruce Ismay.

Taft floored the man with one punch. "Arrest him for questioning!"

"Yes, Mr. President." Agent Bowen holstered his pistol and quit the chase.

"Mr. President, he's getting away!" shouted Jervis.

"I know!" Leopold disappeared down the hallway, which was now thickly congested with panicking people. As Taft surveyed the scene, he realized the hopelessness of the situation. "We have to get every woman and child off this boat. Make it happen! And offer sidearms to anyone willing to fight."

"Yes, Mr. President." Agent Sloan holstered his weapon and rushed into the first cabin he saw. "Excuse me, ma'am?"

"I heard him!" shouted Mrs. Margaret "Molly" Brown. She was searching for the pepperbox pistol she had packed in her hatbox.

She was the first of many passengers to join the fight for the *Titanic*.

Meanwhile, along the port side of the boat deck, a thick wave of passengers was running away from the bridge of the ship.

"GET OUT OF THE WAY!" shouted Chief Wilkie, with Robert Todd Lincoln racing closely behind him.

The J. P. Morgan automaton was plowing a path of destruction through the ship, knocking through wall after wall of the officers' quarters.

"Why the hell is it after me?" cried Robert.

"I don't know! It wasn't doing anything until you showed up! Hey, wait a second. . . ."

Wilkie leaned over the edge of the First Class promenade and looked back toward the bow. U.S. soldiers were hurriedly loading passengers onto lifeboats while simultaneously fighting a fierce battle against Leopold's forces. Although there were not nearly enough lifeboats on the *Titanic* for its thirteen hundred passengers, the cunning officers aboard Airship One were able to improvise a solution. Shortly into the battle, Captain Young spotted an iceberg nearby. Major Butt was directing lifeboats there via searchlight so they could unload passengers and then return for more from the steamship.

It was a completely ad hoc and unorthodox maneuver, but for the time being, it worked.

"Looks like Archie is doing all right!" observed Wilkie, completely unaware of the Maxim machine guns being brought out beneath him.

"John!" Robert grabbed the Secret Service chief and pulled him backward. The two ran across the deck from the automaton and into the *Titanic*. "Move! Move!" the duo shouted to the ship's first-class passengers as they raced across a white tiled floor to the ship's grand staircase. As they hurried down the majestic oak centerpiece of the ship, Robert glanced at the great clock engraved on its wall: "Honour and Glory crowning Time." It was well after midnight.

"This is taking too long," said Robert. "John, find the president and get him off the ship. I'll take care of the superweapon."

"You can't!" shouted Wilkie. "King Leopold is alive and onboard. He said the weapon cannot be shut off."

"Leopold?" Robert gasped.

"Yes. Back from the dead. He was behind everything this whole time!"

Robert's eyes gaped and his mind wandered inward. "He may not be relying on time-dissolving capsules this time. John, I need to go downstairs and shut off all power on the ship."

"Mr. Lincoln," Wilkie said sternly, "if I leave you alone against this nightmare, you will die."

Robert, aware that he was standing on a vessel floating toward a vast, unknown shore at fantastic speed, responded, "Then it was meant to be."

Just above them, Robert and Wilkie could hear several passengers screaming. The two looked up to see the J. P. Morgan automaton walk off the overhead deck and land atop a tuxedoed passenger, killing him. Oddly enough, the man appeared to have been chasing two other passengers with a gun.

Robert and Wilkie raced their separate ways while Leopold's agents hastily assembled their Maxim machine guns.

Once the deadly weapons were loaded, the villains turned them against Airship One.

Chapter XXXIX

"Major Butt!"

Y es, Captain."

"Sir, they're bringing out heavy weapons!"

The major looked through his binoculars and saw machine guns being assembled from crates.

"Kill their crews!" he ordered. "Before they use those guns on the passengers!"

"Yes, sir!"

The sharpshooters opened fire while Major Butt hurried back to the airship's bridge. "Everybody take cover!" he ordered.

The zeppelin crew hid behind their equipment while Major Butt continued to observe through his field glasses. Captain Young's sharpshooters took out two machine gunners before their belts were assembled. Dozens of relieved passengers witnessed this and cheered the zeppelin. They then rushed at their fallen enemies and seized their weapons, which included entire crates full of firearms, so they could join the fight for the *Titanic*.

Through the major's binoculars, the tide appeared to be turning against Leopold's forces. He smiled, but then spotted another machine gun.

Major Butt ducked as the weapon tore a mighty wound through Airship One. Bullets and broken glass raked through the bridge until Captain Young personally fired the rifle that put the enemy gunner out of commission.

"Damage report!" called the major as he returned to his feet.

"Sir, we need to gain altitude!" shouted a crewman.

"No, we don't!" ordered Butt as he helped an injured man to his feet. "The more fire we draw, the less damage will be dealt to the passengers and our men on the deck."

"Sir, we're *losing* altitude!"

The major's eyes widened as he saw the airship slowly descending. "We need to lose weight. Drop all our bombs! Keep us in the air! And make sure we don't hit any lifeboats!"

"Yes, sir!"

At the major's order, a sinking Airship One repositioned itself and dropped all sixteen of its bombs off the *Titanic*'s starboard bow. Seconds later, the bombs detonated, causing a tremendous explosion that shook the whole ship. The *Titanic* careened portside on its keel, nearly capsizing. For one terrifying moment, everyone on the enormous steamship had to hold on for their lives.

Airship One shot back up into the air while Major Butt looked below. Not a single soldier or passenger had been thrown overboard, but all three of Leopold's machine guns slid into the ocean.

The major breathed with relief. The crisis was averted.

Until . . .

Less than four miles away aboard the *Californian,* a white flash filled Nellie's binoculars.

"Did you see that?" she asked Attorney General Wickersham. Every man and woman on deck was observing the spectacle. A bright light lingered over the *Titanic* like a firework.

And then another.

"Madam President!" shouted Arthur Brooks from the bridge. "The *Titanic* is using its signal flares!"

"But why?" she asked.

A tremendous explosion illuminated the southern horizon, flooding half of the *Californian* with light. Nellie Taft and her entourage watched in horror as a fireball nearly a thousand feet wide came crashing down on the *Titanic.*

"Archie . . ." she whispered with tears running down her face.

"ABANDON SHIP!" screamed Captain Young. Once the stricken airship was level, all its soldiers were scattered like playing cards across the main dining hall. "Everyone to the windows! Leap once we hit the deck, then start running! Leave no man behind! Everyone—Major!" A bruised Major Butt struggled to stand using his broken sword. Captain Young rushed to his aid, but the fallen skipper shooed him away.

"Don't you dare rescue me, captain! Save yourself! That's an order!"

"Sir, we're getting you out of here!"

"I'll be fine! I'm a good swimmer!"

"Sir, you're coming with me!" Captain Young forced Major Butt to his feet.

As the two officers raced to the ship's shattered windows, Major Butt turned his head for one last look at the spectacular zeppelin. His eyes fell on the great outstretched eagle he saw Robert Todd Lincoln reflecting on earlier. In the fires, the towering bird more closely resembled a phoenix.

The burning airship hit the bow of RMS *Titanic*. All of Nikola Tesla's inventions in the wireless room were destroyed. The Surprise cabinet was crushed and its contents exploded. The recording of Nora Bayes singing "Hail to the Chief" was shattered. The celluloid in the viewing machine Robert Todd Lincoln built for the Tafts ignited. The ship's mighty horn sounded one more time before it was silenced forever. And beneath the great eagle that Major Butt and Captain Young rushed past, the words *Una natio fatum unum* glowed brightly in gold letters until they were swallowed by flame.

Airship One, Earth's most awesome machine, was no more.

Chapter XL

Wilkie

Secret Service Chief John E. Wilkie shoved, shouted, and occasionally shot his way through the bustling halls of the *Titanic* only to have his search for the president interrupted by too many good deeds. First there was a young lady. And then a baby. And then a young lady with a baby. And then several strapping young men in steerage the chief simply had to recruit to join the fighting upstairs. In total, Wilkie managed to kill precisely twenty-six enemy soldiers, personally rescued more than twice as many passengers, enlisted enough auxiliary forces to fill a platoon, and ran nearly two miles through the eight-hundred-eighty-three-foot ship in under half an hour. However, before he was eventually drawn to the sound of Robert Todd Lincoln's screams, it is worth mentioning that one of the above incidents involved an encounter with Miss Knox.

"This way, Mrs. Brown."

"Just a second." The unsinkable Molly Brown emptied her revolver at a cluster of Leopold's agents swimming toward an overturned lifeboat. Once the villains were floating dead in the water, she turned back to Miss Knox. "Thanks, darlin'." Out of all the passengers to join the fighting, Molly Brown seemed to be enjoying herself the most.

The incognito Secret Service agent smiled and then ran to assist another lifeboat that was returning for more passengers to unload. The rescue operation had been chaotic and many lives had been lost, but not a single soldier or passenger who fell in the fighting died in vain. Thanks to their selfless efforts, more than a thousand passengers had already been saved. However, as Miss Knox led the last of the passengers to their lifeboats, her life was nearly cut short by a team of pirates sneaking up behind her.

The crisis started when one of the fiends grabbed Miss Knox by her hair. She immediately grabbed his wrist and snapped it, spinning around in the process. A gang of ten thugs stood against her: far too many than she could handle alone. And to make matters worse, every one of them was brandishing weapons. Miss Knox's situation appeared hopeless until the heroic band on the *Titanic* interrupted their music and rushed at the villains, carrying their instruments as cudgels. Tragically, these men were minstrels, not pirates, and their rescue attempt was an act of self-sacrifice. Nevertheless, their ambush was enough for Miss Knox to leap into the fray with her razor-sharp hairpin and her Apache revolver. When the battle was over, Miss Knox emerged as the only person left alive, having stabbed the last villain through the heart with the tail spike of a cello.

It was in this quiet state of post-battle exhaustion that Chief Wilkie found his greatest agent standing alongside a lifeboat. He ran right up to her, thrust a bundled baby into her arms, and rushed back inside the *Titanic* without saying a word.

Just when Robert thought he'd eluded the J. P. Morgan automaton, something unexpected happened. The walls around him slanted as if the seemingly unsinkable steamship was capsizing. He struggled to regain balance and his old muscles were aching, but he refused to turn back. Robert was determined to end this conspiracy against the United States once and for all. And so, with his shining rifle in his hands and his father's gold timepiece hanging freely, Robert charged sideways through the rotating halls of the RMS *Titanic*.

But then, just as the enormous ship righted itself, Robert heard a menacing thud above him. He took a step backward and the automaton came crashing down through the ceiling. The accursed machine was blocking his way and *still* slowly marching toward him.

Robert reached for the door to his left. Locked! He reached for another door. Locked as well. The only way out was back up the staircase at the end of the hall behind him. Robert spun around and sprinted from the relentless machine until something even more unexpected and terrible happened. A spectacular crash shook the steamship, and every board and bolt on the vessel groaned. The floor dipped downward and water started flooding the hallway.

The *Titanic* was sinking.

Robert turned around and saw the unstoppable automaton advancing. He knew his unusual weapon would be no good against it. He still needed to find a way to shut down all power on the *Titanic* to guarantee Leopold's weapon could never be used. However, he did not want to be killed by an automaton in the process.

He raced down the other end of the hallway toward the stairs to escape, but then . . .

The floor dipped and the door leading to the staircase slammed shut. Again, locked. Gravity had just become Robert Todd Lincoln's mortal enemy.

"NO!" he shouted.

Robert was trapped and the automaton was almost upon him. He had nothing but an endless hallway of locked doors around him. He was standing in a rising pool of cold water, and the rifle he was holding operated on high-voltage electricity. Tesla had upgraded the weapon to lethal levels for this mission, and it was only seconds away from becoming the cause of Robert Todd Lincoln's death.

Then a fireman's ax broke through the door beside him. "Bob?" a familiar voice inquired.

"John!"

Wilkie demolished the door and pulled Robert up a spiral staircase. There was no way the automaton could reach them now.

But as they ran up the steps, Robert got an idea. "Hold on!" he told Wilkie.

The chief turned around and saw Robert aim his weapon at the brass menace standing in the water.

"Does that thing conduct electricity?" asked Wilkie, pointing his ax at the android.

"Yes, sir."

Robert pulled the trigger and Nikola Tesla's electronic gun fired, knocking out all power in the *Titanic*.

The whole ship plunged into darkness.

"What do we do now?" asked Robert as they stood in the Cimmerian staircase.

Ever ready, the Secret Service chief lit a cigar.

Chapter XLI

Taft

M r. President!"

"He's here! I know he's here!" Taft shouted in near darkness.

No, the president was not racing after King Leopold II. He was digging through the smoldering, sinking remains of Airship One, searching for his best friend.

"Mr. President," pleaded Sloan, "the *Titanic* is sinking!"

"I don't care!" Taft screamed with tears in his eyes. "I'd rather die than live knowing I left Archie behind!"

It had been more than twenty minutes since the mighty airship went down.

"Mr. President!" called a woman's voice behind him. Taft turned to see three flashlights bouncing toward him. It was Miss Knox rushing alongside an officer and a passenger. "Mr. President,

Captain Young was with Major Butt when the airship went down. He says the major died in the crash."

"No!" Taft cried. "That can't be!"

"Mr. President," said the captain, "when we landed on the deck, the major gave his life to rescue a mother and her child from the debris. I saw him disappear under the shattered decks of the ship just as the water rushed in. He's gone, sir."

"But . . . he could be below deck! We could search the ship!"

"Mr. President," spoke a grief-stricken Francis Davis Millet, "Archie would have wanted nothing more than for you to return home alive. Please, come with us. We need to leave Archie in peace."

"It's not right," sulked Taft. "I feel I should go down with the ship."

"Mr. President," said Miss Knox, "we were able to get nearly every passenger off the *Titanic*! The only ones we couldn't save were those who died in the fighting."

This surprised the president. "We have that many survivors?"

"Yes. Mr. Millet is the only passenger left on the ship."

"Mr. President," Agent Sloan spurred impatiently. "The sooner you leave, the sooner we can, too."

It was at this point Taft realized he was nearly knee-deep in water.

"All right," said the president. "Let's get out of here."

"Mr. President," begged Sloan, "we can't wait here forever!"

Taft stood with his arms folded on the sinking vessel. "Archie may be gone, but we are not leaving without Mr. Lincoln or Wilkie."

But then there was movement. Wheeler and Jervis shined their flashlights on two men running out of the ship.

"Mr. President!" shouted the fuming-mad Wilkie, who was still holding his ax. "You're leaving without us?"

"Not at all! Hurry aboard."

The two ran up the slanted deck locked in each other's arms.

"After you, Mr. Wilkie," offered Robert Todd Lincoln.

The chief shook his head. "Age before beauty."

The president and his bodyguard assisted Robert into the last lifeboat, but as the last son of Lincoln descended, he spotted vultures circling Taft. "Behind you!" he shouted.

The two remaining men on the deck turned around to see a row of rifles aimed at the lifeboat. Wilkie leaped in front of the president, carrying his fireman's ax.

The villains opened fire, as did all the soldiers and Secret Service agents.

Robert Todd Lincoln fell backward into the lifeboat. He had been shot in the stomach, and the force of his fall sent the small vessel violently into the ocean. Captain Young had been shot in the shoulder, causing him to drop his gun. Agent Sloan had been shot through the wrist and could no longer fire. Poor Francis Davis Millet had been shot in the chest and fell overboard, and the sinking *Titanic* sucked him under the water. As for Wilkie, who was the only person left with Taft on the deck, he absorbed four bullets that would have otherwise killed the president. One bounced off his bulletproof flask and another was deflected by his ax. The other two bullets, however, hit the Secret Service chief hard in the chest.

Wilkie collapsed on the deck and his head split into two pieces.

"WILKIE!" cried Taft. The chief's body started to slide down the ship, but Taft grabbed him by the foot while holding on to the railing. There was no stopping Wilkie's ax, however, which slipped silently into the Atlantic. Wilkie's scalp, meanwhile, remained stuck on the deck of the *Titanic*.

Or was it a wig?

"You are in a hopeless position, Mr. President!" boomed Leopold from the ship. Taft could not see his enemy; he could only hear his deep, pitiless voice. "You are unarmed and exposed. Your life is ours for the taking. However, since I am in need of that lifeboat, I am willing to offer a trade. Tell your soldiers and agents to throw their weapons in the water, and I will only kill you. If you do not, then you will all be as dead as that man in your hands."

"It takes more than that to kill a bull moose!" a familiar voice coughed.

Taft looked down at the late John E. Wilkie, more surprised than he had ever been in his life.

Chapter XLII

Taft and Roosevelt

At that moment, a foghorn sounded and a bright searchlight shined on the *Titanic*. The SS *Californian* arrived to collect the remaining *Titanic* survivors. Or rather, Nellie Taft arrived to decide who should survive the rest of the evening. Miss Knox signaled the first lady using Morse code with her flashlight. Every man and woman on the *Californian* put their lethal weapons to work.

Gunfire erupted, hitting some but not all of Leopold's men. Taft knew this would be his only chance: He slid down the *Titanic* with the man he now knew was *not* Wilkie until they reached the dome over one of the ship's smaller staircases. Both men came crashing down through the glass.

"What the hell is the matter with you?" Taft shouted to Roosevelt.

"Nothing!" Teddy insisted as he spit out his false teeth. "See! I am not coughing blood. That means I'm still fit for a fight!"

"No! What have you done to John Wilkie?"

"Oh, he's fine!" assured the former president. "I accidentally shot him with a Fox shotgun before I 'went on safari,' but he's enjoying his retirement. I just wish he didn't smoke so damn much!"

"My God . . ." Taft realized. "Nellie was right. You didn't go to Africa; you've been spying on me this whole time. My whole presidency! You sick egomaniac! I'll kill you!" The sitting president lunged at the seated former president.

"Please, Will! We'll have plenty of time to sort this out in November. For now, we still have a country to save. Hurry!"

"Come back here, you . . . Roosevelt!"

Taft crawled after his predecessor up the floor of the First Class Smoking Room. It was near-total darkness and the president could not see any further than he could punch. "Teddy!" he called out.

"Don't call me that," a voice whispered.

Taft found Roosevelt huddled in the corner of the room's darkened bar. "How are we supposed to get out of here?"

"Hand me that whiskey."

Taft complied. "Are we going to blow our way out?"

"No, this is for me." Teddy took a long swig from the bottle and then poured it over his bullet wounds.

"Wilkie!" Taft shouted, but then corrected: "Theodore! What's our plan?"

"There's no way the ship's hull can handle any more stress," said the former assistant secretary of the Navy. "The ship should break in half soon. When it does, we'll leap off the stern and swim away."

Taft's curly mustache drooped. "If we do that, we'll freeze."

"Will, if you were to land in the lifeboat, you'll kill everyone in it. Honestly, how on Earth did you gain so much weight? You told me you would exercise!"

"I do exercise!"

"Golf is not exercise!"

"I took up boxing."

"You box once a year!"

The hull started creaking, so Teddy discarded his bottle and drew his only available weapon: his puukko knife. "We'll have to continue this later."

The two climbed over the bar and up into the *Titanic*'s Verandah Café. For a brief moment, its tropic palms very much reminded Taft of the White House. Only slightly more sideways.

"Once we level out," said Teddy, "start running."

As the mighty ship moaned, several more gunshots rang out. The two men could hear bodies falling around them.

"Colonel, if we don't make it out," Taft began, "please know that I always loved you."

"And I always loved being president."

The two friends smiled at each other.

And then, the collapse.

Just as Roosevelt predicted, the fifty-thousand-ton boat reached its breaking point before completely submerging. The *Titanic* broke in half between its second and third funnel, causing the stern to level as it came crashing down into the water. The Verandah Café shook violently and nearly every window on the steamship shattered. But for the moment, the two U.S. presidents could run once again.

"CHARRRRGE!" the colonel shouted, swinging his puukko knife like a saber.

Taft and Roosevelt raced across the sinking ship as if it were

San Juan Hill. They sprinted from the café onto the A Deck, leaped onto the B Deck, and then . . .

Taft turned around, realizing that he was alone. "Colonel, what is it?"

Roosevelt dropped his puukko knife. "Something's not right. I—" He collapsed onto the deck, vomiting yellow bile with spots of blood in it. "Oh, that's not good."

"Teddy! Can you stand?"

"Don't call me that. And no, I can't stand. I can't even move."

The stern shifted upward as the bow continued pulling the ship under. Roosevelt's knife slowly slid down the deck and into the darkness behind him. "I can't go any farther. Please tell the world that no man has had a happier life than I've led."

"You tell them that!" Taft picked up his friend and carried him across the twisting stern of the *Titanic*. The ship careened on its port until it was touching the water, where Taft was relieved to see Miss Knox waiting along with everyone else in her lifeboat. Taft let go of his friend and let him slide down the deck. The former president landed in the freezing water, shouting "Bully!" as Agents Wheeler and Jervis pulled him into the lifeboat to safety.

But then, before Taft could jump, the *Titanic* shook violently. The president was thrown backward as the double-keel connecting both halves of the ship snapped completely. Taft was able to grab on to some railing, but the stern continued to rise until it was nearly vertical. The president held on for his life until he was suspended in the air far too high for him to jump. The only option was for Taft to climb the railing with all of his strength, and he was never that strong a climber.

As Taft made his final ascent up the *Titanic,* an injured Leopold II looked up. He stared furiously at the president who had ruined his plans for world domination and was now hanging on to a flagpole at the highest point of the *Titanic*. Searchlights from the *Californian* were shining on Taft, and Leopold could see him clearly. There was also a knife and a rifle resting in front of the villain. Though mortally wounded, the former monarch reached for the rifle.

Someone seized the puukko knife and stabbed Leopold through the hand, impaling his palm against the deck of the *Titanic*. Leopold screamed with defeat until he was finally silenced. A stunned Taft looked down to see a watery figure leap onto the villain and cover his mouth.

"You've killed enough people with that hand," Major Butt whispered into the ear of the king. "Now, don't make a move or I'll break every damned bone in your body!"

"Archie!" Taft shouted with delight from the sinking stern. "You're alive!"

Major Butt looked up at the president and smiled. He wanted to salute him, but he refused to let Leopold out of his grasp. Instead, the gallant officer stared straight into Taft's eyes, and then dutifully bowed his head.

The president's smile disappeared. "ARCHIE!" he screamed.

Major Butt closed his eyes and let the Atlantic wash over him. His last thoughts were of his mother.

The ocean claimed him.

And it was rapidly approaching Taft.

"Good lord . . ." gasped the president, whose nighttime operation was not going anything like he planned. He tried to kick off his shoes, but his laces were too tight. He tried taking off his coat, but that only made him cold, so he stopped. And he did not have a lifejacket and never prided himself at swimming any more than he did at climbing.

The distressed president looked down at the lifeboat, which was rapidly becoming eye-level. His immediate thoughts went to Robert and how badly he was hurt. Would Taft live long enough to find out? He shook his head. He then looked to the *Californian,* where everyone on its decks was watching, hoping, and praying the twenty-seventh president of the United States would some-how survive the coming fight for his life against the Atlantic.

Including Nellie. Dearest Nellie . . .

Seeing this was the end, William Howard Taft performed what he expected would be the last act of his presidency. He blew Nellie a kiss, waved good-bye, and took a deep breath.

Sir Arthur Conan Doyle was right, Taft quickly realized.

The waters were freezing.

Chapter XLIII

In Memoriam

There were no smiles at Washington's National Park four days later. The nation was still mourning the *Titanic* disaster. There was no zeppelin at the ball game, and such a feat would not be repeated for decades. There was no celebration, no confetti, no special rendering of "Hail to the Chief." There was only a sparse crowd of unhappy attendees, and chief among them was Vice President James S. Sherman. It was Opening Day for the Nationals, and Sherman was there to throw the ceremonial first pitch. It was a recent tradition that he imagined few people would remember.

Before he threw the ball, he took a moment to recite some lines he had prepared in case the *Titanic* operation did not go as planned.

Both Major Butt's seat and President Taft's slightly larger seat were empty.

———

The twenty-seventh president of the United States did not die on April 15, 1912. Instead, he was reeled aboard the SS *Californian* clutching a life preserver he could not fit inside. Although the president swore Major Butt saved his life after the *Titanic* went under, there was no sign of the officer after Taft was pulled from the water. The president was devastated by this, but just as deeply relieved when he learned that Robert was alive and unhurt after being shot. A rather miraculous gold pocket watch caught the bullet that would have ended his life forty-seven years to the day after his father's assassination.

Thanks to the heroic efforts of so many U.S. soldiers, Secret Service agents, White Star Line crew, and countless ordinary people who joined the fight for the RMS *Titanic,* the entire world was spared the fate Leopold II intended with his ultimate weapon. More than one hundred million lives were spared on both sides of the Atlantic, along with all the women and children aboard the *Titanic*. Nearly all those who died had fought so those who did live would live, and the president personally presided over every one of their burials at sea. As did his wife, Nellie Taft, and Robert Todd Lincoln, and a heavily bandaged but still very active Theodore Roosevelt.

There were still many questions surrounding King Leopold and the most elusive partner in his conspiracy, Basil Zaharoff. For the sake of security, the true events of the *Titanic* disaster became a closely guarded secret. When the RMS *Carpathia* arrived in New York on April 19 with more than seven hundred survivors, the SS *Californian* arrived completely unnoticed in Boston with another six hundred people. Many of them were immigrants who simply wanted to start life anew in America. Others were too frightened to return to their former lives knowing what they experienced on the *Titanic*. In both cases, the U.S. and British government complied, providing these passengers with new names and identities, new family histories, and lifelong protection from their enemies. The president also ensured that all their children received good educations at institutions such as the Taft School and Yale.

As for the idea of the *Titanic* sinking after hitting an iceberg, the U.S. government lifted this nearly verbatim from the 1898 novella *Futility, or the Wreck of the Titan,* by Morgan Robertson. There were concerns over how this story would hold after Senator William Alden Smith discovered the armor plating Leopold and Zaharoff had secretly built into the ship. Fortunately, he was humiliated by the British press with nicknames like "Watertight Smith" and "Bombastes" as a result.[44] The heroism demonstrated by White Star Line employees, however, needed no embellishment. Prominent figures like Sir Arthur Conan Doyle proudly defended their valor, particularly that of the *Titanic* band.[45]

It was clever of J. P. Morgan to send an automaton aboard the *Titanic* rather than secretly board it himself. Otherwise, he might have suffered the same fate as Benjamin Guggenheim that evening. But with the full extent of King Leopold's conspiracy exposed to the president, Morgan could no longer hide from his questionable business partners. In the midst of congressional and parliamentary investigations into the *Titanic* disaster, the U.S. House of Representatives formally investigated the so-called "money trust" Taft and Wickersham always believed Morgan was in the center of.[46] Morgan, who hated public appearances and despised

---

44 "Hard Names for Smith," *New York Times,* 29 May 1912.
45 Arthur Conan Doyle, "Mr. Shaw and the Titanic," *Daily News,* 20 May 1912.
46 "Money Trust Inquiry to Have Wider Scope," *New York Times,* 23 April 1912.

the democratic process even more, was forced to testify before this Pujo Committee in December. Three months later, J. P. Morgan died in his sleep in Rome. Allegedly from the stress of testifying before the committee.

Unlike King Leopold II, the king of Wall Street stayed dead.

However, there are some names that cannot be erased, certain histories that should not be rewritten, and select people whose heroism must not be forgotten. Among them were the soldiers of the Ninth Cavalry Regiment, who continued to serve their country even at a time when their sacrifices were never fully appreciated. After the sinking of the *Titanic,* they fought with their fellow countrymen through two world wars, witnessed the desegregation of the U.S. military, and helped usher a new phenomenon over future battlefields: air assaults. A special detachment of one hundred soldiers would remain at West Point until 1947, after which their old grounds would be known as Buffalo Soldier Field.

There was also Captain Charles Young, who, though born into slavery, became the third African American to graduate from West Point. In 1912, Young published *The Military Morale of Nations and Races,* a detailed examination of national identity throughout military history.[47] It was a daring book that challenged racial discrimination in the armed forces while praising the heroic qualities of people of all races, as demonstrated by his fellow Buffalo Soldiers. The book received the full endorsement of Theodore Roosevelt. Captain Young eventually died Colonel

47 Charles Young, *Military Morale of Nations and Races* (Kansas City: Franklin Hudson Publishing, 1912).

Young in 1922. He was the first African American to achieve that rank.

And then there was Major Archibald Willingham Butt, whose body was never recovered from the wreck of the RMS *Titanic*. When President Taft spoke at Archie's memorial service on May 2, 1912, he did not need to lie about the circumstances of his death. "If Archie could have selected a time to die," said his friend, "he would have taken the one that God gave him, and he would have taken it because he would have felt that there before the world he was exemplifying the ideal of self-sacrifice that was deep seated in his nature, and that had become a part of that nature in serving others and making them happy his whole life long.

"The void he leaves to those who knew him; the flavor—the sweet flavor—of his personality; the circumstances of his going, are all what he would have had. And, while we mourn for him with tears that flood our eyes, we felicitate him on the manner in which he went, and the memory which he leaves to the widest circle of friends—a memory which is sweet in every particular."[48]

That same day, a funeral service was held in Boston for Francis Davis Millet, Major Butt's very good friend and housemate. One year later, a fountain was erected in honor of both men in President's Park in front of the White House.

The fountain still stands there.

As does the Major Butt memorial in Arlington National Cemetery.

---

48 William Howard Taft, "President Taft's Tribute to Major Butt," quoted in Archibald Willingham Butt, *Both Sides of the Shield* (Philadelphia: J. B. Lippincott Company, 1912).

And the Butt Memorial Bridge in Augusta, Georgia: proud home of the Butt family.

Taft could not have chosen his words more appropriately. Archie's death was not a tragedy; it was a triumph. He died as one of the most beloved soldiers in United States history.

But did he need to?

Taft tortured himself with this question shortly after his friend's service. In the Blue Room of the White House, Taft confided his deepest guilt to the one person who truly understood him.

"What if I was always the wrong person for this job?" he confessed to his wife. "If Teddy had been president, would Archie still be alive?"

"No matter who was president," Nellie assured her husband with love, "Archie would have been willing to give his life for his country."

"But he saved *my* life." Taft sobbed. "Me! He didn't have to, but he did. If only I had caught Leopold sooner, Archie would still be with us!"

"Will," Nellie whispered to her husband, the president, "as long as we are together, I will always have Archie to thank. He saved the man I love."

Taft turned his head to Nellie, and the couple embraced. "You will always love me?"

"Yes, Will."

"Even when I'm not president?"

"Of course, Will."

Although Nellie could not see it, her husband was smiling for the first time in two weeks.

Chapter XLIV

Justice

It is hard to picture any story involving William Howard Taft having a happy ending. Theodore Roosevelt lived up to his promise on the *Titanic* and challenged Taft to reelection, crushing both men's chances of returning to the White House. On November 5, 1912, Taft carried only two states and 23 percent of the vote: the poorest showing for any president ever. Nellie took the historic defeat well. The outcome was so obvious that she started packing her things early. Had Theodore Rex been content as a painting on the wall, Taft would have been elected to a second term easily. Maybe even a third. Maybe the Great War could have been avoided, or at least won under Taft. Maybe Prohibition never would have happened. And maybe Nellie would not have had to go thirteen years without alcohol.

Thirteen years without beer . . .

Nellie hated the Roosevelts.

However, Nellie was not the only Taft with a political agenda in the White House. On December 12, 1910, around the same time then-Captain Butt took Miss Knox ice-skating, the president announced that he had chosen Edward Douglass White as the next chief justice of the Supreme Court. Why was this so sly of the president? Because Edward Douglass White chose to die on May 19, 1921, and wouldn't you know: the Republicans were back in the White House by then. With the chief justice's seat vacant, President Warren G. Harding decided to ask the former president if he would like to step in. Although Harding was a complete and spectacular failure as a president, he apparently possessed a remarkable gift at making Taft's lifelong dream a reality. The former president graciously accepted and, at long last, had the job he always wanted. William Howard Taft was now chief justice of the Supreme Court, after appointing more justices to the court than any president since Andrew Jackson. More than any Republican president in history. And all in one term. And while doing so many other things.

The first and only president to serve as chief justice. Even Nellie Taft liked the sound of that.

It was in this perpetual state of euphoria that Chief Justice Taft was reunited with a seventy-eight-year-old Robert Todd Lincoln on May 30, 1922, for the dedication of the Lincoln Memorial. It was a pleasant, sunny day with more than fifty thousand attendees there to share, for the first time, a monument President Harding described as "less for Abraham Lincoln than for those of us today, and for those who follow after."

Taft and Robert sat next to each other during the ceremony, and within the shade of the stone temple, the two shared a brief exchange.

"How do you feel, Bob?" whispered a significantly slimmer Chief Justice Taft.

"Old," Robert acknowledged in a drier, raspier voice than Taft remembered. "But well." He smiled.

Taft grinned brightly and asked, "Is there any chance I can talk you into spending the afternoon with Nellie and me? We are having George Wickersham and John Wilkie, the real John Wilkie, over for ice cream. Would you like to join us?"

Robert contemplated behind his old, tired eyes. "Yes, I would. I think it will bring back some pleasant memories of our old friend." Theodore Roosevelt died peacefully in his sleep three years prior, not that he would ever boast that.

"I still can't believe you outlived him!" Taft chuckled.

"Yes, well. I had an unfair advantage."

Taft expected to see Robert reach for his father's pocket watch, but instead his hands rested comfortably on his lap. "Did you bring it?" asked the chief justice.

Robert shook his head. "I never could get it open after it caught that bullet. I considered recasting it, but thought that would rob it of its history."

Taft was surprised but not too surprised to hear this. "So, where is it?"

"I left it on my father's tomb last time I was in Illinois. It may not be there anymore, but I'm not too worried about it."

Taft's whiskers curled with curiosity. "That doesn't sound like you at all!"

"Yes, well. I did not leave myself empty-handed." Robert reached into his jacket and pulled out his father's dazzling watch fob on a chain. Even in the shade, its gold-bearing quartz was as captivating as always. "I think I prefer it this way. It leaves me with precisely what my father had."

The former president smiled at this just as President Harding finished his speech. The fifty thousand spectators in the Mall applauded, as did Chief Justice Taft and Robert Todd Lincoln. It was a beautiful day for the city. And for the nation. And for its people.

"Made in America?" Taft asked.

"Made in America," Robert affirmed.

Epilogue

Clockwork

I n Monte Carlo's lavish Hotel de Paris, Basil Zaharoff had
every reason in the world to be thankful. Even without King
Leopold's mad dreams of revenge, the Great War had made Basil the wealthiest man in the world. He had a beautiful chateau
in France, a casino in Monte Carlo, and even two knighthoods
to his name. He had access to everyone and everything he desired.
And most importantly, despite being eighty-seven years old, he
was in fantastic health. He was showing signs of possibly living
into his hundreds, and his timing could not have been better. It
was 1936, the world once again seemed primed for war, and a
Belgian company called Union Minière du Haut Katanga enjoyed a virtual monopoly of the world's uranium market. The
company's mines were located in the Belgian Congo, primarily
in the southernmost parts of the Lualaba River.

There was a knock at the door, and a maid let herself in. Basil admired the woman as she moved into his bedroom. She was very attractive for her age and looked quite healthy as well. It was one of the reasons Zaharoff hired her. He thought she might make a fine wife some day, or at the very least a mistress. As she arranged his breakfast and poured him tea, Basil helped himself to the morning newspaper so he could leer at her from behind it. Like a gentleman.

She offered Basil his morning tea, and he accepted it.

A clock chimed.

As Basil flipped through the newspaper, a thought occurred: It was Thanksgiving in America. Or was it? He glanced at a wall clock and then checked his pocket watch. He turned out to be partially correct. It was still Thanksgiving in America, but only in Alaska.

He sipped his tea and, for a moment, allowed his mind to revisit some of the many adversaries he had outlasted: Taft, Roosevelt, Lincoln, and, naturally, Major Butt. All four men were dead. Basil smiled with satisfaction. However, as his thoughts turned to some of his former partners, his expression shifted to one of disapproval. Working with Leopold had been a mistake, Basil understood. The monarch relied too much on lunatics like Leon Rom. And Morgan had to complicate matters by bringing Nikola Tesla into it. Why would a man as wealthy as J. P. Morgan pirate Tesla's telegraph lines when he could have just as easily used his own? And Guggenheim was a stooge. He always was. A businessman who knew little about his own business and even less about whom he worked with. It proved a fatal mistake for him at the end.

But then, Basil's mind turned to the new German chancellor. Basil had an approaching meeting with some of the chancellor's men, and he looked forward to continuing his conversation with them about the many, many uses for uranium.

The gentleman folded his newspaper and reached for his teacup, but his usually steady hand quite unusually knocked the teacup over.

What?

No!

A deep, wrenching pain coursed through Basil's chest. He tried to scream for help, but quickly found himself unable to speak or move. He collapsed to the floor, gagging as if he were hanging from a noose.

His body went rigid, his eyes bulged, and his face froze in a horrific contortion.

The maid, meanwhile, finished cracking the safe Basil had hidden behind a painting and quickly emptied its contents: shipping manifests from the White Star Line, Yale's missing blueprints for their steam tunnels, maps of uranium deposits in the Belgian Congo, experiments on chemical warfare, and, beneath them all, designs for a rather unusual pocket watch from the House of Fabergé in Saint Petersburg, Russia, dated 1865.

The maid hid these items beneath her apron and walked over to Basil. As he lay helpless on the floor, she searched through his pockets until she found a heavy, bulky object: a silver pocket watch.

She flipped it open and quickly translated its inscription:

PROTOTYPE.

655321

A. LINCOLN

The maid snapped the timepiece shut and slipped it into her apron. She then bent down on her knees to finish things with Zaharoff. As the struggling, gurgling arms dealer stared desperately at the maid, she took out one of her hairpins, slipped it inside Basil's open mouth, and pressed a hidden plunger on the pin. A liquid dripped down Basil's throat, and the maid removed the hairpin. Within a minute, Basil's breathing became shorter and more rapid, almost as if he was panting. And then, panicking.

The maid stood up and left the room, shutting the door behind her. She did not appear to be in a hurry as she walked down the hall and turned a corner. From behind the corner, she could hear the gentleman's screams grow louder and louder, attracting the attention of a valet at the Hotel de Paris. The maid watched as the valet opened the door. A screaming, flailing Basil Zaharoff threw himself at the man, writhing in pain.

The maid walked calmly to the powder room, and from there she left the hotel.

In a café not too far from the Hotel de Paris, a seventy-five-year-old widow was sitting at a table smoking cigarettes and drinking coffee. She wore a large, black hat with matching sunglasses. Beside her was her forty-five-year-old daughter, Helen, who was now a professor of history and dean at Bryn Mawr College. The ladies sat patiently and talked about unimportant things as they awaited a third woman.

Miss Knox, now out of her maid uniform, joined the two ladies at the table. "It's done," she reported.

"How did he die?" asked Nellie, savoring each syllable in the sentence.

"It was quick, but painful."

"Good," said Helen, holding her mother's hand.

"Did you find everything we need?" asked Nellie, returning to her cigarette.

"Yes."

"Excellent. Please make sure you include this with your parcel." Nellie slowly pointed to her daughter, who produced a folded letter for Miss Knox.

The agent took the letter and sat quietly, looking back and forth between the two ladies. After this brief pause, she asked, "May I read it?"

Nellie thought for a moment, then responded, "I imagine now would be a good time."

Miss Knox unfolded the letter and looked it over.

THE WHITE HOUSE
WASHINGTON

Lyman James Briggs
National Bureau of Standards
My dear Sir:

Please find enclosed a little something for your engineers to examine. From what I am told, it is a most unusual device that the Bureau should find interesting. (If you can believe it, it was originally made for President Lincoln!)

According to former Secretary of State Stimson, who as you may know was President Taft's Secretary of War, this pocket watch was the basis for a weapon of unspeakable power that was used as part of a plot against the United States. Stimson will brief you on the details.

Please take me for my word when I say that the Bureau must treat this matter with the utmost secrecy. This device was intercepted from an apparent arms sale with the Germans. If the Reich is interested in developing some sort of uranium-based weapon, should we be as well?

Let me know if anything worthwhile comes of this. Consider it your special project.

With every best wish,

> *Very sincerely yours,*
> *FRANKLIN D. ROOSEVELT*

Miss Knox folded the letter, bowed her head with gratitude, and then left the two ladies at their table. The mother and daughter sat quietly until Helen asked, "Does this mean we're working with the Roosevelts again?"

Nellie reflected on this question behind her sunglasses. "Yes, we are," she decided. "I like these Roosevelts."

For further reading...

Carl Sferrazza Anthony, *Nellie Taft: The Unconventional First Lady of the Ragtime Era* (New York: HarperCollins, 2005).

Paul F. Boller Jr., *Presidential Campaigns: From George Washington to George W. Bush* (New York: Oxford University Press, 2004).

Paul F. Boller Jr., *Presidential Wives: An Anecdotal History* (New York: Oxford University Press, 1999).

Michael L. Bromley, *William Howard Taft and the First Motoring Presidency, 1909–1913* (Jefferson: McFarland & Co., 2003).

Archibald Willingham Butt, *Taft and Roosevelt: The Intimate Letters of Archie Butt, Military Aide* (Port Washington: Kennikat Press, 1971).

James Chace, *1912: Wilson, Roosevelt, Taft, and Debs—The Election That Changed the Country* (New York: Simon & Schuster, 2004).

Ron Chernow, *The House of Morgan: An American Banking Dynasty and the Rise of Modern Finance* (New York: Grove Press, 1990).

Robert Cowley, *What Ifs? of American History* (New York: Berkley, 2003).

David Herbert Donald, *Lincoln* (New York: Simon & Schuster, 1995).

Arthur Conan Doyle, *Dangerous Work: Diary of an Arctic Adventure* (Chicago: University of Chicago Press, 2012).

Jason Emerson, *Giant in the Shadows: The Life of Robert T. Lincoln* (Carbondale: Southern Illinois University Press, 2012).

Doris Kearns Goodwin, *Team of Rivals: The Political Genius of Abraham Lincoln* (New York: Simon & Schuster, 2005).

Doris Kearns Goodwin, *The Bully Pulpit: Theodore Roosevelt, William Howard Taft, and the Golden Age of Journalism* (New York: Simon & Schuster, 2013).

Lewis L. Gould, *My Dearest Nellie: The Letters of William Howard Taft to Helen Herron Taft, 1909–1912* (Lawrence: University Press of Kansas, 2011).

Adam Hochschild, *King Leopold's Ghost: A Story of Greed, Terror, and Heroism in Colonial Africa* (Boston: Houghton Mifflin, 1998).

Rhodri Jeffreys-Jones, *Cloak and Dollar: A History of American Secret Intelligence* (New Haven: Yale University Press, 2003).

Richard Lewinsohn, *The Mystery Man of Europe Sir Basil Zaharoff* (Philadelphia: J. B. Lippincott, 2004).

Edmund Morris, *The Rise of Theodore Roosevelt* (New York: Coward, McCann, & Geoghegan, 1979).

Henry F. Pringle, *The Life and Times of William Howard Taft* (Norwalk: Easton Press, 1986).

Brian Shellum, *Black Officer in a Buffalo Soldier Regiment: The Military Career of Charles Young* (Lincoln: University of Nebraska Press, 2010).

Edward Steers Jr., *Blood on the Moon: The Assassination of Abraham Lincoln* (Lexington: University Press of Kentucky, 2001).

Gideon Welles, *The Diary of Gideon Welles: Secretary of the Navy Under Lincoln and Johnson* (Boston: Houghton Mifflin, 1911).

Jay Winik, *April 1865: The Month That Saved America* (New York: HarperCollins, 2001).

Marc Wortman, *The Millionaires' Unit: The Aristocratic Flyboys Who Fought the Great War and Invented American Air Power* (New York: Public Affairs, 2006).